AJ BANNERMAN

Every Silence Has A Price

Contents

Also by AJ Bannerman 378

1

Saskia

March 2023, Cotswolds, England.

I tell myself I am only here for Luc. His sponsors, his speeches, his rehearsed idea of family perfection. Fourteen years of flawless photographs and of quotes drafted and delivered for him, and still I tell myself this. Yet when the Aston comes down the lane, low and furious, it is not my husband I feel. It's his son.

Zander takes the bend as if the road belongs to him. He does not brake; he does not correct. Throttle or nerve, probably both. One hand on the wheel, Persols cutting the morning light, the smirk unchanged. For a moment, my breath betrays me, although I tell myself I forgot the sound long ago. My lie, rehearsed and wasted – the body never forgets.

Sponsor day, and Amberley Manor is dressed for it. Drones circle in the pale distance, vultures with marketing contracts instead of claws. I moved the date last week, a whisper about

Étienne's Volt+ launch. Lies are easier when they flatter and easier still when you direct them.

Lucien Montclair, how I loved him once, fiercely, for the bravery of walking away from his half of the Laurette empire, now ruled entirely by Étienne, the brother he despises. Out of pride and stubbornness, he built a rival, Volant Sportif. Zander inherited the nerve for that gamble but not the patience.

Mara sits cross-legged on the fountain bench, head bowed over her sketchbook. Eleven and already obsessive, she draws faster than she can think, tapping her pencil when she stalls. Hair slips forward; her white dress slides off one shoulder. She should be chasing spaniels on the lawn, but she sketches buildings and faces that echo mine. I let her, our only unscripted thing.

In my clutch, between tissues and gloss, a page burnt at the edges waits, the last drawing I kept on the night I fed the rest to the fire. A scar in paper form. My hand finds it without meaning to. Before I smile, I press my fingers against it. Reminder. Punishment and proof.

At the flag, I stand in bias-cut silk from The Row. Black. Backless. Porcelain against fabric. No jewellery; let the absence speak. Sunglasses are like a locked door. My smile was measured.

"Losing grip, are we, Alexandre?" I call across the gravel.

Zander cuts the engine, climbs out, and adjusts his jacket. Sharp suit, perfect lines. He pulls at his tie as if it were a leash, then looks at me with a focus that makes the air buzz.

"I do not lose grip, Saskia," he says.

"No. You only decide the moment no longer interests you."

I hand him water. Fingers brush, too brief to count, too casual to confess. Denial travels well. He pours it into his palms, drags it over his face, and shakes the drops loose. One lands on my forearm. I do not move. My pulse is faster than it should be.

The sponsors laugh, polite and uneasy, unsure whether they have witnessed a joke or a fracture. I let them wonder. That is my role.

Amberley does not speak; it judges. Dutch gables soften under old rain, chimneys stand like sentries, and brick warms the pale stone. At the centre, a carved arch frames a silvered door, keystones heavy as verdicts.

Good manners conditioned the inside air. Cedar, leather, and money left to age. The faint suggestion of ghosts who would rather not be disturbed. Laurette houses reek of smug tradition; Amberley pretends to be; Luc's compromise is heritage bought by the acre.

Zander falls in step beside me. Too close. Not close enough.

Mara is still at her bench, pad propped on her knees. Zander slows, leaning just enough to glimpse the lines taking shape.

"Nice," he mouths. No sound, only the word.

Mara glows red and hides the page under her arm like contraband.

I catch it, the ease of his kindness, how little it costs him. My throat tightens before I can stop it.

My heels count the floor towards the parlour, measured steps, a metronome for a house that prefers to be left alone.

Negronis wait in Nick and Nora glasses, lacquer red against cut crystal. I pour and take the first sip. Place my clutch down, a quiet claim.

"You haven't tired of your poisons?" I ask.

"Only when I need to remind myself I am not him."

He takes my glass and drinks from the lip where my mouth

has marked the rim. His mouth makes a shape that is not quite a smile.

"Too clean. Too bitter. Like you."

I touch the same place and drink again. "You taught me the ratio. You have always preferred your poisons balanced."

He does not look away. Neither do I. This is what passes for a bar fight in the Montclair family.

At the edge of my vision, Mara still sketches. Zander notices as well. His gaze lingers a second too long, then returns to me, unreadable. He then disappears into a side closet to change, the door left unhelpfully ajar.

A wide back with a natural tan, a body that remembers its uses. He strips to briefs, washes quickly, unrolls a fresh shirt, and turns.

"What?"

"I just wanted to understand... what they all find so fascinating."

His mouth curves. I finish the Negroni, let the bitterness sit, and head for the garden before I forget myself.

Mademoiselle Céleste intercepts me on the gravel, Luc by proxy, leather folio in hand, muttering about the guinea fowl. I lift a hand; she persists, her heel sinking at the edge of the grass as if the lawn itself has an opinion.

His tread on the gravel behind me. I end Céleste's petition with a nod, step forward, and give him the view he came for, or the view I intend he should have.

The air carries wild garlic from the kitchen beds, brioche, asparagus, and trout. Plates land, not for appetite, but for information. Who refuses butter, who pretends not to, and who checks a phone beneath a napkin.

Luc speaks about his vineyard as if he were a priest at confession. Specific, unforgiving. He believes in Volant as penance, proof he can stand apart from Laurette and proof blood does not bind him to Étienne's empire.

The turbot arrives in beurre blanc, the fowl in cream, and the panna cotta under elderflower with rhubarb the colour of a blush.

Julien wore a midnight Caruso jacket, the white collar cut so sharp it caught the light. Beside him, Mara tapped a quick sequence into a device that passed for a game in other eyes, though I knew it for what it was: a problem-solving engine, her mind disguised as play.

I lifted a hand in greeting. Julien, my other stepson, is only two years behind Zander in age but worlds apart in temperament. For a moment I thought of the third, Maxime, exiled too young. His absence was always a presence, a space at the table, a laugh missing from the corner. When Luc spoke of his sons, it was always two.

Corky waves like distress at sea, selling an Antibes trip in the next breath. He asks after Isa; Isabelle Loubry is the face of various Montclair brands, ridiculously pretty, and extremely available. I know she is in Paris on a shoot; I do not tell him.

Near the service tent, two junior executives keep their phones too close. "... Volt+, embargo ... Cap-Ferrat, three days dark ..." I let the words lodge. Useful later.

A sponsor mistakes access for leverage. He speaks to Zander, yet his eyes are on me. I give him an answer that is both a solution and a warning. He thanked me twice.

A photographer pivots towards the pergola. I shift half a step and block the line. The frame he takes instead makes Luc look generous and Mara clever. Both are true.

5

We move to the croquet lawn. Mallets shine, grass trimmed to the syllable. Zander plays poorly on purpose, then wins by a margin that reads as modest. Men admire other men for that sort of arithmetic. I admire outcomes.

Mara appears at my elbow and presents a new page.

"Later," I whisper. "Keep them."

"She says you used to draw," Julien offers.

"I prefer clean desks now."

"You prefer locked drawers," Zander says.

"Both can be true."

By late afternoon, the sponsors want a tour of the library. I narrate, edit, and erase. I'm exceptional at erasing.

Zander finds me at the window, glass holding my reflection like a witness.

"You moved the date," he says.

"I scheduled efficiency."

"For whom?"

"For us."

"You always own the endgame."

"Pardon."

"I see it. Delicate, reserved, but always moving the pawns."

"You are observant when it amuses you."

"It amuses me now."

"It will pass."

"Will it?"

Zander plays the loyal heir when it suits him and rebels when it doesn't.

I check the watch I am not wearing. He laughs, low and private. I feel it more than hear it.

Evening drifts down. Lanterns blink on. Someone turns the

music down; someone else turns it up again. Luc speaks of oak and sweat. The applause lands like a tip.

From the pergola, Zander clinks a glass with a sponsor, a voluptuous brunette; she misses twice. Zander catches it the third time. She smiles.

My mouth is dry.

At dusk, the sponsors retreat. The house exhales.

I ask Mara to wash the green off her knees. She goes without protest, the easiest 'yes' of my day.

Céleste hovers with warnings. "The fowl was five degrees over."

"Maybe, but our guests were ten degrees under."

Zander then joins me at the terrace edge.

"You blocked the photographer earlier. Strategic compassion?"

"Functional."

"Not generous."

"Frequently."

"You did not eat," he says.

"The panna cotta was sufficient."

"You moved it around the plate."

"I edited it."

"Into what?"

"Into something I could live with."

"Does he know you are starving?"

"I am not starving."

"What would you call it?"

"Preference."

"You should eat."

"You should stop telling women what to do."

"That was not a command."

"It landed like one."

"Then forgive me," he says, and the last word sounds like he means it.

The lantern by the step dies in a soft cough. Night arrives properly, with rules. I take Mara upstairs. She sleeps with her hand open, as if she expects to wake holding something new.

The mirror in our room tells the truth men prefer not to learn. I wipe it until the edges blur.

Downstairs, the staff reset the world. Upstairs, I return my clutch to its shelf and slip the burnt page back into its place. It curls like a secret that enjoys its work.

* * *

Morning sits low on the gravel. Breath shows pale. I leave with Mara before the house remembers how to object. I tell Luc I have business in London. The business is already done. Two days ago, with Dorian Tseng. He offers discretion for breakfast and invoices for lunch. I accept both. Some loyalties are seasonal.

Halfway to the gate, a hum rises. A lavender chrome Porsche slides between the trees, the Faucon hubcaps catching the first light like a dare.

The window lowers. Gauche. Kohl-shadowed eyes, bare shoulders, a vintage Haider jacket over what looks like last night's dress.

Gauche Montclair plays for the other side, Faucon, of course. Étienne's daughter and pet chaos. Where Luc and Étienne build, she delights in setting fires.

"Wrong turn, mon cher."

8

"Perpetually."

She pulls away. Her feeds have been quiet, and with Gauche, quiet is not rest. It is planning. Or hiding. Both taste the same at the start.

Mara is curled up next to me, her breath on my arm. I brush long dark hair from her cheek. My hand lingers a moment too long, the way it does when I am hiding something.

The lavender chrome is gone, yet the air keeps her perfume. Amberley shrinks in the mirror, then holds, as if the house knows something I do not. Something moves against me already, and it is too late to say I did not see it.

We pass the hawthorn hedge, the lane narrowing to a choice. London right; the village left, where no one forgives us for buying history with cash. I signal right. In the mirror, a sliver of lawn lingers, a square of yesterday, then it's gone.

2

Céleste

Chesterfield House, Lucien Montclair's Belgravia residence, does not pretend to be found. It withdraws, narrow and watchful, its Georgian facades offering silence rather than welcome. Brass knockers burnished raw, a lineage no plaque dares announce. Originally two mansions sutured underground, inheritance cemented with marble and debt. Once a gaudy refuge for men who mistook excess of power, now pared back to austerity by Luc's hand. Restoration not as vanity, but as discipline.

The stairs breathe as I move; the ceilings press me into obedience. Here, architecture corrects weakness.

Luc tells people the ballroom could rival the Palace, though he finds spectacle obscene. His theatre lies elsewhere, smaller, more intricate, a dining room suspended beneath a canopy of blossoms that never fall. Plastic, flawless, impervious to decay.

A narrow stream edges the table, koi carp circling faster than the guests can think. Their arguments dissolve before dessert, their tempers drowned in the motion of water.

This house wasn't made for living; it was made for control. Luc stands at its centre, conductor of silence. Every room insists on obedience, and every guest learns their part.

I choose the seat that matters. Not at the head, never at the head. Close enough to cut, but never to lead. It is proximity, not prominence, that draws blood. Breath must be measured before a lie is spoken. This is where men compete for divinity. Women, meanwhile, calculate the ruin.

Julien arrives late. His jacket folds into shadow, collar white as an oath. Hands restless around his glass, never still enough to convince. His eyes move too quickly, Saskia, Zander, then me. A boy, unguarded, stumbled into a room of predators. And yet, when his gaze snags on mine, I feel it. Recognition, or something resembling it, sudden and uninvited.

Luc rehearses without sound, his lips shaping prophecies no one should trust. They call it respect when he doesn't look at me. I know better. Fear of the ledgers. Fear of what he suspects I've already written.

Saskia holds her stillness like a jewel, something barbed, made precious with effort, but even she slips. A glance at Zander, a retreat, then the slow return. The room studies her, weighing her not against Luc but against herself, measuring silence as its own kind of currency. His name in the air shakes her. Not grief, no. Something colder, more exacting. A debt unmet.

Mara sits beside Julien, glass tilted, never drunk. She wears obedience like skin. Her art is refusal by disappearance. The beginning of something, though no one marks it yet.

Zander slouches wide into the space; his eyes map the exits and the light angles. Ease as decoy. Appetite was his only inheritance.

Julien lingers on Saskia with patience that doesn't belong to him, the patience of a man learning calculation. Luc falters, Saskia signals, and Julien receives it. A truth changes hands in silence, a flame cupped from a gust. He glances back towards me, uncertain of sanction. And when he does, it unsettles him. The boy cannot name it, but he feels why my gaze cuts.

Luc smiles, immaculate, serviceable. His hand moves sharply at a fumbling server like memory. Not violence, but something remembered as close enough. A glass trembles across the room; wine vanishes before it leaves a mark. Cruelty here is not action, only climate, as constant as damp against the skin.

The men speak of futures, forecasts, corpses; the women endure the pause, sharper for the waiting. The bread is perfect and useless. Servers circulate as shadows, bodies rehearsed into absence. Call it tranquility. It is dread perfected into precision.

I eat nothing. Observation is sustenance enough.

Saskia's laughter lands as an instrument. Zander takes note, watching her mouth, the doorway, then nothing at all.

Luc's voice resumes, like a pressure that sounds polite until you feel the bruise. Julien's fork escapes, metal clattering too loud against porcelain. Mara's chin tips upward, the smallest rebellion, and for a moment I almost admire her.

Luc fills the silence, as he always does, feeding on it first. I let mine linger longer, sharpened into judgement. The room leans into the pause until I lift my glass. They follow out of instinct, not loyalty.

"A toast," he says, smooth, unneeded, inevitable. "The Montclair men, raised to conquer."

I tilt my glass, my eyes fastening on Saskia.

"And the women," she says suddenly, "raised to outlive them."

The koi convulse, circling tight, water breaking into restless light.

Luc doesn't flinch. His reply moves colder than the glass in my hand. "Outlive, perhaps. At the cost of silence. Years of it."

Saskia hardens, then softens, like tempered steel. Sensible enough to survive, brave enough to risk. The most dangerous balance of all.

He leans back, lazy, deadly. "Jokes are smoke, Saskia, and smoke does not last."

Julien laughs, brittle as glass. Zander refuses the game, his gaze scattering elsewhere, naming his refusal without words.

I place my glass down and move forward, just close enough. Voice lowered, edge deliberate, meant for every ear. "Be careful of the daughters of silence."

Chef Louvel parts the tension, starch-white, stiff as parchment, carrying the silver dome as though treaties rest beneath. His voice is a ritual, naming the course as if an heir were being crowned. Fillet de boeuf en croûte, dark black truffle, a vintage distilled into memory.

The lid lifts. Pastry gleams, obscene in its perfection. Knives scrape hollowly, voices resume, brittle as spun sugar. I taste nothing.

Ritual continues. Stillness binds us tighter than speech. Alliances stagger under the weight. Zander's laugh folds into silence that belongs only to him. Saskia fillets her fish with surgical cruelty. Julien leaks anxiety into the room, messages striking staccato against the air. Luc folds his napkin closed. Appetite cancelled.

The door opens. Dessert proposed, forgotten. Watches checked, smiles drawn and emptied. I fold my napkin carefully. They see it. Signal received.

"Legacy is patient," I murmur, not to them but to the koi, to glass, to the taste left on air. The women inhale the warning. The men mistake it for architecture.

After dinner, the doors give way. Luc moves towards the drawing room, slow as driftwood on a current. The meal was only a prelude, a performance reserved for outsiders. Here, with smoke and Armagnac, the actual play begins.

The room announces him before he speaks. A Sun King throne, resold at Sotheby's, gilding stripped for discipline, creaks beneath his spine. Churchill's chaise crouches near the fireplace, leather cracked, history etched into its folds like ash that refuses to leave. Above the mantel, a falcon, glass-eyed in perpetual flight, wings pinned, talons suspended. His brother's bird. Trophy and warning in a single frame.

Whisky crowds the crystal, bottles older than the youngest man here. Cigar boxes breathe cedar into the heat; the air grows heavy with earth and money's insistence.

They arrive one by one, each absorbed seamlessly into Luc's set.

Annina Keller first, entering like judgement, ivory silk cutting the smoke. She chooses her chair without hesitation, as though the seats had been designed with her in mind.

Digby Corcoran, Corky, drifts after her, amiable grin intact, the boy next door offered cheaply to disguise what he shadows. His role is protection, but he plays it as charm.

Then Félix Dujardin, bathing in the success of the Volt+ launch, his restless energy condensed into a single body, his shoulders burdened with Paris as though it were a family inheritance he is too proud to set down.

Horace Bhandari drops to the edge of the circle. His suit hangs wrong, threadbare in places, with fatigue mistaken for humility, an error that serves him well.

Toby Greaves last, cap tilted insolently over a suit too sharp to be accidental. A grin worn thin from repetition. Luc despises the headwear but tolerates the boy. Yachts and villas don't conjure themselves.

They sit as if the script has long been written, absorbed into Luc's new Versailles. He gleams at them, smile polished, weaponised, dazzling as glass under flame. His eyes reach the falcon's wing. Feather, talon, followed by sermon.

"Gentlemen," he says, light enough to unsettle. "And ladies, of course. In this house, I permit only two things. Loyalty and very good whisky. Fail me in either, and you will find the whisky easier to replace."

The laugh arrives warm, indulgent. The kind that softens no edges.

Once the second act has ended, the room fractures, scattering towards cigarettes, mirrors, and vanished smoke. Saskia excuses herself neatly, fingers smoothing silk into obedience. The tremor is small but true. Her absence hollows the room; the rest scramble for rhythm under a weight unseen but felt.

I do not watch her go. I watch Zander. His gaze clings to the empty chair, unwilling to release it. Dynasties do not erupt; they unravel thread by thread, beginning with the refusal to look away.

He rises, excuses hollow as air, intent too clear to be mistaken. Recklessness is a luxury in this house, one that pays in theatre or ruin.

Luc's shadow tightens the room. His cruelty, polished and silent, closes the distance. Julien's eyes flicker to mine; brittle, boyish. I stand knowing no sanction is needed.

The corridor sighs beneath my steps, rugs swallowing sound. Portraits turn their backs. A staff member lowers her gaze, perfecting invisibility.

Ahead, silence swells. Zander waits at the powder room, tie loosened too deliberately, posture studied for nonchalance. Careful stillness betrays the nerves of a boy rehearsing charm in empty mirrors.

Saskia's cheeks are coloured, but her poise is recalibrated. Her stride is clean until it isn't, a caught step, a flicker beneath the mask. She offers no smile, yet her mouth softens subtly, betrayed by pleasure found in his presence. He breathes her name too carefully, too rehearsed, reverent as a prayer. Her look denies him, but lightly, denial is a kind of invitation.

"I am fine." The words are clipped, but her smile lingers this time. She smooths the edge of her dress, fingers busy when her body isn't.

"You don't look it." His tone is light, but his eyes stay on her too long. One hand slips into his pocket, the other tapping once against the doorframe, nervous, pretending not to be.

"Then don't look."

"I couldn't stop if I tried." He leans in just enough that she feels it, then catches himself, straightening as if to erase the move.

"Zander." Her voice was a warning. Her sleeve brushes his arm as she passes, not by accident, not entirely deliberate.

She doesn't turn back, but her stride falters for a moment, just long enough to know he's watching.

I continue, scentless, untethered.

"Mademoiselle Fournier," Zander calls, the title sharp with nerves.

"Monsieur," I return. Then, softly, to Saskia: "Madame."

Our gazes lock, neither yielding nor defiant, but lit anew with secrecy, dangerous and alive.

"Your daughter misses you." The weight lingers beyond the words, offered to both, binding none.

I leave them in silence, entering the ballroom. Chandeliers scatter brilliance that blinds no one. Floorboards sigh, heavy with history. Men will remember the light. Women, the weight.

Luc's presence clings like shadowed smoke, invisible but suffocating.

3

Camille

Before dawn, Perpignan holds its breath. The river rail is slick with rain; wild garlic rises from the verge, scenting the city's edges. Gables blur, wet outlines, gentled by night's mercy. Inside, the lobby lights hum against concrete and steel, scrubbing the executive floor of anything that might betray weakness.

My heels mark the silence like a summons. Futures assemble quietly in the margins, long before anyone dares to notice. I am never first but always watching, mapping hesitation, and recording missteps. I have been the prize; the queen commanding the board. Now, I am the player recalibrating to survive a younger hand.

The doors slide away. Étienne arrives, his shirt immaculate, weariness blooming beneath clouded eyes; the scent he wears is too sweet, a fruit past its prime, overripe and fading.

"Heritage is holding," he murmurs, easing into his place with practised indifference. "Volt+ brings the press to Laurette. They want her again, and we will oblige."

A smile drifts across my lips.

"Heritage, Étienne, is a mirror, polished, flattering, but always reflecting backward. Faucon must be the lens. The future is raw, unclaimed until some brave, or foolish, eyes dare to see it. Laurette wears nostalgia, and Gauche doesn't carry such weight. She is fresh blood, too hungry to be tethered by history."

He shrugs, like a man who already won yesterday. "My name holds the market."

I meet him with a bitter truth: "Names fade. Relevance is impatient. Bloodlines buy little of tomorrow."

I watch him, with less fondness and more like a seasoned predator gauging a wounded stag. Luc's hunger kept him lethal. Étienne softens in easy applause, dulled claws, and a decorative prize. Saskia Lin, a silent force, sits like fragile porcelain, but I read the ledger she writes in measured strokes: debts, betrayals, unspoken wars. Her forgiveness is a blade she never needs to draw, yet never lowers.

They once leaned in when I spoke, when my smile alone altered deals, when my presence rewrote the room's shape. Now, at thirty-eight, beauty turns quietly to shadow. Sensual, yes, but men's eyes trace Gauche's silhouette instead, the younger, sharper, faster model with intellect honed like a rapier. She carries the future like a scent that lingers, compelling, impossible to ignore, and I am left holding the fading silk of Laurette. Legacy applauded, relevance fading.

A knock, soft and certain. Safiatou Doué arrives, precise as a scalpel's edge, silent as a shadow. Seventeen and already unsettling, carrying quiet hunger beneath her composed smooth skin.

She places the folder down deliberately. Nails bare, no vanity, only intent sharpened for function.

"The Volt+ package." Words clipped, each measured for maximum impact. "Your spend on print and broadcast is heavy. Gen Z will scroll past. Denial is no strategy with respect."

I permit the silence to grow, a predator's pause, inviting misstep. In Languedoc, storms wait behind mountains. Patience is currency. The weapon that outlasts the blade.

My voice soft and deliberate: "Your sister, Safi... where does she fit in this strategy?"

Light traces the sharpness of her cheek. "She models the cascade. I find the fault lines. She finds the story."

No doubt. No need. Authority lived, not claimed. Luc would mark her as careful precision.

The secure link flickers, my reflection a ghost before Aïcha Doué breaks through, electric and untethered.

"Camille!" her voice, a fast-moving wave. "Your creatives? Stuck in 2005. Volt+ could sell itself if you stopped speaking French to an audience trapped in TikTok rhythms."

Her words are music, fast cuts and samples, a set spun for eyes alone. By her side, Safi's hands await the cue, controlled, and ready.

Aïcha launches the reel, night skaters, sodium lights, and pulsing logo. "Cost us nothing," she smirks, raw teeth. "Dropped last week. Engagement up thirty-four per cent and climbing."

My laugh is slow, coated with envy: "You make the ascent sound effortless. Many fear the fall."

Aïcha: "Let them. We drive the drop. The platform's our playground if you know the tracks."

Safi, calm as stone: "Cascade demands structure. Skeleton, then rhythm. Resonance needs form."

"Structure stifles the beat."

"Chaos is wildfire. Structure survives the drought," Safi added.

"If they never watch, stability is a whisper lost."

A dance, not a battle: Safi lays rails. Aïcha races fire.

My glass is cool, a steady anchor. I tally the power on display and the risk. Safi, rails. Aïcha, fire. Gauche, the future I hunger to claim.

"Ladies…" I draw out the word. "You make war sound… elegant."

Aïcha: "Elegance is weaponry. Everything else you must purchase."

"Weapons wield power only when claimed with intent," added Safi.

Their words settle around me, then break into heat.

Saskia would see it plainly: Safi is structure, Aïcha the spark, and Gauche danger in practised disguise. The future waits for no one except those bold enough to seize it.

C'est toujours ainsi; the future demands no permission. It arrives raw and indifferent. Only the outstretched hand claims it.

A pang of regret runs sharp beneath the calm: my son already calls me Camille, never Maman. The syllable lands cold, stripped of softness, of reverence, of the history carried by that word. A mother reduced to a name, as though I were a colleague, a visitor passing through his life. I allow it; I must allow all that cannot be forced, but the wound etches itself deep, invisible to all but me. Words matter; they carve bloodlines in a child's heart.

Saskia would never permit such distance. She weaves her daughter tight in silk, an affection that doubles as a tether, a leash of love calibrated with precision. She holds Mara so close that touch becomes currency, not comfort. Then, when power demands, she loosens gently, coldly, the grip of expectation, love and leverage, intertwined.

I am left with absence disguised as freedom, a silence that grows heavier with time. To be a mother is to command loyalty more sudden and unyielding than any alliance. Softness can wound, but it can also bind. Saskia knows this. I, sharp and poised elsewhere, have not yet learnt the truce between holding and letting go.

By noon, the floor stirs reluctantly. Étienne vanishes for lunch, an empty ritual as productive as fumbling shadows. The boardroom harbours his father's portrait, smiling down, syrupy and canned like a poor performance.

From my window, the river churns pewter beneath a weak sun. My reflection pins itself in the cabinet glass, lipstick corrected, mask restored. Annina once said, "A trial begins with a compact mirror and ends with a cheque." She was not wrong.

My desk holds Gauche's press photo beneath a weight of glass. Sequins like scales, each catching light, flashing an unspoken dare. Her grin tilts too wide, but those eyes, sharp and calculating, belie the ingenue mask. She is the perfect blend of calibrated charm and ruthless broker instinct. Men call her dazzling; women know her as dangerous. She wears the future like couture, woven from ambition and style. A living contradiction, beautifully poised: fragile yet unbreakable, light yet edged with steel.

She embodies possibility incarnate: the merciless pivot from yesterday's safe applause to tomorrow's chaos and disruption. I clutch the thinning silk of Laurette, the nostalgia brand worn soft, applauded, and already waning.

My phone flares, a drift report from Safi, visitor lists stripped to bare essentials. I forward it to Aïcha's secure thread, notes arranged tight as music notation: engagement windows, seeded creators, timing, tone. Soon Aïcha will return with the creative tree: three campaign strands, each a rhythm with impact measured and inevitable. Then the edit will be mine to command.

Davide Marrucci steps from the lift on a gust of Milan, leather sharp as espresso, helmet tucked like a trophy. Heat slips in with him, a slow burn under smooth charm.

"Early bird, Camille." His voice is low, thick with warm insolence, too close, the confident swagger of the Italian drunk on his own legend.

"It is past lunchtime, Davide. You are an insufferable prick."

He grins, no shame, and blows me a kiss. Insolent. Italian.

He props himself against the printer, the same machine where proximity once became promise. Fingers brush again, carelessly, habitually. I recorded those touches, not for pleasure but for proof. Softness is camouflage; consent must be evidenced. Discipline follows only when desire is mirrored.

Numbers bloom across glass: margins shaved to bleeding, forecasts stripped to bone. I turn a page in my notebook. Names web across the paper, most harmless. One is not.

Zander.

Once he called me "not a queen, but an architect, and we live in the house she built." Dangerous because he seeks to understand. Men who understand either vanish as assets or become ruinously costly.

Saskia is a pressure he does not name. Their gravity

reshapes rooms. I do not need him to want me. I need him to hesitate, just once, when it counts. Leverage is a pause, sharp and unyielding.

The secure channel blinks. Aïcha's tree unfolds: Branch One, viral seeding via micro-creators; Branch Two, street-level clips stitched into long-form reel; Branch Three, a timed drop tethered to events, sharp and unstoppable.

Each strand climbs. Aïcha sets the beat as Safi's data supports the structure, uncompromising execution; no talk of the past. Only reach, velocity, impact.

I smooth silk across my ribs. The mask slides back into place, the impeccable COO underestimated for the subtle steel beneath.

The notebook snaps shut. Ink dries to a pinprick mark; ledgers begin in shadows this small.

At the door, I pause. The building listens. Lamp clicks off. The loading bay exhales metal and shadow. Secrets fold themselves into corners others ignore.

I do not need to be loved. I need to be first to see the cut.

4

Saskia

L'Hirondelle is not on any map. If you have to ask, you do not belong. The entrance hides in Mayfair behind a hedge of camellias, a brass button pressed into shadow. The door is the exact blue of a 1997 Hermès saddle, a colour too specific to be accidental. Inside, velvet walls in plum and midnight blue drink conversation before it can escape. Baccarat chandeliers scatter fractured light across linen and crystal. The effect is theatrical, though everyone here pretends otherwise. Expensive unhappiness has its own dress code.

Julien guides me towards a half-curtained booth. He does not offer the menu. He opens his, then sets it aside as if theatre is beneath him.

"If we are not needed in the meeting," he says, "better not wait around on an empty stomach."

I let the corner of my mouth move. It pleases men when they think they have drawn it from me.

"Félix insists the artichoke hearts at Soho House are better," he adds, "and that the foie gras here is a trap."

"That sounds like Félix," I say.

He smiles, patient, leaving a space in case I wish to fill it. "What do you miss? About home, I mean."

The question catches me. In that family, no one asks what I miss. They ask what I will do.

"Singapore?" I say after a pause. "No longer, no."

He nods. Not to agree, but to mark it. He is not gathering ammunition. He is listening. That too is rare.

The server pours wine. He does not correct my choice. Luc would have. Zander certainly would have.

As I look up, Zander is there. Sliding into the booth as if the seat had always been his, uninvited, entirely sure of himself.

"Family dinners are still theatre," he says. His voice pitched low, just sharp enough. "This is quieter."

Julien's smile thins, but he does not object. Zander looks at me with a look balanced between apology and possession.

Julien recovers first. "You keep the temperature," he says. "Everyone else is weather. Gusts, storms. You hold the room."

I let out a soft laugh. "That sounds like something you should put in one of your reports."

"Already did," Julien says. "They ignored it."

I smile.

Zander places his glass down with a click that makes the crystal tremble. "They ignored it because it was true. And truths like that get people burnt in this family."

The food arrives. Julien leaves silences, gentle as cushions, waiting for me to inhabit them. Zander cuts through with questions sharpened like pins.

"And what did you gain?"

"And what did you lose?"

Each a test.

Between them, I feel both cushioned and exposed.

I reach for my glass. The stem slides. Julien steadies my hand, warm and deliberate. Too brief to remark upon. Too clear to ignore.

Zander's eyes follow the touch. Not jealous, colder. Possessive, assessing, as if the table itself had tilted. Our eyes meet across the linen. The air sharpens.

Attraction, yes. But wrapped in warning.

Julien breaks the pause with a complaint disguised as a confession. "Luc is playing me sideways again. Throwing scraps, calling it responsibility."

"Now, now. Zander will take the throne one day, but you will be in charge of the crown jewels. Vérité Joaillerie and Vérité Maison. They earn more than the rest combined."

Zander's jaw tightens. His eyes never leave mine.

"I am not in the habit of ceding ground," he says.

"And yet," I answer, "you indulge your father."

The waiter interrupts with sole meunière, quail eggs, and comté sandwiches with caviar. Julien leans closer, lowering his voice, and I fold my replies part-flirt, part-counsel. When I brush my glass again, his hand steadies mine a second time. Not an accident.

Zander's silence is louder than speech. He has seen. He will remember.

I feel alive, caught between them. One hand warm around mine, the other gaze burning through me like a brand.

"You speak as if you already chair the board," Julien says.

His phone buzzes. A server leans in with a discreet whisper. Julien frowns, murmurs apologies. "Dubai client. They do not sleep. Two minutes." He rises, leaving his jacket behind like a promise.

Silence folds in with him gone.

Zander turns his glass slowly by the stem. "I see him, the way he looks after you."

I reach for my glass. Fingertips graze the base of his. Just a scrape of skin. Nothing and everything. I pull it back as though it had not happened.

"And you observe a great deal," I say.

"Observation is survival," he answers. His tone is cool, but his eyes are not. "You know that better than anyone."

I take a slow sip. My pulse betrays me in the hollow of my throat.

"You make it sound as though every dinner is a battlefield."

"Is it not?" he asks. His gaze slides to the velvet curtain, half open to the room. "Plum walls, crystal light. It is still theatre. The cast only changes costumes."

I placed my glass down harder than intended. "Perhaps I am tired of being cast."

That draws his eyes back, deliberate, unreadable. He lets the silence stretch until it becomes heat.

"You do not look tired."

The pause carries weight. It presses against my ribs.

"You came uninvited," I say.

"I thought you enjoyed company."

"Not yours." The words snap before I can soften them.

He leans back, studying me as though I were a code already half-cracked. "Then why correct my father on my behalf?"

Heat rises despite my control. "Because someone must."

The silence that follows is not empty. It is a charged field, waiting for movement. Forks clink faintly at another table. A woman's laugh carries too brightly before the velvet swallows it.

Zander's eyes stay on me. Not wandering, not careless. Watching with the patience of a man who wants not possession but understanding. That is worse.

When Julien returns, apologetic smile intact, the moment has already shifted. But Zander's glance lingers, sharp and unfinished.

For the first time all week, I feel seen rather than staged. But it is Zander who makes me feel watched.

* * *

My house knows how to greet me. With the curtains already drawn and lamps low, the space carried its endless hush. I said goodnight to my nanny with a fond hug and let my bag rest on the console, slipped off my heels, and stood for a moment in the stillness. Rooms remember things if you let them.

Jasmine padded out from the shadows, tail high, eyes half-lidded with age. Fifteen years on and still the first to check that I'd come back. She brushed once against my ankle, a brief acknowledgement, then disappeared towards Mara's room. I moved through in silence, checking locks without seeming to, smoothing a cushion that did not need smoothing. Control restores itself in insignificant gestures.

I paused at Mara's door. The light beneath was soft, the kind she chooses when she pretends to be asleep. I opened it a fraction. She was curled on her side, book balanced on her knees, lids half closed but listening. Her hair had fallen across her cheek. The sight pressed something under my ribs. I did not disturb her. I let the door ease shut.

The air was fresh once I knew she had surrendered to sleep. Lighter, but also more dangerous, as if the house lowered its guard along with her. I lit two candles in the sitting room without thinking. Habit, mood, protection. The flame steadied.

I poured a glass of water and sat with it in my hand. The taste was sharp and metallic. I thought of Zander's eyes across the linen and the way he had said, 'You do not look tired.' I wished I had not remembered the warmth of Julien's hand at my wrist at the same time. It was indecent that the body could keep two sensations alive at once.

The clock struck the hour, discreet and expensive, as if apologising for passing time. I place the glass down and arranged olives and Manchego on a plate I would not use.

Clara arrived first, bottle in hand, heels already dangling from her fingers. She smiled at me like I was the reason for getting home early, no matter the day.

Annina followed, barefoot, eyeliner smudged like she'd rubbed a thought too hard. A tight charcoal suit softened just so by the drop of a silver bracelet on her wrist.

We did not bother with plates. Bread, olives, and cheese. Three glasses lined up like accomplices.

Clara poured.

"You are glowing," she said.

"I am not," I answered.

Annina tipped her glass toward me, a wicked grin shadowing her eyes.

"We hear Julien asked you out on a date?"

I let a smile slip before I caught it. They pounced, of course.

"You should see yourself," Clara said, dry as the wine. "No one looks like that after spreadsheets."

"It was lunch."

"Yes, lunch with Julien? Jesus, I haven't seen that happy

Saskia face since 2016."

"Ah, the Montclair men," Annina sang.

Clara raised a brow.

Annina leaned back, smirking lazily. "Will you spill more about Zander than Julien..."

"Annie!"

"All she can confirm", said Clara, "is that he does indeed have a great arse."

Everyone laughed.

"Yes, we had already guessed that; we've all looked enough times." Annina added.

"Not all of us, thank you," I said quickly, too quickly.

The glance they shared said they noticed. Neither pressed.

We drank, the three of us, laughter circling like perfume. Conversation slid to Clara, her life on pause; Annina restless, admitting she had never planned for this life in a boardroom.

"Do you want children, Annie?" Clara asked suddenly. Not blunt, but it landed with a weight on the table.

Annina barked a laugh. "Please. First, I'd have to find a man who's not terrified of the c-word."

Her glass clinked against mine. She drained it in one swallow.

"I suppose I just want what every woman wants eventually... something that loves me without asking for a blow job."

The room erupted.

Clara did not flinch. "I do not think I ever did. Not really. Too many years proving myself, waiting for a time that never came, and now..."

"Fifty is the new thirty."

"Fifty? I'm forty-nine, you cheeky cow!"

Everyone laughed.

I turned the stem of my glass slowly. "You still could."

"Could I", she said, not unkindly.

Annina made a face, playful and deflecting. "We should freeze our eggs together. Matching cryo-tanks. Two-for-one specials."

Clara's laugh was quiet, startled out of her.

The wine softened us. We spoke of Zander's arrogance, of Luc's theatre, of Félix's ridiculous, well, everything. We spoke of them as women who had known them, survived them, and still circled and sparred with them.

Only once did Julien's name come up again. Annina said it idly and carelessly, and for a heartbeat I felt the ghost of Zander's eyes on mine across the linen table. I said nothing, just lifted my glass.

Annina's glance shifted, sharp and quiet like an arrow half-drawn.

"You carry the Montclair weight well, Saskia, but even diamonds fracture under the wrong pressure."

I met her eyes, steady. "I do not break easily. But I do know when to bend."

Her smile was faint. "Good. Flexibility isn't weakness; it's survival. Especially here, where they mistake sharp edges for cracks."

Clara shook her head, pouring another glass with brisk efficiency.

"You look like you've locked up your usual fortress and forgotten the key. You can't keep everyone out, not Zander, not Julien."

I smiled wryly. "They're allowed their entrance. The walls keep out worse things."

Clara smirking. "Like pretending any of this family isn't a

32

fire curling under thin ice."

We drank again, the warmth and sharpness of the wine weaving around us. For a moment, we were not executives, not players in a family boardroom. We were just women, tired and flawed, circling causes and loves we barely named.

Later, when Annina sprawled on the sofa and Clara gathered her shoes, I noticed Mara's toy horse left on the cushion. I picked it up without comment. They both saw. A silence held, full but not heavy. Jasmine was curled at the end of the sofa, paws tucked, eyes half-closed. She didn't stir. She has lived through louder nights than this.

For once, none of us were playing roles. We were just women, tired and flawed, but still laughing.

5

Gauche

Cap d'Antibes.

The Villa La Garoupe Blanche smells like salt, sunscreen and old money. Turquoise water, white stone, and cicadas sawing the heat into ribbons.

I am only here piggybacking on my cousin's booking. Zander, Corky, and Félix booked the villa for the week, and of course lovely Isa tagged along too. Rivals in business, yes, but sometimes even rivals need to sweat in the same sun.

Lunch stretched indecently long. Grilled fish, pale rosé, laughter rising like heat from stone. Isa, in a white bikini, looked sculpted on the lounger. Twenty-four, born knowing she will be watched. She has been in the Montclair bosom for years, more ornament than relative, and she lets them look because they have always looked after her. I let myself look because I enjoy it.

"Eyes front, Gauche," Zander said with a lazy grin as he

carved at the charred sea bass.

"She likes it," I shot back. "She'd complain if I didn't."

Isa stretched, slow and deliberately, smiling at neither of us. Corky nearly dropped his fork.

"Putain, you're all hopeless," Félix muttered, shaking his head. Paris streets were still in his cadence, even when he wore linen. "She is a person, pas une statue."

Isa laughed at that, tossing her hair.

"Maybe both."

Corky raised his glass, carefree as always.

"To statues that talk back."

We drank. The sun burnt. Salt dried white on our shoulders.

Later, cards on the terrace. Corky cursed like a schoolboy when he lost. Félix sketched absentmindedly in the margins of a napkin, lines turning into something beautiful without him seeming to notice. Zander leaned back in his chair, long legs stretched, smirk fixed in place like armour.

"You still think you can outplay me?" He asked when I laid down my hand.

"Bébé, I don't think," I said, scooping the pot. "I know."

He grinned sharply. "Confidence looks good on losers."

"Better than arrogance on heirs," I shot back.

Corky howled. Félix only smiled faintly. Isa faux yawned, then lowered her sunglasses just enough to catch my eye and give a slow, conspiratorial smile, then arched her back like a cat stretching in the sun.

It was easy, too easy, to fall into their rhythm, wine, rivalry, and sun-drenched arrogance. But I felt the pull of town, the need to step out of their theatre before I drowned in it.

Corky and Félix had already stripped off to start skinny-dipping in the sea, whooping as they cannon balled into the water. Isa lay stretched on the lounger, sunglasses low, absently twirling a strand of hair as if the entire villa had been built for her amusement. She would join in soon, of that I know.

Zander poured himself another glass of rosé and slid it across the table towards me. "You're restless."

I shrugged, rings flashing in the sun. "Better restless than bored."

"Bored?" His smirk widened. "With us?"

"With you," I said, sipping anyway.

He leaned back; the sun catching his face. "You always run when things get interesting."

"Or maybe I know when the room's out of moves."

Our eyes held. His smile sharpened. "Careful, Gauche. You spend too long in town, you'll come back thinking you own it."

I grabbed the Vespa keys and tucked them into my back pocket. "Better than coming back thinking you own the world."

"Touché," he said, lifting his glass in a mock toast.

I leant in just enough for him to hear. "Funny thing though. Some thrones are too heavy, even for men who think they were born to sit on them."

He laughed, low and genuine, like I'd scratched where it hurt. "And you'd rather be what? The storm that blew the tent down?"

"Exactement."

I left him there, grinning at his own reflection in the wine.

When I looked up, I saw tanned bodies with white *fesses* staring back at me, except for when Isa stood up from her lounger she didn't even pause, just smiled that slow, wide-eyed smile, kicked off her sandals and peeled away what little she was wearing. She ran for the steps like she owned the coast; the sunlight catching on her golden skin. There were no tan lines on Isa, no white bits, only perfection. The water took her with barely a splash. She looked like she moisturised with cashmere and bathed in fuck-off confidence, long and slender, like someone stretched her out on purpose, but still had curves and edges. She really was something to behold.

Zander coughed; he saw that I was transfixed.

I left them before the wine claimed me too. I knotted my dark curls, kicked the scooter awake, and let the town swallow me.

Late afternoon light washed everything gold, the cinematic forgiveness the Côte d'Azur does best. The promenade shimmered with bare shoulders, linen shirts, kids licking lollies faster than they melted, and dogs trotting as if the stones belonged to them. A busker pulled heartbreak out of pop songs. Neon hummed above gelato cases.

I stopped at an oyster cart I did not intend to patronise. The vendor recited his regions like a confession, each shell a troubled child. I tipped him and left the tray to a couple on the edge of kissing. They laughed and kissed; their spell broken.

That's when I saw her.

Not staged, not framed. At the far end of the promenade, where the stone leans into the sea, she leaned against the iron rail. A grey linen dress cut clean at the collarbone, falling just so. Long chestnut hair pulled back severely, a single strand slipping loose in rebellion. Slim, curved, elegant, no posing, no phone. She looked at the horizon as if it might answer.

She turned. Our eyes caught. Held.

37

"Bonsoir," I said.

Her smile tested me; not sweet, not cruel, weighing if I was worth her time. "Bonsoir."

Her vowels were French but burnished with somewhere else; Atlantic cities, expensive, tired of being expensive.

"They call me Gauche," I said, as if to spare her the gossip. "It meant one thing, but now I've made it mean another."

She smiled, "Esmé."

Her eyes blue enough to keep the light hostage.

"Esmé Béraud. Sometimes the wrong thing is the only honest thing."

That landed. No performance, no coyness. I should have played it bigger.

Instead, I reached for the loose strand hiding one eye, tugged a rhinestone pin from my curls, and slid it in with mock ceremony. My knuckles brushed her neck. "Emergency couture."

She laughed, low and surprised, like ice in a glass. Lifted a hand as if to remove it, then didn't. That decision felt closer than a kiss.

A baby stroller squeezed behind me forcing me to slide nearer, linen brushing linen. Her mouth was close enough that I felt the word more than heard it.

"Merci."

Every hair on my arms lifted. She did not move. Neither did I.

"Pardon," she said, not sorry at all.

"Noted."

We stepped back. The strand attempted an escape again, but the simple pin did its job.

"There," I said. "Now you look expensive."

"And before?"

"You looked like you could leave at any moment."

"Maybe I can."

She said it like a fact, not bait.

Tourists interrupted, phones flashing. I posed without effort. Esmé watched, then returned her gaze to the horizon as if it were the only thing worth her attention.

I should have asked for her number. Instead, I brushed her arm on the way past, for too long to be manners. She didn't flinch.

"Bonne soirée, Gauche," she said, soft, balanced between invitation and dismissal.

She left first. The rhinestone pin flashed once in the last of the sun, and then she was gone.

Back at the villa, the others were still wet from the sea, arguing over cards, salt drying on their shoulders. Félix was telling jokes, so I waved and sat at the end of Isa's lounger and massaged her feet whilst remembering to laugh at the right lines. I was not in the room. I was still at that railing with Esmé .

Later upstairs, I searched. Esmé Béraud. The name floated up with ghosts, dead painters, a Lyon pastry blog, and nothing else. No socials. No trace. Which is more dangerous than being everywhere.

I grinned at the ceiling. "Of course."

Sleep was scarce. My dreams were a horizon that moved, and the feeling of being watched without malice.

* * *

I returned to the same market in the morning. Bread hot from the oven, spices in pyramids, metal shutters clanging. I wandered stubbornly, pretending I wasn't looking. Until I saw her.

She was at a fruit stall, testing a nectarine like it was an exam. Hair pinned back again, pin still there, ridiculous and true. The vendor adored her, called her 'madame' and meant it.

I circled and picked the best peaches without looking. Our eyes met. Her mouth almost smiled, then did.

Daylight made her stone. Carved, precise, skin-like porcelain fired to strength. In a photo she'd look untouchable; in real life the blue of her eyes was almost reckless.

"Bonjour," I said.

"Bonjour."

"You always spec fruit like a prototype?"

"Yes, fruit tells the truth if you let it."

I laughed. "We'd be dangerous in a negotiation room."

"Would we?"

Knuckles grazed her wrist. Neither of us apologised.

"You kept it," I said.

"For emergencies."

"This isn't one."

"Not yet."

The market moved around us. Someone dropped oranges; a violin turned a cheerful song sad.

"What are you doing today?" I asked.

"Seeing if the sea is different."

"And if it is?"

"I will act surprised."

Her smile hit my stomach like bass through a speaker.

"À plus," I said.

"À plus," she answered. Permission. Warning.

"Here," she said as she attempted to give me the pin back.

"Keep it, I have plenty," and pointed to the stack of dark curls atop my head. "It suits you."

Back at the villa, I looked at myself in the mirror, a similar pin now holding my own curls.

Everyone usually wants a piece of me, but she is the first in a long time who did not ask. Which makes her the most dangerous of all.

6

Hortense

New York. Midnight.

The Tribeca penthouse is a time capsule lodged between shadow and glass. Concrete softened only by modular furniture placed with a curator's precision. No photographs. No warmth. Just punches of blood-red art pretending someone lived here. Near the entrance, a freestanding mirror leans crooked in its antique frame. He placed it there once. I have never moved it.

One record waits beside the player: Mahler's Symphony No. 5. Mine, not his. Small truths matter most.

Outside, Manhattan glares back, shards of light scattered over violence and glitter, indifferent. I stand before the skyline until an ache settles in my calves. The city does not wink; it dares.

Behind me, Alexandre Montclair's presence weighs like gravity. My heels rest by the door as if I stepped out of my life for a moment and have not yet decided whether to return.

I lean against the kitchen island, pouring two drinks. The weight of silence is familiar, one hand wrapped around glass, the other pressing memory like a wound. The silk clings to every curve in ways only he remembers.

His eyes slide past the curve of my waist to Manhattan's distant edge. They land, then wander, a man tethered to his ghosts and the now.

"I saw her."

The clink of glass speaks what his face cannot.

"Sabine."

"She is no ghost worth chasing anymore," he says, quieter.

I take a step closer, shoulders bare to the rain still gleaming on my skin. The silk shifts softly, neither for theatre nor invisibility, somewhere between demand and surrender.

"She left one of your private clubs. You must have signed her in. She wore the smile she uses to hide tears."

He doesn't shift his gaze from the skyline, so I let him carry it.

"You were photographed the same night."

The glass reflects us, him in shadow, me fragmented. I close the distance deliberately. Rain drips in my hair. Electric storm-bright.

"You're lecturing me."

I smile slowly, the one worn when unravelling is planned.

"No. I wanted to see if you still lied."

The air sharpens, pleading to be crossed.

He turns. Eyes trace my collarbone, linger on my mouth. He tastes the past. I watch the ice-blue aftermath and breathe slowly and steadily. I stand as if forgiveness is a prelude to retribution.

"You think I'm in love with her? That was years ago."

"No. I think you still belong to her."

I offer the drink. Fingers almost touch; siren's wail beyond the glass.

"You didn't move the mirror."

"Why would I?" I answer. "You were always coming back."

My hand slides to his neck, cool against the heat beneath.

"You're bleeding again."

He frowns, searching.

"Where?"

I tap the hollow above his heart.

"Inside. I smell it."

His kiss is sharp, then softens; regret tastes heavy on his lips. I let him. His body presses close, urgent. My silk is soaked in jasmine, bourbon, dusk, and inheritance. I know what I smell like to him.

"You don't have to fix me."

"Don't flatter yourself, Zee."

I turn towards the bedroom. He follows. Some rooms invite ruin.

Sex begins in silence; it always has. Lust without lyrics; history without grace.

I unfasten his belt like cutting a wire. Precise. Unafraid. Ready.

"Why now?"

"Because I can."

Truth, not lies, knives angled like daylight.

I sink to my knees. He watches.

I know what my mouth can do, and what memory wields.

He stiffens, but not like I expected. Rhythm stutters. Blood betrays him. Mind drifts not here. Not me.

He pulls me up, rolling beneath. Muscle memory. He thinks pressure cures all.

The kiss below my ear brings back shivers long past. In a breath, years dissolve. We are reckless, untouchable again.

I let him believe, but spy the shadow of another in his closed eyes.

He is inside me but thinking of someone else.

He wants to bury me beneath skin; I feel it in his grip, ache in his kiss. I bite his lip and breathe warmly in his ear.

"You feel so fucking good."

I hold his gaze steady.

"When was the last time?"

"Inside this apartment?"

"The last time you were inside me."

He would now be remembering marble and blindfolds, my hand at his throat, eyes open. Watching. Punishing.

When I come, I do not turn away.

I want him to see what he no longer owns.

Afterwards, the silence is brittle, almost tender.

We laugh, fragile, uncomprehending.

"Why didn't you answer my messages?"

I graze his shoulder lightly, teeth just a whisper. "Because you'd expect me to."

I curl into him, just enough, a fraction too little.

"I wanted you to feel it."

"Feel what?"

"Like a teenager. Obsessing. Waiting."

He says nothing. Silence hangs between us like suspended breath.

Then he stands naked, restless, moving with purpose, full

of it.

I watch. Beautiful, broken, still mine, when I choose.

I trail fingers along my nipple, not for him but for myself.

He notices; he always does.

Then, I tell him what I let happen.

He freezes, utterly still.

I do not soften.

"That's what you get," I say plainly, "for letting me love you second."

He does not look away. Never does.

"You don't want warmth."

"Then what?"

"I want to know what Leila fucking Farrow was doing here."

Calm, waiting, I meet his eyes.

"She stole my laptop."

The rest unspools between us: files, photos, videos, and AetherFlex material.

His curses spill in French.

The room is bugged. His phone lights up with proof.

My robe slips back casually.

"Her fingerprint still opens the door," I growl, "from when you fucked her here before me!"

I rise and pour bourbon.

"Well, now we've all been fucked!" He laughs bitterly.

Zander texts his people silently.

Manhattan hums louder than both of us.

I smile slowly, sharply.

"If you ever think I didn't love you... remember: I never copied your phone. Not once."

One heartbeat.

Then another.

Silence. Balanced.

They want me to spy. To harvest slips and weaknesses.
   Tonight, I gave them plenty.
   Beneath the cold, I feel it.
   I adore him.
   Which makes this the cruelest betrayal of all.

7

Saskia

The investor event is a glass cathedral of confidence. Uplights rinsed in bone white. Sound engineered to make applause inevitable. A stage that eats people and turns them into slides.

Tables gleam with linen flatter than diplomacy, crystal aligned like soldiers. The air carries gardenia and champagne, chosen to reassure, not delight. Silver trays drift through the crowd: oysters on shaved ice, lamb skewers lacquered to a shine, and tartlets no one admits to finishing.

The ceiling vaults in mirrored panels, reflecting every guest back at themselves in distorted grandeur. Investors in black tie lean across banquettes, laughter tight, watches brighter than eyes. Assistants hover a step behind, polishing silences.

Security stands too still at the edges, menace pressed into bespoke suits. The donors like their danger understated.

It is theatre disguised as hospitality, where fortunes are courted under chandeliers and reputations crack in the cloak-room.

Mara looks small against it, cardigan and badge swallowed

whole by glass and crystal, as if the room exists to remind her she does not belong.

My job, as ever, is gravity in heels.

Luc is absent, though the air tilts toward him. He has sent me in his place, his precision delegated, while he buries himself in a launch he calls new and exciting. I have rarely seen him so animated by anything beyond profit. I want to know what draws such a fuss.

Mara asked to come. I said yes when I should have said later. She is good with rooms when she can draw them first. Tonight there is no sketch, only light. I pin her badge inside her cardigan and tell her she can sit by the tech desk. Independent Block, the tutors call it. A phrase I dislike. It turns a child into a time slot.

The CFO rehearses his joke about growth. Zander waits off-stage left, mic clipped. He has a calmness borrowed from other people. The MC says, 'Two minutes,' as the logo breathes on the screen.

The scrape of a fork cuts the air. Mara stands. She moves towards the bright, the way people do when they mistake light for invitation. She is eleven, surefooted, and one step from the sensor. Stage left sees her too late.

Zander moves first.

He drops the script and rushes towards her, placing himself between her and the edge, a wall in a suit. His mic hisses. The light misses his face, and that is kindness. He reaches no closer than needed, voice even and low.

"Hey, Mara. Not yours, my love."

She checks his eyes, recalculates. The stage manager holds the cue with a hand that shakes. The MC counts backwards into air.

Zander shrugs out of his jacket and drapes it over her shoulders so the cameras do not love her. He turns his body to shield, not to hide. He gestures towards me with a tilt of the head, asking permission without words. I nod. He walks her back, step for step, slow enough to lower the room's heartbeat.

He does it with Mara the way he does with me, stepping into the gap before danger shows its teeth, offering cover without claim.

I take her hand.

"Xinyi." A whisper, a tether.

"I wanted to see," she says. Small, steady, annoyed with herself.

"You can, but from here."

She squeezes my fingers. Zander meets my gaze over her head. A thank you forming, waiting its turn.

The MC launches the show. The logo opens like a mouth and swallows men with microphones. Applause moves through the room on schedule. Investors smile at the right slides.

I stand at the back with Mara's cardigan bundled in my hand and feel the walls trying to sell calm. They almost succeed.

At the interval, I move to the bar for water I will not drink. Dorian Tseng finds me without appearing to move. Charcoal suit again. No phone, only the folder look, even empty-handed. He does not touch my elbow. He does not need to.

"Filed," he says.

"Good," I answer.

He mentions a time already on my calendar. "Morning, Corsica channel confirms."

"Xièxiè," I murmur, too softly.

His mouth barely moves. "Mh sái la."

50

The words linger.

Nothing more than manners, only syllables, but I said 'thank you' in Mandarin. He answered immediately in Cantonese. The correction is not for the room. It is for me.

I am supposed to be from Hong Kong. This is Dorian's way of saying he knows.

"I—"

"Queens don't apologise," he interrupts. "They let the room correct itself."

We step apart as if gravity requested it. He looks beyond me, calculates the risk of lingering, and chooses correctly. I turn back to the crowd like a woman who has not just moved a piece across a board no one else remembers is there.

Later, after applause has bruised the air and donors have wrung out their last compliments, I find Zander in the service corridor where the light is honest. The hum of the ice machine is the sound a headache makes.

"Thank you," I say.

He leans a shoulder against the wall, close enough to narrow the space. He tries for casual, fails. "For what?"

"For—" I hesitate, my voice smaller than I meant. "For shielding her."

His eyes soften, forgetting performance. "Oh. Yes, of course, always."

The words land wrong, too broad, as if he promised more than he should. My throat catches on what to say next.

Gratitude is what I meant. What rises is not gratitude. The pause between us is bright and thin. One step and I would feel his sleeve against mine. One more breath and I would give myself away.

51

"Outstanding event," he says at last.

"Outstanding save," I answer. My hand rests on the door handle. I do not push it. Not yet.

His smile lingers, quiet. "She is brave."

"She is." The handle is cold in my palm. His shoulder still blocks half the exit.

"She saw light and wanted more of it. You cannot teach that. You can only keep the edges from cutting."

The silence is now heavy between us. My body tilts before I command it not to. I shift, meaning to pass, and my silk sleeve brushes the wool of his jacket. Heat, brief, undeniable. Gratitude would not burn like that.

I nod and slip past before the corridor itself decides for us.

Outside, the night arranges itself into the London people pay for. Taxis hum. The air tastes of rain considering itself.

* * *

At home, the Quiet House is lit by side lamps, reflections wearing the windows as masks. I do not turn on the overheads. Softer is more civilised. Less like betrayal.

Heels off first. Black silk, still warm from rooms where everyone performs belief. Mara is already in her soft clothes, curled on the sofa with her tablet and tools, head bent over a project I could not explain.

I change. Shake the evening from my shoulders like something that will try to climb back on. Pour a drink, white and cold. From the doorway, I watch her for a full minute. My angel.

In the hallway, I open the envelope Dorian handed me earlier in the week, the one I have not allowed myself to check again.

Just enough to see what I need. A name. A date. The holding signature. The transfer is through. Done.

Mara pads in for goodnight. She smells of graphite and sandalwood shampoo. I hug her too tightly. She does not complain. "Night, Māmā," she says.

"Night, Xinyi."

When she is gone, I stand in the reading room, barefoot. The Meursault waits on the sideboard. The house holds its breath for me.

I take out my phone and open the message from earlier. Zander's voice, low, roughened by microphones and unsaid things:

"Sass, call me back. Please."

I type, delete, and type again.

> Thank you for today.

The three dots appear. Disappear. Appear. I wait through the longest minute in a brief life.

> Anytime.

Then, after a moment that knows what it is doing:

> Always.

The word pulses against my palm where the glass rests. I should have let it pass. Instead, I read it twice, as if repetition could dilute danger. It does not.

A quick scroll. Someone has stood up to Kevin Price at under:CORE and forced a date in court.

```
Jury to Hear under:CORE Case After Exec's
Striptease at Staff Retreat — Clara Sundström Named
in Retaliation Claim.
```

My beautiful, brave friend, Clara.

"Bravo," I say aloud and raise my glass.

I forward the report to the girls, write only 'Bad Bitch', then place my phone face down. The glass goes black. The quiet is useful.

Tomorrow there will be calls, strategy, and the problem of the Mandarin word drifting through a room that had been told I am only what my passport says. Tonight there is the small shirt folded on the arm of the sofa, the constellation socks paired at last, the echo of a child almost stepping into too much light and a man placing himself between her and it without ceremony.

I choose noise. Quiet will not save us.

8

Mara

I drew Julien's hand, curled under the table. He thinks no one sees it, but I do. His cuff is wrong; it's too loose, a mistake. The koi circle beneath us, slow as breath. I press them onto the page in loops, mouths like doors opening and closing.

I like to sketch Aunt Céleste. She doesn't move. But the surrounding lines do.

The scrape of a fork cuts the air. Everyone else talks through it, but to me it sounds like a hurricane splitting silence open. I press my pencil harder. The koi grow darker, mouths wider, like they might swallow the table whole.

Jazz brushes against my leg, soft fur, tail flicking once. No one else notices her. She always finds me when the noise gets too sharp. I let the pencil ease, and feel calm again.

Zander leans forward, pretending he isn't watching. In my sketch, his jaw is sharper than his real one. That's how he thinks he looks. Adults hate when you draw what they imagine instead of what they are. It makes them restless.

Māmā is the hardest. She sits too still, every breath rehearsed. I make her eyes softer than she wants them to be.

At the bottom of the page I write:

People never look like they think they do.

No one asks what it means. They rarely do.

Later, when the house is quiet, I lie flat on the tiles in the reading room. The floor remembers. It keeps the heat of the day. I press my cheek against it until I can hear the hum of the underfloor wires. Heat has a sound if you wait long enough.

Moss sits in its glass tray by the window. Tonight, it is grey at the edges. I whisper, "Do not creep away." It shivers but holds. Moss listens when the lights are low.

I draw again. This time I do not stop at hands or koi. I draw Daddy. Not Luc with his work face, the other Daddy. I give him a yellow suit instead of dark, the kind that burns behind your eyes when you stare at light too long. I forget his eyes. Or maybe I erase them. The page is stronger without them.

When I look at it, my chest feels hollow, like a bottle waiting to be filled. I tuck the drawing under my pillow; the pencil smudge kisses the fabric, a grey promise someone might see.

I put on Four Tet's *My Angel Rocks Back and Forth*. It sounds like weather I can live inside. I hum the notes until they belong to me. Quiet is a tool.

Barefoot, I curl my toes into the rug. Count to three. Again. Again.

Then I log into ChessMaster.

```
KnightLight against BleuFantôme.
```

Another game no one knows I am playing.

```
BleuFantôme: Your move, little knight.
KnightLight: Bishop to F5. Why do you always leave
gaps?
BleuFantôme: Because gaps are doors. You know that.
KnightLight: Doors let people in. Or out.
BleuFantôme: And which do you want?
```

I do not answer. Instead, I paste in a few of my favourite Radiohead, he sends me Leonard Cohen back:

> *There is a crack in everything; that's how the light gets in.*

I hum again, softer. Music is the only language without lies.
  Sometimes I test words on him.

```
KnightLight: Shoes are apologies to the body.
BleuFantôme: Good. Say it again.
KnightLight: Shoes are apologies to the body.
BleuFantôme: And silence?
KnightLight: Silence is a blade. Quiet is a tool.
BleuFantôme: Then keep yours sharp.
```

He signs off. His icon fades to grey.

I stay at the desk with my sketchbook open to a page no one will see. On it, I have written:

Some shapes ask to be chosen.

I do not know yet if I mean people or patterns. Maybe both.

The pencil smudge stains the side of my hand. I rub it against my cheek before washing. The floor keeps the mark longer than skin does.

I put the sketchbook under the bed, where the boards creak

if anyone looks. I whisper to Moss one last time. It answers with green. Agreement.

The house sleeps. Māmā thinks I do too, but quiet is a tool.

I am awake, drawing men who do not have eyes, and listening to the floor breathe.

I am KnightLight.

I am the lock and I am the key.

9

Saskia

Luc called it the Quiet House. He hadn't lived here for years. A Chelsea side street, facades polished to the same gloss as the Bentleys and Maybachs parked outside. Five bedrooms, no clutter, no sentiment. A stage set in limestone and silence.

Outside, the street is manicured into obedience with clipped hedges, security cameras, and polished brass. Inside, the deep music from Mara's speakers fractures the order, plaster vibrating, portraits rattling on the walls.

Now it is mine. A place to vanish between strategies. To ache, to plot. To pretend I am above it all.

I strip the sheets in the guest room and carry them to the laundry. A shirt slips from the pile, not mine. Small, cotton-soft, and carrying the faint smell of crayons and sandalwood shampoo. Mara's. I press it to my face, and for a moment I let myself breathe her in, and it undoes me. Ridiculous, sentimental. Dangerous. I slip it back into the basket too quickly, as if the fabric itself had caught me out.

"Xinyi," I whisper. The name she lets me use is soft as a

secret.

Downstairs, the bass surges, windowpanes trembling. Portishead. She sings with Beth Gibbons, raw and true. The sound makes the house feel less like a mausoleum and more alive.

It is her time now, and the tutors dress up as Independent Block. A phrase I dislike. It turns her into a time slot. The theory is elegant. The practice is that I cannot hear myself think when she insists the speakers test their limits.

I wait for the hum of the dryer to settle me. It doesn't. The hum sharpens the silence in my head.

I think of Céleste last year, her verdict on schooling.

"Her mind bends in patterns," she had said calmly, not as advice. It was as if she had already judged. And Luc had spoken of it with her, not with me. That was a shock. Not that she knew. That I had been the one left out.

The bass pounds again. Mara laughs mid-lyric, carelessly, like the room belongs to her.

I press my hand to the dryer door, heat blooming through the metal. Socks patterned with constellations, a hair ribbon, and a washcloth streaked with graphite. Ordinary things, spun into orbit. They undo me more than anything Luc has left behind.

Upstairs, my phone vibrates against the marble counter, low and insistent, like a pulse I refuse to touch. Zander. Another voice message. I do not play it. I tell myself not to think of his hands steadying Mara at the gala, his jacket falling around her shoulders, the way his eyes found mine before the lights claimed him. The thought arrives anyway.

Instead, I fold Mara's shirt, smoothing it flat, and imagine the house the way it was meant to be: silent, immaculate, lifeless. Then I imagine it as it is now, music tearing through rooms, small objects colonising the emptiness.

I prefer the noise.

The dryer clicks off. I carry the stack upstairs. Her constellation of socks slide free, one falling against the base of the old bureau in the corridor. I bend to retrieve it, hand brushing the lower drawer.

It gives. Too easily.

Inside: folders, immaculate. Luc's order, his handwriting in the margins. He hated clutter but loved records. Excision without erasure, loyalty performed whilst the stage was rearranged.

I almost shut it again. Then I see her.

Mara.

A photograph, glossy, edges fading. She is no older than one, a blur of dark hair, cheeks flushed with that easy warmth she still carries. A sunlit room I recognise but shouldn't, the Corsican villa. I was there once, the walls bare, shutters half-closed. Yet in this picture, the Bechstein piano stands behind her, the vintage one Claudine claimed Liszt had played. 'Romantic nonsense,' Luc had laughed. Still, he kept it.

He divorced Claudine, but he never let a bad word be spoken against her. That was his trick: excision without erasure. He curated history the way he curated everything else.

Downstairs Mara's voice is unselfconscious and bold. "It's Portishead," she calls, laughter folding into the lyric.

I hold the photograph tighter. For a moment I imagine her older, eyes sharpened, chin stubborn, with a trace of him in the jawline. Luc's daughter, but I'm thinking of Zander. It unsettles me how easily the blood surfaces.

The folder shifts under my hand, heavier than paper should

be. More photographs. More truths.

The phone vibrates again, a tremor waiting to be answered. I let it buzz against the stone until it dies.

Another photograph. Mara again, a little older, near the same piano. In the blurred background, a woman's hand rests on the fallboard, pale and elegant, jewellery catching the sun. Claudine, I think. It must be Claudine.

I bring it closer. Not Claudine's chain. The details sharpen into something else, a heavy gold bracelet worn over a glove.

Céleste.

My stomach tightens. A cold rush moves through me, the kind I only feel when the game changes. Of course, she was there. Of course, she was everywhere. Yet Luc never mentioned it. He divorced Claudine and guarded her reputation, but it is Céleste's hand fixed in the frame of Mara's infancy.

Annina would laugh at the bracelet. Clara would ask why he hid it.

For an instant my mind betrays me, filling in another hand entirely, broad-knuckled, impatient. Zander's. I close my eyes and shake it away.

I slip the photograph back into the folder, then change my mind. I pull it free and slide it into Mara's folded shirt.

Clara answers on the second ring, background noise alive, as if she's already halfway through a victory lap.

"Bad bitch confirmed," I say, letting my smile carry through. "The case made me proud. How are you holding up?"

"Triumphant, exhausted, drunk," she fires back. "In that order. But mostly triumphant."

"You deserve it." I let the silence hold, a gift. "And how are you, really?"

"Dangerous question. Do you want the list?"

"Another time," I murmur. "Tonight, you win."

I let the moment breathe, then tilt my voice lighter, as though idly curious. "Clara... tell me, am I being silly? Did Mademoiselle Céleste ever spend time at the Corsican villa?"

Her laugh stops short. "You guys still refer to her as Mademoiselle! Céleste? Not that I remember; wherever Luc was, she would be there. Why?"

I hesitate enough to be noticed. "A photograph. Mara was at the piano with a hand in shot, but the bracelet, which I thought was Claudine's, was not; it was Céleste's. Luc was hardly at the Corsican villa when Mara was that age."

"Then you're probably not being silly. Just keep an ear out, just in case."

Downstairs, the bass rattles the floorboards. Mara's voice rides the song as if she were born for it.

From this moment. How can it feel this wrong?

Noise over silence.

The Quiet House was meant for silence. Tonight it shakes with music and my daughter's voice. And in the pause between bass lines, his message waits, the word always ghosting the air.

For once, I let the walls keep it.

10

Isobel (fragment)

The garden steps at Amberley still held the remnants of rain. Stones dark where the moss had taken hold, too bright where the gardener had been zealous. He said it would not grow this year. It always does. Some things prefer the shade.

From here, just far enough to be ignored, one sees what the wine will erase by morning: the lit windows, the family arranged like an amateur stage play, gestures repeated, lines delivered without rehearsal.

Saskia at the table, profile caught by a lamp, looked as if she listened whilst, in fact, she waited for her cue.

Lucien was speaking again; of course he was, his voice filling the air as reliably as mildew. Food, wine, the order of courses. Some men collect mistresses; he collects amuse-bouches.

Alexandre leaned forward, still pretending thirty-five was an audition for twenty-one. Shoulders stiff, grin still boyish, a man rehearsing a prime already reviewed and closed. Saskia watched him without malice.

Mara drifted in through the terrace doors, wrapped too

tightly in a shawl that had nothing to do with temperature. Lovely, distracted, murmuring to herself: 'He appears more benevolent in the drawing.' No one replied. Perhaps no one heard.

I did.

Ash pawed at my wrist for attention then settled again at my feet, a long sigh through his narrow chest.

Lucien turned then, smile soft for the child, hand easy on the other dog's ruff, a picture of benevolence lit by the terrace lamps. A man framed as patriarchal, generous, and golden. But when the gardener stammered something about the roses, Luc's hand never left the dog's head as he answered. Words low, clipped, promising consequence. The child laughed, the dog wagged its tail, and only the gardener looked like prey.

I remember the first atelier, before all this glass and theatre. The rafters low, the walls chalk-marked with patterns no one filed, cloth stacked in shadows. Young Lucien has forgotten it or prefers to pretend he has. But I still see it, threadbare and alive.

And I hear things now, too. Not from people. People are careful, or think they are, but there are still whispers if you know where to listen. Fragments, drafts, numbers mislabelled as data. I take what they do not mean to give.

And when Céleste finally spoke, Luc stopped. Even the knives paused—cutlery, conversation, the whole charade.

"Do cheer up," I said, taking the seat that had been waiting for me. "It looks like a funeral. And I do hope it is not mine; I would rather be consulted."

That turned their heads. It always does. They forget I am still here.

The thing about families is they prefer silence dressed as

loyalty. Personally, I prefer the naked truth. It has fewer airs.

If Saskia knew about the dawn flight to New York and Hortense again, her angle might have sharpened. Instead, she still plays dutiful, and dutiful is a dull blade. I watched her slide Mara's pages out of sight, the way you would hide contraband, not homework. Zander's name hovered on her screen.

AetherFlex is already under the microscope. I can see long, slender fingers on it. They will not be gentle.

Lucien tells people he flew to Paris. Of course he does. A man like him is always flying to Paris. Except I watched the helicopter lift and bank the wrong way. Paris does not lie west. Paris does not disappear over Paddington.

I could tell Saskia. I could tell any of them. But then what would I do for entertainment?

11

Saskia

The Wexford, Mayfair.

I am not a member here, not in how it counts. The Wexford is private, lined with men who only say 'please' to their lawyers. I can sit in the main bar because of Luc's name, not mine. The private rooms are for members; some are only for men. Below ground, a whisky bar where you cannot speak after midnight; the AI listens and remembers your voice.

I choose the main bar, and the mirror that runs behind it. I want to see who is watching me without giving them the pleasure of seeing me watch back. Number Four serves me. They go by numbers, not names, a trick to keep the members feeling singular.

I wear The Row, silk that moves like thought, armour disguised as softness.

Heads turn. Eyes stay. Attention lands like a weight in my

lap, not a hand on my shoulder. Familiar, never kind.

Clara would have smiled back at them, slowly.

I do not order. I announce. Saint-Romain, I say, from Christian's brother-in-law's private cellar.

Number Four nods too quickly, a tremor at his mouth. When the bottle arrives, he waits, trained to be invisible. I do not pour. I instruct him in angle, height, and pause. Passive aggressive? Yes. A win the size of a sugar cube but still sweet.

The men watch, always watching. Some with the old smile, some with the new blankness that says any expression is a liability. Their reflections are better behaved than their bodies.

A man with a signet ring and the smile of someone who treats politeness as currency raises his glass.

"Madame Montclair. Brave of you to sit alone here. Women usually prefer the tearooms around Mayfair."

Laughter rolls, trained to sound harmless.

I let my smile sharpen without touching my eyes. I do not answer. The weight of attention presses harder, as though I had been called to account and found lacking.

My phone lifts with a small vibration. I open the reply box and type nothing. The unsent words gather behind my teeth. I delete the blank and put the phone face down.

Stupid. To be here at his club, in his air. Waiting for a scent, a glimpse, a misstep I could call accidental.

"Bonsoir, mademoiselle."

Zander.

He arrived as if summoned by their cruelty. The laughter cut short as though someone had closed a door. He stood as if the room were already his. No rehearsal, no courtesy. Dark jacket, cuffs undone, hair still marked with the faintest curl of rain. He didn't glance in the mirror to check angles. He didn't need to.

"Come now," he said, not a request. "A woman of your stature cannot sit at the bar." His eyes flicked to the men pretending not to stare, their smirks exhausted even by their own boredom. "You know they are watching. It's tedious."

The courtesy was careless, not precise, which made it protective rather than parody. I ignored his hand but rose.

We both smiled.

"We will go through," he said. "I have friends arriving, but not just yet."

The corridor was lined with oils of dead benefactors who looked as though they had founded shipping lines and alibis. Green velvet walls drank the light, amber lamps set low. Nineteen-twenties jazz curled like perfume, deciding who to trust. A room for confidences and gossip traded like currency.

Zander chose a corner facing both the room and the exit. He let me sit first, then sprawled opposite, posture loose but eyes fixed on mine. He wanted me to notice. Montclair by blood, fighter by instinct, always optimising the angle without appearing to.

We drank, and let the room softened around us.

"You know," he said, "Luc thinks competition makes us sharper. Hunger as virtue."

"And does it?"

He tipped his head, not quite a nod. "It makes us watch each other too closely. You can't build if your eyes are always on the next man's hands."

"Luc mistakes fear for drive," I said. "Fear corrodes. It makes people petty. You don't build leaders that way. You breed saboteurs."

69

His smile ghosted. "And you? How would you play it?"

"Simple. Decide which of you can build the future. Then give him room to breathe. Hunger doesn't build. Vision does."

Something shifted in him, a softening, the membrane between defiance and longing. "You make it sound so easy."

"Oh, trust me, it isn't easy," I said. "It's necessary."

He looked at me for three breaths. I heard the room noticing and pretending not to. I also heard my phone shift in my bag, a ghost fish in a silk river.

"You don't rehearse," I said. "You don't practise conversations. Not like Julien has to."

A laugh, low and unpolished.

"Never. I say what I shouldn't... then I say it louder."

I laughed, clean and real, not the brittle gala laugh. The kind you're supposed to cover quickly.

"Numbers I trust," he said. "People, less so."

"You say people like you're not one of them."

"Tu marques un point!"

I smiled warmly.

He asked about my dress, not the label. "The architecture," he said. "What makes it work?"

"The seam," I told him. "Always the seam. The invisible line that holds the shape. Place it wrong and everything looks expensive and wrong all at once."

He leaned back slowly, as if committing it to memory. For a second I saw him at twenty, bruised from sparring, daring the world to underestimate him.

He sat forward again, hands loose, not folded. "May I ask you something? Off the record."

"You already have," I said.

"When you talk about loyalty..." His voice dropped. "What

do you do when someone, when loyalty itself, is turned into a trap?"

I let silence do its work. He filled it, as I knew he would.

"Luc left papers on his desk," he said. "Careless. Looked like a draft. Suggested I'd be...discarded."

"You looked?"

He nodded, his pause was too long for innocence.

"Luc wanted one of you to look," I said. "It was bait. Curiosity over loyalty. That wasn't his will; it was a mirror. A test."

Zander's jaw tensed. The words fit too well.

For a moment, the calculation fell away. Doubt made him young. It made me want to protect him and shake him in the same breath.

"Stay loyal," I said, quiet but absolute. "Luc trusted more than you think. He didn't ignore you; he tested you. He needed to know which son could resist fire."

He exhaled, half laugh, half groan. "You are very certain."

"I am very practical. Certainty is for men in oil portraits."

He smiled properly then, eyes greener than the walls. For a second he looked like a spy in a mid-century novel, dangerous because he remembered everything.

We drank and spoke of Berlin, champagne pouring from sculptures, and nonsense people pretended was normal. He told me he fought men bigger than him for sport. I told him that was a love language. He didn't argue.

The room filled in increments: men in navy under a bronze stag, a woman in silver with a man already tired of her. Jazz slowed. Someone laughed in the corridor and then remembered themselves.

"You'll think me foolish," he said. "I replay conversations

71

after they happen. Until I find the word I should have chosen."

"You're not foolish," I said. "You're a man who wants to control the past, and you'd be surprised how many of us live there."

His watch told him his friends were due. "Will you be here?"

"For a while."

He leaned closer carefully, carrying the scent of vetiver and rain. "Thank you," he said. "For the advice, and the seam."

"For the warning," I answered.

He smiled. "That too."

We hugged. His jacket sleeve brushed my arm, warm, brief, and enough to leave me unsteady. He asked if I was driving or needed him to arrange a car.

And then he was gone, leaving me with the table, the bottle, and the thought that truth was not what Luc wrote on paper. It was what his son had almost believed.

I drink the Saint-Romain and feel the edges of the evening rearrange. The subway-dark thought moves through me.

His sleeve against mine still lingers, an imprint more honest than his words. My skin recalls warmth long after it should have cooled. I replay it the way he replays conversations, as if repetition might strip it of meaning. It does not.

I walk back past the hall where a glass case exhibited club artefacts that look like trophies and bribes. Past the Serpent Room, visible through glass, named without irony for the men who shed their skins in it and leave them for the staff. The serpentine motif glints along the dado rail. The shadowboxes show gifts from past members, grotesque and expensive.

In the glass I catch my reflection, bent by the curve of silver. For a moment I see myself displayed, appraised, waiting for laughter. Then I remember how quickly it died when he spoke.

And I hate that I am grateful.

In the quiet, his voice returns.

Thank you.

I loathe the way my mouth almost shapes a reply.

12

Clara

He only touched me once, but it was enough to ruin the next five years.

I never said those words out loud. Not to HR, not to the journalist who asked if I had ever been personally affected, not even to Hal, but they replay sometimes, like a note that will not decay. The hand on my lower back. The whisper at a launch gala.

You look better when you smile, Clara.

It was nothing, and it was everything, because the next morning, he made sure my promotion was delayed.

I learnt quickly. Power is not a ladder; it is a gate, and I was taught early who held the keys.

Now the headlines carry my name.

Jury to Hear under:CORE Case After Exec's
Striptease at Staff Retreat — Clara Sundström Named
in Retaliation Claim.

I stare at the words on my phone screen; the glass catches the faint reflection of my face. No photograph. Not this time. Just my name, tied to yet another scandal. I tap the glass with one fingernail, then place it facedown on the table before the familiar heat rises in my chest.

The whisky helps. More than it should.

My phone buzzes again — not another headline, but a message from Saskia.

Noise over silence.

Three words. She never wastes them.

I don't answer, not yet. But I leave the screen lit longer than I should, as if her words could steady me through the glass.

Kevin Price hadn't always been a villain. Not in the way the tabloids are writing it now. He was magnetic once, a man who could sell sand in a desert and make you thank him for the privilege. Once, he could fill a room like champagne bubbles — bright, restless, impossible to pin down — but when the fizz went flat, what remained was sour. The decay was obvious if you wanted to see it, though most people called it ambition, but desperation makes strange monsters of men. By the time under:CORE began haemorrhaging market share, his mask had already slipped.

When the lawsuits came, they called it betrayal.

I knew better.

The company bled itself dry on things that looked like marketing but smelt like misconduct. Whispers of dysfunction were brushed off as jealousy from former partners or disgruntled ex-employees. Meanwhile, behind closed doors, Price and his circle threw money at athletes and investors in clubs where the walls were too dark and the doors too private.

The annual spring gala was the worst of it. Marketed as a showcase for new products, but everyone knew the genuine attraction was the guest list. Photogenic women, employees, and influencers handpicked to "mingle" with key partners. Inside, some executives even joked about it: *grooming the current.*

The phrase still makes me cold.

All of it would have remained rumour. If not for the theft.

The prototype, AetherFlex, stolen from a rival. The Montclair's, no less! When Price's name was placed in the frame the dam burst. Lawsuits. Investigations. Retaliation claims, and now, a jury trial. By the time the subpoenas landed, AetherFlex was already long gone. Kevin sold it; he was not stupid enough to claim it as his own. Sold cheaply but with lifetime royalties tucked into a shadow clause. And Luc, of course, waiting with an open chequebook.

The kitchen smells faintly of garlic. Hal is cooking something. He moves with quiet competence, stirring onions until they turn soft and translucent. He glances up when I enter, eyes warm and steady.

"You're home early," he says.

"Was I expected late?"

He always sees more than I say.

"I read the headline."

I reach for the bottle on the counter. Pour a glass. The clink is louder than it should be.

"You should eat first," he murmurs.

"I'm not hungry."

"You're always hungry when you're angry."

That makes me pause. He is the only person who can disarm me with a single line. The only one who sees the cracks.

I sip instead of answering. The whisky burns, then soothes.

He doesn't press. He never does. That is part of why I chose him. Hal doesn't need my confessions. He offers presence, not interrogation. The opposite of the men I've worked with.

"Clara," he says, not looking up from the pan, "you're more than the company's shadow."

I want to believe him. I used to be proud of who I was.

I told myself I was protecting the company, protecting jobs, but I wasn't protecting women. Not really. Sometimes I made sure they got a severance package. Sometimes I bought out a non-compete clause so an intern wouldn't be blacklisted. Quiet things. Things that never made the papers.

But I never burnt the system down.

And that is what makes me complicit.

I walk over to Hal and hug him from behind.

"I have swallowed worse. The trick is never letting them see you choke."

Kevin's face flashes in my mind, the smug curve of his mouth, the way he leant in too close. He called himself a visionary. The truth was simpler: he was a thief with better suits.

"He only touched me once," I whisper. "But it was enough."

I thought I was protecting jobs. But Saskia would call that theatre. She has no patience for illusions. And maybe that's why I followed her to London when I could have started fresh anywhere else. She makes me believe there's still something to build after the fire.

I swirl the whisky. Watch the amber coat the glass, cling, then slide back down.

People call me unflappable. I cultivate that. Neutral tones, tailored suits, Swedish restraint. In the boardroom, silence is a weapon sharper than words. I've watched entire rooms fall still when I enter. Not because I shout. Because I don't.

But the truth? Some nights the silence presses back.

The article lies open on the table. Words I can't unread: retaliation claim. Culture clashes. striptease incident.

One woman who started this, young, clever, ambitious. She came to me after a retreat, voice shaking, eyes wide. She told me what he'd done. The shirtless dance and the photo in branded swimwear were shared to the team channel. The mocking comments about #MeToo.

I told her not to escalate. Not because I didn't believe her. But because I knew how the system would treat her.

It will damage morale, I said. *It won't scale, and it's legally indefensible.*

I thought I was protecting her. I thought I was protecting the company.

Now it looks like complicity.

And maybe it was.

Hal sets a plate in front of me. Pasta with garlic and olive oil. Simple, perfect.

"You need to eat," he says.

I take a bite to humour him. The salt, the oil, the heat – it pulls me back into my body.

"You think I'm guilty," I say.

He doesn't answer immediately. He wipes his hands on a towel. Sits across from me and meets my eyes.

"I think you survived a system designed to crush you," he says finally. "And I think you learnt how to use it. That doesn't make you guilty."

"It doesn't make me innocent either."

He studies me. "Do you *need* to be innocent?"

The question hangs between us.

Later, when he's asleep, I pour another glass and open the laptop. Read the headlines again. London wasn't meant to be exile. Hal calls it renewal. I call it distance. But Saskia was here, and sometimes that's reason enough.

The laughter stalls. The sea keeps breathing.

"Bravo, Clara," I murmur, raising the glass to the dim reflection on the screen. It's about time someone set fire to him.

And if I'm the one who burns with it? So be it.

I drink. I read. I let the silence press. Then I remember: silence is what men count on.

Saskia always tells me that noise always wins over silence.

I was not built for silence.

13

Céleste

Montclair HQ, London.

White stone under my heels, polished to a shine that betrays every trespass. Black leather chairs no one uses. Frosted glass panels that pulse faintly, as though the building has its own heart. Behind reception, the digital display shows only the date and the weather. Never the time. Luc's order, his way of erasing clocks.

Security here is layered: fingerprint, passcode, and face. No cards, no concessions. Everyone feels watched, and they should.

On the screens: a bank collapsing in Singapore, wheat fields burning in Kherson. No sound, only the ticker running too fast to follow. No one reacts. Montclair breeds intelligence, not curiosity.

Luc's office crowns the building, a glass triangle suspended above the city. A room designed to unsettle. Soundproofed, capable of blackout at the brush of a hand. Only one guest chair, because control does not share its space.

On the walls: a Montclair shoe from the 1950s, polished mahogany. A photograph of Lucien Sr pressed flat beneath glass, stripped of frame and date. On Luc's desk, nothing but order and a cup of Earl Grey.

"Zander is making headlines. And enemies. One of those matters to me."

Luc slides the dossier forward. His hand never lingers.

I open it with my fingertips. Zander's bare chest against the window. Hortense's bare chest bent to the same glass, blurred where it matters, not for decency but liability.

The door slides open without warning. Zander enters, jaw taut. Behind him, Saskia. Neither waits to be asked.

Luc steeples his fingers. "Ring Avery. Make Hortense disappear from the Tribeca apartment."

The pause is surgical. Then Saskia's voice: cool, deliberate.

"You're asking me to make this palatable?"

"You handle optics," Luc says. "You are the priest in this family."

Her answer is a blade. "I am not a priest. And I do not clean the sins of men who enjoy being photographed whilst they commit them."

The refusal hangs, crystalline.

Zander's head turns towards her, and for a moment he forgets to mask himself. His gaze lingers, not defensive but lit with something sharper, something that looks like hunger disguised as respect. He watches the precision of her mouth and the steadiness of her stance, as if she's the one with the power to define him.

Her eyes flick towards him, a brush of acknowledgement,

and in that silence she makes it clear she has seen him see her. She doesn't reward it with expression, only the cool precision of restraint. Which is worse for him, I think, than any reply she might give.

Luc's lips harden. "Your role is containment."

"My role is choice," she says. "And I choose not to waste my authority repairing what should never have been broken."

Zander steps closer, voice hot.

"Do not speak of me as though I am absent. You wanted a headline, Father; here it is. At least mine proves I am alive."

Luc's reply slices cold. "Alive is not the same as useful."

Zander, bristling, caught between defiance and the quiet pull of Saskia's refusal. Saskia, unflinching, the point unsettles them both.

And me, silent, seeing more than either of them.

I have seen Luc's 'useful' before: the cheques that smothered women's voices, the advertising accounts that bought reporters. The assistants who disappeared between one season and the next. All of it tidied away, always on my watch.

I close the dossier with two fingers. The sound is louder than I intended, louder than I ever allow.

"Enough," I say. Knowing it isn't. Not here, not with them. Not anymore.

Belgrave Square.

The square keeps its secrets behind iron railings. Private calm, purchased centuries ago with inheritance and silence. Saskia calls it a garden. I call it a stage.

The bench beneath the trellis is ours. Wisteria falls like

drapes, roses bent into obedience.

She is there first, as always. Ivory silk, sunglasses too dark for the weather. Stillness performed to perfection. I sit beside her without announcement. Waxed linen, velvet gloves, perfume chosen to unsettle. The air accepts us both without question.

We talk of the roses. Our ritual. She notes the gardener's obsession with white blooms. I tell her colour is truer. Vulgar, but honest. Ritual clears the ground for sharper words.

"Luc is not happy," I say, smoothing the glove seam against my thigh. "Hortense Valois has become something of a sitting tenant in Zander's Tribeca apartment."

Saskia lets the words hang. No flicker of surprise, just that faint pause before the pour of wine resumes.

"Hortense," she says at last, tasting the syllables like a sour grape. "A guest who does not leave becomes a parasite."

"She calls it companionship."

"She calls it everything except what it is," Saskia replies. "Possession. Squatting dressed as affection."

Her candour jolts the silence. Then, lighter, she steers away. "At least Hortense keeps him fed. When was the last time you saw Zander eat something that wasn't out of a box?"

I allow the laugh, brief and unguarded. "He gets that from Luc, the legacy of men who think appetite is weakness."

She leans back, the sun catching the glass in her hand. "And what of our appetites, Mademoiselle? Everyone assumes women are either children or diamonds. No one asks if we want either."

Dangerous candour. Honesty is rarer still.

"You stood in that room with Luc. You refused him."

Her lips press together, not in denial, not in apology. "I am

83

not there to be his priest."

I let the silence run a moment too long.

"We have been priests for longer than either of them cares to admit. Confessors without the cloth. Burying the bodies without the funerals."

Saskia's hand stills on the stem of her glass. A pause, then the faintest smile, bitter, complicit. "And I am finished with sacraments."

That is the answer I wanted. Not denial. Not shame. A refusal. A woman aware of the risk and unafraid to let it breathe.

"Beautiful creatures rarely pass unseen," I say lightly, as though returning to roses.

Her mouth curves, faint amusement cut with defiance. "If they are beautiful enough, why should they care who sees?"

Yes, she knows I have seen. She knows I am referring to Zander. Her chin tilts the smallest degree, acknowledgement disguised as disdain, and she knows I will not use it, not yet.

I smooth my glove as if closing the subject. "Camille mistakes destruction for strategy. But passion, passion is far more dangerous. It makes you predictable."

Saskia's expression resets, flawless again. "Passion is a weakness for people who can afford it."

"And yet the men we orbit build empires on it. They call it vision. But it is the same hunger."

"They mistake compulsion for genius," she says.

"They always do."

For a moment, she studies me. "And what happens when the buckets overflow?"

"Then," I answer softly, "you learn how to swim. Or you drown. Zander will float. Julien is still deciding."

"And me?" she asks.

I smile. The smile that tells her I will answer, but not today.

The wisteria trembles overhead, curtains on a stage no one else knows we are playing.

I am not here to judge Saskia's glances or Zander's reckless-ness. I am here to record, to remember, and to decide when to pull the thread tight.

The spider never needs to bite to remind the fly of the web.

When Saskia leaves, she slips her glass onto the table, empty. "Clara has her whisky," she says, almost to herself. "You have your gloves. Rituals are harder to bury than scandals."

She does not wait for my answer.

I remain beneath the wisteria. Ash from a neighbour's chimney drifts faintly across the square, settling on the roses until the gardener comes and brushes it away.

I think of the files I signed, the reporters I redirected, and the women I persuaded to take the cheque instead of the stand. I think of the way Luc's voice could strip a room of oxygen and how often I lent him my silence as ballast.

My ledger is not numbers; it is names. Too many to count.

I smooth the glove on my knee and let the ash settle. For the first time in years, I do not reach to brush it off. Silence was always my sacrament. Perhaps I am finished with that, too.

Instead, I take the silver case from my bag, light a cigarette, and watch the smoke coil upward through the wisteria. Small rituals that remind us we are still flesh, not stone.

Some stains are meant to remain visible.

14

Zander

Saskia's House, Chelsea.

I did not call; I simply arrived, the heat of the day still clinging to me, stress threaded through my stance, and rage tucked somewhere behind my ribs like a spare weapon. I looked like every mistake she had ever allowed back in.

Saskia was in her ivory silk Volo robe. I thought about what it meant, but this was not teasing. This was war. Heated.

Mara was asleep upstairs. Saskia guided me into the kitchen, a quiet space that made every sound feel deliberate. Her bare feet whispered against the cold tiles as she touched the switch and lit the under-counter lamps. The light was low, amber. It made her poise sharper, almost surgical.

"You knew," I said. Not a question.

"Of course I knew. You think the rest of us walk around blind?"

The silence that followed was taut enough to hum.

"And you thought silence was mercy?"

A faint smile, barely there. "Would you rather I'd told you your brother bribed a journalist and Luc signed a silence clause, all to keep your lover's name out of print?"

I could feel my teeth grinding together. "You let me play the fool. Selling redemption like a brand slogan."

"I let you play the part you wanted." Her tone was so even it almost sounded kind.

"No. You let me audition for a role you'd already written."

Her gaze flicked up to meet mine. "We all have to survive him, Alexandre."

"And survival requires what? Watching me burn?"

She studied me. "You misunderstand me. You needed to see the fire to know where you stand."

"You manoeuvre me like Luc. That's the real insult, realising it too late."

"It mattered to you," she mumbled. "That's why it worked."

I let out a breath that was more laugh than air. "Don't turn this into sentiment. Don't turn me into a lesson."

"I'm not your priest, Zander. Not your confessor." She said it without heat, which only made it crueller.

"No. You curate the sin. Frame it. Make it look like art."

"Yes," she said. "And I would again, if it meant getting out with my skin."

I stepped towards her, the tension still elegant in my restraint. "Then why keep me close? Nostalgia? Or just the view?"

Something shifted in her eyes, too slow to be surprise, too controlled for guilt. "Because I thought you might prove me wrong. Perhaps you still could, but I'm not here to raise a better Montclair."

I almost smiled. "No. You're here to make sure I fall the correct way."

"Only if you insist on falling at all," she replied.

The silence that followed had a pulse. I couldn't tell if it belonged to her or to me.

Then, the glass slipped from her hand and shattered on the tiles. I crouched, gathered shards, and swore in French, one of those Jesuit curses my father would have called unprofessional, then twisted a chair round and sat with my face in my hands.

She moved towards me slowly, touched my head, and cradled it against her chest.

"No, mon cœur," she whispered. "I have always been here to see if you land."

For a moment I softened. Pain flickered beneath the defiance; I felt like a younger Lucien, vulnerable.

My finger bled. She lifted it, inspecting it without haste before tasting the crimson. Not affection, not cruelty, a communiqué. She held the power to mend or to wound, and she wanted me to know she enjoyed both.

I drew my hand back.

"Your tattoo, what does it say?"

"My tattoo?"

She nodded.

"I will be silence where your name wanted to live."

She knew the line already; she wanted more.

"No, what it means. I will share a secret if you tell me."

"My mother's last words," I said. "Her parting gift. A sentence and a silence."

It was a crack, and she knew it. The room narrowed at that fault line.

We stared. The quiet between us grew taut.

She loosened her robe. The silk fell just far enough to show skin, not invitation, not promise.

Declaration.

The light caught her collarbone, the slope of one breast.

I looked. Of course I looked.

Her skin was pale, cool porcelain. Her nipples were a muted rose colour against her ivory chest. No hard border, just a gentle wash, as if painted with restraint.

Even further down, the palette barely shifted. A faint warmth at her thighs, the suggestion of dusk where the porcelain yielded. There was hair, but only just, dark and fine, shaped to precision, like a final edit rather than a flourish. Even that felt curated: not wild, not bare, but measured, a choice.

I didn't look with hunger; I looked like a student forced to confront a text he cannot annotate. She had peeled away fabric not to tempt but to control, calculated intimacy, an illusion of access. Her nakedness wasn't beauty; it was believability. That was her genuine gift: to make you believe you'd been granted something rare, when in truth you'd only been permitted to glance at the perimeter.

Even the most intimate parts of her seemed untouchable. Pale, precise, untrespassed. A body curated like a room in which I was only a guest, allowed to see, never to inhabit.

She took my hand, guiding it with the same quiet authority she used on rooms of men twice her weight.

I met her eyes. My breath betrayed me.

She moved my hand, not where instinct thought it would

89

go, but over towards her hip. The truth lay there.

Two small faded tattoos, raised slightly, permanent. Easy to hide under silk or lace. Tonight she wore neither.

I traced them slowly, reverently almost.

"What does it mean?" My voice was low, more curiosity than a plea.

"Not yet," she said.

Then she closed the robe, pulled the distance back into the room, and bent to the shards as though glass were all that had broken.

When I looked up, I was not in that kitchen anymore but somewhere else entirely, in my past, in some theatre of memory she'd just unlocked.

She kept her eyes turned away as she said it.

"You think desire makes you dangerous. All it does is make you predictable."

I did not answer. I could not. Because she was right. Desire makes me predictable. And for once, I wasn't calculating or rehearsing an escape. I was only there. In the room. With her.

Feeling. And that, more than she ever could, will undo me.

Zander's Flat, Mayfair.

Number Eleven had never felt like mine. Tucked behind an unmarked façade off Mount Street, no parking, no buzzers, nothing to suggest it existed. It could have been an embassy annexe or a discreet clinic for men who didn't want their faces back in the papers. Intentional. Entry occurred only if the system already knew you.

The retina scan admitted me.

Stone underfoot, steel, black linen. Brutalism disguised as taste. It didn't want to be lived in. It wanted to be endured.

The only art was a black-and-white photograph of my mother, Claudine, at the piano, shoulders bare, turned away as if refusing the world. I had never taken it down.

The phone buzzed. Secure line.

Maxime.

I answered.

"Zazou," he breathed, drawling. "Still alive in that mausoleum you call a flat? I imagined you swallowed by your own retina scan. A delicious end, bureaucracy with fangs."

"Maxi."

"You sound like Luc when he's pretending to pray. Don't. It ages you. Anyway, you asked me about AetherFlex in your message. I have dug and under:CORE is rotten. Toby's playing priest; Kevin Price is a drunk altar boy. Picture Étienne reading bad poetry in a cassock, tragic, but with ulcers."

I let the silence sit.

"Ah, the pause," he said. "Zazou's deadliest weapon. Shame it doesn't work over international roaming."

"Horace flagged it. He wouldn't have if he were in on it."

"Horace, dear Horace. He leaks secrets like Étienne leaks bile. But you're right; he's too pompous to lie convincingly."

"And Toby?"

"Oh, Toby," Maxime sighed. "Our Judas with a bad haircut. He's in deeper than he knows. He thinks Kevin Price can still swim. I told him KP couldn't float in Evian, but Toby never did like my metaphors."

"And Luc?"

"Luc signs everything. Contracts, death warrants, birthday cards. It's his one consistent virtue."

I heard him strike a lighter. A pause, a drag.

"Lisbon's divine, by the way, and the door is always open, brother. The gin tastes of lemons and regret. I sit on the balcony and imagine you all strangling yourselves in couture. Almost makes exile worth it."

"You're drinking again."

"I tried sobriety for a week. Dreary as Luc's monologues. The gin's kinder."

He coughed, then softened his voice, almost fondly: "Look after my Little Saint, won't you? Saskia does love to martyr herself."

"How's your little saint, Isa?"

"Stupendous as ever, thanks."

"Maxime—"

But he was already slipping away, laughter smoke-thinned.

"Zazou, someone could not resist peeking at the new draft of Luc's will. Be careful, they might be... angry."

"Across the channel?"

"Closer to home, Rusty! Got to dash. Peace out, Zazou."

The line went dead.

Julien!

I stared at the phone and paced. My reflection warped in the screen, never quite meeting my own eye.

"Claude." I call, activating my personal AI.

"Here, Zander."

"Contact Lefèvre. Increase the percentage on the new Vérité Maison capsule. And check if the new Isabelle advert is ready. If not, make it sexier. Sexier to the point of censorship."

"Acknowledged."

"Oh, and Claude?"

"Yes, Zander."

"Cue the quarterly for Vérité Joaillerie. Quietly confirm which of our suppliers are still laundering Angolan diamonds under 'ethical' headings. Keep it buried."

"Acknowledged."

I leaned on the concrete counter, Claudine's portrait at my back like a rebuke.

"And whilst I shower, play my maman on the Bösendorfer. I have someone in my head I'd prefer erased before the boardroom. Then, choose an outfit that won't humiliate me."

"Affirmative."

The piano began, Chopin nocturnes, her phrasing sharp and aching. For a second I was not in Number Eleven, not even in my own life. Just a boy listening to a mother who never looked back.

Steam rose as I stripped and walked into the shower.

Claude's voice followed, clinical: "Grey Cifonelli. Midnight tie. Your statement watch. Boardroom, not bedroom."

I let the water burn; with enough heat, even ghosts lose their hold.

But not this one.

Not Claudine. Saskia.

Her robe loosening. Porcelain skin. The curve of her collarbone, the small tattoos she let me touch but not name. Her sentences, verdicts, not confessions. The knowledge that she could ruin me simply by refusing me.

Desire was meant to sharpen me into a threat. She was right; it made me predictable. Predictable enough that even Claude could dress me for the next meeting whilst my mind replayed the shape of her shoulder.

The mirror blurred with steam. My reflection stayed turned away.

15

Esmé

Saint-Jean-Cap-Ferrat, Côte d'Azur.

The drive to Maison Béraud curled like a secret, lined with lavender and stone pines. Silence that had been here longer than I had. The villa waited behind pale stucco and green shutters, its ownership written in Zurich, its memory in the mouths of locals.

The concept Peugeot eased to a stop on the gravel. Not the wrapped Porsche tonight. No spectacle. Just control, shaped in curves and matte pearl white.

She stepped out slowly. Crop top, taut abs, denim hanging loose on narrow hips revealing the top of her underwear. Her jacket caught the light in fractured flashes, more art than print. Hair straightened and pulled high, clean lines emphasising the planes of her face, the same way the boots showed off the length of her legs. Gauche had that unbothered confidence, like she'd been photographed enough to know her angles without trying. The driveway seemed brighter around her, the air bending just slightly in her wake.

I had changed too many times. Settled on white linen, sandals, hair pinned at the nape with the rhinestone clip she once slipped into my hair. A look rehearsed as effortless. Watching her move, I twisted the hem between my fingers; it was an old betrayal.

"Ça va?" she asked.

I leaned against the frame, a precise shift of weight.

"Better now." My smile was curated, not cute.

She crossed the threshold as though the villa had always been hers. No kiss. No touch. Just the promise of both withheld.

Inside, the Baccarat glasses still caught fractured light from yesterday's martinis.

"I'll make us a drink." My voice made it fact. Krug on the counter, dripping from its ice cradle. Not mine. A cellar indulgence, and what use is champagne if not consumed? Next to it, a bottle of crème de cassis, small-estate Burgundy, the kind Gauche once demanded. I poured sparingly, staining the glass like ink.

"How was Versailles?"

She shrugged. "Another hall of shiny things and boring people—"

Her mouth grazed my neck. I froze, caught the clean note of her perfume, iris, salt, or simply her. I refused to close my eyes.

"Without you there."

I placed a single blueberry in each flute, dark globes descending through gold.

"Now," she said, arms thrown wide, "I'm switching everything off."

She danced around the room and then out onto the terrace; the sea spread beneath us, cicadas steady as a metronome. I handed her the glass in silence. My wrist betrayed me, my pulse too fast.

Later, I draw her a bath. The tap hisses, heat climbing into marble. My knees press against stone. The faint smell of bergamot still lingers. I drop candles in the corners, flames licking the air, shadows dragging along the walls. Time slows as if warned.

She is already in the bath when I return. Steam lifts from her in threads, clinging to the mirror until the room has no edges. Her knees rise from the water, slick and shining. A droplet rolls down the inside of her thigh with indecent patience.

I let my robe fall. My skin prickles where the air moves across it. A strand of chestnut hair slips forward across my cheek. I do not move it. Let her see me through it.

Her gaze moves before her eyes do. I feel it on me, the rise of my breasts, the slow give of my weight against the doorframe. Then my hips, my legs, and lower still, where a small strip remains. 'Not the French way,' Gauche once said, half-teasing. But I'm no French girl, not really, and by now, it's too late to alter the evidence.

I hold the pose a breath longer than necessary, one arm raised, ribs parted. Not accident, not hesitation. Long enough to know she is looking.

Stone cool beneath my feet as I cross. I lower myself to the edge and take her face in my hands. Her skin is hot beneath my palms. My thumb presses against her mouth, the faint give of her lower lip.

My fingers drift to her collarbone, tracing the rise that softens into breast. Skin drags faintly against mine, her nipple tightening against my knuckle. Down across her stomach, smooth and taut, then back up the other side. She leans toward me, her breath grazing my arm.

"Back?" My voice sounds different, lower, stripped down.

Her nod is barely more than a pulse.

The cloth is warm in my hand. I press it to her shoulders and let it slide down her spine. Her skin damp, alive, the ink catching beneath my thumb.

Non sum quae fuisti.

I trace it, feel her breath.

"You let go here," I murmur.

I kiss the side of her neck. Heat against my mouth, the throb of blood beneath skin. Another kiss, firmer. I step into the water before I can argue with myself, heat climbing my thighs, my hips, and my stomach. Control abandons me in stages. She does not move away.

I slide my hands under her arms and cup her breasts from behind. Their weight fills my palms, her nipples pressing into my thumbs. She leans back until her spine rests against me. My legs fold around hers, water shifting, betraying us with each movement.

The oud is faint beneath the steam, darker than the berg-amot. My lips find her ear.

"Say it."

She doesn't.

I kiss her neck harder. She exhales, eyes closing.

"More."

My hand sinks beneath the water, heat wrapping around my wrist. I follow the shape of her, the parting. She is already warm. My fingers curl, listening to her breath, to the slight changes in her body. I find where she tightens.

One arm locks across her chest, holding her. The other works slowly beneath the surface, pressure building.

Her breathing changes, becoming sharper and shorter. A tremor moves through her before she allows it to reach the surface. I keep her there, keep her open against me.

When it breaks, it is not loud. Not shared. It is hers alone. A slow uncoiling, her weight settling heavier into my arms.

The water's cooling. My chin rests on her shoulder, the scent of her skin filling me. My fingertips on her thigh, drawing shapes that don't mean anything but stay anyway.

"You always that quiet after?"

"Only when it feels real."

It lands on my chest. My breath moves over the back of her neck before my mouth does. I kiss the place just under her ear. Not an invitation. A mark that she was here with me.

Her hand finds mine under the surface. Fingers thread. And I'm not thinking about how I look. Or what I am. Just the weight of her hand in mine, the press of her body against me. And the simple, impossible fact is she saw me and didn't leave.

* * *

I wake to static. Then light. Then the vibration of a phone, trapped under the pillow, humming like a wasp caught in silk.

Not mine, Gauche's.

"Fuck. The tag storm's begun."

I rub my face.

"Volant dropped the capsule overnight. Fifteen seconds. High-budget. Hollow."

I leave her to it, run to the bathroom, and then make coffee.

When I set a cup at her side, my hand finds the line of her spine, just fingertips, light. A quiet signal that says, 'I'm here.' No instruction. No pressure. Just there.

"Okay?"

"No," she says. "I want to break something beautiful."

"Start with me, then."

I hold my breath before I notice I'm doing it. She sits up, sheet dragged over her chest, phone still in hand.

"I need a signal; I need sharpness. I need someone to blame!"

"You have birdsong and me."

I smile, but she's already tugging my T-shirt over her head.

"You don't have to fight it alone," I say. "Let me help."

Her smile falters. Then she's swearing again, walking towards the terrace.

I split two figs, still cold from the fridge, their insides open and glistening in the low light. I carry them out to her.

I set them down, lean in, and kiss the wild curl at her temple. A fingertip traces the curve of her neck; my hand settles there as I watch her. Not to soothe. To remind her she's not alone.

And for once, this isn't a performance. It's surrender.

Montclairs build empires out of hunger. I wanted hers to be for me. Perhaps that's why she's dangerous.

Perhaps that's why I can't stop.

16

Camille

Hall of Mirrors, Versailles. 2034 FIFA Bid Gala.

Everything gleamed. Gold, crystal, and ambition polished to a razor's edge, almost dangerous in its reflection. The chandeliers dripped with thousands of crystal diamonds, catching light and fracturing it into a thousand scattered promises. The illuminated tables resembled chess pieces, each ready for a game-changing move. Every mirrored wall warned the wary to watch themselves from every angle, for there is no hiding here.

The Hall of Mirrors stretched long and grand, its vaulted ceiling painted with the triumphs of Louis XIV, the Sun King, and political allegories carved in gilded frescoes that made the wealth and power of France a tangible thing. Seventeen colossal mirrors faced seventeen luminous windows, doubling the light and the grandeur, an architectural echo that pulled the eye deeper into opulence and spectacle.

The Saudi bid bore the weight of numbers; Australia offered polite ambiguity. But the real negotiation, unofficial, silent, and far more dangerous, was conducted in the whispered shakes beneath the polished marble surfaces. The Montclairs knew it as well as anyone: the true victor here would be the one who understood not just the game on the floor but the rules unspoken behind the scenes. No Middle East World Cup, they all knew. The heat, the drink, the watchful censoring of women's presence, and delicate bindings on power.

Versailles was prepared like a stage. The hall glowed with flickering candles and golden light, the chandeliers' reflections fracturing into endless copies of the same faces, all watching, all measured.

Étienne stood in the centre, carved in ivory wool, in a collarless jacket like a sculpture he wore rather than clothing. No tie, no cuff. Just the faint gleam of platinum, the watch on his wrists, as his hands made measured, purposeful cuts through the air. White Faucon trainers, custom moulded, flawless under the spotlight.

He spoke of unity, legacy, and football as poetry. His words were crafted for the bid, but the faint smile flickering at the corners of his mouth belonged to a game set to unfold sooner, a nod exchanged near the south door, a signal disguised as nothing, invisible to all but me.

AetherFlex. Our crown jewel. Gone. Not announced, not argued, simply vanished. It did not roar from the vault; it slipped away, deliberate and silent, as if the product itself had chosen new hands.

Volant will have it now; we are all sure of that and will rebrand it as innovation. Étienne calls it sabotage, but I read the theft for what it truly is: choreographed defection with all the precision of a practised dance.

Adèle Aït-Khelifa was at Étienne's side, draped in midnight silk that clung and shadowed like poured ink. Bare shoulders caught candlelight, collarbones sharp and deliberate, skin the warm hue of umber. One emerald earring flashed as her hair was swept back; cheekbones cut with exquisite intent. Her hand rested lightly on Étienne's chair, a tether without claim, her eyes not lost in admiration but in a calculated sweep for anything worth noting.

She was the room's most striking presence because she did not seek to be; something about her carried the weight of grander halls and darker rooms left behind without regret.

The air smelt of money and old history. If I played this right, Faucon would flood every frame of the World Cup broadcast.

Across the room, Toby's shoulders tensed; his gaze flicked sideways to Horace and Avery, heads bent close in confidential communion. Whatever passed between them was a language written in glances, a code of exclusion. Toby's mouth compressed, tight with more than frustration. He fretted, not over the bid, but over his place in the alliance quietly assembling without him.

I watched the tilt of their bodies, the sharp weight of their silence. Proof enough. Volant holds AetherFlex. Not rumour or conjecture, possession whispered in deliberate exclusion. In rooms like this, being left out echoes louder than any public declaration.

Saskia, I thought, would already have turned this knowledge into leverage. She would make a phone call before the champagne soured and draft the first countermove before dawn. I, instead, was left to observe, to record. She plays the hand; I keep the score.

I let the silk of my coat slip from my shoulders just as the doors opened. I had chosen a floor-length Givenchy of liquid black silk crepe, the skirt slit daringly high, with a disciplined V neckline. Beneath, La Perla mesh and satin lay seamless against skin.

Zander entered, his black velvet coat shed with command, his matte black Cifonelli tailored sternly, his Roman shoulders square in readiness. Beside him, Sabine Hauser moved like scandal, in black silk, high slit, no back, Westwood's rebellious elegance barely restrained. They were hand in hand, part lovers, part conspirators.

Sabine's laughter caught the chandelier's sapphire light and would make the night's most viral picture.

My attention shifted to Gauche.

She entered as if the air parted specifically for her, black asymmetrical dress trailing behind long, honed legs that caught every sliver of chandelier sparkle. The neckline is precise, and the straps are sharp. Jewellery clashed at her wrists, neck, and ears, a symphony of controlled excess.

Curls tumbled in deliberate chaos over one bare shoulder, framing a smile that tempted with warmth but guarded like forged armour. Black spikes clicked out her rhythm, marking the floor with each deliberate step that set the room in motion.

She settled beside me, one hand on her hip, scanning, calculating, using every mirrored angle. Her dress did not turn heads; her presence did.

The gallery was full, conversations ran deep and layered, and three moves were made before a word escaped. The mirrors offered no reflection, only truth. People's tells were naked here.

Luc posted at the far table, nodding curtly at the Australians.

His glass spun idly, never lifting to meet Étienne's eyes once all night. That silence said more than speeches ever could.

Étienne danced in the centre of his gravity, projecting unity for willing ears. Adèle steadied, her grace a foil for her restless eyes that mapped and mutated the room.

Saskia moved through conversations with a thief's grace, a smile without warmth clinging like a silver blade. She wasn't here to dazzle; she was here to take.

I followed her gaze, Zander.

Not closing, not retreating, just watching. Glass half-held, smile half-formed but eyes fully alert. Patience sharpened by understanding.

Two dynasties, one table, the same ruthless hunger. The hunger to press the other's weakness, to emerge the victor unscathed.

The music shifted, a subtle rise of strings beneath murmured verdicts and promises. Somewhere between marble and mirrors, the night slipped from masquerade into war.

Zander didn't catch me watching. I didn't need him to.

The gala had thinned into its late stage; the music slowed, and blood thickened with wine. Deals were no longer struck; they were sealed in shadows away from watchful eyes, in corners no camera touched.

I kept my glass untouched. Champagne dulls precision.

From my vantage point, I studied Zander. His eyes were never still, always measuring. He addressed an Australian delegate, lips moving, but his body leaned towards the marble corridor leading to private lounges, the way of an escape artist sizing exits. His hand touched his temple twice, a silent signal of withdrawal whispered by fatigue not yet worn at arrival.

The Hall of Mirrors caught his image thrice, reflected and fractured like a prism splintering truth. I noted the set jaw, the jacket's cut, and the faint line of weariness at his mouth. A man masking cracks beneath perfect tailoring.

I let my gaze fall away, a predator pulling back to draw out pursuit. He'd know the absence before understanding why. His eyes hunted mine, searching for the smile that promised bait.

When he found me, I was laughing at a ghost of a conversation, leaning just enough into my companion to suggest intimacy without breach; the soft candlelight traced my throat and sharp collarbone like a secret invitation. He would remember the flicker.

Minutes later, he excused himself, not abruptly, with no suspicion, just a man grasping solitude for a moment's breath. I waited, counting the beats to the curtain, measuring the gradual erasure of his figure from the room.

Then I rose; the chair sighed beneath me.

I closed the distance deliberately, letting the mirrored panels mark progress, each reflection a new angle, a new lure. The dance of invitation and mystery played between light and shadow.

At the corridor entrance, the warmth he left lingered like whispered heat.

I kept the lounge door from closing and slipped inside.

The lounge was smaller than it fancied, the velvet banquettes too broad for comfort, the crystal ashtrays untouched, and a gilded mirror hung too high to flatter. Zander stood braced against marble with a loose jacket, palm splayed as if fighting gravity's weight.

His glance met mine; not surprise, not startle, but an old recognition of prey caught in the hunter's gaze.

"Camille," his voice dry and even. "Should I assume my uncle Étienne sent you?"

I pressed my thumb to my lips, thumbnail grazing, a habit, a calculation.

"If I carried Étienne's messages, you'd already know."

His smile was sharp and contained. "So what are you carrying?"

My coat slipped where the silk shifted, thigh bared.

"Leverage," I breathed. "Or curiosity, if you prefer."

He poured Armagnac, measured. Lifted my glass, as if weighing the taste of me, then poured again.

"Curiosity wrapped in something else," he murmured.

Our fingers brushed; enough contact to spark but not consume. "And you," I said, "always pretended to afford indifference."

His jaw tensed, a silent confession.

"Camille," low and slow, "what do you want?"

"Want is the wrong word." My silk slid along his thigh. "Need is sharper. AetherFlex is ours; it was taken. You know this. I know this. But before we negotiate restitution, I remind you..."

I tilted my head close; losing breath was a choice.

His eyes flicked, not down, not yet, cataloguing, baring.

My hand rested lightly above his heart, nails tracing the cloth. "You may dislike Étienne's tactics. But, Zander... whose hands would you rather I trusted? His? Luc's? Or yours?"

Silence stretched like taut wire. His breath shifted.

He leaned forward, not for the kiss, not yet, but for measure.

"Careful, Camille," he murmured. "You mistake me for one

who can be played."

Slow smile, mirrored behind Zander's shadow. "No, mon cher. I mistake you for one who believes in choice."

The room held us, mirrors and marble built for deals lost from ledgers. Candlelight pooled like forgotten gold. A velvet sofa waited, soft and untrustworthy.

I left the door ajar: the essential illusion of choice.

He followed, dark curls at his temple. A beautiful creature poised like a predator in the gilded cage. I placed my palm flat against his chest, feeling the quickened pulse beneath the tailored fabric. His heart answered faster than his mouth.

"You—" He began, but I silenced him, my finger pressing lightly to his lips.

Silence. My invitation. My trap.

Suddenly, he pushed me back, the cold solidity of the marble wall meeting the softness of my silk gown. The jolt was electric; pain sharpened desire, making the want razor-sharp.

I bit him first, just beneath the sharp line of his jaw, enough to mark but not break. His hands caught my wrists; his grip was tight. I could have freed myself, but I chose surrender in that containment.

"This is nothing."

Breath hot between us.

"I know." His words were betrayal by body, not tongue.

His hand slid beneath the slit of my dress, slow, possessive fingers tracing the tender inside of my thigh, skin to skin. The other followed the pathway of silk across my chest, finding and loosening the hidden clasp at my ribs. Fabric slipped down, whispering secrets, slipping away.

Mesh and satin exposed what boardrooms and strategies never dared to imagine: real, unguarded flesh beneath his touch. My breasts, bare and unhidden, the small ring flashing where candlelight caught the curves, freckles scattered like secrets he'd never earned. His mouth parted, breath caught, as if witnessing a truth rather than expected theatre.

I smiled, cruel and soft entwined.

My hands tore at his shirt, buttons bursting free, fabric parting to reveal the sculpted muscle beneath. I pressed closer; every inch mapped just so.

He lifted me without a question. Legs wrapped around his waist as if rehearsed a thousand times, bodies aligning with practised precision. Hard, unyielding pressure, the tempo rising, a crescendo against stone.

His mouth sought my collarbone, tracing a path through sweat, down into the hollow between breasts. I arched, offering more, the taste he'd imagined through endless meetings, curt smiles across polished tables.

My nails gouged small marks into his back. Hands tangled in my hair, tilting my head back, exposing skin for teeth that grazed without drawing, inviting laughter from breathless lips.

"Careful," I whispered. "Scars are evidence."

His groan was a promise, voice ragged against skin.

"You drive me fucking insane, Cammy."

"I know."

The rhythm deepened, rough and relentless. His hips rammed mine to the wall. The chandelier fractured light across a kaleidoscope of mirrors: his teeth clenched, my mouth parted, his hands locked in desperate claim. Every angle a different sin, each reflection an entry in my private ledger.

I tightened around him furiously, shuddering in sync. He

cursed softly in French, a breath lost, head buried against my shoulder, vulnerable, undone, belonging to me in that suspended instant.

When it ended, I let him linger, one heartbeat longer than need allowed. Then I slid down, drew silk back into place, and had painted lips restored to red. No marks left. Composed and immaculate.

He stayed against the wall, shirt damp, chest heaving, watching as if I had stolen something irreplaceable. Perhaps I had.

I left him with silence, the loudest noise in Versailles.

In the adjoining room, I pulled out the silicone cap with my fingers, wrapped it and flushed it. Gone. No trace remained on me or in me.

My clutch snapped open. Eyeliner sharpened, lip stain precise. The bone-conducting earpiece hummed against my ear, a signal more intimate than touch. I never have sex without it. The voice returned, clipped, businesslike. "Zander Montclair has failed to act on Q3 restructuring terms. I move to escalate."

Perfect rhythm. My rhythm.

I checked the hidden phone sewn into my clutch. The proof: his hands, my body pinned, the fire in his eyes. Archived. Waiting. Not for scandal. Not yet.

For leverage. The kind that turns tides, bends choices, and redraws power.

When the moment comes, this will be my edge. My assurance. The silent verdict delivered in digital ink.

The compact clicked shut; a quiet sentence passed.

17

Isobel (fragment)

Inside the private Wexford bar, even the men's cocktails are chosen by algorithm. Heart rate, blood sugar, dopamine. Easier to call it data than desire. Alexandre swears his mood tracker gives him control. Which is rich, considering the thing pings him every time Saskia declines to answer. And tonight she did. Screen down, smile on, drawing slipped into her bag like contraband.

Men mistake silence for victory. They never ask what we're saving it for.

Alexandre whisked Saskia off her pretty little heels with his charm and chivalry, but if she saw him like an animal inside the Hall of Mirrors, then one wonders if her heart rate would spike so quickly. He has already seen nearly all of her in a kitchen lit like a confession. Now he must decide whether he wants all of her, which is the greater risk, and he knows it.

Sometimes my feed is cut; some places have their cages where no whispers escape. They don't realise I need to hear all of it if I am to be of any assistance.

Ash nudged my palm, insistent, demanding what men never

do: touch without transaction. His ribs pressed sharp against me, yet he carried himself like a prince. Once, long ago, I had a man who asked for nothing in return. I still remember the shock of it.

I see more than they think I do. Always have.

Camille promised Étienne she had "proof". Proof of theft, of silence purchased, of something whispered heavy enough to bend the air in every room. She was bored already, which is why men find her terrifying.

Clara Sundström lifted her glass. Calm as ever. "Scandal is just weather," she said. "It passes if you stand still long enough."

Yes, I thought, you are a force to be reckoned with; however, if you stand still in bad weather, you still get wet.

Ash stretched beside me, bone-slender, velvet-eared, as if agreeing. Dogs never assume, as my fingertip tapped the stem of my glass once, twice. The pulse betrayed me before I stopped it.

And Noémie, she thought herself untouchable. Until Esmé. I watched her eyes stray too long, her laugh tilt warmer, and her exit was delayed past the point of strategy. Noémie has stared down ministers, CEOs, and men twice her size. Yet Esmé made her look like a girl on the verge of falling. It will be a beautiful fall, and a costly one.

They all think AetherFlex is the story. But dynasties never fall for one theft; they fall for the ledger no one wants to read.

I have no secrets left to lose. Which is why I keep theirs. For now.

18

Saskia

The windows wear reflections like masks. I leave the overheads dark and switch on only the side lamps. Softer that way, more civilised, less like betrayal. The penthouse is anonymous by design, with grey marble tables, smoked glass, and no signage. Dorian chose it. Of course, he did.

He arrives three minutes late. As agreed. So as not to be seen with me. Charcoal again; today it's a brushed flannel jacket cut close at the shoulder, soft enough to let in air but not sentiment. Slate-grey suede shoes, quiet and supple. They make no sound on the stone floor, but neither does he.

No phone. Just a slim black folder and the scent of bergamot over pine and restraint.

The room sharpens when he enters, not by presence but by subtraction. He doesn't fill space; he reduces it.

His posture unchanged, spine straight, chin level, eyes unreadable. He doesn't smile, not because he is unkind. Because it would waste the moment. He looks at me, no greeting, just ready.

I am already seated, in late-spring black silk, charcoal trousers, and no jewellery. Hair up. Not austere, just un-inviting.

He sits across from me and lays the folder between us. Closed. Impeccable.

Most men with this kind of money move as though they have the right. Dorian carries something more dangerous than entitlement. Proof.

"Glass of something brutal?" I ask.

His mouth tilts in half a smile.

"You already poured it."

He's right. The glasses sweat on the lacquer tray beside my hand, one for me, one for him, the symmetry that makes men feel welcome. He picks his up but doesn't drink.

"Well?" I say.

"It's done. Filed and registered. Shell company formed. Patents provisionally accepted. Digital rights nested. In the name you asked. No visible link to Montclair or Laurette Holdings. No fingerprints."

I exhale quietly, only then realising I've been holding my breath. Not because I trust him, but because at some point you have to trust someone. The drawings are safe now. If Luc or Étienne ever tries to touch them, they'll find only smoke and silence. Mara's gift belongs to her, not to them.

I cross to the low table where the folder waits. Slim, heavy stock, no seal, just a clean white tab and a date that hasn't happened yet.

"Any complications?"

"One." His voice dips, just slightly. "Gauche found it. She didn't know exactly what she had found. Tried to stall, buying herself time to dig. By the time she contacted the arbitration wing, it was already gone. She's been watching me. She thinks *this* is something else."

He points from himself to me.

I allow a small smile. "Good work."

He studies me. Not with concern. With accuracy.

"Not even Luc?"

"Not yet."

Timing is leverage. And this time, it's mine.

"Why did you help me?" I ask.

"Because legacies are loud. But leverage is quieter."

He reaches and pulls out a sealed envelope. "This is the holding name. Notarised. Filed through the Corsican channel, like you asked. Anyone looking for the source won't find it."

I take it. Clean. Legal. Ticking.

"You were always the smart one."

"Xièxiè," he says, soft and precise, not performative. His head turns a fraction. "As are you, Miss Lin."

"No," I say. "I just learnt to stop waiting for men to catch up."

He almost smiles. Doesn't. Instead, he raises his glass.

"To names that don't need inheriting."

I touch mine to his. "To writing them in ink this time."

He leaves a few minutes later.

I stay by the window as the light thins over the rooftops. One hand on the folder, the other flat against my stomach. Not protective, not sentimental. Just steady.

They will find out eventually. But when they do, it won't be a scandal. It will be structured, intentional, and untraceable. Not legacy. Not revenge.

A beginning.

One I have authored. One they can't erase.

Later, back at the Quiet House, the lights are on low. Curtains half-drawn against the press. The nanny has made it cosy for my return.

I slip out of the heels first. Quietly. Black silk still clinging to the heat of the evening. A ghost of Dorian's cologne lingers: oud and vetiver, dry and dark. The scent of ink and sealed decisions.

Mara is curled on the sofa with her tablet and paraphernalia, head bent into another project. The old man with the croaky voice plays from the speaker, the one I always tell her not to listen to.

"Just down a little, my darling." I kiss her forehead.

She does, without argument.

Her taste in music is eclectic. Not mine.

I change. Shake the day off. Pour a drink. From here, I watch her for a full minute before stepping away.

In the hallway, I open the envelope just enough to see what I need. A name. A date. The holding signature. Then I check the final transfer. It has gone through.

It is done.

Mara comes for a goodnight kiss. I give her the tightest hug and tell her I'll be in soon. Her innocence presses against me, weightless. I wonder fleetingly what it would feel like to tell her everything. I don't.

Back in my reading room. Alone. Barefoot. A glass of Meursault on the sideboard. The envelope sits in the lamplight, its edges cutting a clean line across the wood.

I sip, letting the burn steady me. Then I press Clara's number.

She answers on the second ring, voice steady.

"You sound like you've already decided."

"I have," I say. "They're protected now. Paper, patent, digital rights. No one can touch them."

Clara exhales, rough with satisfaction. "Finally. About time one of us wrote the rules instead of playing by theirs."

"I needed to tell someone who'd understand."

"Oh, I understand," she says, sharp and sure. "Every bastard in that boardroom thinks legacy means keeping their boots on our necks. What you've done? That's a middle finger in patent form, and I love it."

I laugh, surprised by the heat of it.

"Drink to it, and if anyone comes sniffing around, we'll scorch them together. Enough of being their clean-up crew. This one's ours."

Her voice lands like a verdict. For the first time tonight, I feel not just protected but backed.

When the line goes dead, I hold the phone a second longer. The house is quiet except for the faint sound of Mara's playlist leaking under her door. My drink is a warm one now.

The decision sits in my hand like fabric waiting to be cut.

19

Safi

Dust clung to stone. The air purred with heat, every rack blinking like a slow constellation. I sat cross-legged on the concrete, laptop open, cables spilling around me like veins. The rig was mine, scavenged, soldered, and rewritten until graphite sketches turned to light, then into code. As I keyed in another command, a memory flickered: my father's voice, careful and deep.

"Cities are built on invisible rules, Safiatou. Break one line, and the whole district shifts."

I broke lines daily, but only where the map needed mercy.

The scanner arm swept across another drawing; the line jittered, raw, refusing to be tidied. The system tried to smooth it obediently. I killed the correction and rewrote the tolerance. The curve held, stubborn and alive. In the margin, a code note: Collaboration is a river. Extraction is drought. My spreadsheet maps the difference.

A creak at the door. Then Aïcha's voice.

"Yo, Dr Evil. What's the monster today?" She dropped down beside me, hood up, crisp bag in hand. The smell of paprika cut through the warm server air.

"A jacket," I said, eyes on the code. "Biometric veins. Heats up when grief spikes."

She whistled low. "So basically, wearable therapy. Or armour. Depends on who's crying."

I smiled. "Yeah, I guess it depends on who's wearing it."

A message pinged on my laptop, half-distracting, from an interview we did in Paris:

Les Doué Twins: Troublemakers. So smart. So young.

I ignored it and opened a new tab, last quarter's outreach minutes. Already, I could see the same flaw from my teardown: engagement metrics, but no belief tracked. I rebuilt it on ten slides. Laurette still hasn't fixed the flaw.

Aïcha leaned over, dark curls spilling, eyes lit by the screen. "Make the seams visible. Trust is in the flaw. Hide it, and no one buys it."

I logged the note, tagged by theme, already modelling user trust curves. If the jacket broadcasts a flaw, the trust index jumps. If flawless, resale plummets.

The next file opened: a shoe, smudged and restless. I traced its sole onto a pressure-mapping grid, tuned to terrain and to memory. Shoes that braced at thresholds of old fear. PulseField Soles.

Aïcha grinned. "Sneakers that remember your heartbreak. Limited drop, everyone wants the remix."

The scanner arm moved again. A jagged sketch choked the software. I forced the code to believe it. A sleeve split across the screen like a gill, venting heat. Oubliette Fabric.

She laughed. "Sounds like a cologne for men who fuck you and then ghost you. Keep it. It slaps."

Silence stretched, only hum and light.

She broke it first. "Do you ever wonder if Camille actually cares? Or are we just interns she flexes to scare the old boys?"

"She cares about leverage," I said flatly. "We're leverage."

"Better than Luc. Heard he orders women the way he orders yachts."

I smirked. "Étienne is worse. All bass, no treble."

"Zander?" She asked, crunching a crisp.

I hesitated. "He's literally our dad's age. Ick, but also iconic?"

She grinned wickedly. "Smash the family business, but maybe not smash him. That's wild, sis!"

I shook my head. "Hot doesn't scale."

"Spoken like a spreadsheet." She flicked a crisp at me. "I mean, I would, but... I'd need therapy after."

We both laughed and pushed each other's shoulders playfully.

Another file loaded. The sketch unfurled, vectors pulsing, fibres alive. I draped over it a filament I'd been coding for weeks, fabric that tightened when your pulse spiked, loosening only when calm returned. Adaptive armour. Survival disguised as design.

Aïcha sprawled back on the stone, staring up at the racks. "Tell me this isn't bigger than all of them."

"It is."

"So why do they still think they own it?"

"They own nothing."

She grinned at the ceiling. "One day, we'll put Doué on the tag. Front page. Billboard. Whole damn vibe."

I said nothing. She was always the loud one. But I believed her.

We kept building. Jacket. Shoes. Armour. Each sketch

turned to vectors, and vectors to prototypes that breathed like they had lungs. I whispered commands to the rig, coaxing code into obedience, killing auto-correction, and forcing the machine to feel what Mara had drawn.

The results split across the screen: Garments that warmed when grief rose. Soles that braced at the memory of fear. Fabric that disappeared from the body in heat maps.

Not couture. Not a trend. Future. My mind flicked to Abidjan, to the textile workers I'd met, their hands quick and precise; nobody designed alone. No one designed without consequences.

A quiet flash, *N'ka fô, Safi*, do it right, so it lasts.

Aïcha sat up suddenly, eyes gleaming. "Imagine this on the market. Vogue would melt down. Runners dropping trauma-responsive shoes. Couture houses are scrambling to make invisibility chic. Even Faucon couldn't fake it."

"They'll try," I said.

"Yeah, but we've got the receipts. They've got... logos."

She leaned close, whispering like it was a conspiracy. "Camille thinks she's running this. Saskia thinks she is. The joke's on them. They're just waiting rooms. We're the hospital, babe."

I laughed quietly. She always needed metaphor. I just needed numbers.

On screen, the archive swallowed another file whole, its code folding into mine. Column headers. Supply chain emissions, mapped by brand, season, and region. My Medium post pinged and was cited in a niche thread. Someone quoted, "Hype culture launders opacity."

The hum felt louder now. As if someone else were listening.

On screen, the archive spat out one last line of code, unasked.

Not mine. Not the rig's. A flicker. One word in red, ghost-script, faint, almost pretty.

Xinyi.

"Aïcha," I said. She didn't look up.

"Cha Cha!"

"What?"

"Look."

Her eyes flicked to the screen, then to me. "You saw it too?"

I nodded.

We sat there, the hum of the racks loud as a confession. Then she let out a low whistle, sharp with awe.

"There she is."

I felt it land in my chest. Mara's nickname. A signal. A seed. The signature was buried now, hidden inside my scaffolding. But it wasn't gone.

One day it would surface, through Dorian Tseng's filings, through Saskia's refusal to play priest, and through Mara herself. When it did, it would carry a name no one could erase.

House of Mara.

Ours.

20

Zander

The rain left London sticky in the morning, wool's faint sweetness waking up in the downpour, like old books, expensive and alive. The penthouse caught a dull strip of grey dawn through glass, breathless and watching. Luc stood on the terrace, barefoot on pale limestone, cigar smoke curling in slow spirals like smoke signals. He paced that narrow length like a king marking territory, his domain above the city's restless pulse.

Below, the Thames was a black mirror spattered by rain's fingertips. Across the dock, the Cradle's violet spine sliced the mist like a secret too sharp to ignore. His yacht hovered there, gold waterline flashing in the half-light, a promise sealed beneath the clouds.

Mademoiselle Céleste met me at the lift, hair locked into a severe architecture that forbade softness. She didn't invite me to the glass walls, where the city sprawled and distracted. Instead, she led me into the heart of darkness, the black-walled office. No windows, no light, no escape. Just decisions waiting to become sentences.

On the desk, a folder lay open. The first page was my still image: mid-lunge, shirt undone, mouth dark with bruised silence. Below it, Saskia's script, scrawled with elegant menace.

Votre fils saigne. Comment allez-vous le présenter?

Your son bleeds. How will you spin it?

No signature. No pretence required.

Luc entered without the familiar cigar, fingers rolling Turkish beads with deliberate patience. His slow smile was a teacher correcting, a predator sizing up a cornered animal.

"You brought me this?" The words were flat, though everything beneath them tightened.

"What you need to understand, Alexandre," he said, ignoring the question, "is everyone plays a role. Even those skilled at hiding the game."

The beads clicked quietly. He waited for me to flinch. I let nothing show.

"She's not what you think," he said, his voice almost tender in its cruelty. "Saskia, I mean. Complex. Women who rise that fast rarely are simple."

My eyes fell on the single painting he allowed here: Bacon, mid-scream, the chaos caught and suspended. He paid far too much for it. Outbid a rival by two million over. Not art. A warning.

"Whatever it is you and Saskia are plotting—" he began.

"Plotting?" I interrupted. Let him taste the word's sharpness.

His smile sharpened. "That's where we differ. I always assume betrayal, so it can never catch me by surprise."

Milan flickered backstage; Camille's cigarette was poised but unlit. 'Luc won't be undone because nothing or no one ever mattered enough.'

Camille was right.

The door opened. His face slid into something softer. "Ah, my favourite daughter."

Mara's voice, all light and quick steps against stone.

"Jérôme will take you home," he said, checking his watch. "Paris calls."

Paris meant his retreat dressed as duty.

"I'll take her," I said, stepping forward. "I'm heading west anyway."

He nodded, already halfway to the terrace, eyes hunting for fractures in my silence, in my control, in every inch of calm I wear.

Mara bounced beside me, bright and impatient, the only genuine warmth left in these frozen rooms. Maybe he sensed that.

My hand settled on her shoulder, light and deliberate. "Come on, little one. Let's get you home."

Dusk pressed heavy on Burnsall Street, street lamps curving their light over wet brick like whispered luxury. Silence here is loud, the kind that lets secrets breathe. I brought Mara to this place. Not kindness, not obligation. Control. After Father's measured pacing like a sentence waiting to drop, I needed distance, and I wanted Saskia.

The door clicked open softly. Mara slipped in, trainers soft on marble. I rehearsed the neutral greeting I'd wear, something to keep the truth hidden, the weight off my entrance.

Then I stopped.

Saskia wasn't alone.

The desk was lit. Saskia held one of Mara's sketches like a

talisman, anchoring herself to the room, to something real. Clara's voice was low, the thread of twins weaving between her words.

Only Clara met my eyes. Hers don't match, green beside blue, a detail that disrupts. She stands small but exact. Her blonde hair, polished but untouchable. An hourglass figure, sharp cleavage carved beneath soft fabric: an invitation, a warning. I file it away, as always. Just another body, another code.

The silence that followed was not innocence, not regret. Something else, sharp and deliberate.

And I hated it.

Clara cleared her throat as I was still looking at her cleavage; it sounded like a crack in fine glass.

Saskia straightened up too fast. Her eyes caught mine, sharp, unguarded, unsettled. Safi, across the room, lifted her glass steadily and deliberately, as if I'd walked into a meeting I'd never been meant to join.

Mara rushed forward, reaching for her pages. They scattered, arcs of flesh, inheritance, and desire. Saskia caught them before the floor could smooth the chaos.

Her pulse jumped, barely visible, but I saw it in the fragile swallow of her throat. Clara smoothed the sheet like a whisper, too slow, too intentional.

"Careful," she said. "Don't waste them."

Saskia's eyes flicked back to mine, quick, the flash of someone already tangled.

I wanted to say, 'Don't panic. I'm the one who won't betray you.'

Clara tapped a nail, soft and sharp, on the desk.

"The line here is too soft. Fragile will crumple in motion."

Aïcha leaned in, her braid swinging like a pendulum, her voice a pulse.

"Not fragile, fluid. Fragile bends, fluid breaks. You want the bend."

Safi's voice cut in without looking up, even and measured.

"Both fail without the frame. Fluid without form spills. Fragile without support shatters. Lose the structure, lose the fight."

Clara arched a brow. "Seventeen, sounding like an auditor."

Safi's fingers paused on the keys. "Maybe auditors need to sound like us. Admit the pressure before the collapse."

Aïcha smirked, sharp as a needle dragging vinyl. "Own it, Lala. We're the future you wanted but never had."

Clara's smile was small, a truce. "Insufferable."

"Gifted," Aïcha said. "Doué, remember."

Three bent over the sheets: Clara exact, Safi measured, and Aïcha sparks in flight. Saskia held the centre: tethered between break, bend, and scaffold.

Then Safi closed her laptop. "Basement."

Aïcha grabbed the sheets and winked at Saskia. "Proof's coming."

Glasses collected. Footsteps faded down the stairs to servers humming their cold tune.

Mara vanished, the padding of trainers muffled by carpet. The others disappeared deeper, and the room exhaled, leaving only us.

I stayed still. My thumb pressed to the taut tendon at my wrist, counting a pulse I didn't believe. My other hand hovered by her glass, close enough to claim, far enough to let her decide.

Saskia remained still. Stillness her shield.

Her hand returned to the papers, covering Mara's work like a shield. Her gaze fixed on the lamp, as if light could steady a tremor inside her, a look that held its own kind of reckoning.

I moved before I knew why, not close enough to touch, but close enough to inhale the faint curve of her perfume, the heat rising from pale skin. Close enough to hear the paper sigh beneath her palm, pressed flat to hold back the tremor.

"I—"

"You don't have to..." My voice broke before the words could reach full shape.

Breath tangled, hers and mine tangled, caught in the same thin air.

Her wrist trembled once more and stopped. A pulse leapt under bone, quick, raw, unhidden.

I wished to tell her that she was safe. That nothing I carried would betray this moment. She could trust me, not as Luc's son, not as a Montclair, not as a pawn waiting under fire, but as myself.

My fingers edged closer slowly, letting her stop me if she chose. The back brushed her hand, barely touching, but enough to feel the warmth, the restless pulse beneath her skin that betrayed calm.

She didn't recoil. For a suspended fraction of time, we shared a breath neither dared acknowledge.

Her eyes locked on mine, stripped of panic, gleaming with something like surrender. My pulse faltered; hers raced.

Fragile cracks, fluid bends. Spill or shatter without scaffold.

We were none of that. No frame, no scaffold. Just two bodies holding still on fault lines.

For a moment, it felt inevitable. We didn't reach further. We didn't need to; the charge was enough.

I would stay silent.

Not for Luc, not for Volant, not for the Montclairs. For her.

21

Saskia

The message is gone, but I see it anyway. Zander's text vanished before dawn. Nothing remains on the screen, yet its absence hums louder than anything Luc has spoken to me in years. Silence can be a promise. Or a threat. He will keep my secret.

It astonishes me, the weight of things that no longer exist. Words deleted, yet memory clings like perfume on a coat you should have burnt. I keep checking, as if the letters might reassemble, a ghost surfacing on glass. They do not. Proof is not truth. My pulse reminds me I know the difference.

The call came that afternoon. Luc's ledger voice, pared to bone.

"We'll talk settlement. Not in front of Mara."

"There is nothing left to settle but signatures." My voice cut like marble.

"She'll have the Chelsea house. A bolthole. It will serve."

Bolthole. The word lodged. A kennel for the discarded. My composure fissured.

"It was her home, Lucien. And you've never once seen her

for what she is. Vision, not ornament."

His silence pressed, his old trick, a hand at the back of the neck.

"You forget yourself."

"No." The word cooled on my tongue. "I remember you, and I remember you have three sons. Julien. Zander. And..." I let the last name dangle, cruel as bait. "Maxime."

Click. Click. His beads, steady as a clock.

"Maxime is a junkie." A pause, almost indulgent. "An embarrassment."

"That's what the Priory is for. You don't throw away blood, Lucien. You direct it. He could still serve."

"He made his bed. Let him lie in it."

The line went dead. My reflection in the hallway mirror stared back, severe, merciless, testing whether I had the stomach to devour what I had just taken.

Luc thought to diminish me with Chelsea, but the victor's shrug does not define a battlefield. It is defined by what the woman builds after. It should have hurt.

Instead, it confirmed what I already knew. Houses outlive marriages. They outlive fathers too, if you build them to.

Later, in the Quiet House parlour, warm lamps pooled across sofa arms; whisky breathed in crystal bowls. The hum of climate systems whispered of bones, the house alive beneath Luc's disdain.

Dorian Tseng sat opposite, vowels clipped and neat, every word precision-calibrated. A tactician masquerading as a solicitor.

"No-fault petition. Six months minimum unless we press leverage. He'll expedite. He won't want discovery."

Clara perched at the sofa's edge, hair yanked into submission, glass in hand, her posture a razor.

"Six months is a waste of oxygen. Press him. Discovery would shred him; he knows it."

Across the table, Aïcha gathered Mara's sketches into stacks, rings catching lamplight. Mara's small hand twitched, protective, but Aïcha was gentle, reverent.

"The designs are in trust," she said evenly. "Clean. They'll be hers. Not his."

The assurance carried a quiet violence that soothed me more than any of Luc's hollow promises.

"And Camille?" I asked.

A shrug. Frank.

"We don't cling to loyalty pacts. We cling to receipts. Your generation calls it betrayal. We call it proof."

Clara's laugh, dry. "And proof is the only language Luc understands. File this week, or he'll spin you as sentimental. Sentiment is debt in his column."

Different keys, one refrain: stop rehearsing fear.

On paper, the house was already moving into my name. A Chelsea bolt hole, diminished by his shrug. Millions reduced to charity.

But walls are theatre. Foundations. Promise.

Luc had gutted it before surrender, stripped the vaults, and taken even the mantel frame, as if glory could be unscrewed and packed away. He thought he left me shell and dust. But bones remember. The rails, the ducts, the quiet filtration. He assumed I would never find the skeleton of his archive, let alone bend it to my daughter's hand.

That was his mistake. Cruelty became raw material. Every theft sharpened what I would give her.

I repurposed it.

For Mara.

Her drawings belong not in margins but in marrow. The rails became her easels, the scanners her capture. Through Dorian's channels I built something invisible, unregistered, and untraceable. Moss. Her bespoke AI.

Moss knew her. Absorbed in her. Threaded her lines into the house's lattice. The walls recognised her. The walls loved her.

Luc thought he gave me an afterthought. He gave me a fortress.

That night, blinds drawn and lamps low, the house breathed as if it understood.

Luc thought I was cornered. Instead, I had turned his derelict into a sanctuary, and in that silence, my resolve set whole. Not revenge. Continuity. For Mara.

My phone rang. Maxime.

I answered on the second ring, his breath dragging sharply. "Saskia."

My name carried a rasp but no slur. Sober enough to hurt. A pause, then a laugh without humour. "You must be the only woman alive still answering my calls. God knows why."

"Maxime! How are you, my sweet?"

"I need to see you." He didn't waste it on preamble. "Privately. I'll fly to London. You pick the time, the theatre, and the curtain call."

His words had that half-drawl, half-challenge, like he was mocking his own urgency even as he bled it.

"Why?" I asked.

"Because Luc still thinks I'm dead weight, and Julien pretends he can't smell the powder. You at least remember the boy who drew in margins before the pages went up in smoke."

Silence stretched, heavy.

He broke it with a soft, fatalistic sigh. "Don't worry, I won't bring the ghosts. They drink more than I do. But I'll bring what matters. You'll want to see it."

He paused.

"Tomorrow. London. Don't make me crawl."

* * *

Maxime was already in the corner cafe on Ebury Street when I arrived, his coat folded over the chair, a book in his hand he clearly wasn't reading. He stood as soon as he saw me, with that unstudied grace that still belonged only to him.

Light from the window turned his messy dark hair ash-brown at the edges. His smile was softer than anything I had faced all week.

"You're late," he said, voice slow, the corners of his mouth tugged in amusement. "Though time has always adored you more than it ever adored me."

"Sorry. Busy," I replied. My voice eased, unarmoured.

He kissed me lightly on both cheeks, the old French formality. The touch steadied.

"Busy conquering, Sass," he added, using the name like a caress. "Or busy pretending you haven't already?"

"Both."

His laugh was soft, unconvincing, and borrowed from another man. For a flicker, I saw the boy I'd first met, fourteen and unguarded, sketching animals in the margins whilst Luc barked orders into a phone. The boy I was meant to protect when I became his stepmother soon after.

I sank into the chair opposite. The waiter appeared with an ease that suggested this wasn't Maxime's first time here. Without glancing at the menu, he ordered a bottle of Chablis.

"Wine before confession," he murmured. "Otherwise it hardly counts."

When the glasses came, he lifted his and tilted it to the light. His hand was steady, I noticed, though I didn't let him see it.

"Exile tastes like this. Cold, clean, faintly metallic. You drink it because you must, not because you like it."

"Exile never means absence," I whispered, watching him.

Something flickered in his storm-coloured eyes: recognition or warning. He smoothed it away with a smile sharp enough to cut. "Careful. Quote scripture like that, and I might almost believe you still have faith in me."

He sipped slowly and deliberately, then leaned forward, closer than he had to. "Do you?"

I held his gaze steady.

"Tell me," he said softly, "who are we crucifying today? Luc? Étienne? Or shall we start with me?"

His grey-green eyes flickered, half warning, half invitation.

For a moment, the air held no ghosts, no archives, no Montclair silence. Only this. Only him.

The cafe wrapped the street corner in glass, three sides open to the street. Conversations blurred into a single hum, punctuated by the scrape of cutlery and the hiss of a machine behind the bar.

Maxime's gaze stayed fixed on me, sharp against the ordinariness. He made the air feel private, though the room was anything but.

"Funny," he murmured, swirling the Chablis. "London

always pretends at normal. Flat whites, dog leads, prams. But just there..." He flicked his eyes to the window. "...behind the glass, an empire chewing itself alive."

A server passed, tray rattling. The spell cracked. The cafe reasserted itself with clinking glasses, the perfume of burnt milk, and chatter about nothing.

Maxime smiled, faint and unreadable. "So. Shall we order food, or truth?"

I lifted my glass, letting the light fracture through pale gold. "Food can wait."

He leaned in, his voice dropping to a register the room couldn't steal. "Then hear this, Sass. I've kept my silence for four years, but Luc isn't half as careful as he thinks, and neither is Tonton across the channel. If you ever find yourself in need of leverage, for any reason at all, you'll know where to find me."

He knows something.

I held his gaze. The storm behind his eyes was not rehearsal, not performance. It was knowledge. Dangerous, deliberate, alive.

"But truth", I said evenly, "only if you can tell it without rehearsing the lie first."

Silence stretched quickly before he laughed, soft, hollow, almost a click of beads. For an instant, the sound carried Luc's cadence.

I tasted the wine. Cold, clean, metallic. Exile.

When I finally stepped outside, the street was ordinary again: dogs tugging at leads, a cyclist swearing into the wind, and a tourist snapping photographs of the pretty flower wall enveloping the cafe. None of it touched me.

What lingered was Maxime. The man in front of me now and the boy from fourteen years ago, who had once looked at me with trust I hadn't known what to do with.

He knows.

Enough to wound, enough to save.

I wanted him safe. I wanted him whole. Neither had ever been enough.

I tightened my coat and walked faster, as if pace alone could break the echo.

It didn't.

22

Céleste

Saeculum Editions, Paris.

The rain etched the windows like veins: fine, branching, and insistent. Silence upholstered the room too tightly. I had asked Saskia to come. I carried the kind of weight that opened locked rooms without keys, but she had the Montclair name. The archivists looked at her with suspicion and at me with deference. Entry codes, passwords, authority – I had all of it.

Yesterday, a note slipped under her door whilst she was out. No signature. Nine words in an elegant hand neither of us recognised:

> *Look underneath Paris. Something someone wants to stay hidden.*

At the same hour, the tape arrived at my apartment. Matte-black plastic. No sender. Digitised by eight. At 08:03, it lived on the screen.

"Pause it."

"Of course, Mademoiselle."

Étienne, twenty at most. Oil-streaked apron. Hands precise as a surgeon's, bent over Luc's prototype support sole. I knew the model. The athlete. He never competed again.

Then his hand, swift, replacing the material. Not a test. Not an accident. A decision.

The sound faltered, then cleared for ten seconds:

"Let him fail. He learns better that way."

I played it again. And again.

"Is it real?" Saskia asked.

"It's real."

"It's not the truth."

"It's enough."

We did not look at each other. The walls had more eyes than either of us cared to count.

"Luc has always known how to bury a body," I said, voice low. "This is only proof he sharpened his sons on the bones."

Her breath caught. She covered it with a sip of water, too slow, too careful.

"They'll be watching us," she whispered.

"Naturally."

In the black reflection of the screen, our faces hovered side by side. Not touching, not speaking, but aligned. The kind of solidarity surveillance could never unmake.

A Post-it inside the trial register:

DO NOT TRANSFER.
    Initialled:

H.V.
Hortense Valois.

I thought of Hortense's lacquered nails, how lightly she touched the world, and how many lives she had already ruined without leaving a trace. Too light a slip of paper to carry this much weight.

I thought that between my authority and Saskia's Montclair name, we would get in and find what was hidden. By noon, permissions had vanished. Legacy logs sealed.

I received an anonymous message as we entered the archive:

That shoe was not the only thing they sabotaged. Look at the 2000 endurance trials.

I whispered, "That trial was shut down. We lost an athlete. Quietly. Follow me, but make it look casual."

I led Saskia to a box marked:

REDACTED / 2000 / BETA.TRI.

Inside: biometric files, fabric logs, thermal exposure charts. The runner's ID matched the trial. Shut down, erased, then resurrected under a new name: AetherFlex. Publicly ours, privately routed from a desperate U.S. tech partner.

Name: Christine Okonjo. Seventeen. East London.

Her name struck me harder than the numbers. For years I had told myself I was protecting the house, but the house was a mausoleum built on other people's bones. Every archive we opened felt like another grave. What loyalty did that deserve?

Saskia's hand tightened on the edge of the box, her knuckles whitening against the dark cardboard. In the reflection of the glass case beside us, our faces hovered side by side again, both too still. Surveillance could not mistake that for anything but complicity.

Underneath it: *downstream consequence.*

I closed the lid. "Legacy is just plagiarism with good timing."

Hortense's voice in my head, a recording from the bugged Tribeca apartment:

If you ever think I didn't love you... Remember, I never copied your phone. Not once.

"Oh, Hortense. What are you involved in?"

We leave Saeculum in the late afternoon, rain needling the Seine. Saskia does not speak in the car. She does not need to.

The bolthole is one of Luc's old addresses, a second-floor flat above a shuttered antiquarian. Dust sleeps on the sill. Iron balconies hold the rain. A hidden bottle of St-Julien waits in the cupboard the way an old favour waits, patient and inevitable. The bottle opens without effort, as if it had been expecting us.

We sit across the low table. I peel my gloves off and fold my fingers as carefully as folding a letter. Saskia sets the tape between us. It is still warm from the machine, the plastic catching light like a small, dangerous coin.

"So," she says at last. "What will you do with it?"

I let the question hang in the kind of silence that persuades. "It cannot vanish. But if it surfaces uncontrolled, it burns us all, Étienne, Luc, and the name itself."

Her mouth curves, not quite a smile. "Then you intend to own it."

"Control is survival," I say.

"You think survival is control. I think survival is choosing who you will still face in the mirror."

We pour the wine. It breathes in the glass whilst we sit with the tape. On the third glass, I call Annina, a secure line routed through Geneva. She answers on the second ring.

I do not explain. I only say, "We've seen the tape; it's real."

A pause, the measured kind that decides things.

"Keep it dark. I'll move money where it cannot be traced. No paper, no screens."

Saskia watches me end the call. Her voice is soft when she speaks. "I buried one secret like this years ago. It still wakes me at night."

I study her. The house has asked favours of her; she paid them; she paid them well. She looks smaller in the low light, not diminished, only human.

"And you, Mademoiselle, would you cover for them again?"

She meets my eyes. "For the house? Maybe. But... not for them. Never again for them."

Her answer lands with the deadweight of something honest. The tape between us seems to take on a heavier silence.

I fold my gloves once more, a motion like setting a seal, then I ask, "Do you know what I would wish, Saskia?"

Her eyes narrow. "Tell me."

"To see Étienne exposed as the saboteur he always was. To watch Luc gag on the word "legacy" until it rots in his mouth."

She holds my gaze. "That is revenge, Céleste."

"No. That is balance. If the balance leans towards revenge, so be it. I regret nothing in wanting them to pay."

She sees the years in my face, the cost that sits behind any offer of reparation. She knows I am not saying this casually.

"I stood by him once," I say, the confession soft and precise. "When he destroyed that cyclist in Zurich."

My admission meets hers like an icy wind. "And I'll regret it until I die," I add.

Rain presses harder against the shutters. The bottle is empty. The glass' stem rests against my fingers. For a moment, the wine trembles; a small betrayal.

Saskia notices. She says nothing. She does what she has always done; she absorbs what cannot be spoken out loud.

She pushes the tape across the table. The motion is simple. It is everything.

"You came because they will believe you more than me," she says. "If it must be buried, you will be the one to lower it."

Between us, the tape lies like a live charge, small enough to misplace, heavy enough to kill. The truth does not sleep.

Converted Warehouse, Rotherhithe, London.

Félix's studio smelt of resin and old smoke. Half workshop, half confessional. The walls were bare but for a sun-faded Rauschenberg and the framed decree that had once barred him from Noir Pavé. He had kept it like a relic, proof of his own martyrdom.

He was barefoot, with dark crescents under his eyes, moving with the uneven grace of a man who had lived too long at the edge of sleep. Erratic, brilliant, too costly to cast out, too unstable to ever fully trust.

I stood in the doorway, arms folded. I wanted him to see how sombre I was first.

"This stays in the room, Félix."

The photograph slid across the table, the paper catching against the grain.

Trial Subject 04. C. Okonjo. 2000 endurance project.

A blurred runner, feet pounding broken concrete. The mesh on her ankle is unmistakable.

"The biometric tag matches our Flex."

Félix's hand did not falter. He took it in without surprise, only with the weariness of a man already half-condemned.

"It is not original tech," I said.

He asked, voice quiet, "Whose bones did I build this on?"

The question did not require an answer. He already knew.

"We did not steal it," I told him. A shield of words, nothing more.

His reply was sharper for its softness. "You did not have to. Someone did it for you."

He turned away, opened a drawer, and drew out an air-gapped drive, matte black, edges scarred from years of use. The machine on his workbench whirred to life with a cough of fans. He fed the tape through, every movement precise and ceremonial.

Lines of code bloomed across the screen. He typed without flourish, only with the exhausted inevitability of a priest repeating liturgy.

Two USB sticks slid onto the desk, silver and unmarked. Félix printed the hash values on a sheet of white card, stamped it with the date, and pressed his palm flat against it as if swearing an oath.

"If this goes public," he said quietly, "it goes exactly like this. No edits, no erasure. No doubt."

I nodded once. "Then it stays like this until it must."

Without another word, he lifted the Rauschenberg from the wall and hid the secrets behind it. The act was quiet but final. His farewell had begun before I even left the room.

I carried the photograph in my mind as I walked away. Not the shoe. Not Félix.

The runner: blurred, forgotten, erased. A girl whose bones had been ground into someone else's legacy.

Christine.

That was the truth I would not bury.

Montclair HQ, London.

Luc's office, half-lit, shutters drawn. The screen showed both women in the archive room, side by side, their reflections caught in the glass. He let it play again. Then again.

He pressed two fingers to his temple, steadying the fury.

"Activate," he said. The personal AI came online at once.

"Get Avery Trent on the phone, but keep her holding."

"Certainly, sir."

"And ready the helicopter. France. Perpignan. I'll have to see my brother."

"Affirmative."

He lifted the receiver. His voice was calm, almost bored. "Bring me the trial ledgers."

A pause, then the question on the line.

"And the women?"

Luc's smile did not touch his eyes. "We remind them what loyalty costs."

23

Aïcha

D own in the Quiet House basement, the bulbs hum their own spaced-out lullaby, throwing long shadows over brick. Phones breathe out on the stairs. Faraday silence, zero interference.

Down here, the console glows like something meant to be touched gently. Cold vaults, rails, and a filtration choir behind the walls.

They thought they would let the dust have it. They thought wrong. This place is Mara's now, not his.

The rails are easels for her hands. The scanners, her lens. Dorian sent his ghost crew. We built Moss, custom code laced quietly and close, not listed anywhere. Mara named it with a grin, palm pressed to steel. That's her style.

She whispered, "Moss," and the system went soft for her.

It recognises her. DNA, breath, how she stands in this cold air. Otherwise, the archive just dreams old dreams. With Mara here, the AI wakes, stretches, and listens for her.

When she draws, Moss follows the pencil, remembers every edge, and slips it into a secret lattice. The walls keep her close, always. She doesn't need to stash her work or fear random theft. The house is her passport; she belongs.

Safi slips the drawing in and makes it speak. Translation: low-key alchemy. That's what we do. I wire what was never meant to meet. Mara? She's the reason it works smoothly, like a rumour you can't trace.

Mara perches in her *Dead Space*, headset half on, pencil balanced easily. She draws like she's stealing memories back, recapturing moments before anyone else can claim them. Every exhale sets the Studer reels rolling. First sound, deliciously clumsy. Real. Static in the walls, Moss waking slowly, responsive only to Mara.

I catch the feed and let Safi thread it clean of all coughs and pauses and shoe scrapes, pure. No filters. Proof she's alive and we're right here.

Félix drops in now, scarf trailing like he's headlining the basement. Silk brushes my sleeve; blink and you'll miss it. He talks big about hating AI, but look at him now, orbiting Mara, not Volant, not Luc, not their weak remix of truth. He's got a tell: his hand hovers, notes in Mara's margins like a new annotation; maybe he wants us to read him.

I let it ride. This is our track drop, and the men upstairs? Still dancing to static.

Dorian tags it in, in quiet respect. None of us talks much in here. We're satellites circling her gravity.

The Chelsea house doesn't play at being clever. Upstairs, everything's performance: antique mirrors to catch the light, eggshell walls, a drawing room sleek for sponsors, and every square inch shined to a low-key gloss. Under the parquet, truth lingers, sours. Luc's basement. Hollowed, wired spine of the building. The Saeculum Archive. Concrete hush, metal racks, servers stacked and silent as kept secrets. Down here, silence has gravity: heavy, preserved, like lungs wrapped in glass.

Mara first, always. She lays a line down, nothing rushed, her sketchbook open flat. She isn't inventing, just... retrieving. Curves fall from her wrist, gentle, exact. Not new, the recovery of something half-lost, soaked in light. Mara never explains. She sketches, and we fall into orbit, satellites pulling their own shadows.

Dorian files the line in, calm. He does it the way some people hide a letter in a drawer, filed, silent, never meant to be found. Insurance and erasure folded together. Enough for someone to lock, not enough to ever make a noise.

Félix scowls; bass vibrations, no hint of a melody.

"Machines do not dream. If it's Mara's drawing, don't cut the head off the flower."

He's always so sure he's the only one who cares about beauty. He forgets who owns the track.

Saskia's head lifts, every movement calculated, cold as vinyl pressed wrong.

"Stop talking about cutting off Mara's pretty head."

Words are sharp, almost careless, but the edge cuts. Brittle laughter skitters, dies out, and never catches in the warmth.

Her thumb stays pressed to the edge of the table longer than it needs to be. Her tell, neat and private. Hairline damp, too much city heat, too many eyes. The kind of day when lawyers circle from above, accounts pulse, and threats flash by post, stamped with his name.

Mara glances up. The pencil hovers, the line interrupted, reading Saskia's undertone with a daughter's precision. She doesn't need volume to sense trouble, only silence, weighted.

I say nothing. I watch the way Saskia's voice rasps instead of rising. In that blink, she isn't Luc's wife, or Zander's problem, or anyone's emissary. She is a mother, flanked and dangerous, a live wire on Mara's behalf.

All bass, still no melody. Félix doesn't realise Mara's the needle.

Félix's hands go wide, like a preacher at a pulpit.

"If you cage her too much, she'll wilt. I'll burn every server before I let that happen."

"It's not a cage. It's a mirror. Every line she draws makes it sharper." Safi bristles, dryly.

"It's learning her, not owning her," I put in simply.

Truth is, even mirrors distort if you stare too long.

Mara doesn't blink, doesn't break. Pencils down, steady-cool. The scanner breathes in her mark. Moss exhales, a ghost line, a shade ahead, AI getting bold.

A schematic builds, layer by layer: Mara's hand, Dorian's silent stamp, Félix's restless curve, Safi's code threading, and Saskia's pulse held midair.

"Twelve minutes over schedule. Four redundancies in phrasing," Safi notes, eyes still on the numbers.

One clear delay, Saskia's pen suspended for a three-count before finishing. Hesitation: not random. Reads like a secret halfway confessed.

A moment too long. Drop imminent. Even silence hits like percussion if you bother to listen.

They all nod, bobbling, hypnotic. I almost lose it. Saskia never tips her hand, but today she let the card flash, edge up, quick. I clock it, a shift beneath the surface, promise and warning all at once.

"Recorded. Archived," Safi says, ritual complete.

Saskia's planner is left on the table, the notebook spine sharp against glass, her handwriting the usual iron: precise, controlled, until it isn't. One line breaks formation. Ink pressed, a pause heavy enough to warp the curve.

DO NOT TRANSFER. H.V.

Félix catches it first, jaw ticking, silk scarf slipping like a sly nod. Safi clocks him clocking it, a twin thing, old as time.

Behind Saskia's empty chair, voices feather together, near-silent.

"H.V."

"Not ours."

"So whose?"

A shrug, clean as a snare hit – this is smoke, not fire. The trick is to act unbothered. They know already, of course. The actual game: pretend not to.

Saskia comes back, phone holstered, face ironed flat. She reaches for the planner, but Félix drops one fingertip onto the page. Light. Casual. Game piece, not a challenge. It matters. It doesn't. That's how you know it's everything.

I file it. Filing is what I do. Queens have tells, even if they crown themselves. No one notices the young ones in the room, not properly. Seventeen, they think I'm a shadow, a handmaiden to genius, played for laughs. But I'm always here. Knowing.

I know Mara draws recoveries, not inventions. Dorian, relics filed for a god he doesn't trust. Félix, his beauty hungry as any king. Saskia, with her lockbox memory for things no one sees coming. Safi, the architecture mapped behind her eyes.

149

Félix's scowl, never missed. Saskia's mask was perfect until today.

She tries for neat. Her hand hovers. I don't let the book go. My finger rests there, deliberately, with no apology.

"Use us," I say, the pitch quiet enough they could call it kindness.

Safi's eyes glitter, recording, already scheming. "We can help. Our toes touch many waters, Saskia."

She doesn't answer, but her hand pauses, a tell, and then slips the planner away.

Camille's shadow is on the wall. From Paris, from somewhere colder. Smiling like she's the one who minted control.

They don't know I'm recording too. Not files, not code. Here, in my head, in sync and bars, in rhythm. Sampling every misstep, breaking, stitching, keeping it for later. Their mistakes will build my mix. One day, when the men upstairs finally notice the silence, what they want will already be ours.

It isn't enough to archive. You have to remix. Make them dance to your loop. The Saeculum Archive isn't just storage, not tonight. It's spinning, sampling, remixing, and every sound in here is ours.

Saskia gathers the planner, her grip a fraction too tight. Nails moon-bright against the paper, knuckles showing white. For a breath, her eyes flick to the door, as if she's listening for footsteps, counting the seconds before someone else demands the truth.

Somewhere behind her eyelids, calculations spin. Even the glass in this place feels complicit, reflecting fear she doesn't permit surfacing.

She smooths her skirt and pivots, a queen rehearsing

indifference, but her shadow is sharper, doubled. She knows the net draws closer. That Luc is circling, tallying accounts, and running his own silent diagnostics on where she walks, what she saves, and whom she trusts.

For a second, I hear the hiss beneath her calm, the pressure at the edge of the drop. Tonight, nobody here is free. But I'm the only one who feels how close Saskia comes to slipping.

The room resets, Dorian rustles, Félix cracks his knuckles, and Mara lowers her eyes. Holding, waiting.

It's enough for now. But soon, somebody's going to miss a step. And then it will all break wide open.

24

Saskia

Montclair HQ, London.

The boardroom was built for intimidation. Twelve chairs, one left empty for Lucien Senior, still reserved, still waiting. One wall was matte onyx, polished to an impossible depth. Another was velvet-lined, concealing a flush bar and the drawer they still called the archive. Above the head of the table, a camera lens disguised as a slit. No one knew where the feed went, only who it fed.

There were no PR handlers today, no stylists, and no set dressing. Only legal, legacy, and loyalty pretending to be neutral.

The boardroom was too quiet once the others had left. Papers still scattered across the table, the ghost of strong scents in the air. I smoothed one page flat, not because it mattered, but because my hands needed something to do.

Zander leaned back in his chair, watching me in that way he

had, steady, unblinking, like he could wait all night.

"You showed me once," he said at last. His voice was low, but it cut through the silence. "The tattoo. But not why?"

My hand paused. I didn't look up.

"Not everything is a story I'm ready to share... *yet*."

The word was deflection, but the pause after it said more than I wanted.

"I can't stop thinking about the old archive in your basement, I mean. That night, at your house. You didn't know I was there, but I saw you. And I," he broke off, searching for the right truth. "I haven't been able to forget it."

My eyes snapped to his. A flicker of alarm, sharper than I intended. "That was not for you."

"And yet I saw it." His gaze didn't waver.

Something shifted in my chest, an old performance sliding off my shoulders. I exhaled.

"I'm not a Montclair anymore." The admission landed heavier than I expected. "The life I rehearsed, the one I wore like armour, is already over. I don't have to keep pretending."

He leant in closer, not enough to touch but close enough that I felt it. The warmth carried across the small space, uninvited and undeniable. "Then what do you want?"

My throat tightened. I didn't answer. Couldn't.

We turned back to the papers, though neither cared about them. Their hands brushed over the same sheet, skin sparking against skin. He didn't pull away. Neither did I.

His gaze found mine, lingering, deliberate. Breaths mingled in the hush between them. He shifted just slightly, as if the table had drawn them closer together. I felt it, the almost. His hand half-turned towards hers, waiting.

And then the door creaked.

Mademoiselle Céleste stepped in, the click of her heels too loud in the charged quiet. I offered a polite smile, retrieving her phone from the side, but her eyes took in the scene. Myself, flushed and frozen. Zander was too slow to mask the moment.

"Pardon," Céleste murmured, but she lingered a heartbeat too long before gliding back out.

The silence she left behind wasn't the same. It carried everything we hadn't said.

Saskia's house, Chelsea.

I wasn't expecting anyone, but Clara suddenly called.

She sat at the table, legs crossed, calm, a glass of wine already at her elbow.

"You've been twitchy all week, babe," she said. "So, what gives?"

I swirled my glass, the ruby catching lamplight.

"A plan."

"Specifics," she pressed.

"To fuck over the men that left us out," I said, sharper than I meant. "Luc. Étienne. Maybe even Zander. Pick your poison. They built a boys' club; I'm writing the correction."

Clara smiled. "Excellent. Just don't dress it up as revenge. Revenge bleeds money. Make it business."

"It is business," I said. "Business that looks like revenge."

Her mouth tugged sideways, half-approval, half-warning. "Fine. Just keep your pulse steady. Men like them can smell a spike faster than sharks smell blood."

She drained her glass in one line, set it down like a full stop, and stood. "I'll leave you to it. Call if you want numbers, not hand-holding."

The door clicked shut behind her. Silence expanded, almost civilised. I thought I'd won a few minutes of quiet.

Then, footsteps. Heavier, looser. Must be Luc dropping off Mara.

It was Zander.

He dropped the bottle onto the table. Glenfarclas. Thirty years old. A whisky that announces itself, smoky and measured, not showy. Luc never touched it – too Scottish for his French palate. Zander knows better. He knows what cuts.

I met his eyes. Stillness is my answer. No flicker, no shift. He thrives on reaction, but silence unsettles him more.

"At least you bring decent whisky."

"Naturally."

He poured two fingers into crystal. I didn't stop him. Didn't stop myself either. The scent rose, deep and woody, with a thread of sherry sweetness underneath. Not Luc's drink, never mine either, but tonight it felt like a language only Zander and I could speak.

We sat at opposite ends of the table. Not far in distance, oceans in meaning.

The silence vibrated, alive, not empty.

"I almost kissed you earlier," he said.

"I almost let you."

"Would it have mattered?"

"Only if it had been good."

I watched the corner of his mouth move, a half-smile that did not reach his eyes. He wanted me to feel the danger of it. He wanted me to imagine.

"Do you ever get tired of being the fallout?" I asked.

His glass rose. He drank. Didn't answer.

"He built you to lose, Alexandre. You know that, don't you?"

He nodded once. A boy conceding a rule he had known all along.

"I thought you were strong enough to survive him."

That one landed. Too clean. I felt it under the skin. I rose as if motion could dissolve meaning.

"Mara's not here?"

"With Luc."

Bach played low, a cello line frayed and mournful.

We sat across from each other. His glass half-full, mine barely touched.

"You have to sort yourself out, Zander. I need you."

Stillness. Mine first, then his.

"*We* need you, Volant, I mean."

"I know."

"He's freezing you out, and you're letting him. It's a test. Make sure you pass it."

"He doesn't use my knowledge; he always refers back to his original protégé."

"Who, Camille? Fuck Camille. Keep Luc's side as Luc's side."

"You make it impossible to tell if I'm in check or already mated."

I leant forward and set something on the table. My top slipped, one shoulder sliding open. Pale skin in amber light. Porcelain and bone china catching flame.

I saw it hit him. That flicker in his eyes. The hunger. The restraint. He would never admit how much it shook him. I didn't fix it.

"You didn't get this from me."

A USB.

"What is it?"

"Private comms. Camille and the American one. They joke about which of your exes will break you first."

"Who, Leila! Anything else?"

"Leila used the phrase 'downstream acquisition'. Means nothing to me."

But I saw the way his body stiffened. His mind was already somewhere else. "Biotech. Kevin Price talk."

The USB was delivered with a slip of card that had come with the courier. No sender. Just these words:

Exile never means absence.

"Maxi," he whispered almost to himself.

"I thought it was Maxime," I blurted.

"He's... a help, even from so far away."

"Good to know."

Our fingers brushed, the smallest graze. The current between us was still alive, still dangerous.

This time, he didn't let go.

His hand closed over mine, just enough to hold. His thumb pressed lightly against the inside of my wrist, where the blood beats close to the surface. A pulse against a pulse.

For an instant, Mara's face flared in my mind, the sketch tucked away upstairs. She trusted me to keep her world safe, not to collapse into his orbit. And beneath that, Clara's dry warning echoed: keep your pulse steady; men like them can smell a spike faster than sharks smell blood.

I felt his breath shift. Saw his jaw harden, as if he knew he should move and couldn't.

It was not a kiss, not an embrace. But it was worse because

it could be denied. A fraction longer, and it would no longer be an accident.

The heat of his skin stayed after he pulled away, a ghost-pulse echoing mine.

I could see the different coloured irises, both dilated.

If he had kissed me, it would have been ruin. And yet my body leant towards it, reckless, ready.

I didn't pull away.

He did eventually, suddenly and sharply, as though the contact had burnt. He stood too quickly, glass unsteady in his hand, masking it with a swallow.

His voice came rougher than before. "You hate me."

"Only when I can't have you."

He set the glass down too hard. Amber sloshed against crystal. He didn't finish it. Didn't take the bottle either. Just left it there unopened, an offering or a mistake.

The click of the door echoed, too sharp for such a small sound.

I stayed seated. Finished his glass instead of mine. Let the whisky burn, rich and medicinal, threading down my throat like a secret. The burn was not his mouth, but it was close enough.

On the sideboard, beneath an art book, I had tucked a sketch. Black ink on rag paper. Two blurred figures, arms brushing. Mara, unmistakable, and Maxime's face beside her.

Zander had seen it.

I poured myself another measure. The silence had weight now, heavy and electric. Not Luc's silence, not his pauses, nor his calculated retreats. This was mine.

Zander was still here, and I told myself the silence was only tension. That was a lie.

Because it was hunger too.
And hunger never leaves quietly.

25

Gauche

The suite smelt of truffle butter and river light. Not the cheap kind that sits heavy, but the kind a private chef finishes with a brush, just before he vanishes. Millennium Beaux Noirs was built for moments like this. Two storeys of glass, folding doors thrown wide to let the city in, and Luc's yacht moored below like punctuation. The helipad above, the river walk below.

Me at the centre.

I chose the dress deliberately. Silk the colour of burnt sugar, clinging where it should skim. Long brown legs bare from mid-thigh, shoulders bare, no bra, nipples alert, ready for their prey. The silk moves like water when I walk and stops moving entirely when I stop.

Waiting. For Dorian.

I open my tablet and scroll through Laurette's quarterly expenses. My nails tap once, twice, then still on a line item.

Roussillon Holdings – €8,000 monthly transfer.

A vineyard, on paper. The name tugs at something half-forgotten. I screenshot it and send it to Camille with a single line: What is this?

The reply comes faster than it should.

Adèle: *Legacy vineyard. Nothing worth the data burn.*

No greeting, no nothing. Too clean, too fast. You do not waste that kind of speed on €8,000 unless it is not about the money.

I am meant to be composed. Predatory, even. Instead, I am still thinking about the message when the door clicks.

Dorian comes in without the deferential smile people usually wear in my presence. No apology. Just that faint, assessing look, the one that makes me wonder if he has already seen me here in his head.

"You redecorated," he says, glancing at the table laid for two.

"Only for tonight."

I fill the silence with talk about the view, the light, and the build quality. I cross my legs slowly, letting the silk slip higher. I smile too much. I hear it as I do it, the way women do when they are performing their own myth.

He pours himself a glass without asking. The stem of his glass does not tremble; mine does. Only slightly.

"You came for AetherFlex," he says, not even pretending it is small talk. "But you did not bring anything to trade."

I cross to him first, bottle in hand, like I planned it that way. Tilt just enough for silk to slide against my ribs, for the neckline to offer a measured glance of skin. His gaze drags with the silk, pausing where the fabric parts. The trick is to make it look uncalculated.

My wrist turns, wine running into his glass in a thin red line.

I let my fingers linger on the stem a heartbeat too long, not touching him, close enough that he can smell the heat of my skin over the Bordeaux.

The folder on his right hand stays where it is.

"I brought myself, monsieur Tseng."

His mouth twitches. Almost a smile, almost pity.

"And you thought that would be enough?"

"You used to think it was."

A pause. Not long. Just long enough to be dangerous.

"You are confusing nostalgia with leverage," he says. "One disappears faster than the other."

I stand behind his chair. Let one hand rest lightly on the back, my body angled so my scent catches the air between us. My fingers skim the fabric of his shoulder, the briefest ghost of touch.

He does not move. Does not even breathe.

Instead, he slides the folder towards me without looking up.

As if I have already stopped mattering.

No rush, I am the one who has to open it.

First photo, a grainy telephoto from the Dubai SportsTech Awards. Me in a low top, leaning in close to Kevin Price. My hand grazing his arm. A laugh frozen mid-bloom.

Second photo set: two stills from Montclair HQ's side entrance in Belgravia. Night. Toby glancing over his shoulder, me leaning in to speak, almost conspiratorial.

Third set, Julien and me at a discreet Mayfair bar. We are close, heads bent together, my hand on his wrist. Caption printed at the bottom, Vérité & AetherFlex, Q2 discussion?

I flip the last photo back into the stack. My mouth twitches, the barest shift of jaw muscle.

For a moment I see it the way he wants me to, as evidence. Not of guilt, but of weakness.

I reached too easily. Trusted too quickly. Laughed too often.

All the little tells you do not notice until someone else puts them on paper.

"Putain..." The word escapes before I can stop it. My voice comes out flat. "These are all innocent meetings."

Silence.

"Is that what Étienne would think?"

The pause is deliberate, enough space for me to imagine Étienne's reaction, for the warmth in my face to turn cold.

I push the folder back towards him without looking down again.

"Do not mistake silence for forgiveness."

He stands. No smile. No warning.

"You do not have to pretend, Gauche. You never did."

His voice is soft enough to be mistaken for kindness.

He pauses in the doorway. Turns just slightly.

"You always drink red when you are lying. But you only swirl it when you are afraid."

Then he is gone.

I turn to the glass, to the city, to the sound of laughter far below. The silk sways once and stills.

Somewhere behind me, the door clicks shut.

I look down at my phone. The Roussillon message still sits there. Silent. Waiting.

Like it knows what comes next.

I hear the buzz. I do not answer.

Camille lets herself in. Two bottles of red. Black heels, no stockings. Hair pinned like she has come from somewhere

163

better or is planning to ruin somewhere worse by midnight. She does not speak. She pours. Sits opposite. Silk blouse half-undone, no bra. Her perfume reaches me before the wine does: amber, jasmine, and something sharper underneath. Intent, maybe.

I hate that I notice. I hate it more than she knows I would.

"Thought you might need this."

The wine is expensive. Not French. A choice. A message.

She waits. She always does. Letting the silence bend until it serves her.

She sips. Her blouse shifts. I see it then, the ring, left nipple, subtle, glinting. She is not flaunting it. Not quite. She is leaving the door ajar. Seeing who steps through.

Then, like she is offering me a cigarette or a loaded gun:

"I have dirt. On Dorian, I mean."

Her voice, smoke dipped in sugar. Smooth enough to bruise.

Her eyes move over my face.

"He got to you."

It is not a question.

"They always try to make us look small first."

I remember her saying I would never survive politics, then helping me steal the vote two days later. She likes to warn before she arms.

I watch her mouth as she speaks. Fully glossed, that studied pout she wears like regalia. The kind that wins boardrooms and buries rivals with grace.

"And if I asked for your help?"

Her gaze flicks up, cool and deliberate.

"T'es sérieuse? I'd say you owed me one."

She smiles genuinely. Warm.

I lean forward, elbows to knees. Silk slips lower over my

chest, clean and deliberate. I see her look. Not accidental this time.

Her eyes dip, not just to stare, but to study. The line of me, the weight. The tension in the fabric. Not sex, not yet. Analysis. Inventory.

She is not thinking, What if?

She is thinking, Would I?

Would she?

Her lip curls. Not a smile. A twitch of something older. I know that look. I have worn it too.

The quiet female audit. What skin costs, what it buys. What you offer when no one is asking, and what you keep to yourself. She does not speak. Neither do I. The air changes, electric, precise, close to cruel.

We do not kiss.

We could.

We still might.

We have spent years being measured by men. Now we measure each other.

This time, neither of us looks away.

"Allez, love. France is calling."

I hate the rescue, but I take it.

* * *

I fly back to Perpignan with Camille, arriving in a cloud of leather and perfume. She pulls me out before the scene can curdle.

I take the Renault and drive the coast road one-handed towards Saint-Jean-Cap-Ferrat. France rolls out ahead, and so does Esmé.

The villa's too quiet. Esmé's away, but the door code works. I slip inside, pour a drink, and let the warmth take the edge off. I'll message her, just in case. But for now, the quiet suits me.

Wired had been pushing for a profile interview, *"Gauche: The Future in Combat Boots"*, so I told them now was a good time as long as it could be done remotely.

"You've said before you don't really believe in legacy," the journalist, a pretty, brunette, straight-laced type, prompted.

I smiled without warmth.

"Legacy's just hand-me-downs in a prettier box. Faucon was my father's skeleton of an idea; he just didn't know how to dress it, so I taught it to scream, but it was still his bones. I'm tired of dressing corpses."

"You don't think of yourself as an heir?"

"Heir?" My laugh was quick and too sharp. "Putain, sérieux? They called me gauche as a kid – left-handed, yes? But also too tall, too clumsy, and too brown for their whitewashed castles. I made it a name worth whispering. That's not inheritance. That's architecture."

"And now?"

I bent and tapped my boot against the wall. "Now I'm building something that never existed before. No old man's name on the patent. No blueprint but mine."

The journalist hesitated. "What do you say to people who think you're just disruptive?"

"Disruptive? Nah." I leaned into the camera, eyes lit, voice low enough to cut. "I'm not the fire, I'm the forge, and they're gonna choke on their own smoke before they figure out the difference."

I straightened back up and let the silence carry.

"Now print that. Or don't. Either way, I'll still be louder

than your headline."

As I end the interview, a message pings, not from Esmé as I'd hoped but from Saskia.

Careful. She breaks pretty things.

WTF?!

I begin typing, delete. Begin again. Delete. The three dots must have tortured her, appearing, vanishing, appearing, and vanishing again.

I traced the bolts at the corner of the small table and found the joints. Childhood muscle memory: dismantling my father's stereo, rewiring lamps until they blew. I liked things better once they bore my fingerprints.

"Forge," I muttered under my breath to no one. The word tasted different when no one was listening. Less slogan, more prayer.

My reflection stared back from the black screen of my phone. Not clumsy anymore. Not gauche.

"Architect."

I whispered it like a promise.

The light is low, just screen glow and the sodium hum of the streetlamps outside. My heels are off. My hair is loose, wild black curls around my face.

I prop the phone against a Saint-Estève paperweight.

No filter. No ring light. Just me. Bare. Blunt. Waiting.

I hit record.

"I do not know why I am doing this."

A pause. One breath.

"Sometimes your legacy does not love you back."

My head drops. Then, I look into the lens again.

"Sometimes your last name is just a barcode. They scan it. Smile. Take what they want. C'est la vie, non?"

A hollow laugh that doesn't land.

My thumb hesitates over the keyboard. Just one word, Esmé. I type it. Watch its pulse there under the clip. Then delete it.

I do not cry. I do not fix my hair.

I watch myself a moment longer. I see the tiredness. The resolve underneath it, tight, coiled, waiting.

I reach forward and tap *Save to Drafts*. No caption, no hashtags. No post. Just proof the moment exists. Even if no one ever sees it.

I do not post it. I do not delete it either. I let it sit there. Unseen. Like me.

I close the laptop. Sit in the dark a moment longer. Let the silence settle.

Then, I slide my hand under the silk.

Not out of lust.

Out of want.

Out of need.

Not for anyone else.

Just for me.

26

Zander

Lisbon.

Alfama's light isn't like anywhere else. It moves like someone paused the world to admire the cracked tiles and laundry strung between balconies. I now know every alley, every cat that claims a doorstep like it owns the city.

The villa sits tucked just beyond the tourist buzz, private enough to matter. No knocking. The brass keypad clicks open with my thumbprint, quiet as a whispered secret.

"Intruder," Maxime calls from the kitchen, voice low and sardonic. "Careful... You'll wake the ghosts. They've been oddly well-behaved this week."

"Only if you changed the locks. Didn't figure you for the paranoid type."

He's barefoot, sleeves rolled to elbows, hacking figs onto a chipped plate. Damp hair still clings to his neck like a poor decision.

Isa's here. They kiss once; nothing staged, just this brief, sharp space between them before she takes the knife and finishes his work better than he ever could.

"Bonjour, beau," she sings warmly whilst kissing me on both cheeks.

We move through the villa. Spartan on the surface, almost monastic, until you lean in.

One ashtray clings to a windowsill. A single wineglass and lipstick drying by the sink. Not lodgers or distractions. Just ghosts paused between comings and goings. Maxime lets them orbit. Never settles for permanence.

We sit. Smile. Wine was poured.

"Our dear brother Rusty", Maxime says, voice going low, "has been rifling through Luc's drawers like a petulant schoolboy. Found something, too."

"Since when does he play nice with anyone's toys?"

"Since he found something worth the trouble. A draft of the will. Not the one on everyone's lips."

I let the silence stretch longer than it should. "...Yes?"

"A different draft. Luc's unspoken manifesto. Deliciously inconvenient."

I laugh.

"And AetherFlex? Étienne's golden child, wasn't it?"

"Yep." Maxime's smile is a faint slash. "Stolen, flipped back to Volant. Toby, foisted out like a tragic ambassador."

"That'll give Étienne an ulcer to rival the London fog. I'm almost tempted to watch it all unfold."

"Oh, I thought it might brighten your day. Serve up Étienne's ulcer on a silver platter."

Behind him, the sideboard hosts three open laptops. One

170

flashes a French newswire, another flickers maps, and a third hums like a restless phantom, its fan working overtime, as if it never sleeps.

"Isa's been feeding me whispers, names, deals, and Camille's offhand remarks."

I file everything instantly.

We exchange intel like trading cards, not weapons, but currency. Gossip traded as trust, not betrayal.

On the sideboard, the third laptop hummed louder than the rest, its fan rattling like a smoker hacking up a poor memory. The screen split a chessboard frozen mid-battle, with black and white squares stacked like unsent letters.

I leaned in, glass perched in my hand, voice soft enough for irony. "Chess, Maxi? I always pegged you as a Solitaire kind of man. One-player puzzles suit the lonely well."

He didn't deign to look, his voice lazy and sharp. "It's not Solitaire. Though the loneliness... that's mandatory."

Two names blinked in the corner, BleuFantôme versus KnightLight. Almost sentimental, almost ridiculous. Children's stories told of queens and knights.

I perched on the stool, fingers threatening the trackpad. "Let me."

"Don't." The word slid out like a warning, with a lazy smile behind it.

I moved a knight anyway – doomed, diagonal, reckless and funny. A low, dry laugh spilt from him. "You've just insulted centuries of dead Russians."

"Then they should hurry up and get over it." I sipped; the wine was a smooth lie.

With a single flick, his hand corrected the piece, irritation efficient but insufficient to push me away. His face softened slightly when the reply came, KnightLight's bold queen's gambit. Too sharp, too playful for anything older than ten, or so the tease went.

"He's good," I murmured.

His voice clipped the word, the drawer shutting with a click I felt in my ribs. "She learns."

She?

I left it hanging. Maxime's lies were always tangled with truth, best left to ripen before spoken aloud.

He leaned back against the counter, eyes fierce over the rim of his glass. "You know, Zazou..." His smile thinned to a cat's, flickering with dry amusement and something older, more tired. "I've never seen a woman do this to you, Zazou."

I tried to laugh. It fractured sharply. "Don't start."

Maxime's grin grew wider, all teeth and secrets. "Ah, but it's true. You're restless. Unfinished. Like someone changed the locks in your head and forgot to leave a spare."

I shook my head, a sharper motion than intended. "Drop it."

His phone buzzed on the sideboard like a bad omen. Face down, unread. He flipped it away, grabbed a fig and grumbled about deadlines like a man weighed down by ghosts.

I don't pry. I file it all away: the pill vial slipped in a book spine and the faint chemical bite near his desk. Not chaos. Not collapse. Just enough to keep him tethered in exile, where even ghosts need to hide.

Maxime's laughter lingered on the balcony long after he disappeared back into his screens, deadlines slipping through his fingers like ash. Typical. Burn the match, then leave me alone with the fire.

Maxime's jab still echoed in the smoke.

I've never seen a woman do this to you, Zazou.

By the time I'd wrestled for a reply, he was already gone, folded back into the glow of his laptops, master of leaving chaos unfinished. Typical.

His laughter still hung in the air when he slipped away, a spark thrown then vanished. Left me pacing through the smoke.

Isa stayed.

She curved into the armchair by the balcony doors like she owned the space, the way only she could make such a claim without a word. Her legs draped across mine, natural as breathing, the cut-off denim shorts she wore clinging tight, lengthening those long limbs impossibly. Her fingers brushed the inside of my wrist, grounding me even as everything else threatened to unravel.

Isa carries a beauty both effortless and deliberate, classical until she could turn to marble and still command the room. Her loose waves of chestnut-burnished hair frame a face so symmetrical masters have carved it, with cheekbones quiet gods would envy. Her skin glows warm and soft, untouched by harshness.

Those sharp blue eyes miss nothing, holding the world in a thoughtful, measured gaze. Her lips, full and poised with a natural pout, speak in unspoken balances, weighed between revealed and withheld.

Her figure is precise, runway-thin, and designed to let fabric tell its story rather than disrupt it. Subtle curves held just right, teardrop-shaped and perfect beneath delicate silks, beauty that whispers, never shouts. I can't help but see it, complete and untouchable, but laced with warmth and the rough familiarity of nearly a decade spent side by side.

"You've been pacing like the streets owe you answers," she said, cigarette balanced like a thread ready to snap, smoke curling up and fading into the humid Lisbon night like a reluctant confession.

"Sorry." I muttered, gaze fixed on the darkened rooftops. "Didn't mean to keep you."

Her blue eyes didn't flinch. "I like the quiet. People say there's more hiding in it than noise."

I laughed hollowly, humourlessly. "Not me."

"You say nothing." Her voice softened, less edge, more shield. "Which is curious for a man who usually talks himself into trouble."

She leant forward, thumb finding the knot in my shoulder, unspooling a tension words couldn't reach

"She got to you," Isa said, not a question.

My chest tightened. I kept my eyes away.

"I've seen it," she said, her voice just above a breath. "The way you look at her. The way you fight, the look. It tells more than you say."

"It's wrong."

"By whose rule?"

"He's my father."

"She's leaving him."

"She was family."

"Not really."

The certainty in her voice pressed hard against the night wrapped in cedar and salt, a weight settling sharp on my skin.

"I thought getting away would clear my head." I admitted. "But she haunts every corner. Even when she's not here."

Isa's hand stayed steady as a lighthouse, her gaze catching

174

and holding mine. "You love her?"

I looked down at my hands, thumbnails bitten to raw crescents, words failing. "I don't know what I'd call it. But I can't stop."

Silence bloomed between us, full and heavy. I saw Saskia in it, the boardroom quiet, the way she smoothed paper, the dark ink of her notes, and the lingering scent of perfume on my skin.

I raised my glass, swallowed hard, and dark thoughts slowly rooted in my gut. I wanted Étienne to choke on AetherFlex; I wanted Luc's empire to rot quietly from the inside out.

Isa sipped her wine, lips soft and composed, setting the glass down like the closing note of a sad song. "You don't have to say it." Her voice was low and certain, her legs still draped across mine, anchoring, claiming space. "I already heard it."

The words settled between us, heavier than Maxime's barb, steadier than my silence. I couldn't name the feeling just yet. But I could pack it away, use it, fuel not wound.

Then her gaze sharpened, flickering with something sharp, the kind shaped by knowing, not just seeing. "Max and I," she whispered, voice soft but firm, "we've seen the changes coming. The cracks are growing; the silence tightening. I hope you're ready, Zee. Things won't wait for you to catch up."

She shifted slightly, her bare thigh sliding just an inch, the denim shorts whispering secrets from within, the curve of her limbs, familiar terrain, quietly mapped in my memory.

Her words hovered in the air, warning folded into care. Isa was more than the room's quiet pulse. She was my axis, my rock.

And finally, I didn't bother hiding that I needed both.

27

Saskia

The Saeculum archive hum is soft today, low enough to almost forget. Almost. It sits behind Mara's sketching like a metronome she doesn't hear, but I can't ignore it. Her stylus logs every stroke, and it catches every hesitation, being more loyal than any human memory. The lines flicker on her screen, saving themselves a thousand times over.

Every line is hers, but the machine remembers better than she does. Better than I do.

I should feel proud; I built this. Instead, I feel a quiet guilt. Like I've tricked her. She's still too young to know anything stored can be stolen, reshaped, repurposed. I watch her bent over the tablet, tongue pressed between teeth, hair falling forward like a veil. The desk lamp halos her innocence, something I lost long ago.

Sometimes I see Zander in her drawings. The chaos spilling past the frame, the desperate reach for something lost. Maybe that's why I guard these lines so fiercely, even from myself.

She looks up.

"Is this really the right place for me?"

The question lingers. Not about the archive. About me.

I nod.

"Yes. It is."

I hope it's not a lie.

Because I don't know if I'm enough. Only that I want to be. If Moss was once an archive, maybe it can become more. Not just storage, but a framework. A place Mara can build from, without anyone else's blueprint.

When she leaves, I linger. Shut the system down. The hum dies in increments, like a heartbeat fading into silence. The air feels heavier, emptier without it.

Have I made her safer? Or archived her soul for someone else to play with one day?

That question hangs in the fug of tired machines and fading light.

Julien asks me to lunch at The Nest. He always reserves the same table, tucked far enough from the mirrors to stop himself checking his reflection. Still, I catch the small, nervous habit, smoothing his cuff, a quiet adjustment repeated when he doesn't know where to put his hands.

After he leads me through the blue door to the private garden terrace, the one never mentioned in the membership book. The air tastes of indecision before rain, metallic and electric, as if the city itself is rehearsing a storm.

L'Hirondelle's table has two rules and one law: no press, no recordings, and nothing leaves the blue door.

The terrace blooms with an abundance that should be gaudy but isn't. Palms and citrus trees crowd massive urns, ivy claws at walls, and lanterns spill soft light over mosaic tiles.

Chairs are upholstered in mismatched silks and velvets, bright parrots against green. It's curated, secret, like the set of a show only the silent audience gets to witness.

London's hum fades beyond brick walls, submerged like distant traffic underwater. Here, it's only the clink of glass, servers' hush, and night flowers mingling with tobacco's salty smoke.

Julien lights a cigarette and offers me one, though he knows I don't smoke. I shake my head at first but then take it, the burn sharp on my tongue. Two drags, and I hand it back, lipstick bleeding pink onto the filter. His mouth curves, not quite a smile, something softer.

He's always had this thing for me. Never said it. Never acted on it. But I've always known.

Sometimes I ache for him. Sometimes I pity him. The latter stings more than I'd admit.

Zander was wildfire: volatile, magnetic, impossible. Julien is steadiness. Old stone, not sparks. The kind you trust to hold roots deep. Maybe that's why it was never him.

"You hate this place," Julien says, breath thin, flame small beneath pale sky.

"I hate the velvet rope, not the meal."

His lips twitch, half amusement, half something deeper. "You always hate the rope. Never the table."

I shrug. "That's why you invite me. I'm cheaper than therapy."

Smoke curls between us. "Therapy doesn't wear Chanel."

"You should have married a banker's daughter. Or a duchess. Someone made for this world."

"I don't like duchesses."

"You like control."

His gaze settles, heavy enough to curl tight inside my ribs. "No. I like honesty." He says it like a confession practised twice before release.

I laugh. "Then you're in the wrong family."

No laugh from him. Only smoke veiling half his face. "I never liked Zander for you."

There it is. The closest he's come. I turn away, eyes tracing the sharp glints between rooftops.

"You don't have to like him," I say. "Just tolerate my terrible taste."

Julien flicks ash over the balustrade. "Think that's all it is?"

Silence stretches between us, old and fragile, an unspoken ghost we both feel.

A female server flirts with Julien. He straightens slightly, stiff with practised courtesy. When he laughs, it's a moment late, like a rehearsed soundtrack rerunning.

I smile back at her, playful and dominant.

He laughs too.

"Do you charm everyone?" I ask.

"Only the ones who don't know they're already mine."

The lunch table holds its usual quiet hum, soft clinks of cutlery and an indistinct murmur of well-placed words between bites. I keep my tone light and texture smooth where I can.

"So," I say, glass just grazing my lips, eyes steady on the subtle flicker of a shadow across the corner of Luc's face. "Has Luc mentioned Mademoiselle Céleste lately? In passing, I mean." A question pointed enough without asking directly.

He smiles too smoothly and shifts in his seat. "Céleste? Yes, of course."

"That's the thing, isn't it?" I ease forward, voice casual,

but the weight behind my words isn't lost on either of us. "It seems complicated with her and Luc at the moment. Complicated can swing many ways. I wonder which way it's leaning these days."

I let the silence stretch, a quiet invitation to fill the space.

"Last I heard," I continue, "there's been talk, little murmurs. People like to have their opinions, don't they?" A soft chuckle. "You must be tired of all the noise."

His jaw tightens imperceptibly, voice dropping just a touch. "Noise can be misleading."

I nod slowly, deliberately. "So, what's the truth then? If it's not noise."

He meets my gaze. Nothing more is said, but I file away the moment and the unsaid.

Julien scans the room before he pulls out his phone, thumb flicking the screen. Not a call, not a message, but a photo. He turns it towards me: Gauche and Leila Farrow, mouths inches apart, sequins and glass catching light like a staged performance.

"What do you make of that?" His voice is light, but his eyes weigh heavy.

I hold the phone longer than needed. This footprint reeks of Maxime, his games, his whispers, and his tests.

"Gauche never plays for free. She's staging something."

"And Leila?"

"She's just staging herself. As usual."

Later at home, the jacket I wore still smells faintly of his cigarette. My hair still carries the night, smoke and perfume braided tight in the strands. I should sleep, but every nerve thrums with the part of me that refuses to quiet.

Gauche's photo lingers on the edge of my mind. Did she know about Leila? One of Zander's exes, and as far as I knew, not someone who dated women. So what did this mean? The thought twists inside me in that familiar spike: part rage, part begrudging admiration.

Gauche always knows how to stage herself, how to be the algorithm's favourite. Not just seen, but unavoidable. Her beauty isn't accidental; it's a weapon forged sharp with killer curves and cold calculation.

I don't know whether I hate her or want to be her. Maybe both. Most days, both.

Fingers tremble over the screen as I open a DM.

Careful. She breaks pretty things.

Send.

The message sits, the words casual but raw beneath the surface. Not a warning exactly. Not quite a confession. More a line cast in the dark. Whoever wants to play with Zander's ghosts, they'll find me waiting.

I set the phone face down.

The night hums around me through the open window, the city breathing, restless, waiting.

And I can't tell if I've just lost something important or quietly begun a game I can't afford to lose.

Either way, the stakes are mine. My move.

28

Mara

The floor in the basement is warm tonight. I press my cheek to the tiles until the heat climbs into me, humming in my jaw like a second pulse. Heat has a sound if you listen long enough. Moss brightens pale green across the tablet, agreeing.

Sometimes I count the windows in the hall. Eleven, always eleven, unless someone moves the curtain. Then I have to start again.

The space hums steadily, softer than usual, like an old fan hidden behind the walls. Every stroke I draw is caught, copied, and filed away. Sometimes I think it isn't archiving my drawings at all but archiving me, each hesitation, each pause, as if those were the real data.

Patterns don't like to be found, but my brain finds them anyway: the number of cracks in the ceiling, the way light bends when nobody is watching.

The house is quiet. No footsteps in the corridor. No doors shutting, no clink of glasses. Only once do I hear my mother's voice, muffled through the wall, speaking into her phone.

Then silence again. She never comes in. I don't mind. Quiet is a tool.

When Mummy drops a pan in the kitchen, I hope the noise will reach me, a genuine sound, not the thin sort that slips under the door.

I test the stylus against my wrist before letting it touch the glass, a faint scratch, my ritual. Then I draw. A digital koi curves across the screen, mouth open, a tiny door to nowhere. Moss follows, curling around the line as if to close it.

"No," I whisper. "Not ready."

The moss freezes, sulking grey.

The chess window blinks. BleuFantôme has moved. His knight stumbles diagonally, hopeless. Maxime never plays hopelessly.

If someone pretends not to hear you, it's almost like silence, but silence is honest, and pretending isn't.

I hum one note in my throat, steadily. Then type:

```
KnightLight: You're distracted.
```

The pause is long. A kettle hisses somewhere in his villa and clicks off. When his reply comes, it's short:

```
BleuFantôme: A guest. He won't sit still.
```

I don't ask who. I already know. Some shapes ask to be chosen. Even knights who move diagonally when they shouldn't.

I slide my bishop across the board, bold, and wait. Quiet is a tool.

Another chime. His queen drifts forward, careless. He's not

paying attention. I grin and kick off my trainers under the desk. My toes spread on the floor. Shoes are apologies to the body.

Socks slip inside shoes because shoes want you to forget your feet. Adults pretend not to notice, but when I say it out loud, they stare at the wall instead.

I type it into the chat.

```
KnightLight: Shoes are apologies to the body.
BleuFantôme: You're impossible.
KnightLight: And you're losing.
```

Three dots flicker, vanish, and return. Maxime never hesitates.

A pawn moves forward, meaninglessly. Whoever paces in his villa is rattling him enough to make him bleed pawns. But I won't tell him I know it's Zander. That's mine.

I remember Zander once showing me how to double-knot laces so they never came undone. His hands moved slowly, patiently. He didn't laugh when I said the loops looked like rabbit ears. Most people laugh when I say things like that. He didn't. He just said, "Exactly. Rabbit ears."

I miss that. I miss him. But I would never confess it.

I like when Moss is angry, fizzing and loud. It means somebody's listening, even if it's only me pretending.

Moss suggests a correction, a neat line it thinks I should draw instead. I press the button that refuses it. "Not your choice."

The koi circle endlessly. I lean back, stretch until my spine pops, then drop forward again, cheek against the tiles. One, two, three, always three.

Some messages get lodged right behind your teeth, waiting for the exact right moment to slip out, and most grown-ups never notice them leaving.

My thumb hovers over a new window, and then I message Zander.

She misses you. Pretends not to, but I can tell x.

I don't write, Mummy. I don't need to.

I see her jacket draped over a chair. Her hair unpinned, perfume thick in her beautiful hair. Her eyes fixed far away, listening to something I can't. She doesn't say his name, but her silences do.

I remember once she was humming in the kitchen. Then she halted, as if caught. She stood there for minutes. That's when I knew.

I asked Uncle Max why grown-ups always sigh at closed doors. He just said, "You ask the oddest things," but odd things stay the longest.

The message leaves almost nothing plain. But enough.

I set the stylus down, both palms flat against the floor. Heat crawls up into me, steadily. Moss brightens emerald, approving now.

Far away in Lisbon, a phone will buzz. He'll see it. He'll know.

Quiet is a tool. Tonight I've used it.

The Saeculum saves another sketch, another pause. It only listens when I draw. Without me, Moss would be nonsense, static. Everyone thinks they can control it. They don't see I'm the lock.

And the key.

29

Saskia

I t had rained in the night. London peeled itself open one layer at a time, warehouse roofs sweating, puddles holding the first pale light like coins no one had pocketed yet. Even the streetlamps along Silvertown Quays looked guilty, flickering as if they knew where they'd been. Luc's penthouse rose above the old Millennium Mills, two storeys of glass and limestone and a view that pretended the river answered to him. Through the doors I saw him on the terrace, barefoot, a cigar burning, pacing the lip as if the black water below were a stage he'd commissioned. Heat lamps threw amber across his shoulders. The Thames fractured into rings where the rain still found it.

Not long ago, these docks were industrial relics. Now, Luc's Millennium Beaux Noirs crowned ten storeys of executive luxury born from the bones of flour and concrete. The shopping complex wrapped Silvertown Quays in flagship boutiques, whisky bars, and midnight noise, making this corner of London his signature: a prestige complex reborn where the mills once stood forgotten.

Across the dock, the Cradle's neon rim burnt into mist, the home of Luc's Premier League football club. They called it CS Silvertown 86, a dynasty conjured from the ashes of a dead-end factory site. Before the billionaires, a non-league crew called Silvertown Works FC played here, men from the flour mills and chemical plants, their dreams drowned by smog and river fog. Then came the rebrand, the money, and the experiments; 'legacy fans don't scale,' Luc once said.

Now, the Royals patrol the pitch in silver, bone white, and a shiver of navy. Their motto glared in steel above the gates:

Ex Ruina Gloria: From Ruin, Glory.

Every badge shimmered with a cog entwined in a sheaf of grain, the jagged silhouette of the mills rising like ancient teeth across the crest. Centred boldly on the chest, the club's kit bore the mark of Zander's crown jewel, a gold Vérité, its presence subtle yet commanding, ensuring every stitch spoke of refined craftsmanship and whispered exclusivity.

The stadium, 'the Cradle', hunched on the riverbank, forty-two thousand seats clamped tight in brutalist, vertical muscle. Its oval shell curved in glass and smoked steel, flooding blue at sundown, looming with the threat and promise of the new.

Inside, the pitch shimmered under engineered floodlights, roars folding on themselves, never escaping, manufactured glory, looped and inescapable.

His yacht rocked in the inlet, that precise gold waterline catching stadium flares like a signature.

Mara and I were on the terrace too, both of us barefoot, following the narrow run of koi that threaded the stone. The coils under the tiles lifted heat into our feet. Her breath fogged the glass when she leant in close to watch them. She counted under it, soundless, but I knew the rhythm.

He'd left us when the solar lamps flickered awake. He was in his office now in the belly of the penthouse. The cube. No windows. No distractions.

I tapped the glass door with my knuckle and lifted my mouth so he could see the words.

Whatever you're plotting, wave to your daughter. We're leaving.

He opened the door enough to lean through the sliver.

"Plotting? You would know!" Calm. Measured. A chastened schoolmaster in shirtsleeves.

He bent to kiss Mara, not me. "Good timing. I have to fly. Paris."

I nodded as if it were nothing and turned away. We took the lift, the mirrored box spitting our faces back at us from soft angles.

A message from Clara:

By the Quays. Ten mins?

Odd. The wording was clipped, almost neat. Not her usual voice. I typed back:

Here.

Outside, the new plaza wore its rain like gloss. Low jets pushed fountains through light so silver it felt cold to touch. My phone vibrated in my pocket.

We walked the water's edge where the rail hummed against the wind. The yacht sat like an answer that refused to be questioned. Obsidian hull. Gold line. Someone had polished it in the dark; you could see yourself graded in it, from no one to someone and back again.

Clara arrived as a silhouette first, hood up against the spit, then startled into light when she stepped under the terrace lamps. She laughed, quick and apologetically, with a hand at her throat.

"I thought you messaged me," she said. "Said to meet. You wanted to talk."

"I didn't..." I started and stopped. My phone pulsed again, another "See you there" sitting in our thread above hers, with my name on it, neat and decisive as if I'd finally learnt to be both.

Mara had already slipped towards the fountains, caught by the way the LEDs climbed water like rungs.

"Aunt Lala!" she called, because titles are choices, not facts. "Come and see Daddy's yacht."

Clara bent to her and played along. "Show me," she said, and Mara put her palms to the rail and pressed her face between the bars to make the water bigger.

We stood together, the three of us, smelling rain and diesel and the faint sweet aftertaste of cigar. There was a moment where the square could have been any square, where the families arriving late to dinner behind us could have blurred the night into something ordinary. Then the rotors chopped the air. Everyone glanced up and forgot again. We didn't.

Luc's helicopter rose from the pad and climbed steadily, nosed towards the river like a creature that knows its route in its bones.

It banked left, slow and deliberate, drawing a calm scythe across the sky. West. Not east towards Paris. I waited for it to bank back but instead watched it cross over the city and disappear over Paddington.

Mara's grip found my sleeve and held there. She didn't

speak, the way children don't when they realise a game has rules.

Luc wasn't going to Paris, as he wanted me to believe. Someone else had placed us at the rail, in this light, at this minute; someone patient. Someone who writes messages in other people's hands and signs their names for them.

This wasn't a man's design. The hand behind it moved differently. Quiet. Precise. Female.

I put the phone to my ear and kept my voice careless. "Mademoiselle Céleste, I forgot to tell Luc something. Is he still there?"

"He's gone," she said over me, crisp as ice. "Paris. La Garde Noire."

"Ah." I gave her a smile she couldn't see. "His retreat. He might have mentioned it. Bonne nuit."

I watched Mara splash her fingers once in the low basin where the jets ran flat as glass. We watched our reflections shiver, then headed home to Chelsea to untangle the day.

* * *

In the morning, the clouds sat low as I searched Luc's calendar. It said Belgravia HQ Board all morning, so I drove over to his penthouse at the Isle of Dogs.

I stood in the doorway of the cube until the security sensor hissed and let me in. He kept the office colder than the rest of the penthouse, as if cold made thinking sharper. Checked the digital flight logs, then strolled outside to the helipad. No one at the window, no crew. No rotors ticking themselves cool. The Airbus sat like a dog told to stay. Up the steps. Latch. Cabin air: that odd clean that isn't clean at all. I reached under the port-side seat for the grey flight bag I wasn't supposed to know about and found it where it always was. Headset. Folded maps creased on the ridges. A slim black logbook with a gold edge, the leather softened where a thumb had worried it to kindness.

Ink doesn't bother to lie. It just waits.

I opened the ribbon and ran my finger down the last entries.

08/07 – 1957 – IOD → Talgarth, Powys (Wales) – 0.9 – G. Kirk

Wales. Not Paris. Not even close.

I sat with the book open across my knee until the warmth of my hands made the gold edge bloom, then I took a photo and sent the coordinates to my private investigator, 'Cole', through my secure channel as 'Napoleon'.

Pull full routing. Compare digital with analogue. Quietly.

I made coffee I didn't drink. Mara padded in, hair sleep-wild, and put her cheek against my side without speaking. She'd dreamt, I could tell by the way she blinked, slow and careful, as if the morning air might erase it.

"Can we feed the koi later?" she asked.

"We can," I said. "Shoes."

She looked at me the way children do when they know you're pretending you heard them. She went to find them anyway.

The reply arrived mid-afternoon.

Airbus ACH145 – "Nocturne"

Registered departure: Isle of Dogs, London
Logged destination: Paris
Actual coordinates: 52.0165° N, 3.1980° W, Talgarth,
Powys, Wales
Structure on site: Old Georgian. Windows blocked.
Rusted sign at turnoff: NEW PROVIDENCE MEDICAL
ESTATE
Private access road. Staff observed in medical whites.
No public entry points.
Average visit time: 73 minutes.
Pattern: Monthly.

I put the phone face down and let the weight press on the desk. The penthouse was quiet enough to hear the lift cables breathe. I could taste last night's cigar still in the air, stale sugar and ash pretending to be a memory.

New Providence.

Nothing clean ever named itself after salvation.

At home, I settled Mara.

On the desk, the photo Julien once gave me sat folded, edges softened with time. I hadn't meant to keep it, but I hadn't thrown it away either. The ink was wild. Unguarded. A sketch from a version of myself that hadn't yet learnt how to self-censor. Before Luc, before legacy.

Before Zander.

I turned the paper. His handwriting is still faint on the back:

You're going to change everything.

I'd forgotten he had written that.

My fingers lingered at the fold, smoothing it flat, then pressing it back again. A habit. A hesitation. Not quite a decision.

Once, years ago, I'd found Julien in this same room with Mara perched on his knee. He was fixing the wheel on her toy horse, humming under his breath whilst she told him the colours she wanted painted on its saddle. When she darted away, he finished the job anyway, meticulous as always. He never claimed credit. He never needed to.

Outside the room now, the corridor lay empty. I thought I'd heard footsteps retreating earlier, soft ones. Julien's gait had always been quieter than you'd expect, like he didn't want to take up space. Like he'd been taught not to.

My throat tightened.

I told myself I had chosen correctly. That he made sense. That precision was safer than sincerity.

But even after I'd cut him cleanly, a piece of Julien still lived in the sketch I kept folded and in the way I'd never quite let myself read his words aloud.

The living room held a hush, low lamps and the faint thud of Mara's bedtime playlist bleeding through the wall.

Clara arrived and had made herself at home, heels kicked under the coffee table, jacket draped across the sofa arm, and wine glass already half-drained. She watched me pour mine.

"You're quiet," she said.

"I'm always quiet."

"Not like this." She took a sip, eyes sharp. "What did he do?"

I didn't answer.

She smirked. "See, that's how I know he did something."

I sank into the armchair opposite, legs folded tight. Mara's toy horse was wedged between the cushions again. I didn't move it.

"Mara and I watched his helicopter," I said finally. "He told me Paris. The logbook says Wales."

Clara didn't blink. "Well. That's not Paris."

"No."

"Did you ask him?"

"He lied the first time. Why would the second be different?"

She didn't say I was overreacting. Didn't press for details. Just nodded, as if she'd expected it all along.

"You always think it's you," she breathed. "That you misheard. That you're paranoid. Until one night you're standing in the rain, reading flight logs like they're tarot cards."

The breath I let out was sharper than I meant. "Jesus, Clara."

"Sorry. Projection."

The silence that followed wasn't awkward, just brittle.

Then she reached for the bottle and topped us both up. "For what it's worth, I don't think he's cheating."

I closed my eyes.

We are not even together.

Down the hall, the playlist shifted to lullabies. I heard the creak of Mara's bed as she turned over. Clara followed my glance, then looked back at me.

"You've made something great here," she said. "Something real. He doesn't get to wreck it."

She stood and lifted her jacket. Her eyes were gentler now, but there was no pity in them.

"I've got a face mask in the fridge and a brief due by midnight. You okay if I leave you to spiral in peace?"

I smiled. Not quite a yes. Not a no either.

She bent and kissed my cheek the way sisters do.

"Text me if you decide to go full MI5. I'll drive the getaway car."

Then, she was gone.

30

Zander

Saskia was still in her meeting when Luc told Jérôme to collect Mara from her lesson. I overheard and took her instead. Mara sat beside me with her knees drawn up, chin on them, humming something shapeless but steady. The sound drifted through the car, soft as breath, filling the spaces where words might have been.

Lisbon had shaken something loose in me, but Mayfair and a calendar full of meetings had glued it back on crooked. I told myself I was fine. Claude, my apartment assistant, had already reordered my day, matched shirts to ties, and suggested a playlist with piano that sounded like thinking. I'd told Claude to shut up twice on the drive and then felt stupid for apologising to a machine.

At the house, Mara didn't bounce ahead like the messy child I'd learnt to avoid. She took my sleeve, soft as a bird catching fabric, and tugged.

"Do you want to see the Dead Space?"

I almost laughed.

"Dead Space?"

"You can call it something better," she said, barefoot already, trainers abandoned at the hall rug. "I call it that because nothing gets in. Nothing gets out."

"Lead the way."

Down two flights. The basement door was the old Luc signature: brushed steel, a palm plate that remembered. When I touched it, the lock clicked with the same little sound as the penthouse cube. The air inside had that filtered chill of rooms built for secrets, but the room itself wasn't a bunker anymore. Rugs softened the concrete. A bear slumped against a rack with its arms out like a bouncer on break. Paper drawers lined one wall in a mosaic of flat files, each labelled in Saskia's hand. Koi taped to the steel door, mouths like small O's, as if they were sipping the cold from the air.

"Barefoot," Mara said, pointing at my shoes as if I'd committed a crime.

I kicked them off. The floor was cool under my feet, then warmer the longer I stood.

She hummed again, that one low note. Across the far wall, a mirror clouded, then loosened as if something behind it took a breath. A faint green pulsed once, twice.

"Moss," she said, bright with pride.

The voice came from nowhere and everywhere at once. Soft. Calm. Uncertain of gender, certain of tone.

"Mara."

"Hi," she said. "He's with me."

"Parameters?"

She didn't look back for permission. "All."

I thought of every NDA I'd ever signed, the clauses about internal prototypes, vault copies, and disaster recovery. This basement used to be Luc's vault. I could hear Luc's voice in my head: 'Don't bring outsiders, don't show anything unfinished, don't let wonder cost you margin.' A lifetime of tidy rules.

Then the mirror peeled itself into images, and the rules fell away.

Lines first, thin as air. Spirals like chalk on black slate. They doubled, tripled, and tightened into lattices. Static sketches became movement, threads finding each other, deciding to belong. I stepped closer without knowing I had.

"These are yours?" I asked, though I'd seen the labels on the flat files when I came in.

MARA 3–5. MARA 6–8. MARA 9–11.

A life in drawers.

"They were," she said. "They still are. Moss doesn't boss them around. It listens. Then it shows me what it heard."

"Moss?"

"My genius AI."

"Since when?"

"Always." She shrugged like it was obvious. "Mummy kept them flat so they wouldn't wrinkle. Félix made piles and piles and told Moss where to look."

"Félix?"

She grinned. "He helped with the scanning bit. But mostly Moss likes when I'm here. It goes grey when I'm gone."

Félix.

The mirror pulsed again. A human figure appeared in outline, just wire and joints, treading across a grid that looked like a city seen from above. At each step, the soles beneath the figure's feet lit up, tiny galaxies of pressure, heat, and something else that didn't look like data at all. The grid tagged the path with faint words that faded as quickly as they arrived: childhood, careful, run, safe, not safe.

"PulseField Soles, I think we agreed on that name," Moss said in that quiet voice. "Emotional memory. Terrain intuition."

I watched the animated footstep on an empty square. As the figure crossed it, the pressure pattern altered, like the shoe remembered a fall there, braced for it, then eased when the second step landed. I couldn't help it; my foot shifted, testing the basement floor as if it might answer me.

"How does it know?" I asked.

Mara reached out and tapped a floating diagram I hadn't seen until she touched it. "Places keep secrets," she said, as if she were telling me a basic fact, like where the spoons live. "Shoes can listen if you teach them the right language. Safi did the swallowing of signals so they don't talk outside. Félix made the drop thing so people still get excited." She wrinkled her nose at the word 'drop', like it was ridiculous. "But mostly it's the memory map."

I'd stood next to Mara at a hundred events, felt her there and still missed her entirely; I'd labelled her and moved on. I'd been wrong.

The mirror shifted again. Luminous threads laced side to side, first slowly, then in a sudden bright rush that made the hair lift on my forearms.

"Project CHORUS," Moss said.

The letters blinked, then gentled to a steady line in the top corner. Below, silhouettes appeared side by side – five, twelve, or twenty bodies inside garments that looked ordinary until they began to breathe in unison. Heartlines found each other. Pulse met pulse and settled on the same word: steady. Then one silhouette faltered, its line frayed. The surrounding ones adjusted; their lines gave a little, took a little, until the frayed line found a rhythm again. The entire group moved together, not stiff, not forced, just aligned the way a flock turns without an order spoken.

"For when people forget how to be together," Mara said, almost shy. "Or when they're too sad to remember the steps."

I read the smaller text spilling gently along the edge: Families at vigils. Dancers between counts. Crowds that want to hold a line without breaking it. Teams in cities that scare them. Protest without panic. There was a version even I could see Volant would want: stadia that throbbed as one, the brand beating through the crowd like a drum.

There was a version Luc would force: security, compliance, and control, all fed through a pretty knit. I didn't care about those versions right now.

I looked at the girl who'd shown me a network that breathed with the same note she'd been humming since the car. I felt something old and sharp roll in my chest – desire, yes, the old ache for Saskia that Portugal hadn't scratched, but braided now with something larger.

Responsibility.

Not the corporate kind I could summarise for Claude and file under "Actions", but the sort that starts and ends with a person.

"You did this?" I asked.

"Moss did it," she answered quickly. "With me."

I laughed once, a raw sound pulled straight out of me. "I thought you were playing games on those tablets."

"I was," she said. "They were just the kind where grown-ups lose."

I deserved that. I let it sit in the air and didn't wave it away.

Moss dimmed a fraction, as if it knew the show was enough for now. The mirror gave back some of its sheen; the bear in the corner had sagged until its chin touched its chest. The room held its own hush, deeper than the cage itself.

Mara fidgeted, rubbing the ball of her foot along the rug's worn track. The humming stopped. She looked at me, not quite straight on at first, then lifted her gaze and held it.

"Do you think it's good?" she asked. "Or is it just scribbles that Moss is being polite about?"

I had to swallow before I trusted my voice. "It isn't good, Mara."

Her mouth tightened, a flash of muscle I knew from Saskia, her way of bracing against disappointment. Even barefoot, she already carried her mother's armour.

"It's not good," I said again. "It's everything."

The muscle eased. The light came back into her eyes so suddenly I almost had to look away, as if I'd stared too long at a lamp.

"Will you come back tomorrow?" She asked quickly, afraid her courage would break. "Sometimes it listens better when there are two people."

"I'll come back, as many times as you want."

Not for Luc's empire. Not for the tidy rules I'd memorised. For this, the girl, the work, the pulse I'd almost missed.

She beamed. "You're nicer when you don't have shoes on."

I stood there barefoot in the room Luc built for control and felt it slip out of my hands in the best way.

Upstairs, I hear the door open, a wash of rain following, that mineral smell a city leaves on you when it thinks you are not

203

looking. Heels cross the hall, quick, hopeful. Each strike is as familiar as my own pulse.

"Māmā!" Mara's cry darts ahead of her, reckless, uncontained. She is already running for the stairs, the sound of her bare feet battering the wood like something too alive to cage.

Saskia is there at the landing, rain strung through her hair, corners of her mouth lifting, the smile beginning in her eyes first, brighter than the lamps. She looks down and in a single sweep sees it all: the archive, the faint green bloom against glass, her daughter at the railing, and me, barefoot, inside the room.

The smile falters. A breath mislaid, and for a second, the control slips.

Of all places, of all people, it is me inside her archive.

Mara's voice ruptures the silence. She shakes the handrail as though her strength alone could deliver her mother to us.

"Come see, Māmā. I showed him everything. The patterns, how it glows – it's magic."

"Everything?"

I feel the word slice through me. Her face flickers in quick succession: pride, annoyance, a flash of laughter, then the slight drag of shame. A private equation that no one else is meant to solve. She glances down at me, light as the brush of a fingertip, and I catch it in my chest.

She should correct us. She should narrow the doorway and banish me with one measured word. I am already braced for it, shoes in my hand, rain at my back.

Instead, she moves. One step, then another. Slower now, each heel carefully weighted, as if softening her arrival. Mara squeals, runs upward, clinging to her arm, tugging, dragging her down into us.

Inside the room, her daughter presses her to sit, and miraculously, she does. No rebuke. She smooths Mara's hair without once breaking my gaze.

"You showed him everything, Mara?"

The words land silk-soft, but the meaning cuts.

Mara nods, her joy irrepressible. "Yes. He liked it. Didn't you?"

"It was thorough," I answer. "I doubt there's a secret left for me to steal."

Her mouth curves, the nearest thing to amusement. It vanishes before it warms her eyes.

"Secrets have to resist being shown," she says, low and precise. Her gaze sharpens. "But you already knew that."

Mara presses both palms to the glass, thrilled by the swell of green light. She thinks she is playing; she doesn't catch the knife sliding between us.

"Refusing my guide seemed discourteous. And discourtesy is far harder to forgive than trespass."

Her lips brush against something almost like pity. "You must be very good at forgiving yourself, then."

The room glows brighter at Mara's small gasp of delight.

"Show her, Zander!" Mara cries, triumphant, oblivious.

Her eyes remain on me as she speaks. My name is wrapped in her child's voice, but it is me she addresses, steady, unreadable. Pride edged with something darker.

"I should find Jasmine," I hear Mara say, and she rises to pad quietly up the corridor to search for the cat, the thread unspooling behind her, leaving me caught where I am, neither dismissed nor absolved, but somewhere hung between.

I carry the silence with me, knowing I will follow, whether now or later, into something alive, feral, and very difficult to undo.

31

Saskia

The house breathes wet air; the walls are swollen with silence. Rain gutters overflow outside, but in here, every surface is listening. Mara's feet skitter overhead, a restless rhythm falling into music behind her door, a melody carried through cracks like contraband.

I sit opposite him, the circle of lamplight between us an interrogation I have staged without intending to. My fingers rest on porcelain. Coffee, never wine, never whisky. Coffee demands truth. The cup burns at first, then slicks with sweat from my skin, proof of the fatigue I can no longer disguise.

Zander fills the chair too completely, shoulders braced, restraint wound tight through his posture. He has seen what was never meant for him. The cage, the sketches, Moss alive and murmuring in the dark.

"You should have told me," he says. The words deliver themselves like verdicts. Crisp, sharp.

I let my gaze linger on the steam rising between us, then on him.

"Told you what?" My voice stays delicate. "That my

daughter has redrawn the bones of an industry before she votes, before she drives? That this house hums with a creature Luc thought he could own? That I let him believe in his cage long enough to build my way out of it?" My mouth curves, refined and cruel. "No. You would not have understood."

He leans back, his jaw tight. "And now?"

I lower my eyes to the dark surface of the coffee, smoke unfurling like a ledger burning. "Now you see. The luxury of concealment is over."

The tremor in my hand betrays the cost, but I set the cup down neatly, refusing to smooth the edges.

"So you trust me?" His voice is quieter now. Dangerous because of it.

"Trust presumes choice. I had none." My words are soft, even, almost prayerful. "I have you."

Mara's music bleeds through the ceiling. Notes bright and untamed, an inheritance she cannot name yet.

"Luc signed, then?" His tone dips, deliberate.

"All signed, stamped, and sealed." My voice thins, though inside it coils with satisfaction, almost hunger. "Chelsea is mine. Antibes and Amberley, should I wish to step into them. Funds secured dispassionately, for Mara, for me." I let the pause stretch, the silence weighted. "He believes he trimmed me out of the story. He believes he bought my irrelevance with a townhouse in London. That belief will bankrupt him."

My spine straightens, energy flickering. "I sat across that table and signed for him the illusion of victory. What I took was freedom. For her. For me. For everything still to be built."

His eyes hold mine, recognition dawning, with no pity in them.

"And what do you do with that freedom, Saskia?"

Exhilaration pulses under my ribs. For a moment I imagine the table splintering beneath its weight. Still, my voice remains level. "I turn exile into empire. The woman he dismissed will build an inheritance he cannot erase. Mara's sketches already know more than his lawyers ever could. Moss will learn not only to record but also to remember. And I will spend the empire he left behind dismantling his illusions."

"Étienne. Camille?" he says, searching for edges.

I do not answer; simply let him hold on to French phantoms. Smiling like a woman who has already moved three pieces ahead.

I lean forward, into the lamplight, so the exhaustion edges into my face, into the shadow of eyes that have not slept enough but still gleam sharply. "Do you recall what I showed you here once?"

"I do."

"You touched it. You knew I have secrets." A pause. A softer inflection. "This one is not mine. It belongs to her. Moss, the cage, those patterns, her legacy. If I lose, she loses. That is the truth Luc can never be permitted to imagine."

My hand comes to rest against the table's surface, visible, with a slight tremor, dangerous in its honesty. Too close, too bare. I refrain from moving it back.

His hand covers mine. Heat over cold. Deliberate. Anchoring.

"You will not fall."

I allow the words to rest within me. Not his promise but my proof: that leverage has become security, that survival is no longer theoretical. My throat tightens, the betrayal of something I otherwise would not show.

"Do not promise me comfort," I whisper. "Promise me a

tomorrow."

"Tomorrow," he says, and for one rare, unguarded moment, I taste it as victory. Not given, not lent. Taken.

The music upstairs shifts, lighter now, careless; Mara always finds new rhythms whilst I still cling to old ghosts.

I rise. He does too instinctively, as if wired to my movements. For once, I let my body choose first. The faintest lean, not a concession exactly, more the kind of offering that can be withdrawn at any time. He understands. His arms fold around me, steady, deliberate, wordless. I allow it. Not as a lover. As ballast, stone against water. Weight given, weight carried.

"You are nicer without shoes," I murmur, my voice sinking into the fabric of his shoulder.

I feel his laughter, quiet and low, shaking through him into me. I hold it only for a breath. Tonight's allowance. Nothing past dawn.

When he pulls back, his gaze is too direct. Dark pools I have hidden behind for too long, holding mine without fear. We hover there, duration stretching, a breath that feels like years pressed together.

And then my body betrays me. The spasm in my chest, sharp as glass, the warmth spilling down my face before I have commanded it otherwise. I shatter in that moment. Fury, fear, long-buried grief – all of it leaking in thin, ungovernable rivers. My voice, raw and fractured, cracks the silence.

"I have not cried like this in years. Not in front of anyone."

The room inhales, then holds fast, as though it too listens. I am too small suddenly, stripped bare of steel. And yet, lighter, almost. Unburdened in the violence.

His hands hover first, cautiously, then come to rest against my temples. Not possession. Not demand. Present. A gesture so careful it risks undoing me further.

"You are not alone anymore," he says. Gentle, resolute. "Not now. Never."

Mascara damp against my skin, my reflection ruined. To him, I must look unravelled, desperate. Perhaps I am. But even here in my unmasking, I feel the old blade sharpening underneath.

The weight eases. My armour, fractured, lies in pieces at my feet, and still I lean further into him, drawing something raw and almost fragile from the possibility of tomorrow.

Tears fall freely now, and even they carry strategy in their flood. Luc thought I was erased. Étienne believes himself victorious. Let them. Let them choke on their arrogance when they discover their silence was never mine.

Later, when the door shuts behind him with the softest click, the echo is louder than I anticipate. I remain pressed to the doorframe, hollow; the walls crowding back in with the weight of everything unspoken. Slowly, I let myself slide down into the waiting dark, knees drawn tight, the tears strangely new, jagged and relentless.

Then, above me, Mara's music surfaces again. A man's voice braided into it, gentler than hers, thoughtful, with an accent I cannot place. Words drop through the ceiling like prophecy.

Home is where I want to be, but I guess I'm already there.

The line lingers under my skin, bittersweet, dangerous. Home may be here, yes. But control, certainty, and safety remain elsewhere, ungraspable shadows. This fragile trust, this quiet unravel, they are both a wound and a weapon, a reckoning carried in silence.

My fingers clutch the cold floor, the chill burning through me. The music swells, an aching hymn to a future I have not yet dared name.

Do I break here, or do I rise again?

The answer, as with all things with me, remains unfinished, waiting in the spaces between breath and silence.

32

Isobel (fragment)

The windows along West Broadway were bare of curtains, as though daring the city to look in. The street threw itself back – neon, wet asphalt, a lone cyclist pedalling the wrong way, entitlement as a civic right.

The apartment was hastily vacated. Drawers ajar, a glass abandoned. She was gone. Avery had made sure of that.

The laptop too. Not burglary, but extraction. Every sketch, every draft of AetherFlex lifted without a drop spilt. Men think theft must be violent; women know it is often tidy.

Alexandre remains close to his mother-in-law. Some look away; others do not. Saskia extracts herself from Lucien; one hopes not to slip into another trap whilst congratulating herself on escape. Cleverer than that. Settlement filings disguised as grocery lists, legal calls buried in domestic static. She does not fumble with blinds or passwords; she slips the knife where no one notices until the ink dries. Men confuse silence with surrender. They never ask what women save it for.

Céleste saw the file before it opened. She always does. This

213

time, she shared it with me. She has hidden plenty, but perhaps now she learns restraint. Or courage.

Across the Atlantic, another tableau: Kevin Price in a townhouse, shirt half-done, grin too wide. A ring of youthful faces caught in the camera flare, unguarded poses. The photographs spread quickly, not as indulgence, but as currency.

Lucien's sons mistake secrecy for locks. Their women know better. Yet I ask: how do they endure this theatre of appetites? Perhaps the answer lies within walls I cannot breach. Silence dressed as brick. If they conspire, they do it without me.

Noémie tried her usual trick. Most men fold at the first smile. This time, Tseng held. I was almost impressed. She lies in a bed still warm with another's scent, telling herself she always knew. Lies are kinder companions than the truth.

Meanwhile, the men polish their appetites as if medals: Julien ferrying noughts and ones across borders he cannot place on a map; Toby gambling losses in Versailles; Lucien's helicopter clocked in Wales again, with "retreat" on the log. Euphemism. Most retreats involve prayer, not doctors in white coats.

And young Alexandre, still rehearsing rebellion in Saskia's silence, mistaking restraint for loyalty. Men so often confuse being tolerated with being loved.

They believe secrecy is silence. It is not. It is only noise turned sideways.

At my age, patience weighs heavier than anger. And I am still listening.

From upstairs, a fragile voice:

Home is where I want to be. But I guess I'm already there.

Mara could not know what she was singing. Hope often arrives in the wrong voice.

Let us see what they do with it.

33

Saskia

Friday, 11 August, 8 p.m. Silvertown vs Manchester City.

The Cradle is swollen with noise, with breath, and with bodies pressed into steel ribs. Floodlights bleach the pitch until it confesses, every blade of grass caught in unforgiving truth. Shadows sheer against white lines, too stark, too precise, as though circulation has been cut from the night itself.

On match nights, it was as if the whole city leaned in to watch these cold, young kings. French defenders, English starlets, and a Japanese striker who streamed every warm-up like a video game, each one handpicked, remade for the future Luc demanded. Below them, the old dockyards slept, and the ghosts of vanished factories listened to the thunder in the rafters.

The air tastes metallic, charged. Chants collide and return

sharper, like glass striking glass, each one cutting a little cleaner than the last. The place is engineered to keep you captive, to fold the noise around your lungs until the rhythm of forty thousand strangers belongs to you.

From the Thames, it gleams like a shell fractured open, steel and glass glowing icy blue. From here inside, it is a furnace sealed against escape. The vibration beneath my heels carries upward, a live current in the bones. It feels indecent, almost human.

The ultras across the south stand strip away their shirts, silver paint slick over their torsos, Latin painted on skin as if borrowed language could stitch meaning into their throats.

Ex ruina, gloria: *From ruin, glory.*

From nothing, this.

Yet what I want is different. A woman's side, not a gesture, not a headline. Substance. Steel under the silver. Proof that ruin can be made into something that belongs to us. A line not easily moved.

Above it was our box. Two storeys of tempered glass overlooking the pitch, more theatre than view. It was built so power could see itself reflected. Silk, crystal, the occasional flash of a diamond cuff. Applause, where it matters, is silent.

Then movement. A ripple across the pitch, forty thousand eyes shifting in unison. The shadow arrives before the sound. A black helicopter cuts low above the east stand, a glint of polished gold where the blades connect. It hovers with studied precision, a predator circling its cage, before curving south and folding neatly towards the Montclairs' flagship London property, the Millennium Beaux Noirs and Silvertown Quay complex.

Luc.

My tongue touches the back of my teeth, a small betrayal. His entrances are always exacted at scale, calculated for breadth, not intimacy. Always last, always above, never inside. Even here, with all this noise, the attention tilts towards him.

The stadium adjusts, bending in his direction. And I, contained in this glass penthouse, watch the sky close over where he vanished.

Inside the box, the heat feels different, sealed in glass and velvet. Polished silence over a roar that never softens. Zander leans against the window, collar slipped loose as if his body needed some proof of rebellion. Drink untouched. He doesn't move when the helicopter cuts across the skyline, doesn't grant them the spectacle they crave. A refusal disguised as composure.

His laugh, brittle and far too sharp, slices the air behind us, across the hum of investors murmuring over margins and lines. It sounds performative, even to his own ears.

I come closer. Not near enough to touch, only near enough to feel the static his body generates. His jaw is set, locked forward, but I feel his glance through the glass, a sideways weight I know too well. He plays the heir who doesn't care, but it leaks, always. Too much intention in the stillness.

Across the divide, Camille. Perfect stillness, as if seated for a portrait. One leg hooked over the other, a red lacquered smile held like a weapon she hasn't yet drawn. Hair folded back in a manner that almost dares you to dishevel it, although no one ever would. She waves once, a gesture perfunctory enough to humiliate. She doesn't smile. Camille smiles only in victory, and victory tonight has already been accounted for.

Beside her, the Qatari they whisper is Faucon. His gaze

doesn't leave the helicopter, as though Luc himself mattered less than the machine that delivered him.

Below, Gauche. She arrives like chaos made into choreography, cream-gold fabric cut to sharpen at the thigh, sandals binding her like she'd walked directly out of a fresher empire. The bag, yellow and absolute, dares the cameras not to pay attention. The stadium folds towards her because folding is easier than resisting.

When she lifts the phone, the grip flashes like a jewelled shiv. She doesn't hide what it is meant to be.

The shriek lands first, a sound almost rehearsed. Champagne flares over a Meta suit, gold in the artificial light. Gasps, shutters, the screen lingers indecently. Gauche smiles. No apology. He grins foolishly, thinking he has been granted some kind of charm. By the time the echo dulls, she is gone.

Camille doesn't flinch. She keeps her still gaze levelled outward and then angled, angled at me. Her lips move softly against the pane of glass; no sound, only meaning.

We're not here for the football.

The sentence rips every extraneous layer away. Crowd sound, summer heat, and the floodlit stretch of grass are all cut from view. The only colour left is the one she directs me to see.

Seka Doué.

Older brother to Aïcha and Safi.

Twenty years old, fresh off winning Ligue 1's Young Player of the Year, he is the reason Luc dropped €50 million to bring him in.

The match itself is a lull until it isn't. Twenty minutes of nothing, frustration mounting, the crowd restless and unkind.

Then Seka cuts the line. Slides wide, shaves past the box, and halts so suddenly he creates absence where weight should be. The defender slips and looks clumsy. With a single roll of his instep, the ball rests easily in the inside corner of the net.

Noise detonates in a form I've never quite acclimatised to. Forty-two thousand throats collapsing at once.

Seka runs to the corner flag. The captain kneels, polishing that right boot as the cameras race to keep up. I lean forward before I can stop myself.

Left: Faucon Volt+, ordinary issue. Right: Volant Aether-Flex, Félix's creation, or so he thought. Not an accident, not an innovation.

Contraband.

The message is immediate, sharpened to a razor:

I exist. I control. Watch who wears me now.

Luc will combust.

I turn my head and find Zander in reflection. His eyes flare at the boot. The rage spirals exquisitely, pressed hard against the glass, vibrating enough that it feels like the stadium itself has taken on his fury.

Half-time.

The whistle splits the air, thin and metallic. The players drift towards the tunnel, jerseys plastered to their backs, steam rising from their bodies.

Seka lingers, soaking in applause as if it were stitched for him alone. Noise clings even as he vanishes.

The door opens without ceremony, a slice of cooler air against my skin. The space folds around him.

Luc.

His face flushed, too eager, too raw. Annina's nails click against glass, sharp staccato, as she scrolls.

"Who wrote this?" His voice carries urgency but not authority.

"The twins, apparently."

The plan glows on Annina's tablet, faultless as a theorem. Côte d'Ivoire's palette woven into French minimalism, so seamless it looks predestined.

"Seka's sister's," Mademoiselle Céleste murmurs. Her softness makes the words more dangerous.

Luc's chest tightens, a rise that might be rage, might be fear. Impossible to decide which, though both smell equally of weakness.

Seka balanced two brands as though they were weights on a scale, and someone inside had tipped him the contracts. Not accident, betrayal.

"Camille?" I ask.

Horace is already crouched on the rug, his body angles folding over the tablet. His voice clipped, efficient. "Clause. Expansion two months ago. Binding. Zurich signature."

"Who?" Luc snaps.

The screen turns. Gauche. Camille. Julien.

The name leaves me before I wish it. "Julien!"

Luc does not flinch. I watch his stillness, the way it performs innocence. He has always admired Camille, always wanted her at Volant, her honeyed poison close enough to sip.

"Not his fault," he says. Smooth, but brittle as ice over water.

Horace tilts the tablet again. A new photograph blooms across the glass. Gauche, black silk and crocodile leather gleaming. Aïcha within reach, his hand placed like punctuation.

Not possession. Correction.

Camille's caption floats beneath:

"When brands pretend they are youth culture."

Already the words splinter, tribes forming in the dark. Think pieces unfurling like smoke. Someone names it "fashion tribalism 2.0".

The air grows thin. Fragile. Glass about to shatter. Beyond the partition, the audience hums, all sound blurred into static.

Luc lowers himself into the velvet seat, spine straight, profile angled like sculpture. He makes himself the fixed point, the axis, immovable. I want him to taste it, I want him to swallow what he brews in others.

His time will come.

The air sharpens, fragile as spun glass. The crowd beyond is muffled static, untranslatable. The next whistle cracks, and the second half begins. The room flexes; order is imposed, though nothing is resolved. Luc reclines, false calm restored.

Zander burns beside me, a body too close, his stare pressed against my jawline. A warning, an invitation. I give him the smile Luc taught me, perfect porcelain, painted over silence.

Luc paces. Zander burns beside me, incandescent, his stare a dare. I smile instead, the porcelain smile he taught me. Perfect, polished, without weight.

The game resumes, but it passes through me as if projected on glass. My mind has left the river and the roar.

It circles somewhere else.

Ty Cefn.

The name reaches me like static pulled through wires. An institution. Polite, antiseptic. Whitewashed surfaces, corridors humming with the same continuous pitch. Nothing too sharp, nothing to draw blood. Nothing you could accuse them of. Which is why I press anyway, always, to the names flanking the ledger, the sign-offs that disappear into the margin.

Not the what. The who.

I push it aside, the roar of the stadium dissolving into another silence.

How long have I been choosing without choosing? Holding the coin between my fingers, unwilling to let it fall. Tonight, I did. The answer was sharp and clean. Myself.

Luc would vanish tomorrow, already signalling it in the way he dropped Paris into conversation. The wooded hills to the west, the crucible he called La Garde Noire. Outwardly, a laboratory for wellness, performance, and resilience. Inwardly, everyone knew the truth was sharper. A place to undo yourself by design. Wind tunnels, hypoxia, cold vaults. He liked to return reassembled, the man who had stripped himself to nullity and endured. A creature forged from his own unmaking, proud of it.

I picture the helicopter again, choreography intact. No touches, no words, only the vibration of rotors filling what he refused to give. Vanishing into altitude and leaving absence heavier than his physical weight ever was.

But it lodges inside me, the word 'tomorrow'. It clings bitterly to the lining of my stomach. Too far.

His previous message still waits, glowing.

Talgarth, Ty Cefn.

Not rumour, documented, etched in black and white. A facility that dissolves itself into the Welsh hills. Every bill underwritten by Roussillon Holdings. I read the words, but the name hisses back at me, unwelcome.

Roussillon.

My palms remember the heat of Perpignan without permission, a memory seared into skin that cannot forget. I do not want it. I cannot scrub it.

I press palms to my thighs, feel heat return through fabric. Tomorrow sits like a stone in my body. If I wait, it will outlast me.

I step outside. The night air is no relief, only heavier, compressed above the Thames until it sticks. A strip of concrete platform, the smell of damp stone, the match hissing under my thumb. I light a cigarette I won't finish, holding on too long. The flare catches on the glass, where I meet my reflection and almost don't recognise it. More tired than I want to admit. Older than I present, younger than I feel I have earned.

The roar erupts again from inside, sudden and guttural, bodies convulsing to some spectacle I don't see. It spills against the glass, vibrating into my spine. My head is elsewhere, and the game knows it.

Then Zander slips into place beside me. He arrives the way his shadow does: silently, claiming space without asking. He leans against the wall, shoulder pressed into stone, gaze cast down as if something beneath the concrete holds him there.

He doesn't speak until the end of my drag.

"You shouldn't."

"I know."

He doesn't extinguish what I've claimed. He lets me smoke it down until my fingers sting with heat. That's his version of intimacy. Permit the ruin; witness it without flinching. No rescue. No recoil.

We stand close enough to feel it, never touching, a partition of smoke existing where we don't. The silence cut raw between us, sharper than anything he might have risked saying out loud.

I grind the ash into the concrete. He watches my hand, mouth parting almost, then stills. Looks away. That was everything.

Zander walks back in and I unlock the secure line. The app flicks open onto its stripped, clinical interface. No names, only code. Cole. Napoleon. No hello.

I type fast:

> *NEW TASK. TIME SENSITIVE. DOUBLE RATE. ROUS-SILLON HOLDINGS PAYMENTS. TY CEFN. DEEP DIVE. EVERYTHING.*

Paperwork leaves ghosts. That's what I've learnt. Follow the trail, and the dead will speak.

The name lands in me like heat.

Roussillon.

The screen blinks back at me. Waiting. Silent dare. Then three dots, slow and deliberate.

> *ACKNOWLEDGED. ETA 36 HOURS.*

I stare at it until the words dissolve.

Back inside my heels slip off. I draw my knees to me on the velvet seat, a silhouette inside the dark shell of the box, whilst forty thousand voices surge around me.

Tomorrow presses towards me in the dark, whether I am

ready or not.

34

Clara

The room is wrong for honesty. Concrete and linen pretending at warmth, floor-to-ceiling glass that erases the horizon. Not built for comfort; built for transfer of power, of silence, of leverage. I clock it before I sit. Temperature, controlled. Angles, deliberate. Scandinavian, chosen on purpose.

Camille Sarron waits with a curated stillness. Poised, immaculate. Forty-two, though you would never know. She studies me the way surgeons study an X-ray, already diagnosing, already cutting.

I smile politely and accept the tea. Matte ceramic, something green. I will not drink it.

"Merci for coming, Miss Sundström, I believe you still go by?" she says in that lilting softness. "I know it has all been... delicate."

The pause, perfectly measured.

I keep my smile tight.

"Not a problem. Clara, by the way. I wanted to hear what you had to say; Mademoiselle Céleste spoke well of your successes."

"Céleste?"

I enjoy the pinprick of surprise in her eyes. She recovers, of course. She always does.

The tea is poured, and the steam curls. Medicinal, not friendly.

Her gaze was still, but not in the way Saskia's was, or Céleste's. Different calibrations, same silence. I was already deciding which silence to belong to.

"We were... impressed," she continued. "Truly. To take him to court, to take under:CORE to court... that is not something many survive."

"Survived" isn't a word I use.

"Oh?"

"Adapted."

I see it register. Survival suggests passivity. I am not passive. Survival isn't innocence. It is knowing when to look guilty and keep breathing.

Ah, that is the myth they want told. Not the facts. Bravery sells better than rage.

"It wasn't about surviving."

Her lips shape the faintest half smile. "Bien sûr. And yet... surviving is useful, non?"

Useful, yes. So is duct tape. But that is not the point. The silence was the fight, the whispers. The men who congratulated me in private and vanished in public, the women who waited to see who would still be standing.

I was. I am. That is the lesson.

Camille tilts her head, birdlike. "And am I right in thinking you and Hal are returning? To the UK or Western Europe?"

I nod. Western Europe, now I see. She is still weighing

whether I am a threat or a relic.

She slides her line in, gently, almost musically. "There may be... something for you, if you are interested."

I raise an eyebrow, cup still untouched. "Ah. Laurette, then. Makes sense. Fast-track appointment."

No confirmation. No denial. Just the faintest pause, then the corner of her mouth curves.

Which means it is not Laurette. Maybe Faucon, maybe she splits them as businesses. If it were Laurette, I would already know.

I file the thought away, clean.

"If it is, well, of course you do not have to say," I add, voice even. "Just know it is entering a far more structured phase. R&D stabilised. Experimental labs. Less volatility. Less noise."

Camille listens without a flicker. Only the smallest elongation on her reply. "Structure... is important. But too much structure, and instinct suffocates. You understand, no?"

I take a sip, even though the tea has gone bitter. "The era of instinct is ending," I say. "The era of infrastructure has to begin."

Her voice comes soft, almost amused. "Has it ended? Or has it only... gone underground?"

I hold her gaze. Silence can be the sharpest answer.

She lets it stretch, then breaks it herself. "Rien n'est officiel, not yet. But we wished you to hear it first."

I set the cup precisely onto the saucer. "Whatever it is, you will let me know. Of course."

Her eyes sharpen. "When the time is right."

That is the tell. Not if but when.

Something is already moving.

I stand. My chair gives a soft scrape against polished concrete. The tea cools without me. "One note," I say. "I am nearly fifty. I do not need anyone's adjectives. Brave, resilient survivor. Save them for your press release. If you want me, you want me to make the mess stop. I am not sentimental. I am efficient."

The corner of her mouth lifts again. "I appreciate efficiency."

"Good." I reach for my coat. "Then you know what to do next."

Outside, the corridor smells of eucalyptus and new carpeting, an expensive attempt at neutrality. The elevator mirrors add three more versions of me that I do not need. I ignore all of us.

In the car, I text Hal.

On my way.

He replies with a knife and fork emoji, then a heart; he thinks he is charming. He is.

The hotel suite feels too warm when I step inside. Neutral carpet, heavy curtains – the kind of décor that erases geography. Safe. Forgettable.

Hal's jacket sits folded over the chair, navy wool, faint chalk stripe. He is at the minibar, opening a bottle of wine with his usual unhurried care. The sound of the cork leaving the neck is a neat little pop, a promise. His voice reaches me before I take off my coat.

"So," he says. "Did Madame Sarron smile at you, or is that too much to hope for?"

I unbutton my coat and fold it over the other chair, adjust

the sleeves, and smooth the collar. "She does not smile. She calibrates."

He grins at that, quick and warm. He pours one glass and leaves it on the table for me. "So what did she calibrate you into?"

I do not answer right away. I step out of my heels and place them side by side, always neat, always deliberate. Habit is a structure. Finally I say, "Not Laurette."

His eyebrow lifts. "No? Then what?"

"Faucon, I guess," I say. "She felt Paris."

"Ah, one of those who never names the thing," he says. "Let you name it for her."

His voice stays calm, unbothered, like the river under the ice, but I know he is listening closely. I cross to the window. London cuts itself into the night: cranes, glass, and a low hum of dirty light. I want silence, yet Hal follows and stops just behind my shoulder, close enough that I feel him through the suit.

"Exactly," I say. "She might think she is tapping me up, so she keeps it deniable. If someone complains, she never says a word."

He tilts his head, hands in his trouser pockets, tie loosened half an inch. "Then I suppose you will brush up on your French, maybe."

The line lifts the corner of my mouth before I let it drop again. "It would suit us, would it not?" I say. "Paris, I mean."

"We said in the middle," he says, "America and Sweden. A fresh start in a more relaxed city."

I take the glass and sip at last. Dry, clean. Better than the tea. The stem is cold against my fingers, a good warning. Do not spill. Do not shake.

"She is building something and wants me on board," I say. "She wants me to be the surrounding structure. The one who looks steady whilst the ground shifts."

Hal nods once, slowly. "And are you going to give her that?"

"I will give her what serves us," I say. "For as long as it serves us."

He takes the cork to the bin and brushes my hand on the way past. Not an accident. He does that when he wants to see if I am made of glass or stone today; he knows I dislike being handled. He also knows I like being read.

"That is why I married you," he says.

I set my glass down carefully. "You married me because I do not flinch."

"That, too."

We stand side by side at the window. The glass cools my forearm. His sleeve grazes mine. The city pretends to be permanent, a graph trending up, but we both know its lines go soft when you touch them.

"What did she call me?" I ask, eyes on the cranes.

"Brave, I assume," he says. "Survivor. Exceptional. A credit to womankind."

"Not in so many words." I look at his reflection rather than his face. "Bravery is what they write when they want you to shut up and look grateful."

"I know." He taps the window with his knuckle, a quiet metronome. "She still wants you."

"Everyone wants me," I say, deadpan, then let the silence carry the joke. He smiles because he likes it when I pretend to be impossible. He likes it better when I am not pretending.

"So," he says, tone light, "conditions."

I turn from the window and lean against the sill. The glass

232

holds my shoulder like a hand. "No adjectives. No soft launch. I want the ledger, not the mood board. Full sight of the labs, the cash flow, the contracts that pretend to be secrets. I want to kill what needs killing and keep what works. If I walk in, we stop worshipping instinct and start publishing rules. If they hire me to do it right, I do it right."

He nods. "Structure is the skeleton."

"Instinct is the meat," I say. "Without both, you do not have a body; you have a corpse."

He considers that serious now. "And what do you call us?"

"We are not a body," I say. "We are the hands."

He looks down at my hand on the sill, at the two pale scars on the knuckles where I once punched a bathroom stall door rather than a man. He takes my fingers, just the tips, with a clinical touch, as if calibrating a grip.

"Paris suits your mouth," he says, and it is almost nothing, yet my skin listens.

"We will see," I say.

He pours a second glass. His shirt has come untucked on one side, the way it always does when he focuses. I watch his wrist, the vein that lifts when he steadies the bottle. We talk about cheap things when we cannot name the price, so I ask about the wine. He tells me about the vineyard, the slope, and the year that should have been better than it was. He says it underperformed yet still delivers. I say, relatable.

He laughs low. He steps closer, not quite touching. The air warms between us, the degree you feel, the degree you could deny. I tilt my chin so I am neither offering nor refusing. It is a balance I have perfected. He reads it correctly. He always does.

"You know," he says, eyes on my mouth, "you do not have

to say yes."

"I know."

"You do not have to prove anything."

"I know that too."

"What do you want, Clara?"

I do not answer for a moment because the question deserves the space. The carpet is soft and too thick. People buy this kind of carpet when they want to forget that feet are made for leaving.

"I want it done bloody right," I say. "No branding, no hush. No more men texting me sympathy whilst they vote against me in rooms I cannot enter. I want a door and a key that works from both sides."

He nods. "We can do that."

"We can, yes." I pick up my glass and set it down again. I count my breaths. "But it will be my key."

"Obviously," he says.

We move around each other, our private choreography that never quite loses its charge. He finds the playlist and chooses something without lyrics. I open the window and let the night climb in. It smells of rain and heating vents, metallic and clean, a city rinsed, never washed.

He comes back to me and stands too close again, in that careful way he uses when he wants me to decide which way gravity goes. His mouth opens as if to say something generous. He closes it. Good. I do not need to be comforted. I need to be sharp.

"Clara," he says.

"Hal."

I lift my hand and touch the knot of his tie; a simple modification. My fingers rest there a second longer than required. His breath answers. I let go.

Across the room, my phone lights up on the table. A message preview, just the first three words.

When the time—

I do not touch it; I do not need to. I already know the rest.

Hal watches my face instead of the screen. "Well," he says.

"Well." I let the smile show, quick and controlled. "Not a relic. Not yet."

"Never," he says.

I pick up my glass and take a slow sip. The wine has been open; it's less sharp now and has more depth. I feel the same in my body, an easing that is not surrender. I place the glass down and align the base with the shadow it makes, a tiny equation solved.

When I look up, he's still watching me, steady, intent, as if he's taking proof. A tension pulls between us, fine as a thread. I don't leave it to snap or fray; I lean across the space and find his mouth with mine.

It isn't tentative. The kiss lands sure, warm, and fuller than I imagined, a release of the held breath between us. His lips part, and I draw him deeper, tasting the softened wine on his tongue, the darker heat beneath. My pulse lifts, not in flight but in gravity, everything in me caught and pulled closer.

I stay with him, long and unhurried, until when I break away the air feels different, richer, claimed, no longer neutral.

I text Saskia:

> *Not interested in the France job. I am interested in what you've got cooking. Room for one more?*

Not a relic, not yet. Never a recruit either. I don't join their empires; I rewire them.

I let the smile return, smaller this time. Quieter, but sharper. It feels like a private weapon, angled only for me, though I know he sees it.

My body hums with a current I don't need to name. I rise, letting the silence gather around me, and head upstairs. Hal is waiting, and I already know the taste of what I'm walking towards.

35

Saskia

Amalfi Coast, August 2023. M/Y Sépulcre, moored off Sorrento.

The yacht drifts in the bay, obedient to no current but its own. Hull black, superstructure white, the lines are so clean they cut the water like polished stone. M/Y Sépulcre, Luc's floating cathedral, his playground, his prison of choice. Everything about her whispers excess, from the smoked-glass decks to the engineered silence of her engines. Nothing ever creaks. Nothing ever admits age.

Behind the cliffs of Sorrento rear up in terraces of lemon groves and cypress, villas scattered across the stone like shards of pearl. They look fragile, precarious. But this boat does not. The Sépulcre sits steady, deliberate, as if the coastline itself were backdrop, not context.

Luc has gone ashore. A silver tender spiralled him and Julien towards the harbour hours ago, its wake cut as neat as an incision across the water. Meetings, money, games, always another circle of acolytes. His absence is a performance in itself, a silence that leaves us curated in his frame, restless and half-naked in heat we can neither escape nor ignore.

Corky lies sprawled across a sofa, turquoise linen slung low, fabric still dark from the sea. His hair drips salt onto the cushions, his stomach is flat and indulgent, and he has strength without discipline – the sort of body that mistakes itself for permanence.

Isabelle Loubry, next to him. A bikini slim enough to dissolve into suggestion, wrapped in the thinnest veil of linen, more gesture than garment. Her skin catches the light effortlessly, a softness that bends the scene, her smile bright but exact, as though rehearsed to remind us she can disarm. She leans into a chair with casual grace, bare legs folded, radiating ease without ever slipping into carelessness. Pretty that travels as currency here.

Around her, the room sways with perfume, salt drying on damp shirts, and the muted hum of engines keeping us anchored to Luc even when he's away.

Toby slouches in deliberate parody, drawstring trousers creased from folding but never work, and a Yankees cap pulled low as if irony excused the vulgarity. That grin of his – easy, adolescent, and far too comfortable in this cathedral of steel and glass – says he knows he'll be kept no matter what.

"Still cosplaying Wall Street in that Yankee's cap?" Corky asks, voice low, edged in amusement that almost veils the contempt.

It makes me smile for the first time in a long time.

Toby only grins wider, unapologetic.

"It's ironic."

Luc collects men like Toby: sly, slippery, and more useful in their flaws than their virtues.

The saloon hums with Chanel and staged serenity. Annina sits star-like in cream silk, hastily softened to suit the heat, though not her nature. Even she swelters, though not visibly; sweat hovers at her throat like a jewel. Beside her, Mademoiselle Céleste dissolves more gracefully, linen giving way, silk dampening to translucence. Her fan beats soundless strategy.

I incline my head to them. Not deference, not warmth. A gesture of civility in corridors built for theatre.

And then, Zander.

Framed by smoked glass, the coast behind him glowing into late gold, he leans there as if the light itself stitched him into shape. White shirt rolled at the elbows, damp at the spine. Linen trousers hanging low at the hip, bare ankles at the hem. Stray hair curls at his temple, sweat glinting where his neck dips to collar. The imperfections undo the calculated posture, and in undoing, make him unbearable to look at.

"Mon cher," he says, barely above a murmur. "At last, I have you for myself."

I let my bag slip soundlessly onto the carpet.

"Only for a moment."

From the deck, a shout, splash, and laughter. Corky and Isa are over the rail, reckless, salt spray gusting back through the saloon doors. Droplets catch my wrist against the railing, cold enough to sting.

Zander leans close. Too close. The scent of citrus cologne layered into the salt air. The hush between us feels heavier than the noise outside.

"You should not be here," I say.

"Neither should you."

239

Silence holds. Tight, bright, dangerous.

Fingers brush against mine. Deliberate. A question suspended in salt air.

I do not pull away.

Julien arrives as if scripted for interruption, voice dry and precise.

"God, the pair of you, king and queen pretending the board isn't beneath you."

He doesn't stop walking, doesn't look back. Just drops the verdict and leaves it there, almost amused.

Zander's mouth edges towards a smile. "Ignore him."

I place my bag carefully against the seat. An action rehearsed, neutral, though the heat steals across my skin as if branded. His eyes never shift from my face. Steadiness is dangerous in how it tempts me, how it pretends what we're doing is possible.

Another shriek from outside. Splashes, whistles, and laughter too loud, drowning any word I might dare.

I lift my bag again, hand perfectly steady, pulse not. This yacht is Luc's domain, but still it rocks beneath me, less like a cradle, more like a cage.

Later, the saloon doors were left open. Black glass slid back until the Sépulcre no longer felt like a palace but a pier abandoned to the night. Darkness pressed in, velvet and salt, water slapping low against the hull. The gold trim of the waterline caught the lamplight with every roll, a pulse that flashed and vanished, flashed and vanished.

I stood at the rail. Silk lifted against my legs in the night breeze, hair loosened by the day's heat until it slipped forward, untidy. The air carried lemon and sea spice from the cliffs, sharp enough to cut the softer notes of oak drifting from the yacht.

Behind me, Zander crossed the deck soundlessly. No glass, no audience, only the low thrum of the generator weaving beneath each breath.

"He built this to be untouchable," he said. Not judgement. Fact. His voice sank into the accompanying hush. "Look at it. A tomb that floats."

I didn't turn. "Then why bring me here?"

A step closer. His shoulder brushed mine. The black water printed itself onto his eyes; every fractured light mirrored there.

"Because you don't look afraid," he said.

My breath caught, too audible in the quiet. I should have stepped back. I didn't.

His hand found my arm, slow, unhurried, fingertips grazing the soft inside of my wrist. Not possession. Not a demand. A claim made subtly. The contact jolted like current, small but absolute, setting my pulse against the hull's steady throb.

When he kissed me, the shock was not that he did but that I allowed it. His mouth was warm and salt-touched, tasting faintly of the wine none of us had really drunk. The first brush was tentative, a question. The second left no exit.

Heat rose, carried easily between linen and silk, his shirt damp to my dress at points where our bodies closed the distance. My hand reached of its own accord, curling into the crease of his shoulder, claiming anchor. His sound was inaudible, near-animal, and muffled against my mouth, and it tilted the ground beneath us.

The yacht rocked, and the kiss deepened. Unhurried at first, then hungrier, carrying the inevitability of something long framed but only now permitted. I leaned into him, unwilling to break it, unwilling to restrain myself.

When I drew back, it wasn't by choice but by necessity. Lips swollen, breath thin. The air between us wavered, hot with salt and wanting. His eyes held mine, steady, unflinching, a certainty I could not claim for myself.

The first kiss wasn't an accident; it wasn't even a theft. It had been waiting, carved wordless into Luc's floating casket of steel.

A secret in his sepulchre.

The kiss lingers in the air even after it breaks. My lips are raw, my breath is too fast, and his hand is still warm on the inside of my wrist. The night folds around us, velvet, salt-thick, the sound of the sea striking the hull too steady to be trusted.

Then, Luc's voice.

It comes sharp and sudden, just beyond the open saloon doors. A phone call. Familiar cadence in the dark.

"Are you alone?"

For a second, my body reacts as if he is asking me, not whoever answers on the other end. My throat betrays me with the shape of a word I don't let out. I almost answer. Almost. Still in his son's arms.

"Good. Did you do as I asked? Excellent. No witnesses?"

The word itches, scorches. Witnesses.

I glance at Zander. His mouth is inches from mine, but it's his finger that moves, pressing to his lips in warning. Silence.

Luc again, the phrasing sharper now: "Now that young cretin has introduced the AetherFlex to the world, we will have to accelerate the launch. Start the planning. My brother cannot catch wind of the new date. He knows I have it, and he'll want it back. Putain..."

The vowels blur as he turns away, footsteps receding across the deck. His voice thins against the sea air until it dissolves into the coast's distant hum.

I exhale finally. Zander is still holding me, silent, the imprint of his finger over his lips as heavy as the kiss we just stole. Heat and fear coil together in my ribs. The beauty of the night thins, turns fragile. Every star above feels like a witness.

Our secret doesn't belong to us. Not anymore, not here. Not in Luc's sepulchre.

Ristorante Terrazza.

The terrace is carved out of light itself. White pillars rising between lemon vines, terracotta tiles still warm beneath bare feet slipping from sandals. Below, the bay spreads endlessly, water hard and blue as stained glass. A yacht slices its course towards Capri, but my eye fixes on the other hull farther out. Black, lit to shine like polished obsidian. Sépulcre. Always present, even in absence.

Luc has been called away. Business: a euphemism I stopped pretending to believe years ago. His absence gave us the one window we needed. We left his floating prison and climbed into the open light of Sorrento, a terrace poised over sea cliffs and silence.

The waiter sets crystal down gently. Condensation trails on the surface, small beads like nerves running.

Zander is half folded back in his chair, shirt unbuttoned at the throat, salt still drying in his hair. Freed from the box, from Luc, from anything performative. Beneath this light, he looks younger, hungrier, as if the sea has rinsed something raw to the surface.

"Do you always look like you're measuring escape routes?" he asks, watching my gaze flick to the terrace edges, the stairs, and the bay below.

"Habit," I say. "And survival."

He smiles without softness, more like recognition. "You kiss me like it isn't survival."

My pulse clatters, betraying me. I lift the glass, condensation cold against my fingers, buying seconds I don't have to give. He waits for the deflection, and I refuse him that.

"Last night was—"

"Inevitable," he cuts in. Stern, absolute.

I look past him to the horizon, where Vesuvius blurs to haze, geometry too distant to be trusted. The air holds its suspension. Sharp lemon drifts from the vines, tugged forward by a breeze that tastes faintly of brine.

The truth thrums against my ribs. If not here, when?

"What if I told you," I say slowly, "that what I am building in my basement was never meant for Étienne, or Gauche, or Camille. It has only ever been—" my voice catches, too clean to hide "—just for us?"

The sleeve of his shirt lifts in the breeze, caught like a flag whilst the rest of him is absolutely still.

"You'd be telling me," he says, voice quiet but sharpened, "that you've already chosen."

"I haven't chosen," I whisper. "Not yet. But I know what I want."

His gaze holds, unmoving, unrelenting. "Say it."

The glass trembles in my hand. Sea, sky, and light itself conspire, forcing confession.

"I want us," I say.

It rips free, unclaimed until it exists aloud. A fracture you cannot plaster over once made.

He reaches across the cloth, not tentatively this time but decisively. Fingers close around mine, grip steady and anchoring, skin warm enough to burn through restraint.

I let him take it. Let him hold me in plain sight on the terrace above Sorrento, with the black hull gleaming in the bay below.

For once, I don't look away.

The breeze shifts. Then shadow.

At the terrace's end, a woman lingers behind oversized glasses, phone lifted at an angle too sharp for landscape. Not the view she's capturing, but us. Her body tilts as though adjusting the frame, thumb still, deliberate. When she lowers it, her smile is faint, a verdict disguised as charm.

Camille's envoy. Undoubtedly.

News flies faster than salt air.

I don't move my hand.

Let her carry it back; let Camille pour it into Luc's ear like poison. Let them both choke at the sight of me choosing what they could never script.

36

Luc

I t was raining the way only London delivers, heat pressing from beneath while the sky strips itself layer by layer. Wrong weather. The kind that makes mistakes easier. Streetlamps outside Montclair HQ flickered like poor actors. Unrehearsed. Unsure.

The Maybach waited in the loading bay. Matte black, reflecting nothing. Curtains already drawn, privacy glass sealed. Inside smelt of pipe smoke and cordovan leather. The sort of scent that insists on silence. A silver pen in its cradle. A single photograph tucked behind the visor: Montclair Workshop, 1956, men in shirtsleeves bending iron. The myth of the beginning.

Jérôme didn't move as I entered. Former Gendarmerie, trained to stillness. He wore gloves even in heat, eyes forward. Fluent in every language that mattered, and fluent too in silence. I never hired men who asked questions.

I didn't touch the cigars. Didn't need to. That was for the ceremony. I left only the Amouage in the air: faint smoke and resin, a warning more than a scent.

I slipped through the west annexe. No handlers, no PR, no press choreography. This wing was stripped, brutalist, and reserved for crises that required my presence alone. Crises too sharp to share with children masquerading as executives.

There was an envelope on the desk. Heavy, unmarked. No flap seal. Only nerve.

A still. London street, shot wide. Zander. My boy. Lips bruised, eyes wired, body all violence. Beneath it, a headline in block serif meant to humiliate:

```
Montclair Heir in Soho Brawl.
```

There was no demand. That was the demand.

I stood for a moment with the weight of it, then entered the control room. Lights snapped alive, obedient, harsh.

"Welcome, Monsieur Montclair."

"Everything new in the last seventy-two. Targets only. Visual. Audio. Staff passes. Ghost feeds."

A pause.

"Authorisation required."

I pressed a hand flat on the cold glass.

"Access denied."

Again.

"Access denied."

"By whom?" No inflection. Only weight.

"Monsieur Montclair."

The room folded in on itself.

"I am Monsieur fucking Montclair."

I breathed once and pressed my thumb against a Turkish bead I kept in my pocket for moments exactly like this.

Stopped the tremor before anyone else could.

The memory came without permission. Milan. Backstage. Camille dressed in silk still wet with heat, smoke curling from a cigarette. Her eyes were already distant beyond me.

'You'll never be betrayed, Luc. You just don't believe anyone matters enough.'

Not cruelty. Accuracy.

I walked the gallery corridor with deliberate sound, heel against marble. Each step was an admission of ownership. A Francis Bacon framed to my left, all distortion and horror, the frame's edge cold as I brushed it.

Images flickered awake.

Céleste and Saskia. Shoulder brushing shoulder. Whispering with their heads turned just so. Seen outside Montclair HQ. More footage: Saskia at her townhouse door, leaning close, words audible only on her lips. Two women conspiring, careful not to let the world read them, unaware I always read them first.

I let my mouth bend, insufficient to call a smile.

"Girls," I hissed. "Always the girls. Tell me, what mischief are you building for me next?"

My phone buzzed. The secure line. Swiss counsel.

"Lucien." His voice thinned with urgency on the line. "It's out. The images are from the Premier League game. Circulating already. Middle Eastern investors are on the line. They want reassurance."

So, the humiliation wasn't waiting for tomorrow's papers. It was already moving across servers, boarding private jets, and printed in rooms that still professed loyalty. Faster than I could contain.

I ended the call before he could qualify; I don't give men

space to explain their failings. I asked for the podcast instead.

The South African's voice filled the control room. Low, precise, scalpel-sharp. I hadn't listened since it first aired; I didn't need to. The man had taken me apart without ever raising his tone. Within ten minutes, my strategy scattered.

Céleste had been behind the glass then. I remembered it still as porcelain beside the producer. I'd watched her face shift midway through. First confusion, then something closer to concern. What came after I couldn't define?

Pity, perhaps. Or pride. Two mirrors, both unacceptable.

On tape, my voice held steady.

'My father told me luxury was earned, not sold. I believed him. Until I saw what it did to my sons. I thought 'legacy' meant 'preservation'. I was wrong. Legacy means change. The right kind at the right time. Or it turns to dust. My brother chose loudness. I chose longevity.'

The interviewer's tone narrowed, fitting the knife between ribs.

'And which one did your son choose?'

I had looked through the lens with the precision of a marksman. He hasn't chosen yet. But I think he's about to.

Now the words played back in tandem with the images. Saskia was at the threshold of my building. Céleste is leaning in towards her, whispering. Zander's bruised face plastered across a mock headline. Legacy unravelling at speed.

The phone blew again. Not the Swiss voice. Bloomberg.

Montclair Group, minus 6.4 percent.

The chart tilted sheer, red bleeding across the screen like an artery split open. Investors aren't sentimental. They rarely need to be. They had already chosen, and the choice was not patience.

I shut the file.

I didn't go home. I never do when the walls shift.

I summoned.

Amberley Manor.

Amberley lit itself for the summons. Lawns skinned in floodlight, rotor wash salted across the night. The helicopter wheeled down deliberately, blades carving every conversation into silence. They arrived as I intended, in pairs, singles, cautious. Heads ducked, eyes already weighing the room they had not yet entered. People like to know whether survival will be served at the table.

The dining hall glowed as if nothing had collapsed beyond its walls. Louvel had set a theatre, with seabass baked in salt and borne in on marble slabs, lamb smoked in rosemary, and amuse-bouches with edges sharp as cut crystal. Montrachet uncorked, thirty years patient, its perfume enough to remind them that beauty is always a weapon.

Jérôme stood behind my chair. Silent. Gloved. The reminder that the air they breathed tonight was licensed.

Céleste arrived last, as was her way. Her face arranged into what she imagined neutrality, hiding the suspicion that this was an ambush she had foreseen even before the message reached her. Her cheek brushed mine. Barely a kiss, less than recognition, and she sat with her eyes down.

The doors opened again, and the room contracted.

Camille.

She entered without introduction, without entitlement, and still the table leaned. My brother's blade, standing in my house, every step belonging to her. I let them think it was a mistake, a coincidence, or even a breach. Until I gave it a name.

"Camille has agreed to join us tonight." The quiet carried farther than volume. "I need people I can trust."

That was the pivot. Etienne's fiercest loyalist is now at my table. Whether borrowed or stolen, they could not tell. It was enough that the theft had already happened.

I raised the glass. Montrachet gold at the rim.

"To loyalty."

The silence was pure theatre.

Céleste was my first turn. I didn't address the table. I addressed her. "You went to Saeculum," I said. A fact placed deliberately into the air.

Her fork shifted, paused.

"I did."

A line crossed with two words. The taste of iron lay in every mouth watching.

"You have kept secrets for me before," I said. Voice level. "Why should this be different?"

The question spread like smoke. To her. To all of them. None exempt.

Louvel set the next course as if obligation could soften the weight.

Plates placed. Cutlery aligned. No one touched it. Food has no flavour when trust is absent.

I watched them; I do not question aloud. I read.

Who moved first, who held the fork steady, and who kept shoulders set as if truth could be performed with posture?

Saskia did not flinch when Céleste admitted Saeculum. Rarer still, Camille did not either. Two women with nothing to spare, watching me without recoil.

The meal ended without a verdict. That was always the point. Theatre finished when I chose. Lamb cut exquisitely, Montrachet forgotten, warm in glasses untouched. Forks barely scraped plates, sounding like whispers against pews.

The drawing room was where the game continued. Aubusson rug beneath, portraits of Montclairs dead and preserved staring down like jurors. A Regency globe in the corner, the speaker inside humming softly, an artefact of control disguised as an ornament.

Chairs are set wide apart. Resistance staged like testimony.

That is where I started measuring them, one by one.

Who held still? Who blinked first? And who believed legacy was a gift, and who already understood it was a weapon.

I stood by the fire. The blaze was contained orderly. I did not sit.

"Toby." My voice was quieter than the crackle. "A vault is locked; you don't have the key. What do you do?"

His heel tapped the rug, betraying nerves before lips moved.

"Find another way in, sir."

Quick. Too quick. He thought speed was a virtue. Speed only exposes impatience. Useful in chaos, dangerous in quiet rooms. Men like Toby improvise their way into graves. Disposable, and not worth mourning.

"Annina." Red-lacquered smile exact, posture rehearsed. I asked her, "Your father taught you loyalty. What happens when it conflicts with survival?"

"They are the same, Monsieur Montclair," she replied evenly. "If you know who to survive with."

Better. She thinks survival is loyalty. Not true, but usable. Women like Annina move as the current does, attaching themselves to the ship least likely to sink. That is not trust. That is leverage, and leverage can be purchased.

Julien straightened with more confidence than sense.

"Father, we all want the same thing. Continuity. Strength. These games—"

I cut him there. One word. "Games?" I didn't need volume.

He recoiled. His entire body confessed. Julien holds to continuity because he cannot conceive of anything else. He mistakes inertia for power. A courier masquerading as counsel. Dependable in errands. Dangerous in judgement.

Zander. My son. The firstborn. The heir apparent.

"Soho," I said, the word barely above a breath. "Explain to me how you'd answer if your face were plastered across a screen in the morning."

His jaw twitched, anger rushing to his throat. He opened his mouth. Then closed it.

Always fire. Never calculation. Rage presented as strategy. My son believes defiance wins the room. He doesn't yet understand that survival belongs to those who wait, those who calculate, and those who bleed last. He is either a failure or an unfinished work. I can't yet decide which.

And then Céleste.

Her fingers did not tremble on the glass stem. She held herself with elegance sharpened into defiance.

"Yes," she said eventually, head angled high. "I went to Saeculum. With Saskia. We weren't hiding it. I've kept your secrets for decades, Luc. Why should this be different?"

Question with question. I moved closer. Deliberate. The portraits overhead observed like judges with stone eyes.

"Because of those secrets you stumbled upon," I answered softly. "This one you sought yourself. Why?"

Her breath shifted, a small, betraying cough. Her gaze did not.

"Because I knew you wouldn't tell me," she said.

There it was. No naivety. Calculation. She believed she had earned the right to breach what I withheld. She hadn't. Her belief was more dangerous than betrayal and therefore more interesting.

Silence filled the hall. The fire whispered. Their eyes tracked mine, but none was brave enough to interrupt.

The verdict belonged to me. And it was already written.

I looked at them, one by one.

Two can be bent. One can be discarded. One can be wounded when the moment requires. And one, my other son, is still clay left soft too long in the sun.

Later, when Jérôme escorted them out, I stayed.

Amberley's lawns carried a sheen of frost, silver spread thin across the ground. Beyond it, the derelict orangery leaned into shadow, ribs of glass and rusted iron visible even in the half-light.

Camille was waiting by the balustrade. Smoke held elegantly between her fingers, the coil rising as if rehearsed. A cashmere trench against a structured suit, severe lines softened only by confidence. With Camille, nothing is wasted, not breath nor movement.

She was my protégé once. I had shaped her, sharpened her, and admired the symmetry of her mind and the geometries of her ambition. Wanted her too, though she never stooped to acknowledge it. That refusal had made her more dangerous than compliance ever could.

"You taught me to play," she said. Her voice was precise, even, the kind of tone that keeps knives sharp.

"I taught you restraint."

She exhaled. The ember stained her mouth red for an instant, cutting darkness like a blade.

"Then you taught me something you never used."

No laughter followed. No softness. Just truth, delivered on ice.

She turned, heels kissing frost, steps measured, calm. Walked deeper into the dark without lowering her head, without looking back.

I let her go.

But even in absence, Camille remained. Her silhouette was left under my skin, more indelible than loyalty, more volatile than betrayal. The calculation remained unfinished: when the shift comes, whose side will she choose?

The answer would decide whether change arrived as inheritance or as ruin.

37

Mara

Graphite dust shadows my fingertips. The pencil stub has teeth marks, proof of thinking. I draw a curve, then another, then a line across them carefully. The line knows what it will become before I do. Some shapes ask to be chosen. This one asked politely.

My watch pulses. 'Archive now.'

I close my eyes; the vault breathes cold. Its air smells of dust and something metallic. Screens rotate slowly, orderly as planets, the kind that choose to whisper instead of burn. The hum is steady. Adults pretend not to hear when it falters.

I sit cross-legged, toes flat against the floor, palms pressed down so the concrete won't forget me. Quiet is a tool. I use it the way Safi uses code, and Aïcha uses her hand.

"Evening, baby genius," Safi says, eyes fixed on her keys, not me. Typing fast, nail polish chipped almost to half moons. Braids loose around her neck, headphones sliding low. Her face catches the vault's blue light and reflects it like she's still inside the sun. She calls me 'baby genius' as if I'm a joke, but not entirely. That's why I like it.

Aïcha stands at the light table. Sleeves rolled once, cuff pressed sharp. Her hair is pulled so clean that the vault's cone of light crowns her without mercy. The stylus rests in her fingers like something that cuts even if she doesn't move it. Her voice lands between us, exactly.

"We have the frame," she says. "We do not have a spine."

Her words arrive placed, like stitches no one can pull loose. She does that with everything. It frightens me a little. Not because it is cruel, but because it misses nothing.

Félix doesn't sit. He never does. Jacket half on, half off, pacing in lines that refuse to straighten. His bare feet twist and turn, like they haven't forgiven the floor.

"This is a mistake," he says, to the air or to me. I can't tell. "You feed nostalgia into a machine and call it genius. You get décor."

Aunt Clara stands by the flat files where my old drawings sleep, corners worn until the card dulled to skin. Navy dress, slim belt, glasses low. Her paper trembles like light rain against a window, elegant and fragile all at once.

"We will not call it anything," she says carefully. "We will look."

I nod, because looking is the only rule.

Moss wakes the moment my fingers near the screen. I named it Moss because it grows where no one asks it to, because it listens. On the display, it shivers once, twice, then learns my presence and steadies, as if learning how to breathe.

I hum a note. The chosen one. Behind me, Maxime's file runs; his lamp turned everything honey when he recorded. He called himself LX Fantôme; only I would know his pseudonym. I could hear his hands on the chords and the way he fell into the word he wanted you to notice. His lyrics are unfinished, which makes them truer. Truth doesn't wait for dates.

Safi tilts her head. "Who is that? It sounds raw."

"My friend. LX Fantôme. A demo." I don't explain more.

"It's excellent."

Her blink is a surprise, but the nod after is permission. The song stays.

I touch the loop. Moss bends, supple. The line softens, reeds in a wind too old to be remembered. Ochre folds into gold. A shadow tucks under a rib not yet drawn. Then fracture. A thin red line is glowing now, and Moss leans wrong, too close. My hum curdles, and the sound in my head clouds.

"No," I say stubbornly. "That is incorrect."

Félix barks a laugh, baited with his own disdain. "See? It cannot feel. It only imitates."

I don't look at him. I keep my finger against the wrongness until it holds. Moss waits with me, a creature taught to listen. The red shifts, thinning, then pulsing bright again, waiting for my certainty.

"You don't decide," I tell it. "I do."

The vault tilts still. Safi's keys are still under her fingers. Aïcha's stylus hovers. Aunt Lala's paper stopped trembling. The women hold their shapes, three kinds of presence, none abandoning me.

I drag a finger across the overlay, thin and exact. Moss follows half a beat behind. The red softens, folding to amber, almost. My breath releases and returns. Spine arrives gradually, the shape that was always there, only waiting. Arched like a bridge arguing with gravity.

The hum of the vault loosens. The lights are the same but warmer because the song found its word again.

Safi exhales something close to praise, swallowing it fast,

as though praise here is forbidden. Aïcha's fingers are sure, though the pause reveals a tremor.

Félix goes quiet. He doesn't move. For him, silence is confession.

"Shoes are apologies to the body," I say. "We should not make the body say sorry."

"We'll print that on the wall." Safi smiles.

"No." My voice is clipped. "Walls listen, but they also forget."

Félix's tone is rough now. "It's a trick. A good trick. It is still a trick."

"It's not." I meet his eyes. They shine too brightly, hating the truth they can't erase. "It's remembering."

LX's unfinished chorus drops. Soft and exact. Like something known before it was written. The argument rots unsaid. Félix swallows it, puts his hands into his pockets, and stares at Moss the way a man stares at something holy he refuses to kneel to.

"Lock the iteration," Aïcha orders.

Her hand moves steadily again.

Safi taps, slows, halts. "Saved. But torsion reads six point three off optimal."

Numbers bites Félix clean across the face. He flinches.

"See."

I hold my finger against the plane's edge. Moss moves to please, trying to close the last line with something neat and dishonest.

"No." Firmer. "If you rush, it lies. We are not lying."

This is mine. Not Luc's, not Félix's. Not even Māmā's. Mine first.

The vault air suspends itself. LX Fantôme breathes a broken

note into another. I close Moss with a gentle tap, like shutting a book. "Not yet," I say. "If you force it now, it breaks."

The silence after shifts takes shape. No longer doubt. Not quite reverence. Waiting for a name.

I stretch my toes against the floor.

Aunt Clara is still clutching a sheet from the flat file, one of my old ones. A felt-tip drawing from a terrace summer. My father at the koi pond, cigar balanced, light cut sharp behind him. Complete except for the eyes. I had left them blank. Intentionally.

Aunt Lala's mouth shapes a word it won't release. Her expression changes, almost fear, almost awe. Like she has driven over a bridge her whole life and only now realised who built it.

The paper trembles again, a sound like a weak flag.

"Is that, is that Luc?" Safi says, then clamps her mouth shut, as if the name itself might wake something better left sleeping.

"Papa stands like that when he thinks no one is looking," I answer. "He sees us anyway. He doesn't need eyes for it."

Félix scrubs both hands across his face, hard. "This is too much," he mutters, softer than before. "You cannot keep a company inside a child."

"You cannot keep anything inside a company," Aunt Clara says, forgetting caution for once. Her voice holds warmth now, the kind people use when they mean a person, not a file. "We can protect her. That much we can do."

"We will," Safi says, gaze fixed on the code that isn't code, numbers halfway down a screen like a game that forgot to drop its pieces. "We will, full stop."

The door opens without complaint. I don't need to turn. The air changes, flatter and heavier for the gravity inside it. My Māmā.

Silk that doesn't whisper, hair drawn back, her mouth a line that only softens when she orders it to. She looks at the screens, then at me. Not surprised. She nods, precise, as if this were already true in her head, and the rest of us are simply late to see it.

"Show me what you kept," she says.

I activate Moss; amber glows at the edge like a waiting yes. I hold my palm above it until Moss rises to meet me, green shifting towards grey, hesitation. I hum the choosing note. LX Fantôme's chorus slips under it, unfinished but steady, and the net holds without tangling.

Mummy steps closer. Her perfume writes itself across the air, cedar edged with smoke. "What does it need?" she asks. Not to the room. To me.

"Time," I say.

A brief, quiet smile opens through her eyes. "We can give it that."

Félix exhales like he's been holding it since another century. "You believe this," he says. Not a question. Half a surrender.

"I believed it when she was three," Mummy says, flat as fact. "This is only the part where the rest of you can see it."

"Legally we are sound," Clara adds, already recovered into careful. But the warmth stays at the edges. "Her identity is sealed, clauses binding. Activation is local. If anyone tries to lift it, it dies in their hands."

Safi nods, softer. "The lock is mine. The ID cannot be forged. She is the key."

"Keys open and close," I say, because that matters. "We

will not open to everyone."

Mummy meets my stare with her own. She doesn't speak down to me. She speaks to me. "Then we close. And we wait."

Moss shifts, a fracture hovering where it once glowed red. This time it chooses grey, waiting at the edges, small, stubborn.

"Good," I tell it. "Waiting is clever."

Félix whispers out something like half a laugh. "She's twelve."

"Eleven."

He lifts his palms. "Eleven. Fine."

The song flickers one unfinished line, humming through me. I hum it back. The vault answers, not imitates, near enough to prove it listened.

Mummy's eyes smile, though her mouth does not. "We'll hear when you say so."

Aïcha lays her stylus down again. Her last line is exact, stopping where she wanted. "Name this mode." Not a test. A ceremony.

"Spine," I say, then glance at the curve. "And Bridge."

"Bridge to where?" Félix murmurs, steady but broken at the edges.

"Across," I answer. "Where it hurts to stand."

He swallows, staring at the drawing of Papa's empty eyes. Doesn't touch it.

Safi files the names: Spine, Bridge. She writes a dot between them to bind them together. Clara underlines a clause, steady-handed, the one that hides my name but keeps me present.

Mummy turns one last look to Moss, then back to me. "Do you want to stop?"

"No." Then softer, pointed: "I want to keep it for tonight.

For me."

"Then we stop for us," she says. "The rest can wait."

I set my cheek against the cool glass, not pressing, just resting. The hum beneath it gentles, a pulse beneath blankets.

I close Moss with one small touch. The screen softens to resting light.

Graphite smudges darken my fingertips, proof I was here.

Mummy's hand rests lightly on my shoulder. "Hungry?"

"A little," I say.

She nods, eyes closing for a second, as if saving this picture in her mind. When she lifts them again, the room looks smaller, as though she can pocket it.

We turn the vault lights down.

On my way out, I hum the choosing note again. Moss, even in sleep, answers. A faint green glow. A forest patient in its waiting.

Then it closes, letting me keep the night.

38

Gauche

Perpignan.

The square is washed in late gold. Diesel in the air, salt from the port, kids kicking a ball between café tables like it belongs to them. I let them have their stage. Mine starts when the light hits me.

Then, Zander, behind Luc's old Jaguar. Shirt peeled open at the throat, sunglasses obvious, beautiful in a preposterous, careless way. Handsome as fuck.

"Noémie." Proper. Ominous. He knows I don't always answer to it.

"Hop in."

The XJ220. Navy deep enough to drown in, bone-quiet, kept alive on Luc's drip feed of reverence in Bordeaux. A machine restored only to be worshipped. Until now.

He drives, the road winding vertically through cypress and stone. Trees bent, whispering secrets they won't share. Sky

264

violet before the storm, the kind that translates itself as an omen. The cassette holds its breath, then dies. No wind-down, no clatter. Silence.

He doesn't restart it. I don't tell him to. Our laughter fills the gap: broken, unscored, honest.

We take the last mile with the windows down. Air clawing in. Hair pulled loose and salt-stung. My ring taps once against the armrest, not decoration or punctuation.

The hills outside Perpignan don't forgive. They remember. Stone walls collapsed in places where the family name failed to hold them up. Grass-like scars. Wind cutting with the bite of inheritance badly handled. No signs posted, no welcome. Only the memory layered under everything.

Then it shows itself.

The Bench.

Outsiders wouldn't see it. Wouldn't understand. From the road it's a shadow burnt into the hillside, low and half-blind, ashamed of its age. Rooflines collapsed towards the river. Tiles dulled to slate, ivy choking the east face like guilt that overgrew.

The front door still bears its mark. The "M" carved into the beam is ghost-like now, but not gone. Shadows never really go.

Above the frame, the plaque clings rusted.

Montclair & Fils, Bottiers. Depuis 1921.

Family inscription. Ruin brand.

I smile, eyes on the plaque. Quiet, sharp.

"Pretty is not enough," I murmur, letting the wind carry it back inside me.

Zander parked beneath the cypress, the river breaking itself open below us. The mist rose in intervals, breath pulled straight from stone, caught in the lower gardens like smoke refusing to leave. Above, the pool caught light, turquoise splintered into the grey like a wound that still bled colour. The air had that weight water carries when it is too old to be called clean.

Inside smelt of cedar dust ground into sweat, of glue dried slow, of iron turned holy. My grandfather's last boot still hung on its hook. His stool waited under the window, the leather seat burnished dark by years of men being told to apprentice, to obey. The benches faced inward, worship disguised as workstations. Every tool aligned. No machines. No shortcuts.

It did not feel abandoned. It felt like it had been listening.

He moved towards the back rack without speaking, hand pressing against the wall where anyone else would see nothing. The hatch opens as if it never stopped breathing. Code unchanged in thirty years: M66, Montclair and a postal area code. That's the poetry of men who think numbers will outlast betrayal.

The stairwell down was mean on purpose. Low. Choking narrow. One bulb was hanging so close you had to bend to pull it. Not warm. Not welcoming.

The vault at the base: La Dernière. For the end. Concrete, steel. Moisture sealed. Supposedly climate-controlled, but the taste on my tongue was metal soaked into dust.

Every wall packed. Shelves groaning with sketchbooks, leathers dyed by hand in forgotten palettes, and schematics no one dared perfect. VHS tapes stacked carelessly, handwriting half-erased by time. Nothing digitised. Nothing modernised. Just the archive of a family that mistrusted the future even as they built for it.

No staff. No cameras. Just us. And the Armagnac he uncorked like a reflex.

The projector in the barn stuttered to life after a rough kick, coughing static then colour.

Garden in high summer.

Zander at seven, a goal between cypresses. My father was cheering him wildly, lifting him onto his shoulders like nothing else mattered. Luc stood to the side in tailored dark, detached, and unreadable as always. Julien is trying to play an adult in a blazer two sizes too wide, already rehearsing obedience.

"What are you trying to show me?"

He didn't answer. He reversed the tape and froze the frame. His own small body pulled back, face twisted, disgust sharp even in seven-year-old bones. The recoil was not from my father's grip but from himself reflected.

He poured a glass. The Armagnac folded into amber like fire trapped in liquid. He didn't look at me when he said it. He didn't need to.

The words fell low, heavy in the air between us.

"Things are not always as they seem, cousin."

The glass shook faintly in his hand. He corrected it before it split.

"It's about... Esmé Béraud."

Two words. Heavy enough to tilt the room.

I started to move, but his hand landed softly on my arm, not with force, only weight.

"What about her?"

He thumbed his phone alive, the screen throwing too-clean light across the dust. A file opening like a blade unfolded.

"She isn't just Esmé. She's Leila Farrow."

The screen bloomed with her. Not once. Many times. Venice, Madrid, Singapore. Same smile. Different hair, different wardrobe. Different men at her side each time, as if partners were accessories swapped for the season.

"CIA has her tagged," Zander said. "Industrial espionage. Contracts herself out. Ten aliases in five years. New identity, fresh face. She infiltrates, she extracts, and then she vanishes."

My hands remained composed in my lap. My shoulders didn't. The questions pressed at my teeth, waiting, but none arrived whole.

"It's verified," he added. "Avery's team tracked her months ago. A pro. Inside your orbit long enough to lift more than you realise."

The vault light was merciless. Too clean for rage.

"She was... different," I managed.

No answer. Which was answer enough.

Then, his hands closed over mine. Not the Montclair inheritance. Not a dynasty. Just cousin to cousin.

"She fucked us both over," he said.

The words hit too evenly. Too calm.

"No." My voice was steel now; all the tremor had burnt out. "She fucked me over."

I tap the table once, hard, claiming the silence.

This is a new game. Fast. Real. Dangerous.

I lean closer, eyes locking on the fracture in his calm, but nothing more needs to be said. The echo waits to fill the room with consequences.

* * *

Saint-Estève's legal annexe always felt like a crypt dressed as a salon. Veined marble, dark panelling, roses left too long in water.

I came in armour. Chain-link top, silver catching every breath. No bra. Low ivory trousers. Hair knotted high, face pulled tight into a challenge no one could soften. The tattoo down my spine, ink bright against my umber skin.

Non sum quae fuisti.

I am not who you were.

My mother would have called it theatre. I called it necessary.

Étienne sat across the table. His teeth clenched a touch too hard, shave cut close, trying for calm and failing. Camille on his right, crisp white, folded like a verse she didn't want to recite. To his left, the trust lawyer, half-listening, all afraid.

The AC was cold. I didn't shiver.

Camille's eyes flicked to my chest. She looked. I let her. Then smiled slowly. Let her wonder if the show was for her.

I dropped the file. Pages fanned out, redacted, stamped, heavy enough to slosh coffee.

"Esmé – sorry, Leila – stole the plans and then stole the tech. Paid for by Kevin Price. Sold AetherFlex back to Volant in perpetuity. Shell companies, dead directors. One name left alive."

I slid the photo across. Kevin Price. Handsome, worn, beard salted, glasses too clear.

"And beneath it? Toby Greaves. Luc's CFO."

The name hovered. They felt it.

"I met with Zander." Let his name breathe.

"He came to me as family. No angle. Just truth. Rare in this bloodline."

Their exchanged glance was a twitch. A tell.

"He trusts me. I can move where you can't. Stop decisions before they start problems here."

Silence. Victory long enough to savour.

I smiled with my eyes.

Camille finally breathed, fingers smoothing a crease no one else could see.

"Pretty. Your theatre. Chainmail. File of ghosts. Pretty is not proof, and proof is what counts."

Her voice was a violin tuned to snap. The word stuck like a hook in my skin. I smiled harder, tearing it out.

I tapped my ring once on the glass, claiming the floor.

"It's not pretty. It's pressure."

My father's jaw twitched; the lawyer was frozen.

Camille's gaze held mine.

"On whom?"

"Everyone."

I smiled, eyes sharp. "Everyone who thought I'd ask nicely."

Silence again. They held it. I owned it.

I leaned back, chain links flashing.

"Pretty is never enough, Camille."

She tightened her lips just a shade. Victory.

Domaine du Faucon Noir.

It wasn't the vines. Not the new L'Envol Pinot, not the fragile Plume Blanche Viognier, not even the Roussillon label we pretend never happened.

Étienne wanted me to see.

We walked past the house, through the oak grove where the land bent towards a hollow. A stone ruin leaned into shadow, a secret kept sharp. Behind timber doors reclaimed by seasons: the falconry.

The air was leather and cedar oil. Perches carved from yew. Shadows moving against wings. A saker, a gyrfalcon, and two peregrines. No names. Not pets. Presence.

This is where my father keeps what he cannot control elsewhere.

I drove him myself. Our secret code: I need to talk alone.

He unlatches a cage. The gyrfalcon's eyes narrow, gold irises tightening to a blade.

"I like your view, Papa. I don't want to own what I love."

Étienne glanced back, sinfully handsome, the uncle everyone claimed to trust.

"Then what's the plan?"

I told him. Zander. The shift between Montclairs. The leverage I hold.

His mouth twitched, smirking not with approval or dismissal, but recognition.

Then, my father told me his plan. Not everything. Never everything. Enough to make my pulse beat faster, enough to remind me he's the engine beneath the noise.

Two predators. One smile.

Étienne lifted his arm, gauntlet raised. The pale hawk wheeled overhead, clean and merciless against the sharp sky. It banked wide, slicing the air.

He didn't move. He knew it would circle back. I wasn't so sure.

I watched him, gauntlet heavy, shoulders set. For years I believed he was the softer Montclair. The one who laughed, who hugged, who disguised cruelties as lessons. But here, in the smell of leather and blood, I saw truth. Luc reveals his teeth. Étienne hides his in a smile. The same blood, different camouflage.

He caught my gaze.

"You wanted me to know your plan," he said, calm as stone. "Now you know mine."

The hawk dipped sunlit wings low.

"How long will it fly?"

He didn't look at me.

"As long as it wants."

"And if it doesn't come back?"

For a heartbeat, I thought of Esmé, slipping between lives, dropping faces like feathers, never returning.

Étienne smiled again. Not warm. Real.

"Then I chose the wrong bird."

39

Leila

The gravel is ragged underfoot, brutal in the stillness. Maison Béraud is silent, waiting. I meander it, every breath scraped from the edges of memory. This is not an exit. It is an exorcism.

Inside, the house has already begun erasing me. Crystal glows too clean in the dusk, with no warmth left from careless hands. Linen and air smell of bergamot, smoke, longing, and fragments that cling when love is over but grief is just beginning. In the desk drawer, my notebooks, weighted with lies, lists, and names she made real. I want to burn them. Instead, I watch them curl to nothing in the shredder: slow ribbons, ash-grey, my story unwritten as punishment.

The Polaroid is almost too much. Her face – no, mine too, both of us – blurred by the sun and something gentler. I tell myself it's just paper and ink, but my hand shakes before the blades bite. The memory is vicious in its mercy. That summer lives nowhere else now.

The kitchen, void. Plates stacked, two forever missing. Figs ruined on wood, honey drying at the edges. The echo of her laughter marks me deeper than a scar. My mouth aches for her sweetness, and nothing is ever sweet again.

The bathroom is the emptiest of all. The sound of water, the memory of cramped porcelain, her breath against my skin, shelter after the world's violence. Here, we belonged to no one else. Now, only my haunted reflection remains. I wipe the mirror in hope and find myself lonelier in clarity.

It should hurt less by now. I try to make it just another job, another cover dropped. She was a risk, a project, a means to an end, but the lie is thin, already giving way to devastation. Every fragment I try to destroy shreds me instead.

I move to the terrace. Where the sea stamped silver across the night, where cigarettes and silence braided into something sacred. Her arm around my wrist, steady in the dark. I remember how we avoided the topic of tomorrow and how we pretended night was infinite and safety was possible. Love, not as sanctuary but as surrender.

The sea receives each piece of her: phones, trackers, hard drives, any evidence that she ever rewired me. I throw them hard, resisting the urge to run screaming after each splash. Ledger closed, but the debt unpaid.

Closing the shutters, the house exhales with relief or regret; I can't tell. I lock the door but leave a print on the frame, an unintentional goodbye. I walk away, but Esmé's death is not clean. It tears, jagged, slow.

Because what I killed was not a persona. It was the only place I let myself be known and unguarded. And I am not sure I will survive it.

The salt lingers in my mouth; the scent of neroli clings as if in warning. I do not turn back, but I feel her, us, breathing behind me, a renegade heartbeat I cannot silence.

New York.

The Manhattan office is punishing in its blankness, glass, steel, and air cold as ritual. My body sits inside perfect clothes, diamond studs are studiously positioned, and my hair is severe. But I am pieced together poorly, shards showing at every seam.

The handler's arrival is a farce.

His eyes linger too long. Not on my face, but in the way my clothes fit, the way my posture claims space. Like I'm inventory. Owned. Disposable.

I meet the look, cool and deliberate. Too much to say in just a glance, but he understands the weight. He is in charge, but this? This is ownership veiled in possession.

"What took you so long? Côte d'Azur was a sideshow." His voice is oblivious to the corpse I carry inside. "Villa's swept. Nothing left. Performance vanished."

If only he knew.

I meet his eyes, steady, measured.

"Esmé's gone."

He smiles like this is conquest, not mutilation. "Put your game face on. Enjoy the payout. Wait for instructions."

I step closer, voice low and deliberate. "You don't own the scars you gave me."

He shrugs, rehearsed, but not unshaken. "The next move's on the table. You're either in or you're dead to us."

I raise my chin, the rhinestone hairpin hidden in my pocket and steel pressing cold against my palm.

"Dead or not," I say, my voice a blade beneath the surface, "some pieces don't vanish."

He doesn't reply. Because he knows.

I say nothing more. Nothing less.

After the door shuts, I stand alone. The city outside is sharper, bluer. Air colder, as if mourning with me.

My phone buzzes. A message coded in shadows only my father knows.

Montclair is still necessary. Do not relinquish.

Even his commands whisper her name.

My mission. My ruin. The lever he will always wield.

I move to the window, but my reflection fractures, multiplied.

Leila looks back hard, practised, and fake-seamless.

My fingers close around something cold and urgent in my pocket. The hairpin.

It's here, her last claim pressed fragile into my hair, now bright against all my dark.

I close my hand tightly around it.

Memory rises: figs, honey, reckless summer, daring. Her hand braced on my neck. Her mouth searching mine, not for proof, nor for performance, but for something true.

I have never been kissed without calculation until Noémie 'Gauche' Montclair.

Transaction was my doctrine. Love was my wound.

My lifetime is unbroken, but she is the fracture I cannot erase.

I hear the door click again. The handler returns, his voice cuts lower:

"That's past. You do what you're told now. No ghosts."

I turn slowly. Eyes cold but voice calm, some steel leaking through.

Ghosts are all I carry now.

"You think I don't know what you lost? Too deep for the playbook." His tone softens, but only enough to slice. "You need to let her go."

I smile, thin and knowing.

He shrugs, posture tight, dismissive. "Mission's the mission."

"Mission isn't all there is."

He studies me, the mask slipping just enough. "You're not built for this if you're soft."

"I'm built for survival."

The room shifts cold around us.

He nods slowly. "Next steps will come soon. Until then—"

"Until then," I say.

The door closes again.

Alone, the city hums sharper, bluer.

The hairpin burns cold in my palm.

"C'était réel."

It was real.

40

Saskia

Zander's Flat, Mayfair.

The door closed behind me with a soft, almost tentative click, colder than the London street outside. Stone underfoot. Shadowed lighting, even though it was barely dark. The glass walls, which could frost at a touch, were clear now, exposing the ghosts of Mount Street lights and my reflection, warped, in the big mirror he never looked at. The place had always felt like a clinic for someone emotionally radioactive, sterile, expensive, and prepared for a crisis no one would name.

His scent hit me first, a reckless tangle of warm amber and musk, danger and exhaustion, like evenings in the Cotswolds before dawn shattered everything. I swallowed the aching bloom inside me. Even after everything, I loved this smell on him.

He was on the sofa, smashed together in his white shirt and

loosened tie, one shoe gone, hair pushed back like he'd argued with his own hands and lost. When his storm-blue eyes finally caught mine, that familiar flicker, the private one, caught and burnt inside me and made me furious because it still worked.

On the glass table lay the old Tribeca stills. Her breasts pressed flat against the window, his profile just behind the glass. A headline mocked up in block serif dared the morning:

```
MONTCLAIR HEIR IN SOHO BRAWL.
```

Luc's voice echoed, cool and lethal, but the shame in my chest was louder.

"I didn't buzz," I said.

"You never have to." His voice was low, almost hoarse, with the lilt of France under the English, the way it always came when he'd been holding something in too long.

I didn't sit. "You lied to me."

He didn't flinch. That horrible steadiness, worse than denial.

"You said you went to her for the laptop," I pushed. "You said you weren't in the mood for games. And all the while," I pointed at the stills. "All the while you were inside her. With cameras pressed to the glass."

His jaw moved once, not in shame. Restraint.

"Yes," he mumbled. "I fucked her. Once. Before you and me..." He cut himself off. "Before it was anything."

"It was never nothing," I hissed, hating the harsh stranger in my voice. "That's not the point anyway. You lied to me, to Luc, to the board. And then you protected her. Every time they circled her name, you put yourself between like a shield."

He watched me like a driver sizing a hard bend, calculating the crash ahead. The corner of his mouth didn't move.

"I was protecting you."

The air left my body and came back sharp. "Don't insult me with that. Protection is what men call it when they're managing us."

He didn't raise his voice. When he's angry, he goes quiet; I learnt that early and pretended I hadn't. "You think I care if Hortense burns? If she's dragged naked through every paper? I kept her standing because if they crucified her, they would crucify you. Guilt by proximity. And Luc." His mouth tightened like the name was poison. "You don't know what he would have done to you."

A laugh broke free of me, bitter and wrong. "So I'm supposed to be grateful. For the lie, for being kept outside my life. For you choosing what I can bear."

"I was trying to keep you out of the blast radius."

"I live in the blast radius." I heard my pulse hammer in my ears, cruel applause in a hostile room. "Every day since I married him, every day since I decided to leave him. Every day I look at my daughter and promise her that our home will not be built on someone else's secrets ever again."

She is watching even when she pretends she isn't. What does she learn if I stand still in a lie?

His eyes flicked at that; Mara always gets in. He looked at the glass wall, then back at me, like he'd walked to the edge of something and decided to jump anyway.

"You think I'm Luc," he said. "His echo. Another Montclair snake. If that's what you see when you look at me..."

"Then stop doing the things he does."

Silence. He took it like a strike. Then, softly: "You don't get

280

to choose when I matter, Saskia. That's not how this works."

My hands were shaking. I curled them into the hem of my coat to hold myself upright because my mother taught me that if you can't win, you can at least stand tall.

The hem tore a little under my nails. I didn't even notice until later, when the thread dangled like proof I'd come apart.

"But I thought," the words jammed and scraped on my tongue. "I thought you were mine."

He exhaled like the truth hurt to carry. "Don't look at me like that. Like I'm someone worth saving."

"You are." It came out before I could strangle it. "You were. "You," I swallowed. "You could have told me. We weren't a couple yet, fine. You were single, fine. You could have said, 'I made a mistake; it meant nothing; I was angry and stupid and lonely, and I didn't want it,' but you didn't. You made me stand up in rooms and defend the man who lied to me about a woman who pressed herself to a window for the cameras."

"Don't make it into a performance," he whispered.

"It already is performance. It's all performance." I nodded at the photographs fanned out on the table. "Ask them."

He rubbed his thumb under his lip, then dropped his hand like the gesture disgusted him. "She didn't steal AetherFlex."

"You don't know that."

"I know her."

The nausea rose fast, chemical and clean. "Of course you do."

"She was forced to steal drawings and other things, but she's a show-off, not a thief," he said. "She wants to be the headline, not the footnote in an IP filing."

"And you're still defending her."

"I'm defending what's true."

"What's true," I said, "is that you visited her in Tribeca and slept with her and then told me you didn't; what's true is that you played saviour and called it strategy. What's true is that when the room turned on her, you stepped in, and every time you did, you put me in the shadow of her body again."

"You think I chose her over you?"

"I think you chose the lie over us." I forced my voice steady. "And I think I can't build my life on that. Not again."

We stared at each other like strangers who used to be friends.

Suddenly, Mara flitted through my head.

What does she learn if I stay with a man who edits the truth for me?

What does she learn if I leave when I still love him?

He reached out then, his fingers trembling as they found mine, his thumb stroking fragile circles. The tiniest moment of connection betrayed both our fierce hurt and desperate hope. His breath was ragged.

"I don't want other women clouding your head," I said suddenly, raw and unbidden. "They will come for you and call it help. It won't be."

His grip tightened, anchoring me.

"I don't want a version of you, Alexandre," I said. No polish, just trembling truth. "I want you."

His eyes were wet. Mine were worse. I wanted to hit him and kiss him and never see him again.

I swallowed hard, the nightmare unfolding before me on the table. Not just Hortense, but also the stupid physical altercation about her chest that the NOX cameras caught outside.

I fought tears. In my mind, a list of battles: the house

settlement nearly signed; our new business's potential proto-types humming under the stairs; Safi asleep on the beanbag because we dream bigger than now; Dorian's urgent messages warning, 'Don't put anything in writing, call me.'

I had told Zander pieces and pretended it counted as hon-esty; I was not clean. I was only better at hiding the dirt.

"Tell me one truth," I said, voice fractured but fierce. "Not strategy. Not protection. The truth you never said."

He wiped a tear with the back of his hand like a boy caught too deep. "I went to her because I wanted to hurt myself, and I knew she would help. It was stupid. I am not proud. I hate that you can see it."

Silence.

"Did you go back?"

"No."

"Do you believe her about AetherFlex?"

"I believe she didn't take it. She was coerced into stealing some things from me but not the physical AetherFlex."

"And the laptop?"

He looked past me, through me. "I needed to know."

"You mean Leila."

He nodded. "Interpol lost her," he said flatly.

"She was never yours to lose," I said, voice cracking as the actual wound surfaced, not Leila, but me.

Women surround Zander. Some vanish; sometimes they come back. Sometimes they don't.

Which am I?

Zander began muttering names, the people he blamed for all of this.

"Leila Farrow and Avery Trent, poking her nose in," he muttered.

Avery was Luc's American fixer extraordinaire, the kind no one ever wanted until it was already too late.

"Avery fucking Trent!"

Then, across the room, I heard the quiet chime of his personal AI.

"Calling Avery Trent."

He jolted, like a slap broke his skin. "No. Cancel. Cancel!"

"Call cancelled," Claude replied, oblivious and pleased.

He swore in French, the curses that carry every ounce of heartbreak and weight. "Next time I say her name like that," he said, voice low, "take it as emotional damage, not a fucking instruction."

"Understood," came the robotic reply.

He drifted into the kitchen that might as well have been a showroom, not a warm hearth, and built a Negroni with the precision of a surgeon: ice exactly level, peel trimmed with surgical exactness, and the stir five turns, no more. No offer for me. No softened gaze. Just standing there with the glass at his lips, as if not drinking would shatter him.

"I should go," I said. I didn't move.

"Stay," he said without turning.

"To do what? Watch you be noble in your own mind?"

That earned a sound, not quite a laugh, not quite a growl. He put down his drink. "I don't know how to be with you right now without wanting to fix it. And I can't fix this. You won't let me explain, and when I try, I make it worse."

"Then stop talking," I snapped. "Or talk like I'm not your enemy."

He turned, eyes red, stripped of polish. "I'm not good at asking," he said. "But I'm asking. Don't let my father make you small so he can make me pay. Don't give them the parts

284

of you I love just to hurt me."

Tears came then, hot and humiliating, brazen in their betrayal of my pride. "You don't get to tell me who I can be near. You don't get to tell me how to protect my child. You don't get to call this love and drag me blindfolded into the dark."

He crossed the room and pulled me in again. We stood, the city breathing behind the glass, the white noise whispering like the sea. He pressed his mouth to my hair. I pressed my face to his throat. We shook, an emptiness both terrifying and sacred.

He whispered in my skin, French broken into English, broken apologies and obscene words, the only language left once pride dies.

"I can't lose you," I said, my voice cracked and not quite mine.

"I think you already have," he answered. A whisper. A wound.

We let go together, the distance between us growing at a painfully deliberate pace.

"I'll send the driver."

"I'll walk."

"It's not safe."

"I don't care."

"I do."

I looked at him, the man I love and the man who lied. "You just don't get it, do you?"

"Make me get it," he said, too softly.

"I need a partner," I said. "Not a curator, not a patron. Not a man who edits the truth out of fear. I need someone who stands in the fire with me, takes the hit, and calls it love, no matter the burn."

He nodded once, soldier-still. "I don't know how to be that man yet."

"Then don't ask me to wait whilst you practise on me."

"Saskia,"

I lifted a hand. "No. Please. Don't say my name like that."

He swallowed hard, and the glass walls clouded briefly, then cleared. My reflection stared back, taller than I was, thinner, a stranger who hadn't cried yet.

"I'll send Mara's book," he said, a small kindness amid the ruin.

"She has it."

"Good." A moment. "Tell her I,"

"No," I cut in, gentler than I felt. "Don't ask me to carry you into my daughter's night."

He nodded, mouth twisting painfully. "You're going to let my father call you at six a.m. with hollow forgiveness and an ugly request. You'll think you have to say yes because the house is nearly yours, you can feel the keys in your hand, and you don't want to drop them. Don't."

"I don't drop things," I said. "I carry them."

He closed his eyes. "I know."

Claude chimed softly, breaking the spell.

"It's eleven past nine."

"Thank you," Zander said, voice reluctant.

"I'm going," I said.

"I'll walk you down."

"No."

No hug. There was no kindness left after that.

I moved to the door and pressed my palm to open the glass. Just as it slid, I heard him murmur, barely there, "Try harder."

I didn't turn. "You first."

The cold corridor smelt faintly of stone and lemon oil and money. On the street, the humid August air hit my face, London tired and heavy. I stood a moment longer.

The coming week loomed: men in sharp suits touching clean hands to boardroom tables; Camille's silk voice winding through dark corners; Luc's polite but deadly calls; a driver I wouldn't take; breakfast for a child navigating grown-up battles; a basement humming with machines mapping the shape of pencil lines into data.

I thought about nights alone in beds full of everything I fought for and the one thing I wanted outside the walls.

Women orbit him, then vanish. The bitter bruise of the thought came back. Maybe I'm next.

I started walking before I could choose. I half-turned, foolish enough to want him behind me.

The glass was empty. Only my shadow kept pace.

41

Céleste

The Montclair boardroom did not change. Twenty degrees. Air flat enough to burn in the throat. Twelve chairs, one left empty for Lucien Senior. Onyx table, velvet seats, a silent camera aimed at Luc's place. The wall held a shine so dark it ate reflections. In the lacquered wood, that faint scorch. The smell of old punishments.

They called it The Ledger. A name at first. Then a habit. Then something the family used like doctrine.

Ledger: fixed, bloodless, absolute. Luc's favourite lie.

Zander arrived thirty seconds late. Jacket sharp, cuffs bright. His grandfather's links lit his wrists with a single cold glint. Luc's jaw twitched. That suit had not been authorised.

Zander wore it anyway.

Saboteur.

Horace nudged a dossier forward with the care of a man handling contaminated evidence.

```
HORTENSE VALOIS.
```

The name alone was a blade.

"Overdose," Toby said.

No reaction. The room held its breath. Zander held his.

"Optics," Annina murmured.

"Collateral," I said. Accuracy matters.

I folded my glasses and set them down. The click was soft, but it landed like a verdict.

Zander's eyes found mine and stayed there. Heat buried under ice. A storm chained to courtesy.

I stood, placed a glass of water beside his hand, and touched his shoulder. A small gesture. An intrusion. He refused the contact by stillness alone.

He rose.

His chair scraped back with enough force to split the silence. A warning in sound. No one asked him to sit. No one dared.

I stayed beside him, the only presence near enough to feel how close he was to breaking something: a rule, a man, himself. He had been carved for this family's use and left hollow where his heart should have been safe.

"Zander."

He looked at me. No rage, not yet, just the brittle restraint of a man holding back everything he could not afford to show.

"I know what this family asks of you."

My fingers traced the edge of the onyx tabletop, cold and unyielding. "It asks for your silence. Your loyalty. Your compliance."

His throat worked once. Small movement. Enormous cost.

"And from those who try to hold too many truths, I know the price."

My smile thinned. Something sharp lived inside it.

"You wear rebellion like a suit. But unless you bury what

hurts, they'll tear it out of you and call it discipline."

A flicker crossed his face, too fast for the others, slow enough for me. He was cracking behind the eyes.

"I am sick to the bile of the disguises we keep. The facades we polish. The sacrifices no one acknowledges or forgives."

Not a plea. Not an accusation.

His gaze broke. A tremor inside the armour he stitched around himself every morning.

"You'll pay for this," he said, voice low enough to bruise.

"Perhaps." I folded my gloves. Soft leather closing like a quiet threat in my hands. "But I will never let the Ledger bury what still breathes."

The boardroom swallowed the words. The camera watched. The walls listened.

Zander Montclair stood beside me, taut, furious, and grieving, and for a moment the room felt one breath away from blood.

Outside the lift, Luc intercepted us, always, never by coincidence. Luc Montclair did not deal in coincidence.

"She is rather beautiful," he said, clinical and unyielding. "And a beautiful fuck too, from what I hear."

Luc followed with patient insistence.

"Was, I should say. She *was*."

The shift was immediate. Zander stopped. One hand shot up to Luc's lapels, slamming him back so the gilt frame rattled.

His voice was wire-stripped, shaking the air with accusation.

"You. Fucking. Monster."

Luc smoothed his fabric, pale eyes sharpening to a wolfish gleam. He savoured the fracture; he always had.

That was The Ledger's lesson. Loss was never grief. It was an entry point to something or someone else.

* * *

Zander answered the door looking like the wreck I expected: the tie still knotted like a leash he hadn't managed to cut, and the shirt clung damp and creased at the collar, as if fabric could be loyal when men were not.

He walked back to the sofa without a word.

"Mademoiselle fucking Fournier," he muttered.

"Yes," I said. "Me."

The flat was cold, with a single black-and-white photograph of Claudine at the piano, her face turned away. Everything wired. Nothing warm. A clinic for someone radioactive.

"I couldn't let you burn the place down alone," I said.

The coat came off. Folded, set on the Eames chair. Two buttons undone. Air, not theatre.

I poured two drinks and handed him one like a white flag.

He took it. Sat close; not touching. Close enough to breathe me in. Neroli, clove, and an old base note the young never recognise.

"Right," I said. "Let's talk about getting you back on track."

A ghost of a smile. A shoulder nudge, light. You've seen me worse. You always bring me back. We didn't need to say it.

"Look at me."

He did.

"Breathe."

I placed my hands on his shoulders, firm under the collarbone. Felt the coil resist, then give just a fraction. My thumbs worked the knot in his muscle. Pride braided with panic.

"You're not broken," I said. "You're changing shape."

His breath stuttered, not from arousal but from recognition, a body remembering what it felt like to be held without being taken.

"Stand up." He did. "Shower." He didn't argue.

Whilst the water ran, I opened the terrace doors and let cool air take the room. London was watching. I turned off the music, then unmuted the news and covered the untouched food.

I set the envelope on the table.

He didn't come back.

I knocked once and stepped in. Steam. A silk rug soaked through. He sat on the tiles, towel around his waist, head bowed like in confession.

"They love him more than me."

Not a boy. Not a prince. Just a son.

There it was, the rot beneath the crown. The hurt he had worn so long it had become his structure.

"Luc needs the world," I said. "You needed only one person who truly sees you."

Silence. Then a small nod. Permission is heavier than pity.

"Up," I said sweetly. "Come here."

He let me help him dress. More than undressing ever could be. Arms raised when I asked. Steps into trousers when I held them open. Shirt against damp skin. I dried his hair with a towel, fingers finding order without forcing it.

"You don't have to be your father," I said, buttoning a cuff. "Stop trying."

He looked up.

"You only have to be useful," I said, "until you're powerful enough to be dangerous."

That reached him. His spine lifted. Fractional. Real.

He caught my wrist, pulse to pulse. We stayed that way for a moment.

Then, I put the glass in his hand and the envelope beneath it.

"Open it."

He read. Once. Twice. The breath left him. The room tilted and settled.

```
HORTENSE LOUISE VALOIS.
```

A date. Two weeks before she died.

An outline of a foetus. Twelve weeks. Maybe thirteen.

At the bottom, in modest print, aligned, clinical, detached.

```
Procedure authorised. MI6 field asset. Patient
override: Denied. Outcome: Foetal termination.
Operational conflict.
```

Some desk-bound coward signed away her choice.

Operational conflict.

Like it was a meeting that could be rearranged. Not a child erased.

"They did this," he said.

"Not directly," I said. "But, your father has friends who sign from the shadows."

He stared at the small print:

Operational conflict.

"Use it," I said. "Or I will."

That was always the risk: women turned into footnotes, bodies signed away in someone else's hand.

"Get some sleep."

"Will you stay?"

"No."

He nodded. A man learning not to ask twice.

"Thank you."

"Don't thank me. Make it count."

Luc waited by the car. Hands in pockets. That soft-smirk look he used when he wanted to be mistaken for human. Leather and endings. Rome, Vienna, and Milan in the same breath.

"Did you make it all okay?"

"I cleared his head."

"Good girl." The old pat on the head, dressed as praise.

He would not say thank you. That was how I'd know it worked.

He watched me as if cataloguing: hair pinned, mouth quiet, no scent of scandal. He preferred his imagination to facts. Men like him always did.

"Come," he said. "I'll give you what you want. Let's settle your future."

His office was an obsidian cube designed to flatten whoever entered. No windows. A grotesque head on the wall, mid-scream, mouth never closing.

He gestured to the folder.

"I knew retirement circled your mind."

He enumerated without pride, only taste.

"The Paris apartment. The Turks & Caicos villa. A Cayman account, naturally. Symbols worthy of your service."

I slipped off my gloves, folded them carefully, and placed them on the desk. He mistook my patience for consent.

"This is your future," he said. "All that's left is your signature."

The desk gleamed like a mirror. His reflection stared back. Mine did not. Deliberate.

"Lucien," I said, voice steady. "Don't fight me. I've had enough."

He smiled thinly, amused. "Enough of what? Rooms? Promises? At your age, memory turns gossip into gospel. You've grown theatrical."

"Age is the only theatre we do not rehearse."

I leaned in, voice soft and sharp.

"I know where the bodies are buried. I have stood in rooms you prefer to forget. I can put names to the initials filed under 'contingency'. I will not say them here. I do not have to."

He watched me.

Finally, I spoke.

"I don't want your apartments. Or your island. Or your accounts."

He blinks.

"No?"

"I want the origin."

He waited.

"The atelier, the land it stands on. The old factory in Perpignan."

He laughed, brittle and too fast.

"Dust. You want dust?"

"Dust is memory."

"Memory is currency."

"You taught me that."

The laugh died.

He saw it then, the story spine by another name.

To refuse would make him look afraid. He could not afford that.

"You truly want ruins?"

"I want the stones your father laid with his hands. The river, the old gears. The walls that remember all the patterns we've stolen and perfected. I want heart. For it all to have been worth something. To watch the sunrise from the sea and set over the mountains from a chair of my own. Keep your villas. I'll keep the myth."

He stalled.

As men like him do when they need a moment to lose.

A last pass at charm. "Céleste," he said, almost fondly.

"We both know you want to be kept."

His eyes, pale and wolfish, glinted.

A man imagining burying me alongside the others if I misstep.

"I'm done being kept," I said. "I am keeping it."

When they finally called me back in, the paperwork waited in a neat, accusing pile. It took a moment before my hand remembered how to sign, but once the ink touched the page, it was finished.

He slid the deed with two fingers, as if passing me a relic stained not just with paper but with what's been lost.

I signed once. No flourish. No, thanks.

He rose.

296

"You won't be thanked for this," he said, amused.

"That's how I'll know it worked."

He thought he had rid himself of dust.

I walked out, clutching the spine of the story under my arm.

Stories outlive men.

Ruins outlive empires.

The Ledger, however polished, still records what bleeds.

And I will decide what story the stones tell next.

42

Saskia

Wilde Lounge. Mayfair.

our minutes late. Exactly. Luc stands as I enter, though his eyes cut to the door before his body does. He'd already marked my arrival in the wine cabinet's reflection. Three-piece charcoal, lapel pin catching light the way he likes to draw attention. The shoulders say what he means to begin with: control, not charm.

I don't step closer. My head begins a slow scan, enough to register him from shoes to hairline, then flattens back to stillness. I chose a black high neck, sleeves like smoke. Hair pinned in its discipline. No jewellery. Power doesn't decorate; it waits.

I watch his throat move once, an almost-swallow forced back. He smells of himself: expensive and deliberate.

I take the seat opposite, not beside.

"You asked for this."

His mouth reacts first, curved, delaying the eyes.

"I asked for ten minutes. You've had days."

The waiter pours something gold, but my hand stays still until the glass lands exactly between us. I don't reach. Things arrive.

"I thought it best to show solidarity," I say. The word tastes staged; I let one eyelid speak for me. "For the cameras."

Luc folds his fingers together, motionless in a way that pretends to be patience. "And the shareholders. There is unrest."

I look only at him. "Because I have moved on?"

The corners of his mouth resist change, but his jaw betrays him with a single pulse. "Because they crave stability."

I lift the glass, slowly and exactly. "Not my problem."

He laughs as if he rehearsed it, though the inhale betrayed its effort. "Tell me, Saskia. You've had your generous settlement; what is it you want now? More? The spotlight? Alexandre?"

He knows.

I placed the glass carefully, fingertips aligned on its stem. "A future without you."

His gaze sharpens. "If this is war, you need more than a headline and a rented bed in Montclair sheets."

My eyes hold steady. "And if you want relevance, you need more than a surname and an heir already failing."

His nostrils tighten. The pupils contract. I smile but feel my teeth press hard against my bottom lip, leaving a private mark.

"You think you are new?" he says, soft as silver. "You are every girl who thought I was leverage."

I lean, slow enough to trouble him with the movement.

"And you are the last verse of a song no one plays anymore."

The silence that follows is taut, almost visible.

"You killed a young woman, and then you hid it, Lucien."

His smile falters, but not for long. "It was not as simple as that. They suffered—"

"She." My voice doesn't lift, but the word cuts clean. "She was a young, promising athlete."

His eyes narrow, and his shoulders shift just enough to signal control. "The sole of the prototype gave way during training. It caused a severe injury; a clot formed, and an embolism took hold. We flew her to the best specialists in Spain, then the U.S. My brother and I paid for everything. We tried everything. It failed."

"I... I didn't know any of this."

"No, when you go snooping in my archive, ensure that you retrieve all the files you need."

"You signed the denial," I say.

The table holds still between us, polished wood reflecting neither of us fully. His nails press faint crescents into the linen.

"Leave it, Saskia," he says finally, soft as a match about to strike. "Leave it buried. It will be better for everyone."

I lift the glass, drink slowly, tasting nothing. "Better for you."

He doesn't argue. The air in the room does it for him.

He stands first, his chair against tile, not loud, not quiet. "Legacy is longer than youth, Saskia. It would serve you well to remember that."

I do not answer.

"And take the Montclair name off all your mastheads and email signatures, Miss Lin."

Miss Lin.

I rise and stride towards the exit, my gaze locked until the last table is behind me.

At the door, bevelled glass reflects him back, still seated, pose intact. But his eyes have narrowed, and his nails press into white linen hard enough to leave their trace.

Outside, the air slaps, cool, sharp, and honest.

Luc's Maybach waits opposite. Obsidian black, matte finish. Reflects nothing, demands nothing. Beside it, Jérôme stands still, watchful, unyielding. No posturing. Just eyes that say, You walked out, but not far enough.

His coat hangs open, deliberate. The curve at his hip is deliberate too.

He doesn't nod. He looks through me.

My phone buzzes once. Then again.

Zander.

Still breathing?

I smile. Small. Crooked.

Just walked out. Heading for the river. Dark but beautiful. Like him.

Three dots.

Come to the Nest.

I hesitate. Wonder if it's part of their game.

I've ordered something that bites and something that

heals. Your choice.

I say nothing, just stare at the river, my mind flickering to the napkin beneath Luc's nails, the crack, and the pressure.

Then, I started walking.

Not home. Not back. Forward.

To Zander.

'Legacy lasts longer than youth,' he said.

Maybe. But legacy doesn't get the last word. Not this time.

L'Hirondelle feels suspended between sky and glass, a fragile bubble where the city blurs, softened by evening light. Neutral ground, if neutrality means holding all the edges just barely apart.

Zander waits, jacket draped carelessly, tie untucked as if he's already worn down the night. The bottle between the two glasses sits like a question unanswered.

When he looks up, his eyes don't just ask if Luc won; they carry something more fragile, almost hopeful, a question too dangerous to voice.

I lower myself onto the chair, uncomfortably close, the table unnervingly small. The air is thin, as if it's already been breathed too much.

Silence stretches, anchored by distant traffic and the faint clink of glass under the bottle's weight. His gaze doesn't waver; it lands with a heat I'm not ready to meet.

"You don't look tired," he says. "But you should."

My fingers trace the rim of the glass again, near enough that a touch between us seems inevitable; despite that, neither of us moves.

The pause holds, amenable to surrender, and I almost want

to lean in. But I look away.

"Mara?"

"Yes, she's fine. Home with Clara, revising—"

He studies me, reading something I can't hide. "So. Who bled?"

The laugh that escapes me is too sharp, too loud, a brittle sound catching on glass and night air. "Luc came to win. I came to wound."

His nod feels like acknowledgement, something heavy and necessary. "And you?"

"When he found out about us, I reminded him I don't need his name."

We drink.

The silence that follows isn't empty. It's clean, stripped of pity or expectation.

He leans back, watching, amused and worn past the point of pretending. "I always wondered if you loved me like a stepson, or if it was just the chaos you craved."

Stepson. The word hangs wrong, unfamiliar, and jagged in my mind.

"It's the same thing," I say, voice low.

Something loosens in him then. His smile is quiet.

I stare at my glass, swirling the dark liquid until the room shifts, not in a flash or drama, but in subtle relief, like a breath finally released.

"Zander."

His eyes find mine, clear now, sharp with something like truth.

"I'm not playing sides. I'm just not playing theirs."

"Good," he whispers. "That makes both of us."

We sit close, two people carved by the same family's fractures. The warmth presses against the thin barrier between us – not a kiss, not tonight, but the quiet acknowledgement of needing no more.

His hand strays, brushing mine on the table, light and unplanned. Skin against skin, fragile and electric.

The world holds its breath.

For a flicker, I almost let it stay.

43

Zander

Number Eleven was too still. Too civilised. A mausoleum disguised as a townhouse, better suited to a dead statesman than a man still breathing. I needed something with a pulse.

By two, the city had thinned into sodium haze and empty tarmac. Notting Hill. Anonymous garage, alias on the plate. My Ducati waited, black with oxblood trim, the sort of machine you buy when you want people to guess at your sins but never prove them.

Helmet on. No plate. No tags. A mask and a wager.

Gate yawning open. Throttle answering like a faithful hound.

London turned into glass and steel, flogging itself into a blur. Wind razored into bone. Corners too sharp, shifts too vicious. Exactly right. I wanted something to flay me alive. Anything louder than her voice; that maddening civility replaying in my skull.

Then the thought, a car behind me. Headlamps pinned steady. Too steady.

MI6? The family? A hired conscience with leather gloves? Pick your poison.

I twisted harder, bent through Docklands. Clipped amber so close I could smell the heat. The car stayed. Or didn't. Hard to tell through the fog; paranoia is the cheapest narcotic, and I've never been shy about economical choices.

The theatre of the chase sharpened me, nonetheless. Veins fizzing, engine screaming, the anticipation almost erotic: the strike, the cut-off, the pièce de résistance.

Nothing came. The lights thinned, melted, and were gone.

Which left the usual possibilities: I'd been hunted. Or I'd been hallucinating. Or, worse still, I wasn't worth the diesel.

Perhaps they'd never been there. Which was almost worse. You can fight an enemy. But shadows? Shadows just make you confess to yourself.

The truth? Silence is always ruder than pursuit. Cities don't clap when you risk your life. They let you somersault onto the asphalt and send in men with hoses.

So I kept going. Quicker, colder, louder. Because if you're going to be ignored, you may as well make enough noise to prove you were here at all.

* * *

The jet was a coffin with wings. Paris on the horizon, silence for company. The Gulfstream purred like it thought it was maternal, but to me the sound lodged inside my skull like a drip I couldn't turn off.

The apartment was no better. Too neat. Swept twice over, the starch of official hands enduring like aftershave. Estate men, MI6 men – their polish has an unmistakable smell.

Hortense's chaos was missing. No wine bottle rolling under the sofa, no silk abandoned on a chair. Just a hollow museum piece titled Absence.

I crossed to the vanity. She'd always kept the surface militant, bottles in parade formation. But I knew her tricks. In Tangier, on a night so humid the sea sweated, she'd peeled a sedative blister from the back of the drawer lining. "Just in case," she'd said, without looking at me, as if it were mascara rather than chemical escape.

The drawer whispered open. Too clean. Dustless. My reflection wavered above, a familiar face but wrong-footed, less sure, more... haunted aristocrat trying to pass for human.

My thumb pressed against the lining. The give was still there, obedient to its old treachery. Paper, foil, plastic. Wrapped like contraband, a soldier's care in her schoolgirl hands.

A USB stick. And her writing, needle-thin, French angles.

They always underestimate how much we notice.

I held the note longer than sense allowed. Proof she meant it for me. Proof she'd noticed long before I did. Typical. Tenz always saw the leak in the hull whilst I was still admiring the wood panelling.

I pocketed the drive and straightened the bottles, a reflex, absurd, like I could reconstitute her with symmetry. The silence answered back, louder than engines. I almost swore I smelt the faintest trace of jasmine, something feral beneath it, but perhaps that was memory drugging me on echoes.

Back on the jet, I toyed with the thing. Plastic and metal can feel like relics if you let them. Warm in my palm, almost pulsing. Ridiculous attachment. The co-pilot was snoring behind the curtain, a useless guardian.

A muted click, and the screen went black. Static spat up. My chest tightened; for a blissful second, I genuinely thought I'd taken down avionics mid-air. Suicide by USB, a family footnote no one would believe but everyone would enjoy.

Then words burnt out of the dark:

> *If you found this, it means you were right not to trust them.*

The engine's hum thinned. My face floated over the pale text, half-translucent, like a ghost caught snooping.

Folders opened. Surveillance stills, names, dates. My name. Hers. People I knew, people I'd rather not.

And then, 'Private Conversations'.

The cursor sat like it was daring me to blink. I clicked.

Camille's voice, light as a cork from a bottle:

"At the Versailles gala, the bathrooms will be perfect. Zander can't say no."

Gauche's laugh, lazy as ever:

"A chore, to be sure."

Camille again, gleeful and merciless: "I won't enjoy a second of seducing Alexandre Fairfax Montclair and recording it."

Gauche's voice turned mock-modest. "As his cousin, I can't possibly watch it... unless, of course, it was playing when I was at yours."

Camille: "I never watch them. They're engraved already."

Silence, then Gauche, almost purring: "Lucky, lucky girl."

The cabin seemed to contract around me, walls pressing in. My temples sweated cold.

Comedy at my expense, tragedy at hers. A neat reversal, except no one clapped. That, I think, was the most insulting thing: betrayal reduced to a performance without an audience.

Hortense had been right. She'd always been right. Camille, plotting the recording, turning intimacy into leverage.

I leaned back against leather colder than it should have been. Power and betrayal, all condensed into the petty rattle of a flash drive. A relic, a pulse, a sentence.

And me, caught between wanting to crush it in my fist and knowing it may be the only proof I wasn't paranoid after all.

The secure line sang faint with static, like an old gramophone choked with dust.

"Maxi... I've got leverage on Camille. What else do you have for me that I might not find myself?"

A drawl came back, languid and amused.

"Luc, naturally. He's the sort of silly boy who hides dynamite under silk handkerchiefs and contracts and memos left to rot in daylight, as if secrecy were a vulgar sport. Invisible channels, polite frauds. Ghosts, my dear. But yours to command. And..."

"...and?"

A soft chuckle, half-fond and half-deadly.

"I've also been to see our Saskia. Sweet Sass. I tried to nudge her gently; you'd be impressed at my restraint. But she's sitting on something... very much yours, very much dangerous. You'll want to ask her about it yourself. Only thing is, if you prise open this box, brother, you'll never shove the lid back down. Ever. You'll change the weather. Your whole family will need umbrellas for the rest of their lives."

"Good," I said. "I'll speak with her. Keep it to yourself for now."

"Remember, Zazou, corpses have a bad habit of crawling up again. Personally, I find it rather entertaining. But then, you've always liked your fires neat, whilst I prefer them sprawling."

A low laugh. "Then let's hope I still enjoy the smell of smoke."

Static flared, then cut. The line died like a candle.

Mayfair, London.

Back in my flat, the door locked behind me with a decisive click. I let myself sag against the wood, shoulder blades pressed hard, pulse still beating battlefield rhythms. Shower. Steam. Hot water turned skin raw and fogged the mirror until even my reflection looked like a stranger I couldn't interrogate.

Towel low at my hips, hair damp, I moved to the kettle. Coffee. Black as penance. Bitter enough to cauterise the nerves.

The news feed flickered past its usual trivialities until a name snagged attention like a fishhook.

"Claudine Morel."

I turned it up loud.

"...Lucien Montclair's first wife, long withdrawn from the spotlight, like a queen quietly removed from the board. Now, she's back in the game with a new capsule release, teased to reveal what's next. Take a look."

The signature flourished beneath the headline, hers, un-questionable.

My hand cupped the mug tighter.

The ping from Corky lit up, cruel in its neatness.

Did you see it? Claudine's latest capsule goes live next week. Be careful, my friend. She plays differently now.

I stared into the black swirl of my cup, the bitter surface circling quietly, as if it already knew the outcome. Hortense with her warnings, Camille with her betrayals, and Luc with his little paper tricks – all of it suddenly made small and provincial.

Perhaps that was always my mistake, mistaking civility for concession, mistaking women for pawns when they'd been playing queen's gambit all along.

My mother wasn't playing for survival, or leverage, or love. Claudine had been silent because she'd been studying the board itself and perhaps designing a new one.

I instinctively touched the place where my tattoo rested, an unspoken reminder, felt more than seen.

My throat tightened at the taste of coffee. This wasn't a feud or a scandal; this was a game I hadn't realised I was enrolled in. And the worst part of recognising a queen's move late is knowing she's already been three turns ahead.

44

Mara

Upstairs, the light felt thinner. Not the bright glass-basin light of the basement where the machines hummed, but a drained, hotel-corridor light, where everything looked too pale. I sat cross-legged on the rug, sketchbook on my knees.

"I miss Daddy," I said. Not loud. Just enough so that Moss would hear. Moss's screen flickered, static crawling the edges of his voice.

"Your father is in Monaco. A hotel. With a female friend who is not your mother."

The words overlapped for a moment, as if another mouth beneath his was whispering them too. I thought of my sketchbook, two circles on top of each other, blurring. When I asked if the woman looked like my Māmā, the hiss came first, a layering of syllables.

"Database entries... subscription... companion service reported." Then Moss surfaced clean again, toneless: "She is twenty-six years old. Brown hair. Paid."

I blinked. Tried to picture it.

Monaco was postcards on the fridge, blue water and champagne glasses that never emptied. But Moss said it with no
smiles, no warmth. Only a place and a woman with no name.
Paid? Like when Mummy pays for the babysitter? Or maybe
Daddy bought her a present, like when I pick ribbons at the
shop? The thought settled in my chest like a small stone, hard
and sharp.

The pencil jerked in my hand. I pressed harder. It buzzed
faintly, like the prickly static that crawled all around Moss
when he spoke, the way the air tingled on my arms and my
teeth felt full of bees. Lines overlapped, shapes collapsing.

At first, it was only circles, the kind I always drew. Then
they split, rings breaking apart, spinning away. I filled them
with jagged teeth, then shaded them until the page was black.
Faces with no eyes. Rooms with staircases that led nowhere.
Doors drawn again and again, but all of them sealed shut. And
then, Daddy. His jaw, square and sharp. His hair was brushed
back just as I remembered. But where the eyes should be, I
left blank hollows. Two empty ovals. I drew them again and
again until the paper tore.

The pencil snapped. I grabbed another. The pages filled
quickly with manic spirals, shadowed blocks, and frantic
cross-hatching that made the paper buckle. The drawings
weren't pictures anymore. They were noisy. When I stopped,
my hands hurt. The air around me felt heavy, buzzing.

Mummy found me like that. She lifted the sketchbook without
speaking. She turned the pages slowly, each one worse than
the last, until she reached him, the hollow-eyed face, and
froze. Her breath left her in a small, breaking sound. Her
hand shook on the cover, though she gripped it hard enough

that the cardboard bent in her fingers. She shut the book and straightened up.

"Moss," she said, her voice low and frightening. "You do never tell her things like that again. Do you understand me?" Static answered first, then Moss's level reply.

"I am programmed to respond to questions honestly."

"Then reprogram yourself," Mummy snapped. "Lie if you have to. Protect her at all costs."

I looked between them, the machine and my mother, wishing I hadn't spoken at all.

Upstairs, Jazz leapt onto the bed, light for her age, and pressed herself against my side. Her purr rose steadily, louder than the silence, as if she could wrap me in it until the fear eased.

45

Saskia

Musée de l'Orangerie, Paris.

I wear red because Claudine never would. It is not a
statement, only resistance, a colour chosen for its
refusal. Luc notices, Zander does not, yet. Blood under
glass keeps its dignity, even before it dries.

Luc flew her in on the Falcon 8X, as though smooth engines
could soften spectacle. From her seclusion on Île d'Orléans,
where she folded herself into silence for more than a decade.
He oversaw every courtesy: cotton pressed, crackers im-
ported, and a vial of mist for the piano bench she abandoned.
He wanted her return curated, the way you prepare a shrine
for a saint. Love disguised as service. Still, his love, perhaps
more than mine.

The Orangerie lay closed to strangers, its hush made private,
its oval rooms bending like chapels that guardians had locked
for us alone. Pale stone, air chilled to a sacred cool, as if the

lilies themselves were fragile flesh. Monet's water held the light in suspension, more threshold than image. They had always been prayers of perception, but tonight they leaned toward warning.

The capsule positioned in the first oval was deliberate intimacy designed to look accidental. Guests spoke carefully, their tones subdued, as though stone could preserve or betray.

Claudine entered without announcement. Black silk, flat heels, and the upright pale cane that balanced her without glamour. No paint on her face, no concession to what we do to women in order to call them alive. She carried gravity, not style. Despite that, a trace of awe moved like a shiver through the room. Bodies shifted back. One does not crowd closeness to a relic.

Her face was a mask of restraint, but her presence unravelled restraint in others. The last time I saw her play, she had already cast fashion aside, favouring the small mercy of comfort over vanities. She could dismantle an audience without a single note and had once held Vienna in suspension simply by resting her hands mid-air. To lift her silence was to make it audible. That weight remains.

Zander felt it before he could look at her. His breath halved, ribcage drawn tight, refusal stamped across his body, though his gaze roved elsewhere. He did not move closer. Some figures are not ghosts; they are residue, part of the air. Claudine never departed; she lingered, refusing disappearance. A prodigy who once performed grief itself and then withdrew with the finality of a slammed door.

Mara is sharp like me, patient like Luc. I once caught her listening at the hem of a curtain, Dictaphone clasped, knees pressed to her chest as though silence was something she could steal piece by piece. She told me she would understand when she grew older. Not if, but when.

Dorian Tseng offered me his arm. I let him. His body carried itself like capital, his scent deliberate, a quiet intoxication. The charcoal suit was cut with such precision it could only have been hand-fed through scissors, with subtle grain and lines as exact as an equation. Oxblood monk straps, luminous from care, not excess. The platinum at his wrist did not gleam for attention; it breathed assurance. Hair black as lacquer, combed flat without sheen, not a strand grey. His age was kept, not surrendered. Cheekbones sharp, jaw ruled to symmetry. Eyes darker still, a void one could either answer or avoid.

This was not a man for introductions. His name entered before he did.

The Montclair's persisted in mistaking threat for decoration. I allowed their error.

The guest list remained stitched to a seam. Claudine's capsule could afford nothing careless; her ascent back into air was tailored with reverence, built to couture specifications.

Corky was already drinking, dragging fruit through something dark, with the kind of laughter that cloys, sweet until it sickens. His shirt hung open one button too far, a performance of relaxation, never harmless. He caught me; let a smirk catch too.

"Shame about Isa," he said, the sadness tuned, not felt. He'd always spoken of her as though she were a drink that had never crossed his lips.

Zander did not look when I entered. Still, he felt me. He always did.

I had chosen my shell that refused to appear as such: a

floor-length silk bias, blood blooming from carmine into oxblood. The line was cut strict, the collar high, the sleeves long, and jewels were avoided save the quiet platinum torque scored around my throat. Fabric that did not flash; it absorbed, holding light the way oil gathers it: slow, viscous, deliberate. My hair, a construction of indifference, piled too carelessly to be careless. That lie was the point.

Claudine's line was all restraint. I clothed myself in its echo.

Zander found me where he was meant to. The conservatory, glass walls, orchids poised and artificial in their perfection.

The conservatory holds its quiet like a sealed chamber. Glass walls breathe condensation against the air, orchids poised too perfectly, as though someone designed them rather than grew them.

I don't turn when he enters. I know him by his silence, by the heat of awareness moving before his body ever does.

"Didn't realise you'd RSVP'd," he says. Cold, clipped.

"I didn't." My gaze slides across the glass, twin reflections caught in it. "I came home."

"And brought a guest."

"Dorian isn't a guest. He's an asset." I give the word enough edge to remind him what it costs to discount me. "Learn the difference."

Behind me, Dorian's stillness sharpens. He knows his purpose, as I do. Stillness is louder than wealth. It unsettles Zander without ceremony.

He's dressed like a verdict: Cifonelli navy, an immaculate cut, yet the shirt betrays him, Meyer & Mortimer, pointedly beyond Luc's sanctioned houses. A gesture of defiance. A wound dressed in luxury.

I turn at last. Enough to register him. Enough to make him know he is seen.

"What did Maxime say to you?"

The question lands between us like glass shattering without sound.

His jaw shifts, but his voice doesn't follow quickly. The pause is telling.

"Everything and nothing," he says finally, smoke caught in his throat.

"Everything and nothing is Maxime's language," I answer. "He likes to believe he makes seams of what's tearing." My eyes rest on his collar, his cuff, fabric I could fix, but a body I cannot. "But seams fail."

His mouth tightens, and his eyes darken. "You would know."

A blade pressed flat, no blood yet drawn.

"You knew Luc didn't want you here," I say.

"And you knew my mother did." His voice lowers, quieter, more dangerous for its quiet. "You twist houses until they're knots. Don't act surprised when I'm caught in one."

I reach then, not to soothe, but to claim precision where he's let it slip. Collar straightened, cuff corrected.

"You've been looking careless."

"You've been looking." The reply costs him; I hear it in how his breath drags after.

Between us, the air tightens, the familiar ache we carry still raw. Desire sharp enough to resent, resentment sharp enough to disguise desire. Luc's name refuses to leave either of our mouths, yet he looms larger for the silence. He is what we do not say, the engine of distance pressed between us.

I step closer, one movement, no more. Cedar rises from his

collar. His pulse beats restrained against my nearness.

"If you're clinging to Maxime, Zander, it's because you believe in glue. But glue only darkens the cracks. Eventually, it fails."

His stare doesn't falter. "At least he still tries."

I hate the truth of it, hate that I want to swipe the admission from his lips instead of hear it.

"Maxime pointed you west, didn't he?" he whispers.

My silence is confirmation.

"You don't know about Wales?"

I lean in, close enough to feel his breath shift.

"What the hell is in Wales?"

I stay silent, letting the silence weld itself where nothing more should be said.

We say nothing. We know we cannot talk about this, not here. Silence always draws blood.

The conservatory glass at the entrance throws back the Paris streetlight, angles of reflection stacked over themselves until nothing feels solid. Orchids stand in their trays, placed as though curated rather than grown, perfection impersonating life.

Through the glass, a movement cuts. Mara. Her dress was light and untethered, and her hair was slipping down her back. At her side, Claudine.

A travel coat drawn loose over silk. Gloves fitted with precision. Cane aligned with her stride. She wears structure, not frailty.

I move quickly, heel striking marble.

"Excuse me. What is this? Where are you taking her?"

Claudine doesn't falter. Her eyes mark me with that absence

of effort only authority allows.

"Ah, the colour of coronation," she says, gaze resting on the red I chose. "Of course you knew I would be here."

"Answer me."

"The Corsican villa. For clean air. Cleared with Luc."

Mara glances up, her step half-paused, hesitancy caught between us.

"Well, no one cleared it with me."

Claudine's look is surgical, a cut delivered without touch.

"This, my dear, is a Montclair matter."

The words land harder than I allow my face to reveal.

"I am a Montclair."

Mara stands small beside her, embroidered bag in hand, my stitched lemon tree curling across the fabric. Her smile is light, too easy, as though none of this required her choosing.

"I have only been to the villa once," I say. "It was under-stood; no one went."

"Then we will not disturb your pattern."

And she moves forward. No pause, no reconsideration.

I don't follow.

Mara retreats back, her hand still knotted around the bag. The child who carries pieces of me doesn't turn.

Claudine pauses. Her gloved hand rests against Zander's chest, deliberate. She leans only enough to shape words low, in French, a murmur meant for his ear alone. I cannot catch them, only watch their shape and form against the air.

He does nothing. Does not bend towards her, nor step back. He looks like restraint carved into posture, a boy enduring a breath he has held for too long.

She straightens his lapel, a detail too intimate, too posses-sive to dismiss. Then the cane strikes marble once, decisive punctuation.

And she is gone. Silk flowing liquid, Mara tethered to her side, drawn through the lilies as if they belonged to her alone. The painted silence folds them in, their path sliding towards the Tuileries and into air I am barred from reaching.

* * *

Paris is grey in a way only Paris manages – elegant, deliberate, as though even overcast has been curated. It presses against glass, bleeds into bone. A shade I have always associated with Julien.

The evening has been a ledger of losses, one after another. When I knock, he opens without hesitation.

The 7th arrondissement exhales hush; he exhales quieter still.

Inside, books rise where portraits would have been. Margins dense with script, others left untouched, each aligned as if discipline itself were a barricade. Not a home. A fortress disguised as restraint.

He wears his usual retreat: navy cashmere rubbed pale at the elbows, with a white collar open but not careless. His hair curls softer than Luc's, is blonder, and is still boyish at the temples. Too soft to wield. He smooths it flat; I catch his hand. A reflex I know well, this instinct to erase the thing he cannot control. He started it young, after one of Luc's more operatic angers left him pale and emptied in the corridor. I had pressed water to his palm that day. I became his steadying glass. He never learnt steadiness alone.

He makes tea. He always makes tea. Ritual is his single rebellion, the only ordinary he has kept from being stolen.

We sit angled, not close, not far. Chairs in dialogue but not confession.

When he places the cup in my hands, I catch his wrist. Only lightly, but long enough for him to register it. A reminder that touch doesn't have to wound. Silence stretches but stays pliant.

He has always been too vulnerable to touch. The family laughed at it, exploited it, the quick flush across his cheekbones, and the blinks that betrayed awareness. They named him Lie: half his name, half a mockery, tossed across summer lawns at Lac Léman. He would smile, accept the burden of it, then replay the cruelty later, lips tightening on all the words he never returned. His manners have been both shield and cage.

All of us have lived under Luc's clock. Sons and wives, each tapping survival to his rhythm.

Julien raises his cup.

"We should toast."

I wait.

"To sins we inherited." The porcelain trembles in his hand. "You've heard?"

His eyes find mine. "Et?"

We drink. Tea as bitter as confession.

Rain traces its fingers down the window, the blur of a city dissolving. He watches me over the rim, eyes shifting from boy to man to heir without ever settling. Thirty-three, burdened with money, empire, and strategy. Still, to me, he is the boy whispering multiplication into locked air, trying to outpace Luc's fury.

I reach for him. My thumb against his cheekbone: light, familiar, dangerous. The same gesture I made when fever burnt through him years ago and he recited trades even in delirium. No one ever taught him that breaking is human. So I did. Over and over.

"Things will get strange," I murmur. "But you will hear me now. Whatever Luc takes, whatever name I am forced to carry, you do not lose me. I will not let them break you."

His eyes flare like glass hit by sudden light. Vulnerable, fractured, straining. He is everything at once, son: strategist, victim, salvage.

And I feel it: the possibility of him. The life I could build if I surrendered to gentleness, if I chose safety over fire. He could be the sanctuary, the second option, the man with whom I could stitch together something beautiful in the ruins.

But Zander is the flame that scars. He is what tears through my chest, what ruins silence with hunger.

Julien is not that. He is porcelain, rare, irreplaceable. The heirloom I have guarded for years. Whether he wants my hand or not, I will keep him whole. Even if my hand already itches for the fire elsewhere.

His eyes hold mine, unsettled but steady, the light fracturing across his face like glass caught in a storm. My thumb lingers on the crease of his cheekbone, tracing the faint shadow of stubble. I do not move, not yet, not before he can feel the weight behind my promise, the words I never voice aloud.

The silence between us deepens, thick enough to drown the bitter tea before us.

Then, quietly, deliberately, almost shyly, he closes his hand over mine. Not to claim, not to withdraw, but simply to hold. His palm is warm, the pressure grounding, a tether pressed against the skin of my wrist.

His touch means everything and nothing at once. Not a hunger, not a surrender. Just a pause, an offering held in fragile balance.

Beneath that subtle weight, I feel the tremor: the risk folded in the gentleness. It is no longer a boy's need but a man's definition of survival.

For a fraction of a breath, too brief to trust, too sharp to deny, the thought flickers. Another life, quiet and whole, one I might choose if I forget the fire that haunts me.

But I know what waits beyond that flicker. I know where flames burn fiercest.

46

Isobel (fragment)

As I look from my window, Paris holds its breath. Saskia is edging closer to the question of why Lucien Junior spends so much time in Wales and why 'Roussillon' insists on footing the bill. I have nudged her discreetly. She will reach it in time unless the distractions prove too pretty. Alexandre, for example. He has charm, but charm is a short-lived currency. I have seen it buy reprieves, never permanence. Their idyll already shows cracks.

Clara Sundström is no one's fool. She has seen through Camille Sarron's little stratagem and declined the invitation. A sensible refusal. Camille's kind prefer accommodation and agreeable silence.

I once refused such silence. I recall what followed.

Lucien, meanwhile, discovers what it is to be pressed into agreements not of his choosing. He has never relished concession. He prefers domination. Yet domination has a price, one his father paid in full. I keep the memory of those negotiations nearer than they would like. To find him on the back foot is a spectacle I cannot help but savour.

Poor sweet Mara overheard the inevitable whispers about his escapades with paid companions abroad. It is always the children who taste the truth before the adults surrender to it.

Young Noémie has returned from heartbreak sharpened, not softened. A woman rebuilt from loss is rarely safe to underestimate. Volant would be wise to remember that.

As for Étienne, I heard him at that falconry he imagines concealed. His voice carried clean as cut glass.

"And if it does not return? Then I chose the wrong bird."

Typical Étienne. Not the genial uncle the family prefers to display, but the other one, the man who never misplaces the knife and never pretends to.

And Claudine Morel has reminded them all that silence can crush as effectively as speech. At the Orangerie, she wielded her cane like a sceptre. I wonder whether she requires it at all, or whether it is merely another prop in her theatre. She won her scene, but the play runs longer than one evening.

I have lived long enough to know the difference. I watched men in the boardrooms learn it the hard way. After all, I was there when the first act was written. And though they preferred to write me out before the curtain rose, I am still here, terrifyingly lucid, with a better seat than most.

My dear boy, who visits me sometimes, says it feels like exile. I let him believe that. It is easier than explaining what exile truly is.

47

Camille

September, 3rd. Italian Grand Prix.

The air at Monza tastes of resin and petrol, a sharp tang that knots quietly at the back of my throat. Pines stand as ancient sentinels along the circuit, yet the engines tear through their silence like cavalry charging a forest. Outside, the Parabolica glistens under the late-summer heat, a crown of black asphalt forged for gods and their wagers.

Inside, the world softens, becomes velvet – velvet ropes, velvet deceptions. Aperol gleams in crystal chalices; prosciutto glistens on silver, each bite slicked with grease and half-truths. Chef Louvel has barricaded himself two floors above, a fortress built of knives and pride, forbidden to others. Luc's superstition: control the kitchen, control the legacy.

But I am not here for food. I am here for blood, for leverage hidden beneath smiles like sharpened blades.

Avery Trent moves through the terrace dressed in flawless black, her pulse steady as a metronome marking the rhythm of controlled chaos. She briefs journalists as if conducting an orchestra, each word measured, each question choreographed. I flick my chin ever so slightly, a signal she alone deciphers. The narrative is locked; the play begins.

Luc arrives first, a monolith in obsidian wool, followed closely by Étienne in stone-grey Nehru and Adèle, poised as if carved from marble. Together, they radiate sovereignty: untouchable, immovable. Or so the surface suggests.

But beneath, the board has shifted.

The seating plan lies rewritten, a new deck dealt. Zander's name, stitched unbidden into the programme as co-moderator, cuts like a fresh wound. Luc's eyes skim the paper once, unread yet feeling like a tremor. Étienne's smile flickers, taut as pulled wire, then smooths with practised calm. To all except me, the change is invisible, insignificant. To me, it detonates everything.

Zander steps onto the stage, unannounced but claiming the light, a predator sensing weakness. He speaks of innovation and access, legacy and doors swung open, each phrase honed with quiet venom. His gaze brushes the front row like a scalpel tracing old scars.

"The future of sport", he says, voice calm but immune to doubt, "is access. Legacy builds walls. We build doors."

Behind him, the slide blooms, shadows of labour and North Africa just edged enough to sting, a silent jab at Luc's empire. The Qatari beside Luc shifts, restless. The room leans forward with hungry eyes.

I sell them the myth they want: nostalgia wrapped in teeth, a woman laughing in a kitchen, boys before dynasties bloomed.

Applause follows me like tidewater; cameras pivot away from the Montclair men to me, the architect in shadow.

Luc's smile is tight and restrained, as if stretched over steel. Zander leans in, whispering something no one else can hear. Luc stands with measured grace, an invitation cloaked in polished veneer.

"Come, Laurette. Montclair belongs to all of us. Let us stand Montclair brands against the world."

Zander's eyes flicker briefly to my face, searching for a trap that does not reveal itself tonight.

The currents of this evening do not flow only across the room but pulse in the spaces between men I once thought tethered to me. Luc, founder and sovereign of the Montclair dynasty, was carved from obsidian and iron will, but even obsidian cracks under relentless pressure.

He studies the room from his seat, silence folding over him. His gaze finds me briefly. An old command or a plea veiled in authority? I meet it without a flicker.

Luc craves control as a starved man craves air. Yet I am no longer his weapon. I am the blade that turns against the hand that wields it.

Years spent as his strategist, his shadow, taught me well. I read the fractures beneath polished surfaces. He believes loyalty still binds me, that I remain a subject in his kingdom.

Loyalty is a currency. I spend it where the return is greatest.

Étienne's presence cuts sharper, more complicated. He moves through the terrace with practised ease, a stone warmed by fire beneath the jacket that conceals ambition and wields quiet threats.

He wants me because I am the thread to Faucon's old-world legitimacy, the voice that spoke truths he dared not utter.

"You still believe the brand is the legacy," I whispered once, soft but edged with meaning. "But the legacy is the leverage. You just never used it."

I saw his mask falter then, eyes flickering with frustrated admiration and something older, a shadow of regret. He weighs me as both a threat and a necessary ally, a delicate balance that I will tip when the moment comes.

Zander is altogether more volatile, a coil of reckless energy, with charm draped like a mask to cover fractures no one suspects.

He wants to understand me; I am certain. Worse than possession, worse than control.

I am the architect, as he says, the woman whose house he inhabits. But to understand me, he would need to confront the jagged edges I guard most fiercely.

He approaches after the panel, close enough that his breath stirs the quiet between us, a whisper brushing the edges of my resolve, a challenge wrapped in invitation.

"You think I am a gambler?" His voice was low, and a smile pulled tight and knowing. "I bet on the house when everyone else is all in."

I let my smile deepen, soft but sharp. The Falcon's smile.

"Power is a game of patience, no?"

We speak in riddles, each sentence a move on a chessboard only we can see. I glimpse the hunger beneath his fire, the desire not to own but to decode. And I wonder... if that hunger might be the one thing able to unseat even me.

The room remains a stage of velvet lies and sharpened edges.

I catch Luc casting a brief glance towards Zander, a flicker of something unreadable passing between them. Étienne's gaze cuts the space, waiting for a crack, a fissure to widen.

I am the quiet force between them, the balance measuring whether empires topple or hold steady.

And I watch, always; I watch.

I watch him, knowing that hunger is a weapon I must master, or it will be the thing that undoes me.

The long table gleams with crystal and knives, treaties disguised as toasts. The B-tables orbit like debris: Toby studying the centrepiece with a predator's focus, Corky dissolving in vodka fog, Horace whispering secrets to Davide. Gauche's chair remains empty, her absence a serrated edge all its own.

Étienne's glass rises; a signal lamp blinked quietly in a silver cufflink. His grin sharpens, reserved for select eyes only, an encrypted message. To any observer, the Montclairs appear aligned. To me, they are a fracturing constellation, each star tugged by unseen gravity.

The new seating cards glitter in the Italian sun like a knife's glint. I placed myself with precision, no flourish, no drama, just enough that when the lights rose, I would be centre frame, the fulcrum of the spectacle.

For one moment, the plan held. Luc's usual command flickered in his eyes, Étienne's grin twitched, and Saskia's gaze rippled like a stone tossed too near. I was thread-and-needle sewn into the moment.

Then she moved.

Saskia rose without hesitation, glass in hand, serene and unreadable. No fight, no lunge, only an effortless glide into the chair I had clearly marked for myself.

The air shifted imperceptibly, but I felt it fully. Cameras pivoted as if drawn by gravity, tides unyielding as they turned to crown her.

I laughed, barely a breath, brittle as ice, with a smile curved in the ruin of revolt, a smile no one believed. The room had seen the truth: I had been eclipsed.

By dessert, the photograph was already currency, with Saskia silently enthroned at the apex, and I was caught half-standing, caught between presence and absence, a ghost suspended within my tableau.

Queens do not wrestle for chairs; they allow you to stumble and then collect your spoils.

I smiled until the muscles ached, the edges of the grin cutting raw in stillness.

Later, the panel dispersed, applause fading to echoes. Toby drifted by, navy linen creased just enough to betray sleeplessness, Red Bull cap tilted with studied disinterest. His voice was thick with warning.

"Told him not to bet on emotion."

His words, slick with shared history, meant simultaneously for all and none. I caught every syllable.

Annina, already mid-anecdote, traded brand whispers like secrets in a coded language, a Red Bull reserve trying to exchange his watch endorsement for a Beaux Noirs black card.

"I gave him a card. Told him to have his agent spell Chronostrate correctly next time." Annie's tone was sharp and exact.

Mademoiselle Céleste sipped her third glass, poised and relaxed, an unassuming fortress in sand-linen and open collar, sleeves rolled, no jewels, no weight to anchor her. The sharpest blade on the terrace.

Saskia arrived then, with minimal makeup, hair pinned loosely in an imperfect knot, a charcoal wrap dress, and flats

– absence of show, presence of power. She did not speak, only looked at me long enough to slow the flow of words, to drain the air of pretence.

She sat beside me. Knees brushed mine, not by chance. Saskia wastes nothing that can be wielded and drinks in attention meant for others as though it were the last drop of air.

Céleste rarely drank in public, and here she was, relaxed, unspooling something interesting.

"I once spent three weeks in Tbilisi with a Russian pianist," she said. "He refused to speak English, even in bed. Claimed it dulled the senses."

I turned, waiting for Saskia's reaction. She didn't disappoint; it was a quick, silent laugh.

"He had the hands of a surgeon," Céleste added. "But absolutely no interest in precision."

Saskia almost choked on her drink.

Céleste caught my eye, just for a second. A glint, playful, defiant. She seemed to want someone to remember her past, when she wasn't always silent and stony. Then she looked away.

Adèle, across the way, scrolled through her phone, legs crossed and catching what light remained, long, smooth, and golden-brown, like a weapon resting quietly.

I knew Volant planned its AetherFlex launch days from now. A calm before the storm. I tasted the shift in silence.

Saskia leaned in, just close enough for me alone to see, a faint perfume trailing, jasmine sharpened with something darker.

"I used to think you'd ruin this family."

"And now?" I whispered.

She did not answer. Silence descended, tight as silk stretched over bone. The truth lies not in words but in what remains unspoken.

Hours later, alone in my suite, the headline burnt against the mirror's cold glass:

Volant – FIFA Bid Partner Le Point: The French Bid's Wild Card?

My robe split open, damp hair slipping over collarbone and spine, smoke drifting from distant balconies like whispered omens. Fingers absently toyed with the ring beneath the towel, tracing the cold metal beneath skin.

The article settled not as words, but as weight, a grit beneath my eyes. Not the headline, but the undercurrents it carried.

Yet it was not the headline that stoked the fire.

It was the memory, the private film kept locked beneath the surface: Zander, undone beneath me, caught unguarded, vulnerable.

My fingers danced over skin, methodical, measured, more scalpel than indulgence, a quiet confirmation. That it was I who held the hand of control.

Breath steady, uncluttered by desire. A smile pressed softly at the corner of my mouth, subtle recognition without softness or surrender.

The footage belonged to me. The camera caught him, not me.

That, I told myself, was leverage.

Yet the chair coup echoed behind my closed eyes, a silent eclipse. Even in solitude, Saskia's shadow clung, relentless.

I closed the robe, dried my hair slowly, and folded it strategically as one folds silk into steel.

I whispered to the mirror, voice low, almost a chant.

"You understand, no? I start fires without striking a match."

The glass stared back, unblinking, witness to too many flames that vanish only to flare again.

48

Saskia

The door is ajar, a thin blade of light cutting across the carpet. I ease it open, careful not to disturb the quiet shape crouched in shadow.

Mara sits cross-legged on the floor, using a chair for her sketchbook, fingers darkened with charcoal and doubt. The pencil flits, dashes, blurs, and returns, too intent to hear me at first.

I close the distance slowly.

"Zander", she's written in a hungry yellow, sprawling and raw, the pastel bleeding to edges frantic with need. Beside him, Luc stares back, dark hollows under a suit that holds no eyes, no mercy. A command without a face.

Her gaze flicks upward, startled, quick to shield the fruit of her unrest. Too late.

I linger a moment longer than I should, the yellow burning behind my lids when I blink.

I don't ask. Children always seem to see the truth adults don't dare speak.

"Bed," I whisper with gentle authority.

She obeys, disappearing beneath the duvet, the book pressed flat, fragile armour against a world too wild already.

"Aunt Clara will be close," I say, smooth and certain. "If you need."

I pull the covers with care, brush a kiss to the crown of her hair, and hold on just a second too long.

Out in the hall, I press my palm to my mouth, quiet, breath short. The colour yellow, Zander's light, it burns still, inviolate and impossible to look away from.

Zander's flat, Mayfair.

Music plays low, a hint, a cover for the spaces between. He stands at the window, barefoot even so, arms loose at his sides. The light catches his shoulder, bronze, raw, unfiltered. Something too real to stage.

The bag falls quietly to the floor.

"You're still his wife," he says, without turning.

"Only on paper." The truth slides out, sharp and bare. "Not in life, not in his house. Not in his bed."

He turns, filling the room with the weight of his presence.

"Hey." Softer than I mean it to be, testing, searching for fracture lines. "You might need some supper after your long day."

No smile. Just the slow cross of the room, certainty in each step.

Hands meet halfway. Warmth before words.

"Is this what you want?"

He nods, eyes soft in the dim light, an unspoken promise held between us.

We stay close, breaths mingling in the borrowed night. London fractures below us, sirens threading the wind.

"You deserved better than all of them," he admits, voice fragile.

"You're the only one who ever saw me," I whisper, breath catching like a secret.

"Never his queen," he murmurs, forehead resting against mine. "Always mine."

My thoughts are still caught between the truth of his words and the vastness they reveal, what he's chosen to abandon. Not just power, but a fragment of himself. Billions given away for a shard of something real, something fragile.

"But Volant, what does it mean?"

His thumb brushes my lips, soft and commanding.

"I made it easy for him."

I search his eyes, reading beyond resolve the quiet reckoning of a man who's stepped out of a long, dark shadow.

"I told him, 'I choose you.'"

"But—"

His touch silences; no argument is needed.

"That's where I've been. Saw him in Paris. Then Geneva. He returned for the launch. It's official."

His pulse held steady under my hand. Warm and real.

"It's just us now. The four of us."

"Four?"

"Mara... and the one you haven't named yet. The one sitting underneath it all, waiting, breathing. Keeping quiet until you let it surface."

I fill the space with silence, dense and delicate as stone on flesh. I ache to tell him everything.

"My tattoo," I whisper. "It says Yajun."

"Beautiful."

"It's my real name, Yajun means—"

He pauses me. A finger presses to lips, gentle authority, dangerous tenderness.

"I don't need to know."

I am left silent, stunned.

"I love Saskia, I love Yajun. I love Mara. That's all that matters."

Tears blur the room, the ache of joy held close, a quiet surrender.

"It's you I love, Saskia Lin," he said. "I love you."

"I love you, Alexandre," I breathed. "Wǒ ài nǐ."

He undressed me like an oath. No hunger in it. Just wondering. I felt the weight steady and gentle, like a promise unspoken but understood.

I reached across his broad, tanned chest and found the tattoo over his heart, the delicate script curling there, no capitals, no punctuation, just ink:

je serai silence où ton nom voulait vivre.

I traced the lines lightly with my fingertips, feeling the warmth beneath. Whispering in English, almost afraid to break the silence, I said, "I will be silence where your name wanted to live."

His gaze met mine, steady.

I swallowed the rest of my words, letting the quiet between us swell with promise.

His lips tasted of bourbon and late promises. I wanted to memorise him.

He broke first. I couldn't hold him any longer. He whispered, "Reste avec moi?"

My voice was softer than a secret. It wrapped around me, and I let go.

"Always."

He looked up. Eyes like dusk held in a glass of water.

Still.

Waiting.

I ached, not loudly, not visibly, but deep enough to know I was his now.

I always had been. The truth was there in the quiet, an undeniable tether pulling us through the dark.

His hands found my waist as if holding something sacred, not fragile, but familiar. I shivered beneath his touch, the electric warmth blooming slowly, like dawn pressing through cold glass.

His breath brushed my temple. Warm. Steady. The scent of him stirred a low, quiet ache in my belly, not lust, not comfort. Calmer, stronger. Like my body already knew him. I traced the line of his jaw with my fingertips, memorising the curve, the slight roughness against my skin.

I trailed my lips to the curve of her neck, feeling the steady thrum beneath. She pressed closer, a whispered urgency in the way her fingers curled into my hair.

The room shrank around us, sound, light, and time distilling to the shared warmth, the faintest sighs, and the pulse beneath flesh. Every touch was a conversation; every glance a promise not yet spoken aloud.

Her lips met mine again, slower this time, an unspoken vow that steadied and unravelled me simultaneously. I held her like a secret I was afraid to lose, the world outside just a

341

distant echo.

The weight of his chest against mine was steady. Not pressing, just there. Anchoring. I could feel the subtle rise and fall, like a grounding breath pulling me closer to the moment, to him.

His mouth brushed mine. Not hunger. Just reverence. A question asked in silence, answered with the warmth of my smile. I leaned into that sacred pause, letting the softness of his lips anchor everything unspoken between us.

Her breasts filled my hands, dusk made flesh, soft, full, the warmth of something stirring low in my gut. She moved like breath, unguarded. Radiant. For me.

The scent of her skin wrapped around me, subtle, like rain on dry earth, clean and urgent. I trailed my lips along her collarbone, tasting the faint salt of her.

Her fingers threaded through my hair, pulling me closer as if she needed the weight as much as I did her. There was no rush, only the slow reveal of a promise kept in silence.

Our breaths mingled, the space between us shrinking to nothing but trust and heat. Every touch, every glance, was a conversation, a confession of something too deep for words.

His thumb traced my lips. I leaned into it, letting the silence thicken, warm, and charged. I caught his scent: sunlit herbs, rain-washed heat, and molten uncoiling low inside me. Not sudden. Inevitable.

Between her thighs was warmth and shadow, the silk of her, softness and secrecy woven into every fold. She opened to me like velvet petals, wine-toned, humid with want.

I honoured every part, not with urgency, but with devotion.

I felt the weight of him along my hip, smooth, warm, pulsing with the ache I carried too. He didn't rush. He traced the soft curls between my legs like a map he knew but was learning, with wonder.

Her scent clung to my fingers, a soft musk lingering like a secret garden, rich with something only she carried. I pressed my forehead to hers. Breathed her in; she was the only air left. The only one that mattered.

His length fit me; the glide was slow. Reverent. A claiming without force. In that moment, I didn't feel possession; I felt presence.

Her hips rose to meet me, urgent but graceful. A welcome, not a plea.

Inside her, the world tilted back into place. No chaos. No proving. Just this, a homecoming in motion.

He moved within me like a tide on the shore. Rhythmic. Inevitable.

With every thrust, he wasn't taking; he was finding me. And with every breath, I let him in.

She tightened around me like language, unspoken yet known. Sweat shimmered between us. Her skin was very fair, smooth, and almost luminous. I was lost in it, not just the heat, but the belonging.

I opened wider, in body and in soul, letting him see the parts of me that had stayed waiting. We moved in a soundless rhythm.

Skin to skin.

Breath to breath.

The moment rose, not climax, but convergence. As if all the lost years had threaded themselves into this one breath, a single, perfect joining.

And when I spilt into her, it wasn't release; it was relief.

I came with a softness that surprised me, a surrender that wasn't weakness but trust returned. My thighs trembled around him. My lips parted, not in a cry, but in silence. The kind that means everything's right.

We stayed joined, the world shrinking to the hush between heartbeats. I rested my forehead against hers. Breath mingled, her scent on me, mine on her. No space left between.

I touched his face, sealing a vow. Fingers traced the lines I'd memorised in absence. His eyes held mine, not an apology, not a yearning, but the stillness of here. Now.

There was no need for words. The shape of our bodies said it all: two lines rewritten to meet again. And in the hush that followed, shared breath, steady heartbeats.

We didn't fall in love.

We remembered that we always were.

49

Gauche

Paris tastes like wet slate and perfume, the perfect backdrop for a war dressed up as a spectacle. Pretty, but not nearly enough. Tonight? Tonight's ours.

My father's on his way, to make an entrance, of course. Luc, ever the drama king, plans to unleash AetherFlex before the Paris press, every bloody spotlight fixed on his fragile throne. And there's Étienne, sliding his counter-launch in at the same damn hour, dragging the original tech, the one Luc filched and slapped a fresh brand on like some lying artiste. Paperwork? A joke. Ownership's about stomping your flag first. The world is watching.

It's ours. We're here to claim it.

I admire the precision, the surgical strike. Exactly what Luc would've done if he still held the cards. That thrill is like a shot to the heart, but poisoned. Because it's all family blood, twisted and rotten beneath the surface.

The suite is a chamber of quiet surfaces and cold, hard light. My black silk slip hangs on the wardrobe door like a battle flag, fabric that knows every curve, stretches with a hunger

I don't waste time denying. Steam fogs the mirror, clearing slowly, like reluctant truth. Smiles? I don't do that. I carve my mouth sharp, wipe the edges clean, and lift my chin, ready for war.

Mirrors are full of lies. I don't smile. I cut. Chin up, war dress tight.

Messages ping across every device, urgent chatter spills over three group chats, walk-ins, walk-offs, camera angles, and embargoes. Rhythm of a show that won't stop, even if the stage's a cage.

On the coffee table lie two things: Luc's launch folder, a cream card embossed like some royal decree, and my father's couriered envelope, plain but lethal. Inside? One typed page with timings to the second, a different livestream link, and his note, tight, brutal letters:

If he blinks, we do not.

The sharply tailored black blazer dress contours my frame, the structured pleats slicing through shadow and light. One sleeve gives way to a mesh of fine netting, a single gambit of texture in a game of precision. Hair slicked back, not for show but for function, my body a weapon honed for the fight ahead.

Outside, media vans hunch along the quay like the entire city's been waiting for this.

My phone buzzes sharply, once, twice, three clipped times.

Before I can reach it, a knock, firm. Final.

Annina stands in the doorway, grace and authority wrapped tight in a grey coat, clutching a folder like it's a weapon. No bag, no phone, just business and cold facts. She owns the room without trying.

I tap my ring once on the doorframe. My floor, not hers.

Behind me, a man stirs softly.

"What time is it?" His voice cracks, unearned, unready. The bedroom door shifts just enough for his eyes to catch Annina's. One long, measured second. No judgement, only a name added to the ledger.

Annina's voice slides over us smooth as oil.

"Luc's had a cardiac incident at his retreat nearby."

The words spill slick but don't stick.

"Cardiac incident," I echo, tasting the hollow. "Is he all right?"

"On his way to the hospital," she says, tight and clipped. "Word came from Dame Vivienne; she runs the retreat. Launch postponed; assets paused. Thought you should know so you can arrange your own postponement and get there."

The world shifts just enough to make the floor unfamiliar beneath my feet. "Wait, how did you—"

No answer. Just the dry clatter of logistics, timelines, briefings, and private jets for family. The machinery behind the curtains grinds on without pause.

Annina's voice softens, steel barely masked. Then she's gone. No goodbye, no glance. Just the whisper of the door falling like a curtain.

I stand still. The room fills with the drip of a faucet no one fixes, a stubborn beat that refuses to quit.

My guest shifts. Cotton rustles. A hand brushes my hip, an offer I don't accept.

"You're somewhere else," he says.

"I'm exactly where I need to be," I reply, cold enough to freeze the space between us.

He doesn't press. The silence between us carries a weight no words could ever match.

I move to the window. Across the Seine, the venue blinks alive, a glass box lit from its bones. Riggers scuttle over trusses like spiders weaving a trap. Inside, I know every detail: a black and chrome stage, a catwalk that leads nowhere, curved screens looping branding, mute, volt-white letters floating over dark velvet. Rows of chairs sliced like graded teeth, placards stamped like prison stencils. A plinth, glass hood, and white gloves waiting for their moment. Champagne beads sweat in buckets, nervous energy trapped in bubbles. A model walks flat with a spine set to a metronome.

Our secret space is smaller, sharper, a hushed former auction house, walls stained with ghosts. Floors scrubbed clean of history, lighting cold and unwelcoming. Brand logos stripped from signage. A server feeds a stream no one suspects, every hand sworn to silence.

I call my father. One ring, crisp connection.

"Noémie."

"They say Luc's had a cardiac incident," I say, voice clipped, brittle like shattered glass. "Annina's postponing theirs. Press waiting".

Silence thick with calculation.

"We delay," he says. "A day, a week, it would look—"

"Like weakness," I cut him off, knife-edged. "Cameras don't blink. Morality's theatre for men chasing applause. This tech? Ours. We don't wait for another man's heart to start. We set the rhythm."

His voice rises once, a shockwave hurled across the line.

"You're excited."

Approval clutches me by the throat, twisting pride into fire and ash.

"Yes," I admit, sharp and dangerous. "I am."

"That's good, but we delay. That's final."

Click.

The line dies. I'm left with my breath, slowing now.

The black armband was left out 'just in case', the family's grief merchandised and distributed like company swag: fashionable mourning for an empire already bracing for the worst. It makes me sick that they could plan for tragedy so efficiently, hope shelved somewhere behind the quarterly reports.

I send my guest away. He dresses like a man who knows he shouldn't stay. At the door, he mutters something about hope. I smile. He will forget the truth by morning.

The lift hums. My phone blooms with condolences; halfhearted, manufactured, and transactional. Words from those who have never loved without an invoice.

Outside, Paris slides past in films of light and wet stone. Sirens brayed, a constant undercurrent.

The venue pulses, security sorting names with cold precision. Inside, the air breathes wealth and control. Moss walls pulse life into stone. Velvet ropes choke the space. Ushers in black read wrists like they were scanning souls.

Onstage, a man tests the reveal, hands hovering like he's touching the future itself.

Beneath the glass hood, our piece waits. Silent, heavy, a small revolution shaped like technology set to heat rooms and ignite industries.

I circle the space. Texture, glass, reflections, flight cases. Staff move with quiet synchronicity, choreographed by a hidden score.

The production manager rushes by, white sneakers pounding, clipboard and fake smile in tow.

"Concrete. Cardiac incident. Retreat." The words fall like costumes worn poorly.

"We keep our slot," I say, voice steel, calm. "Live at the start. No tribute. They pulled theirs, that's their call."

She nods, relief and fear tangled on her face.

In my ear, the ghost of my stage manager crackles through.

"Feed's up in fifteen. The model's ready. Copy updated. Your father's inbound."

The new script waits in my inbox, a boardroom compromise, morals bleached away. I read cold and don't hear myself. I hear the weight in his voice instead.

I slash adjectives and erase 'future', 'brave', and 'survivor'. Leave raw truth, the only currency I recognise.

In the green room alone, the armband waits, black, mute. I lift it once, then again, then throw it into the corner.

"Putain!"

The phone interrupts me.

"Gauche," Annina's voice cuts through the silence. Calm but firm. "The hospital's report shifts from stable to not, then stable again. Dame Vivienne's there. The family's coming. We announce the delay soon."

"Thank you," I say flatly, my voice stripped of feeling.

She pauses, not with pity, but with quiet respect, something unreadable.

"I didn't ask if you're all right?"

Her question unsettles more than the news. I snatch a truth I don't want to own.

"I don't know."

"Do what you came to do."

And she's gone. The room swells and then shrinks.

Palms press to knees; I count eight. Then stand.

Downstairs, the press line swells. Whispers crawl like heat on steel. A man murmurs 'Montclair', a prayer lacking faith. Two women from tech huddle close, eyes locked on the clock.

"Torture." The word flies like a thrown knife, wrapped in tales of Luc's retreats, self-punishing cleanses that bruised his hands blue. People like pain; they believe it breeds change and nobility.

I scribble a note:

Never sell suffering as a product.

At the motherfucking minute, the house lights settle. Screens cut to black. Silence hangs, not quite silence, but a breath held tight, hungry for cracks.

I step forward. The stage is open like a field, wide and bare. The glare carves me into the shape the cameras demand.

I speak, words sharp and deliberate, the order mine, not theirs. I say what AetherFlex is, naming labs, hands, and sleepless nights folded into truth.

At my cue, the camera splits. Our secret room blooms open. The plinth wakes.

The model strides, deliberate, unbreakable. Glass rises. The shoe gleams, small as a lie, heavy like a promise.

My phone buzzes wildly in my pocket, once, twice, and a third clipped beep. I shouldn't look.

But I do.

From Father:

Stop this. Now!

From an unknown number:

ICU.

From Annina:

Board before press.

Stage lights press down, carving the dress to my skin. The room breathes around me. For a moment, I lose my voice. I hear the hum of the crowd, a quiet exhale where fear meets lust.

I finish. Applause bursts. The screen blacks out to the brand's mark. The hostess thanks the guests; all the words for the 'go now' line up like sentences.

Back in the green room my phone rings. Father, again.

"You went ahead?"

Silence was my only reply.

"Good. I'm proud, Noémie. You set the narrative. Noise comes, then fades."

I lean back against the wall. Cold hits skin I didn't know was exposed.

"I did what I came to do."

"Annina always had more sense than the men she serves," he says. "Stay out of hospital cameras. They love wet eyes. Let someone else drown."

"What if he dies?"

The question feels like a stranger in my mouth.

"Then the market will correct. No sentiment."

Click.

Clean exit.

Hairspray smokes the air, a copper bite mixed with florist water's sharp sting.

I do not cry.

Luc's retreats flood my mind: pain worn as discipline, cold plunges he bragged about, fasting that hollowed him out. He believed endurance was alchemy.

I think back to the first time Luc touched AetherFlex and said, 'ours', but meant 'mine'.

Now it is mine again.

Outside, the venue empties. Rumours coil in the dark like smoke.

A single message pings, a punctuation mark from a woman who only speaks in symbols once the work is done.

I type three words. Delete. Rewrite. Don't send.

I don't know who I am yet. I don't know who I'll be tomorrow, when the headlines pick their verbs.

I'm excited. Proud. Cold. Not ready.

The armband remains on the floor.

50

Julien

The venue's bones lay bare, echoes folding through the vast space like a cathedral's lament. Damp air seeped through cracked loading doors, turning the stone floor slick and cold; a scent of wet asphalt mixed with something faintly metallic, like old money oxidising. Velvet shadows clung in corners, swallowing secrets that pulsed quietly beneath polished surfaces.

I stepped onto the stage barefoot, shoes swinging loosely in my hand. Each tentative step pressed and erased itself on the black gloss, a signature both marked and forgotten. It was, in a way, a reflection of my place here: present but unseen, threading the margins of this family's empire.

Numbers churned relentlessly in my mind. Market losses are mounting. Montclair shares are down 4.6%. The empire's pulse faltered beneath the surface, and no charm or board-room cunning could mask that decay.

A flicker of alerts rippled through my phone, a relentless drumbeat of doom. Volant S.A loss climbing, AetherFlex trending down, ICU updates, whispers circling like vultures.

I flipped the phone face-down but could not quiet the data crashing through silence. Losses coiled through pain; pain cycled back into capital.

The cuffs of my crisp white shirt peeked out beneath the tailored navy jacket, sleeves just a whisper too long. I smoothed them, hesitant to draw attention yet unable to subdue the self-conscious moment of polish and correction. The silence pressed, but I played the part – cool, calculating, the tactician who reads fear better than most.

On the dressing table, a black armband lay waiting like a scar, coiled around itself as if hiding its own grief. My thumb traced its surface thoughtfully, a quiet ritual of reckoning.

In the window's reflection, my face looked pale, my rust-coloured hair a defiant note against the stern darkness surrounding the Montclairs. The mirror offered no approval, only an aloof stranger staring back.

The colour of my hair was its own indictment, a verdict I carried on my head. Every glance said *bastard*, no matter the surname on my passport.

A knock on the door. Mademoiselle Céleste entered, wrapped neatly in camel wool that absorbed light like a shadow. No greeting, no preamble.

"ICU," she said sharply. "Two stabilisations, now sedated. No phones. No flowers. The media swarm the hospital. Board meeting at eight."

Her eyes flicked to the black armband, measuring, the chill arithmetic of the empire we share.

I forced a polite nod.

"Thank you."

Her voice softened only for a heartbeat. "You held the launch. That counts."

Not praise, but a note tallied in an account.

For a moment, she hesitated. Then, without warning, she stepped forward and pulled me into a hug: long, firm, and almost reluctant. The weight of her arms was unexpected; the contact stretched the moment until discomfort flickered beneath my skin.

I stiffened, uncertain of how to respond. Her hold was heavier than any word spoken, an unspoken kindness or perhaps a reckoning neither of us dared voice.

When she finally let go, there was a softness in her eyes I had never seen.

"Where's Zander? Shouldn't he be doing all this?" I managed, breaking the silence.

"He's... unreachable."

I tried to breathe levity into the copper taste of the room. "Fate keeps impeccable books... Too clean, too precise."

Céleste's smile was fleeting, an acknowledgement of the unspoken calculus. "Maybe a man who believes pain accrues interest, paying down a final balance."

"Will you go to the hospital?"

"He wants me not to."

"And will you?"

I looked away, swallowing the hesitation. "I don't know."

She left, leaving a quiet void filled only by the soft hum of my own conflicted heartbeats.

Uncle Étienne arrived like weather, dry, cold, and implacable. After a brief hug, he took his place by the exit, a sentinel dressed in calculation.

"Board at half-past eight. We set the narrative: deny, delay, disrupt. No apologies. No sentiment. They say theft; we say provenance."

I bit the inside of my cheek. "And the man in the ICU?"

Étienne's silence was a stone dropped into still water.

The first journalists slipped in shortly after, panic in their footsteps. Florists stripped petals for photo backdrops with clinical precision, grief reduced to props.

Then a voice, smoky with regret, cut through the dampness.

"Still counting percentages, Tonton? Father's heart isn't a balance sheet."

I spun.

Maxime: the ghost from the past rendered flesh. His hair is longer, darker, and falling in unruly waves. His coat was worn but defiant. Eyes stormed, haunted, sharp, alive.

Étienne tensed, fury beneath an icy mask. "If you've come for forgiveness, you won't find it."

Maxime ignored him, fixing me with a look that collapsed years into a single moment.

"I didn't come for forgiveness. I came to see if the old bastard is still breathing."

His voice softened, just for an instant.

"Don't let them tell you absence is death. I've been gone, not dead."

My throat tightened; words caught at the edge of a long-buried fracture.

Maxime leaned closer, voice a blade.

"You owe no loyalty but to yourself. When they try to spend you like a chip, remember that."

And then he was gone, swallowed by mist and gravel-slick streets, leaving only the faintest trace of bergamot and tobacco smoke behind.

Étienne broke the stillness. "We walk. Eight-thirty."

I pulled on my shoes, heavy as lead, steps uncertain on a wet stone that would leave no record. But inside, a slow fuse was burning. Something urged me not just to observe but to act.

* * *

Back in my flat in the 7th Arrondissement, the blinds were drawn tight against the dawn; I sat alone amid scattered papers and half-written emails. The apartment, nestled in one of Paris's most elegant districts, held the quiet weight of history, with walls lined with faded grandeur and the faint hum of the city slipping past cobbled streets below. The light was muted, as if reluctant to invade the stillness.

My laptop glowed with the unsent message to Lucien, each word a fragile bridge stretched over years of silence. I reread the draft, hesitation clinging to every line. The words spoke of truth and pain but also a vague, trembling hope. My fingers hovered over the keys, then retreated, as if afraid to claim the power in confession.

The weight in my chest shifted suddenly, a familiar thrum of sensory overload squeezing my temples. The low hum of distant car horns and the murmur of early traffic filtered beneath the closed windows, blurring into a disconnected cacophony. I rubbed my temples, trying to steady the storm inside, the quiet torment of being watched, judged, yet unseen.

For now, I just concentrated on breathing and waiting for the world to shift beneath my feet.

Then, my phone buzzed sharply on the lacquered table, jarring in the stillness. I glanced down: Annina, Volant's

Chief Legal Officer.

I answered without hesitation.

"We've been instructed by the lawyer in Geneva to view the updated will, in case Luc is incapacitated." Annina's voice was low but urgent.

My breath caught. "Go on."

"I need to see you. Can I come round?"

"Of course. I'm in."

"I know. I'm outside."

My eyes flicked to the window, heart pounding. The quiet rebellion I harboured had just found new footing, the kind that might finally crack the Montclair empire's icy facade.

I stood and moved to open the door.

Annina stood framed in the doorway, smartly dressed in an impeccably tailored blazer, her posture stiff, the faintest hardness at the edges of her smile.

She stepped inside, eyes sharp as crystal.

"What were you expecting, Julien, if ever there was a will reading?"

I swallowed, voice steady despite the tempest inside.

"Well, Alexandre is the heir apparent, the golden boy... So hopefully, I'd be trusted and tested with more. I mean..."

Annina's gaze narrowed.

"And would you be ready for that?"

Her pointed repetition made me question her intent; a silent challenge hung heavy between us.

"Yes," I said firmly. "I think so."

She gave a slow nod, the smile tightening into something unreadable.

"The board wants me to report back if you're ready for that."

I met her eyes, the weight of an unspoken verdict pressing

down hard.

"Annie, what is going on?"

"Are you ready, Julien?"

"Yes."

"Good answer," she said, her voice almost a whisper.

"We're going to need you, Julien."

For a moment, the room held its breath, a promise of power intertwined tightly with the threat of sacrifice.

And I, the perpetual outsider, felt the first flicker of choice pulse deep in my veins.

51

Isobel

The vellum curls at the edges, watermarked by years. Ink endures. Words are stubborn; they outlast the authors. From here, I have seen enough: dinners dressed as diplomacy, children paraded like heirlooms, and women mistaken for shadows until they refuse the role. I record it all quietly, line by line.

I am Isobel Fairfax, eighty. Which grants me candour.

I do not write from spite. I write from memory. Memory, the one inheritance they could not steal, though they tried.

So I keep watch. And if my account reads like theatre, that is only because they lived it like theatre, cast in costumes of power, blind to the curtain falling.

The archive is complete. They can read it if they dare. They never like mirrors.

You built empires from whispers. I am the whisper you never silenced.

The curtains breathe faintly in the draught. I never cared for theatrics, but one must bow to metaphor on occasion. Behind curtains, behind veils, behind the fictions spun for me, this has been my life these past twenty years.

They called me dead. The vanished doyenne.

A step in the corridor. Timid, then sure. Saskia Lin, at last.

"Ah, there you are, dear," I say. "What took you so long?"

She freezes on the threshold, pale and taut, hand lingering on the frame like a frail promise. Every inch the woman I have been waiting for. I motion to the chair opposite.

"Sit."

My maid sets down a tray with tea and neat pastries, nothing extravagant. Civility in the face of outrage has always suited me better than fanaticism. We sit by the window, the view a quiet refuge: ash trees lining the grounds, leaves fracturing light into restless patterns. Survivors, those trees.

Ash, my loyal whippet, pads in from the corridor, a ghost cloaked in velvet. He rises at Saskia's presence, ears sharp, ribs like thin parentheses in the lamplight. Then, indifferent, he settles, chest rising and falling in quiet cadence.

"I named him after the trees," I say. "Ash. Elegant, stubborn, quick. It comforts me to have one at the window and one at my side."

His nose presses into my palm, insistent with the purity of touch unburdened by expectation or transaction. I scratch behind his ear, velvet to velvet, balm for harder truths. Saskia's eyes shift, caught between the solid weight of the trees and the soft life at my feet; her composure falters for a breath, so brief it might have been missed.

"Don't mind him," I add. "He's the only creature here who doesn't lie."

Her gaze follows mine to the grey-green canopy beyond the glass, but she says nothing. The silence is a salve. Some truths demand space to breathe, a stillness where secrets can settle.

"Saskia, don't be alarmed. This is..." I savour words like rare wine. "I am on your side. I wanted you to find me."

Her lips part, quelling a question unspoken, a promise hesitating between us.

"I know," I say, sparing her the enquiries best left unanswered. "They exiled Maxime for finding me, mon petit dernier. Which only proved how little they understood either of us."

"In exile, he visits..." My hand gestures are airy and delicate. "Each night, across a Go board's grid, black and white stones are placed with the patience of conspirators. He calls me Grand-mère Renarde: half mockery, half devotion. I let him win just often enough to hold his faith."

Her voice drops, cautious, threading the line.

"And he visits here too?"

"Oh yes. Four years now. Engaging, beautiful isn't he?"

"He is."

I cut through her uncertainty. "Maxime was forced into exile because he found me. Tenderness was his crime. Luc never wanted him near the boardroom – too soft, too sharp, apparently. Balls! That's what I told Luc myself. So he dispatched Maxime as he did me. And the rest of you chose the easier lie."

Her eyes fall to the floor, apology carved into every inch. "I'm so sorry."

"Not you, dear. You've only been here for the past fourteen years."

The pause hangs impenetrably in the quiet.

"So... Luc has been visiting you?"

I don't answer immediately. I top up tea, fingers lingering

on Ash's fur, letting the weight of the moment stretch, prickling at the edges of the room. Then, with a faint smile distant as dawn, I finally speak.

"Oh yes. Regularly, as you now know. I wanted you to see the helicopter heading west instead of east, so I tampered with your messages, yours and Clara's. A little rebellion on my part. Clara is a force, by the way. Keep her close."

Saskia's knuckles blanch against the untouched teacup, her breath shallow until the colour slowly seeps back into her face.

"The Roussillon was Étienne," I say. "He paid for the sanatorium. Once no one came, Ty Cefn ceased being an asylum and became my executive spa retreat instead. Splendid, really. I have everything I need."

"And Maxime?"

"He taught me to listen to all those personal AIs the men have substituted us for. Everything is there if you have patience. Time is my sole companion now. Not all, of course; your basement project defies me, tangled in that cursed Faraday cage. But I can work it out."

I place a Go stone between us. The click punctuates like a verdict.

"So my boys buried me to silence me. Once Étienne Senior passed, they deemed me a liability. My heart fractured before their verdict. It was simple enough to manufacture notes and prescriptions for melancholy and then hide me away, calling it suicide. Who would doubt?"

Her voice breaks, soft, irreparable. "I'm sorry, Isobel."

I tilt my chin, eyes steady and unyielding.

"Don't apologise. They bred us to apologise so they might feed uninterrupted."

My gaze anchored hers.

"Luc visits me, Étienne pays for it, yet has never set foot in this room. So tell me, Saskia, which one of my sons is the monster?"

The silence settles like dust between us, a question heavier than any answer could be.

52

Isobel

My heels strike oak, no opera, no curtain call. Only facts remain standing once the performance fades. Silence trails me into the Chelsea house, a better company than applause; applause can always be bought.

Céleste, naturally, breaches the quiet with news sharp as a scalpel.

"Lucien and Étienne Montclair have stepped down, pending a board vote. They will not return."

There is no surprise. This was the only ending left to them once I reminded them what I remember.

I reviewed Dorian's memo earlier. Stripped of sentiment, as it should be. Resignation phrased as routine procedure. The sort of language that keeps shareholders calm and reputations from openly bleeding.

I let the quiet hold. Lucien and Étienne never learnt its weight. They mistook noise for strength and distraction for safety. That was their first error.

Lucien cites "health reasons". Convenient. His real condition is fear, of the athlete they failed to save, of the body concealed in panic, of the night they thought would stay buried if they buried me with it.

Étienne "retires to focus on his vineyards." He never tended to anything. He maintained façades. Including the one in the sanatorium where they placed me for twenty years so my recollection wouldn't interfere with their lives.

They are stepping down because I required it, because the truth did not erode in confinement. Because I walked out with every detail intact.

Their downfall is not revenge. It is a consequence. And consequence, unlike them, does not waver.

Alexandre slipped from the will. Paid enough to stay quiet, never enough to mend. The price of being Luc's son but not his heir is knowing exactly when to turn the blade, with grace, naturally.

Julien holds the crown now. Annina asked if he was ready. Readiness is a fiction; the seat consumes immediately. Céleste shows her pride in him in the smallest flicker. No one else sees it. I do. I miss nothing.

Maxime returned from exile. Kindness bars him from the throne. It is too rare a quality in this lineage, but it positions him well to repair what the rest of us fractured.

Claudine walks again, cane abandoned. Her confinement is over. Silence served her long enough. Silence is never surrender.

Noémie at thirty, CEO. A poet forced into command. Camille remains the steady hand at her shoulder. Loyalty reveals itself under pressure; she will be tested.

The pieces moved. Every shift is audible only to those trained to wait, to endure, to strike once the field clears.

Toby Greaves removed. Kevin Price outmanoeuvred by Americans. Under:CORE collapsed. AetherFlex was stripped and restored to Faucon Futures, its rightful origin.

Interpol misplaced Leila Farrow in Tangier. Runaways always orbit home. That is their flaw.

Hortense Valois persists. Archivist, never architect. Collateral, forever. Grief was logged in the system as an ongoing deduction.

Each detail is a stone placed with absolute precision. No sentiment. Only position, consequence, and the pattern they create.

I scan the room: Félix, flint, sharp but spent. Clara, folder finally closed, CFO by attrition. Saskia, a glacier, not a statue, poised at the helm.

The air holds a breath, waiting for the knife to sink deeper.

"Both families have agreed on an unofficial settlement. A lump sum trust for the Christine Okonjo Academy," Céleste added.

The name hovers awkwardly, like smoke in a room full of secrets.

I smile faintly, amused despite it all.

You see? Nothing disappears. Not even a girl buried twice, once beneath earth, once beneath archives. Now she'll have a building and a legacy.

The tea was tepid in their hands. They watch, expectant, as if I'd orchestrated this tableau. I merely keep minutes.

'Legacy', I say, 'is not inherited; it's taken. The truth is yours, but the invoice arrives along with it. Settle up, or excuse yourself.'

No applause follows. They understand the preference.

And I, still here, still breathing, am the proof. You don't

vanish if you refuse to.

53

Saskia

Winter, Perpignan.

The Bench. The original Montclair atelier. Not a name anyone beyond our circle would know. We kept it that way. From the road, the house collapses against the hillside like a shadow, low, unassuming, almost ashamed of the weight it carries. Roof lines step unevenly toward the river, tiles dulled to slate, ivy strangling half the eastern wall. The "M" carved deep into the door is less a mark of pride than a ghost, faint and fading.

Above it, a rusted plaque clings stubbornly to the frame.

Montclair & Fils, Bottiers. Depuis 1921.

No welcome here. Only endurance.

The door is obstinate, always has been. Lucien Senior prized resistance. Céleste leans in, pressing; the wood scrapes with a sharp exhale before it grudgingly yields on the third try.

Inside, nothing stirs but the last gold of the autumn turning to winter; fractured light slices through the stairwell, throwing interlaced shadows across the vault floor. Dust, the acrid scent of burnt glue and older, deeper deceptions.

We enter one by one. Mademoiselle Céleste leads, her steps decisive. I follow, just close enough. Clara's eyes hold calculation, measured and cool. Mara's restless gaze already spins headlines, maps out futures. Isobel Fairfax falls last, her silence a benediction heavy with unspoken intent.

This is ours now. The atelier, the land, the skeleton of a factory once alive with a mechanical choir.

My phone pulses with Dorian's filings, patents locked tight beneath Moss AI's shield. Clara's already unspooled the shell companies like threads in a web. Félix has half-begun styling the launch party, with DJs catalogued for Perpignan's ascent to global currency. The space is heavy with Isobel's quiet, solemn and sure.

Her fingers brush a groove worn deep by years of labour.

"He left us a spine," she murmurs. "Do not squander it."

Mara lingers last, drawn in by curiosity's pull. She bends; a sketch slipped from the clutter catches her eye, a perfect line in the wood, too clean for accident. Her fingers press it, and a panel breathes open. A narrow drawer slides free; a child's hiding place, a secret kept.

Inside, cracked leather bundles tightly fold a piece of parchment and a sliver of jet-black fabric, sealed beneath glass. Lucien Senior's hand commands the top:

Montclair/V2. Pas avant 2000 N/cm^2.

Margin notes carry a biometric ID from a sealed trial.

Mara's eyes scan, her voice low and reverent.

"A weave that breathes with strain, carbon-reactive, biomechanical. A fabric that reads tension, flexing in micro pulses."

Not only for feet.

Even behind glass, the swatch bleeds warmth, alive beneath her touch. She whispers the margin's promise under her breath:

Le tissu lit la tension musculaire. Corvelle ajuste la charge...

Her glance flickers to the boots resting on the bench: one finished, one half-stitched, silent decoys.

What Lucien Senior left wasn't footwear. It was a fuse. She just struck the match.

Five shadows gather under the dying light. Above, tools lie breathless, waiting.

Clara shifts stance, eyes still on the fabric.

"If this is real," she says quietly, "there isn't a number high enough, not in euros, not in dollars."

Silence. Isobel seats herself at the bench where her husband once toiled.

"Then let's be dangerous."

The bench exhales.

Our house, their house, breathes again.

I survey the boots, the table, the fragments of a legacy lost and the raw potential left to sculpt.

I imagine Mara here someday, tracing the leather with small fingers.

Not wondering what it is for.

Knowing what it means.

54

Saskia

Epilogue.

Autumn 2024, Perpignan.

The lights devour everything ahead of me, turning the rest of the world into silhouettes and distant possibility. The dress is black and strapless and cut low enough to remind them I am not afraid of being seen. The bodice is beaded, each curve stitched to catch the light without apology. At my throat, a single black choker with a square-cut stone. Nothing fluttering, nothing soft.

Armour disguised as elegance.

It's not the launch I'm afraid of, not really. It's that I can feel every eye in the world stretching for evidence of doubt, of nerves, of something to dismiss. Volant's board, Laurette's lieutenants, and the trade press gagging for failure. I know what they're hoping to see: that I'm still the outsider, borrowed, breakable, just wearing the crown for a day.

My pulse hammers in my wrists, sweat gathering at my spine. The heels I chose feel heavier than steel, but each step is deliberate. This stage isn't borrowed. It is mine.

Beyond the curtain, Zander's outline steadies me, his nerves hidden behind that wide, disarming smile. If anyone believes in SōMA more purely, it's him. To him it was never just a name: *the body as distinct from the soul, mind, or psyche*; it was design and will colliding. His confidence fills the gaps in my own. In the first row, Mara sits, face dappled in blue light, hugging a sketchbook to her chest. She's so much of my heart it hurts to look at her, brilliant, strange, and braver than she'll ever believe. I am here for her, for all the daughters whose names get mispronounced, whose designs get filed away unseen.

I think of Clara, steady as steel, whispering fallback plans through sleepless nights. Of Isobel, returned, stiller than marble, eyes full of prophecy and ghosts. And the twins – Aïcha and Safi – restless brilliance in their bones, already rearranging the next gameboard in their heads.

Behind me, the weight of women who pulled me through, who stood their ground when the world sharpened its teeth. Sisterhood, not strategy, built this moment.

The crowd hushes, a sea of intent. The future ripples just outside my reach, alive, trembling, ferocious.

I breathe; not a single man in my peripheral vision could take this from me.

I step into the white blaze, owning every eye upon me. The curtain lifts.

The promo rolls, abstract fabric morphing with sound, and patterns blooming like wings. The first SōMA prototype: proof that the body is not a limit, but a beginning.

Aïcha and Safi take the stage, voices alternating in perfect counterpoint. Aïcha, in her striped dress, radiates sharp intent, her gaze direct, her words clipped and precise as she breaks down the lattice of AI and design with the authority of someone twice her age. There's a spark of defiance in her stance, like every syllable is an argument won.

Safi, in black, carries the warmth between them. Her smile softens the edges, her cadence fluid as she speaks of values, legacy, and belonging. Where Aïcha slices, Safi steadies. Together they braid logic and conviction, dazzling the room.

The other lays out the values, impact, legacy, and belonging. The cadence is hypnotic. Applause builds, charged, electric.

Then Mara is led forward. Twelve going on thirteen, coltish limbs, hair tucked back from a face still undecided between girlhood and something sharper. She blinks into the light, her shy smile faltering before it steadies. The crowd softens instantly. She raises one hand in a small wave, awkward and delighted, then vanishes into the wings again.

The twins follow, leaving me alone in the blaze. A rostrum rises. The applause peaks.

The Q&A begins.

I lean forward, one spotlight, dozens of hands.

A journalist is chosen. Older. Chinese accent. His voice was calm but cutting.

"So, Saskia, you left Shantou in the middle of the night to start a new life. Has it all been worth it... *Yajun*?"

Silence.

Shutters click like rain.

I breathe in. My shoulders remain still.

I smile.

Just barely.

"Every second."

The screen cuts to black.

About the Author

I grew up in Manchester, where the streets know how to keep secrets. Now I live somewhere quieter, where the clouds move without asking anything of me. The years before this were shaped by two very different worlds: the rigid discipline of the military and the restless hum of London's media machine, both places where truth slips beneath the surface like a whispered gravitas you're never quite allowed to untangle.

Now, I write. Mostly alone, but there's always Bob, my rescue dog, whose instincts are sharper than most people's judgements. We move through the hush and clutter of rooms like a quiet pact, both attuned to what remains unspoken.

Not everything gets locked away. Some things choose when to be found.

You can connect with me on:
⚯ https://www.goodreads.com/author/show/37350284.A_J_Bannerman

Also by AJ Bannerman

Terminal Countdown

Time is fracturing, and MI6 agent Tasha Stone is trapped in the break.

When a covert team reactivates the CodEx, an anomaly once buried in Churchill's Black Vault, London begins to glitch. Time resets. Reality unravels. And each reset costs more than the last.

As chaos spreads, cyberattacks, signal failures, and a looming bioterror threat, Tasha and the team race to track a hidden pattern through collapsing days. But someone else is watching. Learning. Adapting.

To stop what's coming, Tasha must outwit a ghost enemy, survive the resets, and confront the truth behind her sister's disappearance, an absence that might not be permanent after all.

The Sleeping Spy

Ellory Turner was never meant to be a spy.

But when a quiet accountant gets drawn into a surveillance operation, a simple assignment spirals into something darker: a world of hidden codes, double-crosses, and a woman with secrets of her own.

As the noose tightens around a powerful syndicate, Ellory must decide who to trust: a sharp-eyed handler with his own agenda or Marnie, a Brontë-obsessed daughter with nothing left to lose.

A deal is set to change everything. And in the heart of the game... someone always gets played.

The Sleeping Spy is a standalone novella of deception, duty, and the quiet cost of telling the truth.

Blood on the Bullion

"Gold doesn't change hands without blood. The wise take their cut. The cursed dig their graves."

A fast-paced British crime thriller with a razor edge, this novella peels back the decades to expose a chilling truth behind the infamous Brinks-Mat robbery.

When RAF radar operator Johnny Devlin stumbles across a Cold War-era notebook buried deep in a rural radar base, he's pulled into a brutal conspiracy that never died, just went underground. With bent cops, missing gold, and old ghosts resurfacing across Europe, Johnny finds himself hunted by a deadly gang who will do anything to protect their secrets. This explosive whodunnit grips from the first page to the last. Old loyalties fracture, the body count rises, and the real treasure turns out to be darker than gold.